W9-BON-241

Tor Books by Walter H. Hunt

The Dark Wing
The Dark Path
The Dark Ascent
The Dark Crusade

THE DARK CRUSADE

WALTER H. HUNT

TOR®

A TOM DOHERTY ASSOCIATES BOOK
NEW YORK

THE DARK CRUSADE

Edited by Brian Thomsen

A Tor Book
Published by Tom Doherty Associates, LLC
175 Fifth Avenue
New York, NY 10010

www.tor.com

Tor® is a registered trademark of Tom Doherty Associates, LLC.

ISBN 0-765-34983-3
EAN 978-0-765-34983-5

First edition: August 2005
First mass market edition: June 2006

Printed in the United States of America

0 9 8 7 6 5 4 3 2 1

In each book in this series I have dedicated the work to four people; this is, after all, a number beloved of *esLi*.

This book is dedicated to:

Lisa, love of my life, without whom none of this would be possible;

Barbara, my longtime friend—look, you finally made Admiral;

Tee, my newfound friend and fellow writer—thanks for all your help;
and

Brad, who's gone on; we still miss you, Captain.

Acknowledgments

The quotes from *The Prince* in this book are based on the Thomson translation published by Collier. Nic derives some of his special charm from *Niccolò's Smile*, a wonderful biography of Machiavelli by Maurizio Viroli published by Farrar, Straus and Giroux.

Jan, the yaminon made it into the book—hope you enjoy it. And Joe—thank you, my friend, for being the inspiration for Djiwara.

The statue described in chapter 17 really exists: it was erected in honor of William Pitt, the prime minister who helped Great Britain win the Seven Years' War. From the pictures I've seen, it's as monstrous as Djiwara finds it to be.

For more information about the universe, visit my Web site at http://www.walterhunt.com.

Author's Note

The Highspeech contains words that are used as modes of address between individuals. These words consist of two or three letters when translated into Standard. These words are called "prenomen" and indicate not only the status of the person being addressed (or referred to), but also the relationship of the speaker to that person.

Prenomen have two forms: one is used when the addressee or subject is alive, and the other when the person is dead (listed in parentheses). The prenomen used in the series are described below.

se, si.   This is the standard mode of address between individuals, when they are of equal status or unknown to each other. *si* is used when referring to or addressing a deceased person. *se* and *si* are also used to address a person of lesser status.

ge, gi.   This mode is used to describe a lover, usually in a non-affectionate or pejorative manner. It is also used colloquially to address a person of significantly lower status, such as a servant (or non-zor), though this form is archaic. This usage can often lead to duels and challenges.

ha, ha'i. This mode is used when addressing a person of superior status (other than the High Lord or a person of equivalent status, such as the Solar Emperor.) The person thus addressed will usually respond using the *se* form.

le, li.   *le* is used between intimates, as a term of gen-
uine affection. It is permitted only when a relationship is acknowledged by both parties;
otherwise it can be cause for challenge. *li* is used
when referring to or addressing a dead mate
only.

hi, hi'i.   This mode is used when addressing the High
Lord of the People. It has also been adopted for
use when addressing the Solar Emperor, though
the standard usage is with the prenomen and title, *e.g.,* "*hi* Emperor," rather than the given
name. *hi'i* is used when referring to a deceased
High Lord, and is generally accompanied by a
wing-position of honor to *esLi*.

na, ni.   This mode refers to a Servant of *esGa'u*. It is
used only rarely, often in literature. *ni* indicates
that the person is deceased.

ra, ri.   This mode, similar to the *na* form, is used to address important Servants of *esGa'u*, usually
Shrnu'u HeGa'u. It is similar to the *ha* form.
The *ri* construction is almost never used, as the
notion of such a Servant being considered dead
is difficult to encompass.

THE DARK CRUSADE

 **Prologue**

May 2404
Port Saud Station

"Djiwara."

The merchant factor was a bit older, a bit heavier, and a bit grayer than Owen Garrett remembered; but it had been seven years since he'd met him, arriving here after escaping from Center aboard *Negri Sembilan*. It was a different universe then.

It was a different universe now.

Djiwara turned from the platform that overlooked the big holo display that showed incoming and outgoing traffic from Port Saud. That area had been a big empty wall with exposed beams, but now it was high-tech—at least for a dead-end backwater like Port Saud. The merchant still had the same scowl, though.

"I know you," he said quietly.

"I bet you never forget a face," Owen answered. "Especially when you point a gun at it."

"Where's your big friend?"

"You mean Rafe? He had a previous commitment with the Imperial Government. He's got *Wallenstein* now."

"Big shot," Djiwara said. He walked toward Owen and then past him, so that Owen had to hurry to keep up. "So," Djiwara added without looking, "to what do I owe this honor? God knows, no one just 'stops by' Port Saud."

"I didn't even 'stop by' because I like your pretty face."

"Right." Djiwara scratched his beard. It had some gray in it as well. "Well, that's no surprise, I guess."

"I have a proposition for you."

"Right," Djiwara repeated. They began to walk along the concourse, still busy as ever. The merchant looked up and down, side to side. "*Everyone* has a proposition for me. Even you, Garrett."

"So you remember my name, too."

"I remember the name of everyone I point a gun at."

Garrett smiled inside his scowl.

They reached Djiwara's office, which was the same overcrowded museum of curiosities he remembered. Djiwara settled himself behind the desk; Owen sat in front of it.

"Is this room safe?"

"No place is safe." Djiwara picked up a comp from a corner of his desk and touched it on its edge; there was a low-pitched hum. "You've got about five minutes before some . . . one notices."

"It won't take that long." Owen looked Djiwara in the eye. "You knew what was going on when I was here last. I mean to do something about it now."

Djiwara smiled. "You want my help with this."

"That's right."

"You're insane."

Owen looked away for a moment and then looked back at Djiwara, his eyes intense.

"That might be, but I want your help anyway. We're going to get rid of the infection on this station."

"Just like that. And how are we supposed to *find* the hostiles? Or do you plan to just shoot everyone you don't like the look of?"

Owen's expression half suggested he might just do that, but instead he said, "I can see through the disguise. I can tell you who the bugs are, Djiwara." Owen folded his hands in his lap. "That must be worth *something* to you."

"Oh, it is, it is. Quite a lot. Of course, I have to believe your story enough to be willing to risk my life on it."

"You believed the last story we told you seven years ago."

"I did, didn't I?" Djiwara settled himself in his chair. "And it turned out you were telling the truth. All right, Garrett. Answer me another question, then. Why now, and why here?"

"That's two questions."

"Answer them both, damn it."

"All right. Why *'here'* is easy: When I was here last, there were a few bugs that really, really pissed me off. I have a score to settle. Why *'now'* is almost as easy: I finally got back here—I've had other commitments."

"Let me guess—the Imperial Government." Djiwara leaned forward. "Wait a minute. The emperor has guards that can sniff out bugs. You've been working with them."

"I *taught* them. For most of the last seven years I've been at the Imperial Court, teaching the Guardians their moves."

"Guardians. Creepy lot, that group."

"Nice of you to say so. Anyway, I've had enough—I turned it over to St. Giles and left."

"Don't know the name."

"Antonio St. Giles. My deputy for the last few years. *He's* what makes them creepy, at least in part: he takes a pretty mystical view of the whole thing."

"So you came *here*. You're pretty desperate, aren't you, Garrett?"

"No." Owen unfolded his hands and grabbed the arms of his chair. "No, I'm not desperate. I'm *insane*, remember? And I'm very, very angry. I'm angry about watching friends die in front of me, I'm angry about the way we're fighting this war.

"I want the bugs *dead*, Djiwara. Every last one of them."

"Starting here at Port Saud. Because no one would notice for a while."

"Very perceptive." Owen leaned forward now, the anger in his eyes enough to scare Djiwara a little bit. "But there's something else. You were Damien Abbas' friend, and I believe you and I could be friends—and partners. You're the perfect person to help me disappear."

"'Disappear'?"

"Permanent vacation," Owen answered. "No more 'Guardian Commander' for me. Tonio can have it."

Djiwara didn't say anything in response, but raised one eyebrow and again leaned a little forward in his chair.

"I'm not going to give you a story about destiny or try to tell you about the future," Owen continued. "That's the zor party line: they want you to think that they saw all of this coming years ago. My old CO, Admiral Laperriere, let herself be pulled into reenacting a zor legend; I don't really know what they expected her to do in the end, but at least she's doing it *her* way. They tried to do the same thing to me, but it turned out to be a lie they made up.

"But I *do* know that I have this talent and that I intend to use it. And I know that I want your help. I *need* your help."

Djiwara looked around his cluttered arrangements, as if he were taking stock of them somehow.

"You know, don't you, that sooner or later the bugs will figure out something's happened here at this piece-of-crap station. When they do, they're going to come looking."

"I know."

"You can't stand up against a whole army of the damn things. The Imperial forces have been at war for seven years and it's all *they* can handle."

"I know that, too; I don't intend to. By the time they come after us, we'll be long gone."

"What about the people here? Aren't a lot of innocent bystanders going to be killed?"

"They can be long gone, as well. Or they can stay and be killed . . . or enslaved. They'll get their warning; they can make their choice."

"One more question. Why me?"

"I can't do it alone. And as I said, you were Captain

Abbas' friend. He died on a planet far outside the Empire for no reason. He was used and thrown away."

"By the bugs?"

"No." Owen looked Djiwara straight in the eye. "By the people who are manipulating the bugs—an enemy we can't really see. Sooner or later we're going to have a reckoning with them, too.

"In the meanwhile, we have to get rid of the enemy we *can* see. Are you with me or not?"

Djiwara looked at the comp at the corner of his desk. "Your five minutes are up, Garrett."

"Are you with me or not?" Owen repeated.

The merchant reached into a compartment of his desk and drew out a pistol, then set it down on an unoccupied place.

"I'm with you," he said.

enGa'e'Li

THE STRENGTH OF MADNESS

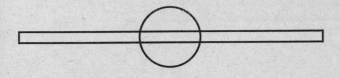

part one

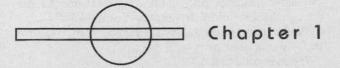

Chapter 1

THE SOLAR EMPIRE HAD SETTLED INTO A POSTURE THAT MADE IT POSSIBLE TO CONTINUE A WAR FOUGHT BY PEOPLE WHO HAD NEVER KNOWN ANYTHING ELSE. INDEED, AFTER A GENERATION OF WAR, THOSE THAT HAD KNOWN IT HAD ALMOST FORGOTTEN WHAT PEACE FELT LIKE.

—author unknown,
The Dark Crusade: A History,
early fragment published circa 2430

February 2422
Tamarind System

In the weird half-light of the alien ship corridor, Sergeant Sam Navarro turned to face his squad of Imperial Marines. His suit helmet didn't show his face clearly; a swirling pool of color a meter away reflected in his face-plate.

"This is it," he said. "Everyone ready?"

Grunts and nods of assent replied on suit-comm. The troopers looked weary—and for good reason: they'd been aboard the half-built hive-ship for nearly four hours, making their way forward from where their landing-craft had breached it.

The most tired figure was Alan Howe, Sensitive Specialist 9. He was standing as still as he could: Navarro assumed that he was working hard to shut out the voices that had been talking to him all the way forward.

"Colonel Howe?"

"Still here, Sam." Howe's voice came softly through the squad leader's suit-comm. "It wants me to run through the door all by myself, but . . . I'm okay."

"We're going to do this by the numbers, sir," Navarro said. "You do your part, we'll do ours."

"Sounds good to me."

"Becker and Czernowski are in place." Navarro put one gauntlet near his right ear, as if to indicate that he was in comm contact with them. "We're all in position.

"On my mark, ladies and gents."

There was a moment of unusual silence. Howe stood straighter, as if he was gathering his strength.

"Mark," Navarro said, and opened fire on the wall in front of them. The rest of the squad fired at the same point and the wall zipped apart. Navarro and the two best marksmen in the squad dove through first, firing and rolling, while the others followed behind. At the same time, another squad—Becker's—burst through, a quarter of the way around the circular room.

Directly after Navarro's lead troopers burst into the hive-ship's control center, Alan Howe dashed through, his weapon held in his hand. His primary weapon wasn't his firearm, however: it was his mind, using it to help fend off the vuhls' mental attacks. From the time they'd come aboard he'd heard the insistent voices in his head. There was one in particular that had eventually supplanted all of the others, crooning to him; it had paused for a moment just before they burst into the control room where they now stood.

The flight bridge was cast in actinic blue light, weirdly misshapen to human eyes, all curves and odd soft angles. The walls and ceiling were intermittently lit by swirls of colored light that moved, stopped, and moved again. There were no viewers, no tables, no chairs, just rounded projections and irregular solid things suspended in midair. The floor was sticky with something that didn't bear thinking about, which lapped up slowly against the soles of their boots.

In the middle of it stood a vuhl Drone, encased in a tight-fitting transparent pressure suit. Alan hadn't seen too many living ones, and none of them this close-up; there had only ever been one captured alive. That was during the first year of the war, and it had died in captivity from some sort of a stroke.

It was black with a gold-flecked carapace, standing on four strong legs, jointed in the middle. Past its midsection the alien stood upright; its two arms, ending in many-fingered hands, held a transparent ball—some sort of control device, Alan supposed; its head was a rounded cone with short eyestalks that darted back and forth within the head-bubble of the pressure suit. Its fanged mouth had large mandibles, and was framed by waving tentacles.

Alan, he heard in his head. *Welcome.*

It echoed from every corner of his mind; it was as if it were coming from every piece of equipment in the room. It came through the soles of his boots and the sticky stuff that was undulating between them; it seemed to flicker along the force-lines of his suit's energy field.

The tech that made it possible for the Drone to throw its power from one ship to another was in full force: From a few meters away, it was almost unbelievably powerful. The fifteen or so Marines in the room were all in its thrall: Navarro's and Becker's troops had all stopped moving, their weapons ready but frozen in place.

Everyone other than Alan Howe had gone completely immobile.

This is not good, he thought.

Come closer, the Drone said.

No thanks, he answered. *I'll stay where I am.* It was like shouting into a stiff wind.

For a moment, Alan had a scrap of visual impression: a transparent cubical box filled with multicolored fog with a silver sphere floating near the top. From within came a rasping, scraping sound of . . . laughter?

The Ór would like to examine you more closely, the Drone said. *It is ready to—*

Ready to what? Alan didn't really want the answer to that question; he wasn't sure what the hell an Ór was, but was in no hurry to find out.

He hoped that General Agropoulous aboard *Kenyatta II* was watching closely—and sending reinforcements.

The rushing wind in his mind suddenly died down. The thought-shape of amusement was replaced by another: apprehension, wariness, even fear.

The weird box-image vanished.

No, the Drone said in Alan's mind. *No—*

He was able to look aside. Sam Navarro's rigid form twitched slightly, as if the Drone's hold was slipping.

There was a flash of light—bright, blinding for a moment, consisting of all the colors of the rainbow. Then all hell broke loose: weapons-fire erupted that had been stopped dead when the Drone had taken hold of the Marines. It crisscrossed the room and struck the Drone in two dozen places.

Within Howe's mind the Drone's screams were amplified by the projection tech. But its last words were seared into his consciousness:

Better to die than to awaken the Destroyer.

Then, mercifully, he passed out.

G eneral."
Jim Agropoulous turned around to see Gyes'ru HeKa'an's *chya* drawn, held a few centimeters from the chest of the patient in the hospital bed.

The patient's eyes were open, but other than the occasional blink he was immobile. He clearly recognized the danger the zor's blade presented to him.

"Name," Jim said, approaching the foot of the bed.

"Alan Cleon Howe," the man in the bed said, looking

from the zor threatening him to the Marine general addressing him.

"Rank."

"Look, Jim, you know—"

"Rank," the general repeated.

"Sensitive Specialist 9. Colonel, Imperial Army."

"Serial number and designation."

"392AH2397-04143-209. Special attaché to Imperial Marine Group 127."

"Recite section 124 of the Uniform Code. Start with paragraph two."

"What?"

"You heard me. Let's hear it."

"I have no idea what the hell is in section 124, Jim, and you know it. Now, would you ask *se* Gyes'ru to put his *chya* back in its scabbard before he hurts someone, specifically me?"

"All right." Jim Agropoulous let out a sigh and nodded to the zor. "Put up your blade, *se* Gyes'ru. It's really him."

The zor warrior sheathed his *chya* and assumed a more relaxed posture, stepping back from the bed. "Eight thousand pardons, *se* Alan. You understand the need."

"Of course."

Jim sat on the edge of the bed. "I swear, if you'd started reciting the Uniform Code, I'd have shot you myself. Gyes'ru said that he didn't perceive you as a vuhl but you can never be too sure."

"Well, thank God I don't have any nervous twitches. And you wouldn't just use a Guardian because—"

"You know the reason." Agropoulous frowned. "Or you ought to."

"Because you don't trust the slimy bastards."

"Not even the ones we like. So how are you feeling?"

"I have a headache like you wouldn't believe, but I'd guess that I'm generally in far better shape than most of the casualties. How long have I been—"

"Sixteen hours."

"What's our status?"

"The battle's over. After you took out the Drone on the bridge, there wasn't much fight left in them."

"After I—" Alan Howe looked at his hands. "I'm not convinced that I 'took it out.' I— Well, it . . . gave up."

"Explain."

"You must've had a report by now. The vuhl Drone was killed by a burst of high-energy fire from numerous autorifles while I was fighting it. But— I was *losing,* damn it. It had me."

"It *had* you? Then why was it distracted enough that the troopers were able to kill it?"

"You wouldn't believe it."

"After this many years, I'd pretty much believe anything. Tell me what happened."

"It gave up. It told me something, Jim. Just before it . . . let itself be killed . . . it said something to me."

"Out with it."

"'Better to die . . .' it told me. 'Better to die than to awaken the Destroyer.'"

"What the hell does that mean?"

"About the Destroyer? Well, you know that they fear the—"

"I know about the Destroyer legend, Alan. What did it *mean,* 'Better to die than to awaken the Destroyer'?"

"I don't know. But I *do* know it was frightened. Something scared it more than the idea of being killed— something that might affect the vuhls as a whole. We know that they don't think of themselves much as individuals, so I suppose that a Drone might give up its own life rather than . . ."

"'. . . to awaken the Destroyer'? Look, Alan, we all know the legend, but who knows what it really means? What did he fear? What the hell was the Drone trying to say?"

"I don't know."

"We have to figure this out, Alan. We *have to know.*"

"*I* don't know."

"Maybe we'd better start from the beginning. All the details."

"Look, I just woke up—"

"I'll order some coffee. I need your report, and I need you to start providing it right now." He drew a comp out of a pocket and set it on the edge of the bed. "Start with the drop."

Alan looked from Jim to Gyes'ru, his fellow Sensitive. The zor's wings did not change position, but he seemed to shrug his shoulders. Outnumbered and outflanked, Alan heaved a sigh.

"All right. We were here to capture a hive-ship . . ."

Tamarind lay at the edge of what had been Imperial space when the war began. There had been three previous battles in Tamarind System: one when the vuhls seized it at the outset of the war; one when Admiral Erich Anderson's fleet had knocked out a base there a few years later but had been forced to retreat; and a third one two years ago—a bloody, costly affair that left the vuhls still in possession of the system and had accomplished nothing of merit, like so many battles in this war.

Unlike the last attempt, however, there was a clear objective this time. Intel had reported that the vuhls were building a hive-ship at Tamarind, at a graving-dock located on an asteroid. The First Lord of the Admiralty, His Grace the Duke of Burlington, initially ordered an expedition to destroy it before it could be completed: if this had continued to be the plan, there wouldn't have been any Imperial Marines involved at all.

But there'd been a change. In twenty-five years of war, the Imperial Navy had never gotten a good look inside a hive-ship. These fearsome vessels, some more than three kilometers long, were the biggest thing in the vuhl navy's arsenal; early in the war, they were frightening not just for their massed firepower but also for their ability to aid the vuhl Sensitives' Domination abilities. They were equipped with tech that permitted Sensitives to project across hundreds of millions of kilometers—tech that had been captured by Commodore Jacqueline Laperriere at Cicero when the war began, then recaptured and destroyed by the vuhls when they took—and lost—Adrianople a few months later. The spooks had no idea how it worked, but if it could be captured and put to use by the Empire it could have a profound effect on the seemingly endless war. The trick was to capture it intact—when the hive-ship was nearly complete.

And *that* made it a job for the Imperial Marines.

I read the briefing. Hell," Agropoulous growled, "I helped write some of it."

Howe ran a hand through his hair. "Do you want me to tell the story or not?"

"I don't see as we need to start with—"

"*ha* General," Gyes'ru interrupted. "Sir, if I may suggest, it is wise to permit Colonel Howe to fly the path. It is possible that something has been overlooked. If the General pleases."

"Fine." Agropoulous pulled a chair near the bed and sat backward, leaning his arms on the back of it. "A point taken, *se* Gyes'ru." The zor nodded, his wing-position moving slightly. "All right, Alan. Go on."

The vuhls realized the strategic significance of the hive-ship, and defended it tenaciously. The Admiralty, for its part, put the battle-plan on the fast track and allocated extra resources to it—in a war that had lasted a generation, there weren't too many things that offered any opportunity to change the basic equation. Admiral Erich Anderson had been assigned a task force of nineteen ships, including his own flagship *Emperor Ian*, to take the system and neutralize any defending force. Still, it took nearly sixteen hours before landing-craft could be launched at the asteroid base where the hive-ship was nearing completion.

I suppose he was at the conn for the entire battle," Howe interrupted himself. "Just like his great-great-grandfather."

"I suppose so. I was on *Kenyatta II* at the time. Can we get to—" Agropoulous glanced at Gyes'ru and paused. "All right, fine. Tell it your way."

Kenyatta II, a sixth-generation fleet carrier, had closed on the asteroid in order to launch a dozen Marine landing-craft under cover of its aerospace fighter wings. The landing-craft were big ungainly things with little in the way of defense or maneuverability. They had one job: Reach the objective, breach, and allow Marines to get aboard. Their target was the hull of the nearly complete hive-ship, where each craft would create its own hatchway through which Marines could attack. The fighters' job was simple: Screen the craft and keep them from being hit.

Twelve landing-craft left the secondary hangar deck of *Kenyatta II*. Ten of them reached the hive-ship intact; the other two were hit by enemy fire, with one able to maneuver well enough to continue and one being forced to go back. Tactical on *Ken*'s flight bridge judged that reducing the fighting force by 8 percent wasn't enough to abort the mission, and soon the remaining eleven had breached the outer hull of the vuhl ship. A few minutes later more than four thousand Marines were aboard, their vacc-suit transponders registering on a holo-model in the Marine command center aboard the carrier.

The Marines were at least partially protected from enemy Sensitives, by field modulators on their suits—similar to the ones mounted on every combat vessel. It didn't completely protect against Domination attempts by vuhl Sensitives; for that, there were human and zor Sensitives among the Marines. One of them was Alan Howe.

He'd been dropping with the Marines for nineteen years, both from atmosphere and in landing-craft like the ones they were using for this assault. He was no infantryman, but he and his fellow Sensitives performed a critical role in a war with aliens capable of controlling minds.

Target, Alan Howe thought to himself as he braced himself against the impact of the landing-craft with the hive-ship. *Big fat target.*

He'd counted to eight before he was through the hatch and had his weapon ready. Most of the regulars were two or three seconds ahead of him; but that was an improvement on his first drop into atmosphere from *Masaryk* at Mashore Reach—he'd taken half a minute to become disentangled from his drop capsule, and had spent the next minute-and-a-half throwing up: all while under enemy fire. At least he wasn't a danger to the troop anymore.

"Report by numbers," he heard in his helmet comm as he moved into position. Troopers began to call out their IDs.

When his turn came, he called out, "24 okay." A few comm signals later, he'd verified that his two fellow Sensitives had made it safely inside. Already he could feel the insistent buzz of the alien mental probes—not that he needed a reminder why he was here.

That's why I'm here, all right, he thought to himself.

That all sounds normal so far. We tracked your progress and saw you establish yourselves inside the hull with minimal casualties."

"We lost half a dozen Marines just getting in—Sam Navarro lost two—but it went pretty well. I don't need to tell you how spooky it was in there: you saw the vid we were sending." Howe looked away at a blank wall, as if he expected it to spring to life. "First off, it was low and tight. Our squad landed amidships, near what would have been starboard gunnery section on a starship. But it was nothing like a starship: it was hundreds of little chambers—and there wasn't a straight line in sight. Everywhere we looked were curved surfaces and shimmering pools of color, like offline vid cquipment."

He looked back at Agropoulous. "I could *hear* them, Jim. In my head, whispering. The hull decompression at our breach point killed a half-dozen of them, but they were in the next chamber, down accessways, on the other side of walls. It was as if I were listening to a thousand comm channels at once."

"Was it affecting the troopers?"

"No, I don't think so. The vuhls weren't focused—it wasn't like a Sensitive team; these weren't Drones, at least not most of them. They were techs and engineers. Workers. They didn't have any trouble disguising their hate, but they weren't able to Dominate us."

"What happened next?"

"Once we secured our flank positions we began to move forward. Everyone that made it over started moving toward their objectives. We'd given up far aft once we lost the twelfth lander, so it left one group without a flanker, but that seemed to be under control.

"But it was slow going. It took us several tries to figure out their doors—there were no obvious controls: the wall would just zip apart and the warriors would charge through. After a while we found some kind of mechanism that would cause the wall to part if we concentrated fire on it. Of course it would stay open then, so we would have to leave a rear guard to watch behind . . ."

After almost three hours, they came through a wall into a vast empty space, unpressurized and with no internal gravity. It was spanned by dozens of metal beams, some of them partially covered by the gray plasterlike material that made up the walls. The scale of the scene was hard to determine: it was hundreds of meters of open space in every direction, like a huge hangar—totally opposite to the close, claustrophobic chambers they'd been fighting through since boarding. It seemed that the vuhls weren't fond of it, either: they were mostly sticking to the walls and away from the vast emptiness in the middle of the unfinished part of the ship.

Far down the curve of the open space, Alan could see worker teams that seemed to be continuing the construction job despite the battle obviously continuing far above—or below—their position. He flipped up the magnification on his suit helmet to watch for a moment: there were six vuhls, moving slowly along an unfinished beam; they seemed to be crawling along, holding tightly as they moved, and in their wake gray plaster was forming up behind. He couldn't figure out at first how they were laying the stuff down; they didn't seem to be carrying any tools or supplies—they were just crawling along the beam, six vuhls side by side.

Then, all of a sudden, he figured it out.

didn't believe it when you first said it, and I don't believe it now. That stuff—the stuff the walls are made of—is coming from their—"

"I don't think they properly have one," Howe interrupted. "But yes, it serves the same purpose. I'd guess that they have a special type of worker that is bred for the task, to make the stuff. Lord only knows what they have to eat to turn it into *that*."

"It's on the inside walls, and it coats their hulls as well. Is it airtight?"

"It dries like granite. It's . . . Look, I don't really want to discuss that aspect any further right now, okay?"

"Fine." Agropoulous couldn't help but smile for a moment. As repulsive as the idea was, it solved a mystery that had baffled intel and the Navy since the war started.

Now, he thought to himself, *we can tell them exactly what that crap really is.*

The vuhls didn't like the open space in the unfinished part of the hive-ship. Intel knew that they were intensely agoraphobic: They designed their ships to be a mass of small compartments, sometimes with scarcely enough room for two vuhls to pass without touching. A generation ago, Admiral César Hsien—one of the first people to be Dominated and live to tell about it—reported that they seemed incredibly frightened of the open spaces aboard human ships.

By comparison, Imperial Marines were used to operating in open space and zero-g. Their orders were to fire at will and eliminate any enemy they encountered.

Alan Howe and the other Sensitives had another mission: to protect the Marines from Domination. Toward the aft end of the ship it had been techs and warriors, but now they could feel the insistent buzz of the vuhl Sensitives' mental probes. They were somewhere forward of the open structure, and they were getting ready for a final assault.

Back aboard *Kenyatta II*, the battle looked like it was going the humans' way, but Alan Howe knew better.

Maybe we should've just blown the fore end off the ship. The admiral suggested it."

"You could've just done that in the first place and skipped the assault. We had nothing when we came out into the unbuilt space: there was nothing new in the aft sections. We were there to capture the tech, remember?"

"Yeah, I remember. But it was a turkey shoot in the open structure—they were awful in free-fall, and the jarheads knew all the moves."

"But it didn't matter. They weren't the *real* enemy, Jim.

It was the Sensitives in the fore section, especially the lead Drone. If they got control of us and killed enough Marines, it would make their deaths worthwhile.

"We were going to kill them anyway. We knew it, you knew it. What happened in the process was what mattered. We could hear them—it was a trap, like the middle of a spider's web."

The sounds of the Sensitives in Alan Howe's mind grew louder and more insistent as his squad moved carefully through the corridors in the command section of the ship. They hadn't gone quickly thus far, and now it seemed like they were moving through some thick fluid. Alan was sweating in his suit, fighting against the probes of the aliens trying to turn him aside, to make him do insane things.

There was one voice that was more insistent than the others. It was not merely a chilling voice looking for an opening in his defenses; it was more like a sly, insidious one that seemed to know him very well. It seemed to bring forth memories of his earliest encounters with the aliens. He was especially reminded of his first brush at Josephson aboard the *Duc d'Enghien,* a lifetime-and-a-half ago, when he'd passed out after the image of a past *Gyaryu'har* had suddenly vanished, leaving him open and unprotected against the onslaught of vuhl Sensitives.

A hundred times, five hundred times since then, he'd faced this situation. It shouldn't have been any different, but somehow it was. Sensitives fight panic all the time: it gnaws at the mind, pulling down defenses and undermining confidence.

There was someone powerful behind this attack. He'd not felt this level of power or skill very often, thank God. It was difficult to keep it from the Marines close by; it was almost impossible to shield it from the other Sensitives. They all felt it.

* * *

It was calling me toward the main flight bridge. It was waiting for me," he told Jim Agropoulous, the hospital room seeming strangely quiet as he recalled the last several minutes aboard the mostly built hive-ship. Gyes'ru and the general were watching him carefully, listening intently now. There was no scope for jokes about where the hull material came from.

"You fought it."

"From a distance. Every step. It was all I could do to take it slow, to let Sam Navarro call the squad's moves. I almost couldn't keep myself from running toward the flight bridge like a crazy man. I was the only one who was managing any sort of resistance against it. We were being pulled—dragged—toward the center of the spiderweb. Hundreds of Marines in the fore section, and a dozen Sensitives with them."

"It must have been the enhancement tech."

"Well, *of course* it must have been the damned enhancement tech. Otherwise it would have had no chance. Too many laser rifles, too many minds to control, and not all in line of sight. But for the tech it would've been overwhelmed."

"So then you reached the bridge . . ." Agropoulous said.

"That's right." Alan Howe shuddered a bit at the memory. "It was waiting for us. And it knew my name . . ."

The flight bridge was cast in actinic blue light, weirdly misshapen to human eyes, all curves and odd soft angles. The walls and ceiling were intermittently lit by swirls of colored light that moved, stopped, and moved again. There were no viewers, no tables, no chairs, just rounded projections and irregular solid things suspended in midair. The floor was sticky with something that didn't bear thinking about, which lapped up slowly against the soles of their boots.

In the middle of it stood a man, wearing a uniform that looked a lot like an Imperial one, but a century or more out-of-date. He had a sort of glowing multicolored aura about him that gave him an unearthly appearance; it must have been some kind of enviro-suit, protecting him against the vacuum. Still, it wasn't like anything Alan Howe had ever seen—it was more like an energy field that surrounds a starship.

"Hello, Alan," the man said. "Glad you could make it."

"You know me," he answered.

"Oh, yes. I've been waiting for you, in fact. For all of you." He spread his arms wide as another group of Marines burst through a hatch a quarter of the way around the circle. They stopped immediately, transfixed.

The Marines with him were stopped as well. It was as if the scene were some sort of tableau, like a still from a vid.

"You can't control all of us."

"I don't have to. I'm not here to do that." He leaned against one of the curved walls, tilting his head slightly to one side as if he were listening to something. He crossed his arms in front of his chest. "In fact, the vuhl whose body I'm borrowing right now is going to be surprised as hell as soon as I give it back to him."

"'Borrowing'—" Alan began, but the man cut him off.

"The best part"—he smiled to himself—"the absolute *best* part of all of this, my friend, is that you're not going to remember a damn thing from this exchange until later. You'll recall getting here, and whatever happens after I leave, but our conversation—" He laughed; it had a sound like breaking glass in Alan Howe's audio pickup. "*Nothing*. At least for a while.

"Things are about to change. They've waited *a long time* to change—since the beginning of the war, really. The vuhls have lost control of their war already—and soon the 'meat-creatures' will lose control as well. In a few moments, my Drone friend is going to commit a self-less act that he thinks will forestall something. But it's just plain inevitable."

"What is?"

"The Destroyer." The man smirked. "The Destroyer is already here."

Alan stopped himself then, his eyes wide. Agropoulous hadn't moved; he had a surprised look on his face. The zor seemed impassive but a motion of his wings betrayed a change in attitude.

"I didn't remember any of that until just now."

"It sure as hell didn't make it into your report." Agropoulous tapped the comp. "We've got it now, though."

"You believe it."

"Do I have a choice?"

"Of course you do. None of it appears on the vidrec. You can send me to the happy farm."

"Tell me what happened next," he answered, without indicating whether sending Alan Howe to the happy farm might be a good idea or not.

"The—man—vanished. There was a bright light, or rather a spray of different-colored light, and he disappeared. Where he was standing was a vuhl Drone. I'm not sure of the markings, but the comp should identify it in some way. It looked around, in the split-second before the troops came out of their stun, and said what I heard. 'Better to die than to awaken the Destroyer.'"

"And then crossfire killed it."

"That's right."

"This man. Could you identify him if you saw him again?"

"I guess so. He was short and thin—gaunt, really. And he was dressed like something out of an old 3-V. Man-zor war era, I'd guess, though I couldn't be sure without some research."

"All right." Agropoulous waved a finger near the comp, then picked it up, and tucked it into a pocket. "Get some rest, Alan. We've already got new orders, and this"—he patted the pocket—"confirms it. We're going to go talk to the foremost expert on the Destroyer legend. Admiral Anderson has detached us to go to Zor'a."

"Jackie."

"That's right, old pal. Your old friend, and my old commanding officer—the *Gyaryu'har* of the High Nest, Jackie Laperriere."

Chapter 2

... THE WAR BETWEEN MAN AND ZOR HAD OCCUPIED TWO GENERATIONS ON EACH SIDE. IT HAD BEEN FOUGHT ON PHILOSOPHICAL GROUNDS, THOUGH THE MEANS AND METHODS HAD BEEN PHYSICAL AND VIOLENT: STARSHIPS, EXPLOSIVES, MARINES, BIOTECH, INTEL. WHATEVER ANALYSIS WAS APPLIED TO IT DURING OR AFTER—TO EXPLAIN, APOLOGIZE, STIGMATIZE, OR JUSTIFY—IT WAS CLEARLY A *WAR*, A SORT OF BACKGROUND PERCUSSION TO EVERYTHING THAT HAPPENED BETWEEN THE DARK DAWN OF ALYA AND THE TREATY OF E'RENE'E, SIXTY YEARS ALMOST TO THE MONTH.

BY THE TIME THE SECOND GENERATION OF BOTH HUMANS AND ZOR HAD GROWN UP WITH THIS CONFLICT AS A COMPANION, IT HAD BECOME ALMOST COMFORTABLE: THERE WAS AN ENEMY AND A PATTERN TO ITS CONDUCT OF THE CAMPAIGN. ONLY MARAIS' WAR, THE FINAL EIGHT MONTHS OF

THE SIXTY YEARS, CHANGED THAT. THERE WAS ONE FURTHER LEVEL OF COMFORT: THE WAR WAS FOUGHT AT THE FRINGES, WITH THE MAJORITY OF THE ACTION TAKING PLACE IN WHAT EVENTUALLY BECAME THE "NEW TERRITORIES," BETWEEN THE EDGE OF THE EMPIRE AND THE ANTARES RIFT.

THE CONFLICT BETWEEN THE SOLAR EMPIRE AND THE VUHLS WAS A FAR DIFFERENT SORT OF WAR. IT HAD BEEN SPRUNG ON THE CONSCIOUSNESS WITHOUT ANY MARKING EVENT LIKE THE DARK DAWN. THE LOSS OF THE NAVAL BASE AT CICERO DIDN'T EVEN MAKE THE NEWSVIDS FOR A FEW MONTHS; ONLY THE CAPTURE OF ADRIANOPLE SYSTEM FORCED THE ADMIRALTY'S HAND. THE SUDDENNESS WITH WHICH IT TOOK PLACE WAS FRIGHTENING FOR BOTH HUMANS AND ZOR.

WHAT WAS MORE, THE TARGETS OF ALIEN ATTACKS WERE NO LONGER SOMEWHERE REMOTE IN A "WAR ZONE." WITHIN TWO YEARS OF CICERO AND ADRIANOPLE, THE VUHLS HAD STRUCK AT DOMINICA, NEW GEORGETOWN, AND JOSEPHSON—ALL WITHIN FIFTY PARSECS OF SOL SYSTEM; NONE OF THEM HAD ANY PARTICULAR MILITARY VALUE. JOSEPHSON *ALMOST* MADE SENSE: IN THE FIRST YEAR OF THE WAR THE VUHLS HAD LOST FIVE HIVE-SHIPS THERE, AND THE FIRESTORMS THEY SET OFF ON THE PRIMARY EARTHLIKE WORLD DURING THE SECOND BATTLE IN JOSEPHSON SYSTEM MIGHT HAVE BEEN SOME SORT OF REVENGE.

THE OTHERS—AND THE MANY ATTACKS THAT FOLLOWED, YEAR AFTER YEAR—SEEMED TO FOLLOW NO REAL PATTERN. SQUADRONS OF VUHL SHIPS, SOMETIMES LED BY HIVE-SHIPS AND SOMETIMES NOT, WOULD EMERGE FROM JUMP AND ATTACK A TARGET. IF THE DEFENDER WAS LUCKY, THERE WOULD BE ENOUGH FORCE TO REPEL THE

ATTACK . . . BUT LUCK WAS NOT ALWAYS WITH THE
DEFENDERS. THE INCURSIONS DEFIED LOGIC OR
STRATEGY BUT THEY WERE NOTHING IF NOT
FIERCE. IT WAS ALMOST AS IF THE VUHLS HAD
STEPPED UP THEIR INTENSITY, AS IF THERE WAS A
DEADLINE: SOMETHING COMING, SOMETHING UN-
AVOIDABLE AND UNSTOPPABLE.

—author unknown,
The Dark Crusade: A History,
early fragment published circa 2430

March 2422
esYen, Zor'a System

Jackie opened her eyes and saw the *gyaryu* around her.
Sergei Torrijos walked out of the darkness. Jackie knew
they weren't alone; sixty-fours of other inhabitants were
out there in the darkness, in case she needed to consult
with them.

"Hi," she said.

"*se* Jackie," Sergei said, inclining his head.

"Admiral Erich Anderson is briefing the High Nest this
afternoon," she said. "*Emperor Ian* came insystem yesterday, jumping directly from the war zone. Something's
happened."

"But that's not what is troubling you."

"No."

Sergei smiled. *He must have been quite a charmer in
his day,* Jackie thought to herself. "I believe I can guess."

"*hi* Sa'a has invited the Talon of *esLi* to attend the
briefing. I have no idea why: She blames it on the Eight
Winds, but insists that *se* Ch'en'ya and her . . . colleagues . . . have to be on hand. 'Important communications,' she says. 'The Eight Winds,' she says."

"You should be accustomed to that by now."

"How long did it take you?"

"To get used to the inscrutability of the High Nest? I never got used to it, *se* Jackie. Eighty-five Standard years and I never did." Sergei smiled again. "I merely came to accept it."

"There you are . . . But my concern isn't that *hi* Sa'a has made this decision: I know better than to question her instincts. I'm just afraid of what *se* Ch'en'ya will say. Or do. Admiral Anderson isn't known for his patience."

"Neither is *se* Ch'en'ya, from what I've seen. But she is a powerful Sensitive, *se* Jackie. Surely *hi* Sa'a believes that."

"I believe it, too, but I . . . I'm not sure. I trust *my* instincts, too, *si* Sergei, and I have this feeling of foreboding."

"About the briefing?"

"No, it's more than that. Lately *se* Ch'en'ya has been talking a great deal about the Destroyer. When she first came to Zor'a, I got a glimpse of what I assumed is the Destroyer; she was standing next to him.

"In the scene she was about this age. I just get the feeling that he's about to make an entrance—and *se* Ch'en'ya knows something about it."

"Do you think she has met him already?"

"I don't believe so."

"Why?"

"Simple enough," Jackie said. "She's still *here*. She's not—wherever she's going to be, standing next to a pile of vuhl corpses."

"You've never told her about that vision—that *sSurch'a*—have you, *se* Jackie?"

"There didn't seem to be any benefit to it. No, I've never told her that she might be the Destroyer's left wing. I've discussed it with *hi* Sa'a and *se* Byar, but not with her."

"What does Admiral Anderson think of *se* Ch'en'ya?"

Jackie thought for a moment. "I don't believe he's given it much thought—but I suspect that he won't be happy to have her present. He probably views the Talon of *esLi*—if he thinks about it at all—as some sort of radical sect within the People."

"And not as the Destroyer's left wing. And friends."

"I doubt whether he's made the association. Are you suggesting that I make it for him? Admiral Anderson must have more on his mind than the Destroyer. He's got a war to fight."

"I don't see how the two are inseparable, *se* Jackie."

Se Alan," said a familiar voice.

Alan Howe turned from looking at a newsvid to see a zor crossing the station deck toward him. Out of courtesy, perhaps, she was walking and not flying; it made it easier to read her wings as she approached. It was an attitude of joy.

Joy? Ch'en'ya hardly knows that wing-position, he thought to himself as she came close enough to grasp his forearms. He kept his face impassive as he returned the gesture.

"In the Name of *esLi* I greet you, *se* Alan," Ch'en'ya HeYen said, releasing his arms and moving her wings to the Stance of Comradeship. "It has been too long since you last visited the homeworld of the People."

Alan and Ch'en'ya had trained together at Sanctuary a quarter-century earlier. They'd worked closely at times, though her involvement with the Talon of *esLi*—a group of young and equally angry zor Sensitives—had drawn them apart within the last few years.

It was all a matter of philosophy, he supposed.

"Admiral Anderson keeps me fairly busy, *se* Ch'en'ya," he answered. "This is a long way from the war zone."

"Indeed." She shrugged, a human gesture. "The war of ships and battles, perhaps. But some would argue that we fight the *esGa'uYal* here as well."

"I . . . suppose so. Still, I'm just here to gather information."

"You will be visiting Sanctuary?"

". . . Not exactly. I'm here to see *ha* Jackie."

"I see." Her wing-position changed suddenly: it took on hostile undertones. "I'm sure that you will find your conversations helpful."

"You don't think so."

"Eight thousand pardons, *se* Alan," Ch'en'ya said, moving her wings again. "I do not mean to suggest anything. The *Gyaryu'har* will be most enlightening, I am sure."

"Tell me what you really think."

Ch'en'ya looked away from him, watching the vid for a few moments. "Friend Alan, it does not serve *esLi* for me to criticize *ha* Jackie: she serves the High Nest as do I. But it seems to me that . . . she does not fully understand the nature of this war."

"She understood it before any of us, *se* Ch'en'ya. She fought the servants of *esGa'u;* she pierced the Icewall."

"Pah."

Still her favorite word, Alan thought. "You understand things in a way she doesn't, I take it."

"*se* Alan. I am sure that the efforts of the Imperial Navy are noble, the acts of true warriors. But ultimately only one thing can defeat the *esHara'y* and the *esGa'uYal* they serve: the Destroyer."

"Oh? What more do you know about the Destroyer, *se* Ch'en'ya?"

Her wings rose to an unfamiliar position; she looked away, down the deck, and then back at Alan. "Only that we are all waiting for the Destroyer to come."

The official residence of the *Gyaryu'har* had once been the home of a stranger, but over time Jackie had made it her own: a small model of the memorial on Dieron's First Landing Hill; pictures of her father, her cousin Kristen, and Kristen's husband Dan; a casual, smiling pose with Barbara MacEwan, taken at Adrianople just after it had been retaken in 2397; one of Th'an'ya, Ch'en'ya's mother and Ch'k'te's mate, whom she never met in life but knew so well from when she went to retrieve the *gyaryu* twenty-five years ago.

Jackie Laperriere received her old friend Alan Howe in the sitting-room. An *alHyu* showed him in, his wings conveying a sense of deep respect; if Alan had had wings, he would've done the same. Jackie did her best to set him at ease, first grasping forearms in zor fashion and then taking his hand and showing him to a chair.

"You're a long way from the front, Alan. Something important must've brought you here."

"I'm here with Admiral Anderson . . . but I still swing a *little* weight, *ha* Jackie. I thought I was welcome to visit anytime."

"Of course you are." She smiled. "But Erich keeps you on a tight leash. Something's happened, so out with it. What brings you to Zor'a?"

"I had an unsettling experience, something you might be able to help with. You know that we took a partly built hive-ship at Tamarind."

"I heard about that. Nice work."

"It would've been, if I could take credit for it. We almost didn't get out of that alive—the Drone in command was out of my league. *Way* out of my league. We got some help."

"What sort of help?"

Alan grasped the arms of his chair and looked away. "I . . . think we got a visit from an *esGa'uYe*."

"Oh?"

"During the final assault, we met a man. At least, he looked like one: a scrawny guy, wearing a naval uniform of the last century. Had a smirk on his face as he talked. He didn't show up the vidrec—but I met him. I *know* it."

"Stone." Jackie's hand strayed to the hilt of the *gyaryu*, lying on a sword-rest within reach. "Stone. What did he say?"

"This is someone you know."

"Your instinct is right on target," Jackie said. "What did he say?" she repeated.

"He said that the Destroyer had arrived— no, that wasn't quite it." Alan pinched his nose, closing his eyes. "He told me that things were about to change . . . and that the Destroyer was 'already here.'"

"Already *where*? Aboard the hive-ship?"

"I don't know. He may have meant it metaphorically, not to imply that the Destroyer was in the room or aboard the ship."

Jackie removed her hand from the sword and folded her hands in her lap.

"Alan, we've known each other a long time. The entire war."

Alan Howe smiled. "Most of it. You didn't think much of me at first, as I recall."

"We've gotten over that," Jackie answered, smiling. "At least *I* have. When I first knew you, I was about the only thing standing between the vuhls and the Empire: and that was because I had *that*." She pointed to the *gyaryu*.

"I know the story."

"Do you? Most people don't, not really." She stood up and walked to the sideboard and picked up the holo of Th'an'ya. "I was *chosen*, Alan. I was sent on a quest to go find the sword, to take it out of the grasp of the *esGa'uYal*. The only problem with the story is that I wasn't chosen by the zor: I was chosen by the *esGa'uYal* themselves to follow a specific course that resulted in getting the sword.

"Stone both helped me and tried to stop me. At First Josephson, where you and I first met, Stone tried to take the *gyaryu* away from me—and then, when he failed, gave me the key to rescuing Ch'en'ya. That was the last I ever saw of him."

"That was twenty-five years ago."

"That's right." She set the Th'an'ya-holo down again and turned to face Alan. "He's been out of the picture, away from the action. It's as if he's been waiting for something."

"The Destroyer."

"Sure. The Destroyer. What in hell does that mean? Is it something like *esHu'ur,* a mystical force that gets personified somehow?"

"There's no way to know. I'm not even clear how you learned about 'the Destroyer' in the first place," Alan added.

"Stone. He showed me," she said. "I've seen the Destroyer—I'll know him when I see him."

"This is the same guy who turned up at the party at Tamarind. Now *there's* a trustworthy source."

"I believe what he showed me. He's never lied to me. If he says that the Destroyer is here—whatever that means, *who*ever that means—then I believe him. I don't know the significance of the statement. Worst of all, I don't know what he's been doing for twenty-five years while we've been fighting the vuhls."

"Helping them, do you think?"

"Stone can walk through jump. He can appear in visions and affect reality. If he—or who he works for—wanted the vuhls to win, don't you think they would have won by *now*? Christ, Alan, they could have delivered us to the vuhls a long time ago . . . if that's what they *wanted.*"

"Then they're on our side. They were at Tamarind."

"That doesn't mean anything."

"It meant my *ass,* Jackie, mine and a whole lot of Marines," Alan said, forgetting the prenomen when he answered. He took a deep breath and continued. "I'm not prepared to pass judgment on the big picture, on what the *esGa'uYal* are trying to accomplish: but on the microlevel they chose to favor us at Tamarind. They wanted us to win there and survive. Lord knows I did, too."

"He chose to help us there as part of a larger pattern." Jackie said. "We're being maneuvered into position for something bigger—the Destroyer and whatever he represents."

"I'd rather be alive to get maneuvered."

The chamber clearly had been designed with both humans and zor in mind. In addition to perches, there were chairs placed in various locations in the room. In lieu of a central table—still a common feature in conference rooms across the Empire—each seat had a small table-surface hovering within arm's reach.

As Jim Agropoulous and his staff entered, they saw Admiral Anderson engaged in quiet conversation with Sa'a He Yen, High Lord of the People. Representatives of various branches of the military, as well as diplomatic representatives and a few Guardians, were preparing for the briefing.

Alan caught Jackie's eye as they approached. She was scowling, her hand resting lightly on the hilt of the *gyaryu*. As he watched, she turned her gaze aside; he followed it, his glance coming to rest where Jackie was looking: at a group of younger zor grouped near the podium at the front of the room. He recognized Ch'en'ya immediately, though her back was turned to him. He'd known that the Talon of *esLi* had been invited to the briefing; when Jim Agropoulous had mentioned it during the trip here, he'd said they should be ready for anything.

"Thanks," Jim had said. "But that's *your* job."

Agropoulous came to a halt a few maters from the admiral and the High Lord, his officers just behind him. The two dignitaries concluded their conversation and turned to face them.

"General," Admiral Erich Anderson said, exchanging a salute. "I believe you have not had the pleasure of meeting *hi* Sa'a?"

"No sir," Agropoulous answered. He offered a salute to the High Lord. She reached out her taloned hands and lightly grasped his arms; he returned the gesture. The High Lord was known for her informality; but the general was still surprised—despite his rank, here at the High Nest he could be classified as "no one of importance."

"In the name of the High Nest I greet you, *se* General." Her wings moved slightly to a position Jim recognized as a friendly one. "I understand that your forces had an . . . interesting experience."

"*se* Alan's experience was the *most* interesting, *hi* Sa'a," the general replied, letting his arms fall to his sides. He nodded to Howe, who stepped forward and inclined his head. "I assume that you read the report."

"It has received wide circulation." Sa'a nodded in the direction of Ch'en'ya. "Things are changing, *se* General. Our war is changing."

"We'll still be fighting it the same way, High Lord."

"Can you be sure of that?" Sa'a's wing-position changed again as she turned away.

Operation Elysium' began four months ago," Anderson began, displaying a 3-V diagram of the Imperial frontier in the center of the room. "After the attack at Evangeline in October 2421, the Admiralty had evolved a plan to remove the threat to the region involving two Imperial fleets.

"At the beginning of 'Elysium,' my command attacked the vuhl forward base at New Harare, while Admiral MacEwan's force moved to engage the vuhl squadron base at IGS 44978. The objective in each case was to remove enemy offensive capability and to prevent attacks into the adjoining sector of Imperial space."

Icons representing the strength of each fleet appeared next to target indicators. They appeared in two columns: one prior to the attack, and one following.

"Both systems were heavily defended. New Harare

cost my force four capital ships and eleven support vessels, though enemy losses were much higher and included two hive-ships under construction. Admiral MacEwan's force suffered fewer casualties, though they required an additional five Standard days to eliminate static defenses and clear minefields.

"My force proceeded to Rivières, three parsecs distant from New Harare. This system served as an intermiediate refueling stop for enemy forces; removing it from vuhl control would give us access to several worlds deeper in enemy space."

"Including Tamarind," Ch'en'ya said, interrupting Anderson's presentation. He had taken a breath to continue but stopped, looking across the room at the group of zor perched together.

"Civilians," Jim whispered to Alan, a scowl on his face.

"*Yes,*" Anderson said. "Including Tamarind and several other systems. We sought to eliminate the threat to Evangeline and its neighboring systems and we were prepared to do it one system at a time. Every star within jump range of Evangeline had to be examined to determine whether it was suitable for basing enemy ships.

"Between Admiral MacEwan's force and my own, we found six small bases. Each had to be reduced and neutralized. In addition, we were forced to respond to a vuhl incursion at Towson, which was repelled with heavy casualties."

The admiral's report droned on. Alan listened with half an ear; he'd read the briefing already. Instead, he cast his Senstitive awareness outward. Slowly, the sounds of Anderson's voice, the background noise of the room, the ventilators, and the faint rustling of zor wings faded away into silence. It was one of the first techniques he had learned from Byar HeShri, Master of Sanctuary, a quarter-century ago.

In the silence, he could feel rather than hear his own heart beating. Closing his eyes would have attracted attention, so he just let them blur slightly as he let his breathing slow. The image of each person in the room faded and was replaced by a faint glow, like a distant star. Each was a slightly different color; for example, Jim Agropoulous was a faintly purplish blue, while Admiral Anderson was of a lighter-hued aqua.

Across the way, the members of the Talon of *esLi* were various shades of green—from a deep-emerald for Ch'en'ya, to pale, almost-transparent greens for some others . . . and there was something else faint and almost unrecognizable.

Unless you were looking for it, Alan thought to himself.

He looked closer, letting his awareness focus on the members of the Talon of *esLi*. He could see something very much like a faint ribbon of rainbow light weaving in and out and around the eight glowing lights on the other side of the chamber.

As he watched, the rainbow suddenly solidified, coiling and rearing like a snake. Across the silence, Alan thought he heard a rasping hiss—

He reached out and swept a reader from his desk to the floor. He didn't hear it hit; but suddenly his vision of glowing spheres and a snake of rainbow light vanished. The room was suddenly filled with sound; Anderson had stopped speaking and was scowling at him.

Alan made a great show of picking up the reader and stylus. General Agropoulous was looking at him, along with everyone else in the room.

"Colonel Howe, if you *please,*" Anderson said, obviously upset at being interrupted. He clearly thought it had been no more than a clumsy move by an inattentive Sensitive.

Ch'en'ya was staring directly at him, though; she'd felt *something.*

"I beg your pardon, Admiral," Alan said, carefully placing the reader on the table.

"If I may continue." Anderson did, returning to a detailed discussion of the battle at Wolfram Minor, the last major engagement before the attack on the hive-ship at Tamarind.

"So?" Agropoulous whispered without turning around.

"There's something there," Alan answered. "Something's hanging around the Talon of *esLi*."

"'Something,'" Agropoulous repeated.

"It's hard to describe, so I won't try. But we've got some kind of company here."

"'Here'? In this room?"

"Around the Talon," Alan whispered. "I think they know, too."

Ch'en'ya was still looking directly at him. Her wings were in a position that indicated affront; he was quite familiar with that configuration.

Comes easy to her, he thought to himself.

"I'll want a report on this."

"You just got it, sir," Alan replied.

". . . which brings us to Tamarind," Anderson was saying, looking again at Alan over the top of his nose. "You have all received vidrec information on the assault on the incomplete hive-ship in the Tamarind System last month.

"An analysis of the hive-ship tech is already under way at the Shiell Institute in New Chicago System. The Admiralty is most appreciative to the High Nest for its assistance in this regard."

Anderson nodded to Sa'a, who inclined her head and arranged her wings in a posture of deference. "The matter of 'the Destroyer' is of prime interest to us, though the data gathered from the current campaign has produced another result."

Anderson gestured above his control pad. A series of lines extended outward from New Harare, Rivières, Wolfram Minor, Tamarind, Towson, and each of the six bases the current offensive had neutralized. They tracked across the empty space until they crossed at a star about fifteen parsecs distant from Tamarind—the farthest the Navy had yet penetrated into vuhl space.

"Additional investigation of jump-echoes going back before the battle at Evangeline confirm the evidence shown on the display. This system"—a series of datarecs appeared next to the star—"is a major base of some sort. Seizure of this base would deal a major blow to the enemy. This system—"

"—is the homeworld of the *esHara'y,*" Ch'en'ya said.

Those in the room reacted to the interruption: the humans, with angry faces; the zor, with wings raised in alarm or affront. If the look Anderson had given Alan was a withering one, the glance he leveled at Ch'en'ya was "shoot to kill."

"*se* Ch'en'ya—" the High Lord began.

"Ch'en'ya, damn it—" Jackie started, but a second later; she stopped, realizing that she was interrupting Sa'a. Anger was radiating from her like heat.

"*hi* Sa'a. With your permission." Anderson held out his hands, palms up.

Sa'a's wings were raised, but she let them lower again.

"*se* Ch'en'ya," Anderson continued. "You are clearly here to test my patience and punish me for my transgressions, but I am quite capable of exercising patience and enduring punishment since you are here at the behest of the High Nest.

"But this is a *military* briefing. We are seeking to make military decisions on the basis of military judgment. We have no conclusive evidence that this is the vuhl homeworld. Indeed, I doubt it: this seems merely to be the source of recent vuhl incursions.

"I do not have an adequate explanation for why this might be the case, but to assume that this system is their homeworld is faulty reasoning, and I don't believe it."

Ch'en'ya appeared ready to interrupt again, and Anderson hurried on. "I am certain that you will speak of the Destroyer, of the Icewall, of the *esHara'y* and the *es-Ga'uYal,* and the triumph of the Golden Circle against Despite. Yes," he continued, "I know all of the words, all of the key players, and I've read up on the legends. But this is a *war,* damn it. This is not poetry: this is strategy. I am not convinced that you have *anything* to say.

"I humbly ask eight thousand pardons, High Lord," the admiral said now, turning to Sa'a and inclining his head. "I do not mean to offend the High Nest in any way."

"Your honor is spotless, *se* Admiral," High Lord Sa'a answered. She glanced at Ch'en'ya, whose wings returned to a posture of deference though her eyes still flashed with anger. "You have shown great tolerance to permit these Nestlings to attend this meeting, and I, in turn, ask eight thousand pardons of you for their behavior.

"Nonetheless, I believe that they have important communications to make at this time. Regrettably, they will refer to the *esHara'y* and the eternal conflict between the servants of *esLi* and the Lord of Despite. It is the way we think; it is the way that we experience the Flight of the People. Whether you find this palatable or not, you must accept this circumstance.

"If you do not wish to permit them to speak, the High Nest is prepared to accept this. But it is the counsel of the High Nest that to choose *that* flight would be an error."

Sa'a settled herself on her perch. She'd said her piece and had left it to Anderson to make a decision.

"All right," he said after a moment. It was clear that he was ready to blow the Talon of *esLi* out of the room, but the High Lord had intervened. "*se* Ch'en'ya, I am ready to hear what the Talon has to say." He waved his hand across his control tablet, transferring control to Ch'en'ya, and sat down.

Ch'en'ya let her wings settle into a posture of amusement. As she extended her hands and laid them on the table in front of her, she appeared to be studiously ignoring the hostile wing-positions of other People in the room.

"*ha* Admiral. *hi* Sa'a." Ch'en'ya nodded to each of the dignitaries. "*ha Gyaryu'har,*" she added, after a moment almost long enough to be insulting.

"The People and their human allies have fought against the *esHara'y* for a generation. Nestling to adult, my generation has experienced war against an implacable enemy with no face. They wield the Sword of Despite with no remorse and with the skill of their *esGa'uYal* masters.

"We are faced with the naked darkness of *anGa'e'ren*, as was the great hero Qu'u in the Mountains of Despite." Again she glanced at Jackie. "This tradition is one that is even known to the *naZora'i*." She paused and looked around the room. "They believe that the cause of fear that *anGa'e'ren* engenders is due to the pulling aside of the Shroud of Despite. This, however, is only a part of the cause.

"There is more to it than that. Qu'u was a warrior of the People, a bearer of a *chya* before he held the *gyaryu*. A warrior confronts the enemies in the reach of his sword, enemies he can face and whose motives and goals are known to him.

"The enemy we now face gives us no indication. Where the *esHara'y* attack, *why* they attack, and what they hope to gain by this war, remain a mystery after these many turns. It is obvious that courage and honor are not enough to defeat this enemy. *si* Qu'u himself, were he here to lead us, could not slay enough *esHara'y* to end this war.

"It is clear that we—humans and People alike—need a power greater than courage, a strength beyond honor.

"We must embrace *enGa'e'Li*, the Strength of Madness."

The word in the Highspeech echoed in the chamber. Those present were now silent and listening carefully. Even the High Lord, who should have by rights been offended by this flight, gave no indication of affront.

The wings of Ch'en'ya, normally so full of anger, conveyed a fierce joy. "Our enemies fear the Strength of Madness. They fear it personified—that it will come as the Destroyer. In truth, *hi* Sa'a, *ha* Admiral, they have every *reason* to fear this.

"We of the Talon of *esLi* believe that the Destroyer has already come."

"Based on the . . . Based on a Sensitive experience on a vuhl vessel," Anderson interrupted. "That does not seem very convincing."

"It is more than that, *ha* Admiral. The omens are all suggestive of the coming of the Destroyer." She turned toward the High Lord. "The High Lord has dreamed this . . . has she not?"

Sa'a's wings now took on a position of anger. Her talons were clenched in her hands as she stood rigidly on her perch. Clearly this was something she had not expected to discuss.

"It is true," she said at last.

"What is more," Ch'en'ya continued, as if the point she had just scored was no more than a mark in a debate, "the pattern of *esHara'y* attacks, coupled with coastwatcher intel and other relevant information that you have not yet presented, suggest to *us* that this system—" She indicated it with a talon on the display, and it was highlighted on every screen in the chamber and on the holo in the center. "—is indeed the homeworld of the *esHara'y*. A strike at this world, with the combined might of the People and the humans, would surely result in the destruction of the enemy and the end of the war."

"And would be tactically unwise," Anderson retorted. "Ardor in battle is admirable, but does not win wars. This— This 'Strength of Madness' is madness indeed. I've read what the Talon of *esLi* has written about *enGa'e'Li, se* Ch'en'ya, and I'm not convinced."

"Pah," she replied. "This is not a warrior's flight you choose."

Anderson did not answer, nor did he let the expression on his face change; but even from across the room Alan could see anger in his eyes as he seemed to be considering a reply.

"Your contribution to the briefing is noted," Sa'a said at last. "You have the thanks of the High Nest, *se*

Ch'en'ya." She inclined her head toward the main entrance to the chamber.

Ch'en'ya looked at the High Lord. It was a dismissal, no doubt about it; perhaps she had more to say, and perhaps she wanted to cross blades—figuratively or literally—with Admiral Anderson.

Whatever her wishes, Ch'en'ya did not seem willing to contravene the wish of her High Lord. Almost at once, all of the members of the Talon of *esLi* inclined their wings in a posture of deference to the High Lord and then took off, flying across the chamber and through the doorway without another word.

Anderson emerged from the room after the briefing was concluded, steam seeming to rise from his head as he walked. Alan had no intention of speaking with the admiral in this situation, but he found himself in the line of fire as Anderson approached.

"Howe," he said.

"Sir."

"Ch'en'ya."

"Yes sir."

"I want to understand," Anderson said, obviously holding in his anger. "I want to know the reason I should have her, or anyone else from her cabal, in a military briefing ever again."

"I'm not sure what you want me to tell you, sir."

"Tell me about Ch'en'ya first. Who the hell is she, really?"

"She's . . . It's a bit complicated, Admiral. She is, or rather *was,* the ward of the *Gyaryu'har*. Her mother was *si* Th'an'ya, a Sensitive of the High Nest who disappeared on an exploratory mission; her father was *si* Ch'k'te, a warrior of the High Nest and officer in His Majesty's Navy."

"Assigned to Cicero."

"That's right, sir. He was posted to Cicero when the

war broke out, and was killed at Crossover during *ha* Jackie's quest to recover the *gyaryu*. *se* Ch'en'ya was found, along with a group of other zor, after First Josephson."

"'Found'?"

"The expedition that included *si* Th'an'ya had crashed in an uncharted system. *ha* Jackie found them and brought *se* Ch'en'ya back to Zor'a. And, before you ask me, sir, I have no idea how she found them."

"And the reason she has a hair across her—across her—"

"*se* Ch'en'ya is mad at the universe, Admiral. She blames her mother for having died in childbirth; she blames the People for leaving her in exile through most of her childhood. She's angry at her own race for being too restrained in their prosecution of the war; she's angry at us for not being warriors of the People. She hates the *esGa'uYal*, she hates the vuhls.

"She wants to pursue this war without recourse to logic or strategy, sir. She wants to drive her *chya* into the thorax of every vuhl, and she wants to do it personally."

"Has she ever actually killed one?" Admiral Anderson asked.

"More than one. And at least one—"

"*—esGa'uYe.*"

"At least one of those, at Sanctuary, when she was an adolescent. She's dangerous, no doubt about it."

"Is she a threat?"

"To what, sir?"

"Let me put it differently: is she a security risk?"

"I couldn't say, Admiral. For the last several years, she and the Talon of *esLi* have pretty much gone where they wanted, said what they wanted, done what they wanted. I don't think they're working for the enemy."

Anderson grunted. "She can be as loyal as she wants and still be a security risk. Will the High Nest be in a snit if I have her watched or followed?"

"I don't think so, sir. I believe *se* Ch'en'ya is a bit of a problem child for *hi* Sa'a at the moment. The greatest danger would be from *se* Ch'en'ya herself."

"She'd be violent?"

Alan thought about the question for just a moment before replying. "She's . . . unpredictable, Admiral. I can't say what she'd do."

Admiral Anderson turned to Jim Agropoulous, who'd done his best to stay out of the conversation thus far.

"Jim, you're to keep her at a distance from all military briefings, sensitive comps, or comm lines. By force if necessary. You read?"

"Loud and clear, Admiral."

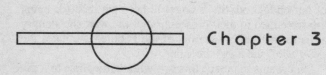

Chapter 3

THE SHIELL INSTITUTE, LOCATED IN JARDINE ON THE PRIMARY WORLD OF NEW CHICAGO SYSTEM, WAS FOUNDED IN 2314 BY LOUISE AND DARIUS SHIELL. IT WAS CHARTERED TO RESEARCH SENSITIVE PHENOMENA AND TO TRAIN HUMAN SENSITIVES. THOUGH RIDICULED WITHIN THE SOLAR EMPIRE, IT WAS PRAISED BY THE ZOR HIGH NEST; IN 2321 IT ADDED A SANCTUARY INSTRUCTOR TO ITS STAFF. IN 2346 THE INSTITUTE CERTIFIED THE FIRST WORKING SENSITIVES WITHIN THE SOLAR EMPIRE; ITS REGIMEN OF E3G TESTS WERE ADOPTED BY THE IMPERIAL NAVY IN 2367.

—*Imperial Encyclopedia,*
2405 Edition

March 2422
esYen, Zor'a System

Third Deputy Director Laura Ibarra touched the comp and the holo-image zoomed to a close-up, showing Ch'en'ya HeYen and a heavyset man. The icon below the image showed that there was audio to go along with it, but they'd been using a scrambler so it was in any case unintelligible.

"Who is he?"

"A ghost." Laura picked up the stoneware mug of tea at her elbow and sipped it thoughtfully.

"You'll be explaining that, I expect." Jackie couldn't help but smile. She'd known Laura Ibarra since she had been an intel officer aboard His Majesty's fleet carrier *Duc d'Enghien;* when they'd first met, the spook had rubbed the *Gyaryu'har* the wrong way, but that was primarily because of circumstance.

And, of course, because of M'm'e'e Sha'kan, who had turned out to be a pretty decent fellow after all. When the rashk had become Director of Imperial Intelligence four Standard years ago, he'd posted Laura directly to Zor'a; since then, Jackie had made her peace with Laura, and now found her company pleasant—and often instructive. Now they sat in a sun-filled chamber of the *Gyaryu'har*'s house in esYen, sipping tea, the holo hanging in the air between them.

"His name is Djiwara. Joseph Michael Djiwara. Goes by the middle name, or did, if he was still alive."

"Well, he's clearly still *alive*," Jackie said, "unless I'm much mistaken."

"What I mean is, we *thought* he was dead. Djiwara is—or, rather, was—a small-time merchant operating mostly outside the Empire. His home base was vaporized by the vuhls almost twenty years ago. Let's see . . ." She touched her comp: "Display dossier entry for subject," she said, moving a tinted patch over Djiwara's head in the image. Another holo appeared, showing a separate head shot and several columns of information next to it.

"His home base was at a place called Port Saud Station," Laura said. "Just outside the Empire, Orionward. Used to be a refueling stop for merchants."

"Pirate port?"

"Not worth their trouble. It's too far off the trade routes; the closest thing to a habitable planet in Port Saud System has violent tectonic activity and a poisonous atmosphere. It was nothing but a secondhand orbital station—at least until January 2406, when the vuhls destroyed it."

"Killing everyone aboard." Jackie picked up her own tea mug and leaned back in her armchair. "Including Djiwara."

"That's what Langley comp recorded, but obviously he got away."

"So . . . what does he want with Ch'en'ya? And where's he been hiding for the last sixteen years? And why would the vuhls have attacked a place as out-of-the-way as Port Saud?"

"You know as much as anyone about how the vuhls think. You tell *me*."

"As Master Byar once told me, 'Despite does not have a point.' But it *does:* We aren't always sure why they attack when it happens, but there's usually a reason we figure out afterward." Jackie smiled again. "Kind of like analyzing the stock market—there's always an explanation after the fact. Still, there must have been something there they wanted—or something they wanted dead."

"Or someone."

"Or someone," Jackie agreed. *And there's something familar about that place, if I could remember what.*

She put her hand on the hilt of the *gyaryu* and closed her eyes. That always drove Laura crazy; she watched closely, but Jackie never gave up any information about what she was doing.

Sergei, she thought, *what do you folks know about Port Saud?*

Nothing, came the reply almost at once. *It wasn't even on the charts. Perhaps you should try using your comp like everyone else.* Jackie heard a chuckle and couldn't help but smile. That usually drove Laura crazy as well.

"Where'd they go?" Jackie asked, opening her eyes again.

"They boarded a commercial ship, *Hellespont,* outbound for Mothallah. From there they could have gone anywhere."

"Do you know anything about the ship?"

"Not much. Captain is a retired Navy man named Rafael Rodriguez."

"Well, *that* narrows it down. There must be only eight billion retired Navy men named Rodriguez."

Laura shrugged her shoulders. "And only eight million named *Rafael* Rodriguez. All right, I'll see what I can find out about him. In the meanwhile—"

"In the meanwhile," Jackie said, "we should try to find out where *Hellespont* went."

Shiell Institute, Jardine City
New Chicago System

The Shiell Institute at New Chicago had never been host to so many dignitaries nor, indeed, so many soldiers. Byar HeShri, Master of Sanctuary, had seen quite a lot of both in the past few years; he wasn't fond of either.

He *was* beginning to be fond of *egeneh,* something he'd detested when he was young. Of course, it had been a different universe then. It had been *si* S'reth's favorite, eights of turns ago—it warmed him against the cold of Despite, he used to say.

I should like to say that I am getting old, he thought to himself. *But I fear that it has already happened.*

He received deferent wing-gestures from People, nods and bows from humans, and maddening, incomprehensible arm-wavings from rashk as he walked slowly along the busy corridors of the Institute. Almost everyone stayed out of his way; presumably his contemplations were too important to interrupt.

Wait until I take my naps in public, he added to himself, thinking again of *si* S'reth, who had become an annoying old Honored One just before he transcended the Outer Peace.

This particular morning at Shiell it was raining steadily and rhythmically, the drops slapping against the windows and pavements; where the ramps and walkways extended between buildings, pedestrians remained dry due to low-power fields that deflected the rain aside. Still, the air was moist and heavy, making the 0.9 Standard gravities seem a bit more burdensome.

Rashk weather, Byar thought with a snort.

As he came up the ramp to Building 9, the doors opened before him and two human Marines came to attention and saluted. As he entered, he saw Dr. Rivendra Wells speaking with two colleagues near the lift. Wells, one of the foremost experts on vuhl tech, excused himself as he saw Byar approach, and turned to grasp forearms with him.

"*se* Byar."

"Dr. Wells. I should like to tell you that I am glad to be here, but I regret to say that I am merely glad to see you."

"That's good enough, Master Byar." Wells steered Byar by the elbow into the lift. "Fourteen," he said, and it began to rise.

"Have you made anything of the technology yet?"

"Yes and no. We know what powers it has, we know what effect it's supposed to have. We've rigged a monitoring comp and a headset for humans and zor."

"But you cannot make it work."

"That's about right, yes. It seems to respond only to certain Sensitive stimuli."

Byar let his wings move to a posture of amusement. "Which, of course, you cannot produce."

Rivendra Wells shrugged. "Not yet." The lift arrived and the two stepped out into a large laboratory/workshop filled with equipment, pieces of alien tech, and engineers in about equal proportion. Wells and Byar stepped into the room and immediately found themselves surrounded by some of each.

"Riv," one of the techs said, turning to Wells, "I can't find the damn—" He stopped at the sight of Byar HeShri. "Oh, sorry," he said. "Didn't mean to interrupt—"

Wells smiled. "Stan, this is Byar HeShri, the Master of Sanctuary. Master Byar, this is Dr. Stanley Komarov, one of our best techs. Stan, Byar is here to look at the alien rig. What can't you find?"

"Nothing important." The tech looked at the zor Sensitive, stuck out his hand as if to shake, then pulled it back and stuck it in his pocket. Byar reached out and grasped both arms, and the tech slowly responded with the same gesture.

"I would like to examine the 'rig,'" Byar said.

"Sure. Right this way, sir, Master—"

"Byar."

"*se* Byar." He managed the prenomen at least. "Come this way, we'll show you what we've got."

"Lead on."

He did. In the middle of the room was a group of twelve oblong metal-and-plastic alien somethings connected by fiber-optic cables of human design. There were two seats and two perches placed in front of them, with headsets made for both human and zor physiques; one of the other techs was sitting at a control console, which had a welter of indicators hovering in midair above it.

"We believe that the device is intended to multiply and project the power of a Sensitive," Stan said. "This part is the actual projector," he said, pointing to the oblong in the middle. "This part is some sort of synthesis device, and we have no idea what the hell these two do. Sir," he added after a moment.

"We were just about to start another test with a WS4 detailed to us, *se* Byar, if you'd like to observe."

"Has the Sensitive had any success as yet?"

"Well, no sir, not yet, but we're still moving through the various frequencies—"

"What is the rating of the Sensitive working with your 'rig'?" Byar asked.

"He's a . . . T6, *se* Byar. He was trained here at Shiell."

"May I attempt it? I believe my T-rating is . . . a few steps above that."

"Now, *se* Byar—" Rivendra Wells began, but Byar adjusted his wings and held up both hands.

"The Eight Winds did not blow me here by chance, my friend. I have come to New Chicago at your invitation; I assume that you brought me here to use my talents." He gestured to the headset. "If I may, *se* Stan," he said to the tech, picking up one of the zor-fitted headsets.

"'. . . a few steps above,' *se* Byar?" Wells said. "You're a T12. Other than the High Lord and one or two others, there isn't anyone in the Solar Empire as highly rated as you. This is experimental tech—if anything happened to you, the High Chamberlain would come here personally and pull my intestines out through one of my nostrils."

"I do not believe he would be moved to violence on that account, even if what you describe were anatomically possible." Byar's wings again lifted slightly in amusement.

"I'm not inclined to take the risk."

"*se* Rivendra," Byar said, turning slightly toward him, "it is not your risk to take." He examined the headset for a moment, then placed it carefully on his head. "Please proceed."

Rivendra Wells considered protesting again, but thought better of it. He put his hand on the tech's shoulder and sat down as the seat was vacated. A group had formed to watch the proceedings; Byar climbed onto one of the nearby perches, arranged his wings, and closed his eyes.

Wells made some adjustments on the console. "You should be getting something now, *se* Byar . . ."

Byar was getting something.

He could sense the minds in the room. There were five eights and seven, though his mind seemed to be processing the number as radix twelve: four twelves and five.

Six of the People. He could identify their Nest and clan almost without thinking—the *hsi*-markings were that distinct.

Five rashk. They were difficult to read, their minds processing three ideas in parallel, selecting two, then one, then all three to consider, synthesize, articulate.

Four eights and two remained. Four eights were certainly human, with five of them clearly Sensitives. Two of those Sensitives were members of that society called Guardians—humans trained to locate *esGa'uYal*.

That left two individuals, who were not physically in the lab, though Byar was not sure how he knew.

He opened his eyes and the two humans turned to him. Everyone else in the room was frozen in position; the light was brighter than he'd thought, and his inner eyelids closed of their own accord.

His *chya* snarled, knowing what was facing him.

"Master Byar," one of the humans said, the tone of his voice conveying exaggerated courtesy. Byar placed his hand on the hilt of his blade and felt anger course through him.

"You are unwise to come here, Servant," he said quietly.

"But we are *not* here, Master. *You* are *here*. You have summoned us—the *s's'th'r*."

The other would-be human nodded.

"That is not a word I know."

The first one raised his hand and opened it, palm-up. A colored pattern appeared in a ball above it. A thought formed itself in Byar's brain.

"An AI."

"Just so. You are the first meat-crea . . . the first 'not–Hive being' to access the *s's'th'r*. None has yet been mind-strong enough to use the capabilities of this device."

"What happens . . ." Byar gripped the hilt of his sword. The humans facing him seemed to shrink in size. "What happens when I desire to end this interview?"

"I do not understand. Please reformulate."

"If I wish to disconnect from it. From you. May I do so?"

"Why—" the Servant began.

Byar grasped the headset and tossed it to the floor. The two humans disappeared; the room burst into motion, like a paused vid ordered to play again.

"Master Byar, what's wrong?" Rivendra Wells was at his elbow at once.

Byar's wings had assumed the Cloak of Guard; three People, noting the position, approached the center of the room, half running, half flying, their *chya'i* already drawn and ready.

"Eight thousand pardons," he said after a moment. "I was . . . The device is disquieting.

"I . . . am ready to continue. Please return to your tasks, Younger Brothers," he said to the People, while the human techs stood back, trying to avoid any sudden moves. *chya'i* were sheathed. None of the three showed any inclination to leave Byar's side, instead standing nearby as if to defend him.

Stan Komarov reached down to the floor and slowly handed the headset to Byar, who accepted it while moving his wings into a polite stance.

"Thank you," he said, and placed it on his head.

* * *

The two human figures reappeared. The lights became bright; the other persons in the room froze in position. "Explain the *s's'th'r* to me," he said.

esYen, Zor'a System

In her *esTle'e* on Zor'a, one hundred and thirty parsecs away, Sa'a turned from inspection of *S'r'can'u* and drew the *hi'chya*. She made a gesture to an *alHyu*, who flew in search of *ha* T'te'e.

With the aid of the *s's'th'r* you can perceive any mind or group of minds. Depending on the magnitude of your power—" The figure let his human face relax into a bit of a smirk, which Byar did not know exactly how to interpret. "—you can extend your *k'th's's* power in any way you desire."

Byar understood the word: it meant "Sensitive ability" in the vuhl tongue. With his heightened understanding, he perceived another meaning—one that implied digestion.

He shuddered slightly; the two *s's'th'r*-beings waited patiently.

"At any distance?"

"I do not understand the question," the AI answered.

"Distance. How—far—can I extend my—"

"*k'th's's?* It depends on your ability, Master Byar. In your case, I should think that the extent would be considerable."

"Show me."

"Very well."

The room disappeared, shattering like glass and falling away. It was replaced by darkness.

At first, Byar felt as if he had been cast into *anGa'e'ren*, the Creeping Darkness of the Deceiver; but after a few moments he began to perceive points of light: eight, then eights of eights, then sixty-fours of sixty-fours. Some were brighter than others; they were a variety of colors and shapes, fading and brightening.

"*Minds,* Master Byar." The voice of the AI came from somewhere and nowhere. "The minds in this city, on this planet. The closer you look, the more you see."

As Byar continued to look, he did indeed see more and more stars. He felt them, as well, and heard their thoughts—mostly alien human ones—and he realized that the mental powers he perceived were small . . . almost scarcely worth noticing. With a thought he could eradicate any one of them.

And feed them to my— he began in his mind:

"No," he said, and the heavens shook.

"Why, Master Byar," the sinuous voice of the AI said from somewhere nearby. "It is true: Your own *k'th's's* power is great, far more than any of the—"

"—meat-creatures," Byar interrupted. "That was how you were going to end that sentence, was it not?" He reached his hand for the headset, intending to tear it off again.

"Semantics," the AI said. "Please don't trouble yourself—if the term bothers you, the *s's'th'r* can be edited to use another."

"It is not the term," Byar replied. "It is what it implies. The device not only projects my mental powers, but it also seeks to twist them. *You* are trying to twist *me,* Servant."

"Master Byar," said the voice, "you have greater *k'th's's* power than any of the minds you see. In fact, the *s's'th'r* perceives a power in you greater than . . . most of those who have previously employed it. With this power, you could accomplish any number of things. Consider it."

"I am well aware of my place and my role, Servant," he answered. "I do not need your advice or your temptations."

"What *do* you need, Master?" the voice said from the

darkness. "Your *k'th's's* is great—great enough to speak with us. What do you need? What do you want?"

Byar took a moment before answering. "Many turns ago," he said at last, "we first perceived the *esHara'y* at the edge of our consciousness. We thought that they were the *esGa'uYal,* but certain . . . experiences . . . convinced us otherwise.

"But *this*—the *s's'th'r*—is clearly a tool of Despite. This is something of *esGa'u* the Deceiver. And you ask me what I *want* from you? Why should I want anything?"

The AI did not answer, perhaps leaving Byar to contemplate the starry heaven of minds. The voice had been right in one respect: the more he looked, the more points he could see; gradually, the scene began to change to a view of New Chicago System. He could see the orange sun and the planets distinctly and clearly.

"There is one thing," Byar said at last. "There is something I want to understand."

"That can be arranged." The voice answered his unspoken request.

Looking closer, he could see something else: a thin twisted cable leading from somewhere nearby and stretching off into the distance—outsystem, into interstellar space.

He thought only for a moment before following it.

In the lab in New Chicago, Byar had not moved for several minutes. The zor had their *chya'i* drawn as if an attack were imminent. Rivendra Wells was watching the indicators on the monitors attached to the alien device reach levels he'd never seen before.

Se Byar is in danger, *se* T'te'e. I sense it."

"*hi* Sa'a, I am troubled as well." T'te'e placed his wings in the Posture of Reverence to *esLi.* "I am not sure what you intend, but I fear that it is an unacceptable risk."

"I require your help."

"I would be dishonored if I did not accede to you, High Lord. Nonetheless—"

"I intend to travel the Plane of Sleep."

"Servants of Despite are free on the Plane, *hi* Sa'a."

"*se* Byar is many eights of parsecs distant," she replied. "We can only reach him through the Plane of Sleep, for that—"

"Eight thousand pardons, High Lord. I know that there is no time. I know also that *se* Jackie can guard our *hyu* and our *hsi* as we fly across the Plane of Sleep. I am ready to serve you however you ask.

"But I am not convinced of the wisdom of this course. The Flight of the People—"

"In *esLi*'s Blessed Name, *se* T'te'e, this is not about the Flight of the People! This is about *se* Byar. His survival is critical."

"As is yours, High Lord."

"As is *yours*. We have spent too many lives because we are willing to sacrifice *one individual* for the greater good. We are going to cross the Plane of Sleep to help *se* Byar. *se* Jackie will guard us, and we will depart now. Prepare yourself."

Seeing that further resistance would be fruitless, T'te'e dipped his wings in a posture of assent.

Byar could feel his body now as he flew along, ethereal, through interstellar space. The stars were a brilliant backdrop, dappling his wings as he followed the trail of the braided rainbow cord.

He could not have said how long or how far he flew. After an eternity that might have been no more than a few seconds, he saw the cord descend into a solar system. As if his mind were changing the view to accommodate his understanding, he saw the system's primary and planets as clearly as if they were in a navcomp display.

The cord did not reach to any of the planets, how-ever—instead it traversed the system and seemed to disappear entirely.

Curious, Byar willed himself closer to the terminus, changing his position and orientation to get a better view . . .

The vuhl ship had suffered a major explosion where the gouge had been, showing empty space beyond . . . and something else.

The pilot's-board view changed, closing in on the vuhl ship; as they watched, the two parts of the ship—the aft and fore sections—fell apart in an additional explosion, tumbling out of view. Across a space perhaps a kilometer wide was a ragged, irregular patch of stars that did not belong.

Unbidden, an alien word came to his mind: *r'r's'kn.*

Other stars. The sky was bright with them. Down, down went the rainbow cord, through the *r'r's'kn.* Down went Byar, following it at an extraordinary speed.

Jackie noted that T'te'e lacked his usual hautcur as he perched beside the High Lord in her *esTle'e.* She had responded to *hi* Sa'a's request—actually, it was a command in the form of a request—as quickly as she could, but she had been on the other side of esYen at the time. She expected *T't'e'e* to upbraid her; instead, he waited silently while she approached.

"*hi* Sa'a," she said. "*se* T'te'e."

"We are going to travel the Plane of Sleep," Sa'a said without preamble. As Jackie began to object, the High Lord held her hands up before her. "I realize that you will think this unwise. Nonetheless, it is the only way to reach *se* Byar."

"Byar? Isn't he off on New Chicago?"

"Yes." The High Lord's wings rose into the Cloak of Guard. "I sense that he is in peril."

Jackie looked from the High Lord to the High Chamberlain, who inclined his wings to indicate that he had acceded to this course of action.

"The Plane of Sleep is unsafe."

"That is why you will guard us, *se Gyaryu'har*." Sa'a said it as a matter of fact.

Jackie thought about it for a moment, then shrugged and drew the *gyaryu*. The light from the dome that covered the High Lord's garden reflected off its obsidian blade; just for a moment Jackie thought she saw a flicker of rainbow color. She wasn't sure whether the two zor had seen it, but didn't want to draw attention to it now.

"I'm ready," she said.

Sa'a and T'te'e flew across the Plane of Sleep. Even since her last visit, Sa'a could see changes: Instead of gray, obscuring mists below interrupted by pillared ruins, the terrain had more the feeling of a dark, roiling swamp with clouds of fog hovering above. Things barely perceived and best not seen lurked below the level of the mist; Sa'a had the impression of long tentacles coiled and ready to reach outward.

All around, she could feel the *e'gyu'u* of the Deceiver. It breathed through every cloud of mist; it twined itself around every upthrust pillar; its voice caressed and whispered in Sa'a's ears as she flew.

One thing reassured her. She could distantly feel the light from the Golden Circle of *esLi;* now that the Plane of Sleep had been breached, servants of the Circle could reach it as well as *esGa'uYal*. The *hsi* of the Golden Legion, trapped in *Ur'ta leHssa* in the time before the High Nest, walked again in the dreams of the People.

Somewhere ahead she could feel the *hsi* of Master Byar as it fell through the Plane, pursuing . . . what?

What was Byar trying to reach?

* * *

The braided cord descended toward a nearby planet, lit bright-blue by the nearest star. There were uncountable numbers of minds there, filled with hostile, alien thoughts. Too late Byar tried to stop his descent; too late he perceived an alien mind attacking him, surrounding him, smothering him with its thoughts.

=This is interesting,= the mind said. For just a moment, Byar obtained a glance: a clear box filled with gray mist, with a silver sphere floating at the top.

=You wish to understand,= the mind continued. =Understand this: You are not to be destroyed. There is too much potential in you meat-creatures to simply feed you to the *k'th's's* of the vuhls. Even they do not understand this.

=But they will.=

No, Byar said, his voice very small. His *hsi* felt as if it was very far away. *In the name of* esLi, *no—*

=Oh, yes,= the mind said. =Yes, indeed. *e'e'ch'n* has brought you here, *se* Byar. What we learn in the next few *vx*tori* should help the breeding program immensely.=

A rush of thoughts invaded his mind—a structured plan, ordering humans and the People under the direction of the *esHara'y.* But the purpose was unseen, and in the talons of *esGa'u* himself—in the talons of creatures such as the mind that now held him and drew him in toward itself.

It called itself the Ór, and it did not serve the Great Queen but rather guided her toward some purpose that she did not perceive—and might not even understand.

Byar felt himself hurtling toward the surface of the planet. Now, somehow, he felt the wind rush past, the heat of reentry singing his wings, his inner and then outer eyelids closing against the pressure—

There," Sa'a shouted. From the mist above, extending down into the miasma below, she could see a wingspan-thick rainbow cord. Somewhere nearby she could feel Byar's *hsi,* and she could sense Byar's distress.

Without stopping to see if T'te'e was following, Sa'a flew at top speed, her *hi'chya* extended. At the last moment she pulled up, swinging the blade across the cord. Foul sparks ran down the blade as she severed it—

In the lab at the Shiell Institute the alien device began to radiate heat. Byar collapsed from his perch to the floor, unconscious.

In her garden in the High Nest, Sa'a launched herself from the perch where she had been immobile for a sixteenth of a sun, flying at high speed toward the center of her *esTle'e*. T'te'e HeYen swayed and then opened his eyes.

The *gyaryu* glowed in Jackie's hands. It might have been simply the way the light from above struck it.

After several seconds Sa'a swept down and landed across from them. Slowly and carefully, she sheathed the *hi'chya*.

"High Lord?" Jackie asked.

"It is done," she answered, "*se* Byar is safe." Her wings slumped heavily, as if she had flown eights of kilometers.

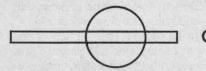

Chapter 4

THE *GUARDIANS*, OR *GUARDIAN ORDER*, WAS ESTABLISHED IN APRIL 2398 BY IMPERIAL DECREE. ITS PURPOSE IS TO PROTECT THE PERSON OF THE SOLAR EMPEROR AND HIS FAMILY, AND HAS FUNCTIONED AS A SELF-GOVERNING SECURITY SERVICE WITHIN THE EMPIRE. ITS ORIGINAL COMMANDER,

COMMANDER OWEN GARRETT (IN, RET.), WAS SUC-
CEEDED BY DR. ANTONIO ST. GILES, PH.D. (SHIELL
INSTITUTE, NEW CHICAGO), IN 2402 . . .

—Imperial Encyclopedia,
2405 Edition

IT IS ENOUGH FOR MOST—INCLUDING MOST
GUARDIANS—TO KNOW THAT WE EXIST TO PRO-
TECT THE EMPEROR. THAT IS A NOBLE CALLING: TO
PROTECT THE EMPIRE, IT IS CRUCIAL THAT WE PRO-
TECT THE IMPERIAL PERSON.

BUT THAT IS ONLY THE BEGINNING OF OUR PATH.
WHAT LIES BEFORE EVERY GUARDIAN IS THE PAS-
SAGE THROUGH THE GATE OF UNDERSTANDING,
THE GATE OF POWER—AND THE TOOLS AND SKILLS
WE ARE GIVEN ARE ONLY THE POINT OF DEPAR-
TURE FOR THAT JOURNEY. FOR MOST IN THE OR-
DER, THE GATE IS UNKNOWN AND INVISIBLE . . .
BUT FOR THOSE READING THIS BOOK, THE GATE IS
THE GOAL. WITH WHAT YOU ARE TAUGHT HERE,
YOU WILL GO BEYOND MOST GUARDIANS . . . YOU
WILL OPEN THAT GATE AND STEP THROUGH. THEN
YOU WILL RECOGNIZE WHAT LIES BEHIND YOU AS
MERE ILLUSION.

—Antonio St. Giles, Master of the Inner Gate,
Opening the Gate,
Green Book edition, 2405

April 2422
In jump en route to ARIEL SYSTEM

In jump there was nothing to see on *Emperor Ian*'s observation deck, so it was largely deserted when the starship

was traveling between stars. Most people who visited there projected something on the viewscreens—scenes from home, star patterns, anything but the inky nothingness into which light never penetrated.

For Alan Howe, there was no need. He could view the Golden Gate Bridge or the Anderhof Chasm on the wall of his quarters, and Astrography was much better equipped to show stellar configurations. The observation deck was as good a place as any to look into the deep darkness that—at the moment, at least—was *Emperor Ian*'s entire universe. Once, during a conversation with Jackie Laperriere, they'd discussed the appearance of jump; she'd gotten a good look at it during her quest for the *gyaryu*, when the hangar doors of *Fair Damsel* had been opened by an enemy onto the nothingness out there. Ever since, he'd had a sort of perverse fascination with it, something that kept bringing him back to look at it from vantages like this.

"There's absolutely nothing to see, you know."

Alan turned at the voice and saw an unfamiliar face and an all-too-familiar uniform: all gray with no distinguishing emblems, no jewelry other than a single earring showing four hands grasping each other at the wrist.

"The zor call it *anGa'e'ren*," Alan said at last. "I don't know you. I'm—"

"I know who you are," the Guardian said, with no trace of emotion. "Colonel Howe. *Emperor Ian*'s WS9."

"That's right. And you are . . ."

"Ah." He walked toward Alan. "Bradford. Cameron Bradford. I've just been assigned to *Ian*." He stopped about five meters short of Alan and gave a little bow, more an inclination of the head than anything else. Guardians weren't strong on handshakes or salutes.

"Really? What happened to Tom Jimenez?"

"Assigned somewhere else." Bradford looked away and out the viewscreen, then down at the console. It indicated that they were looking at a projection from *Emperor Ian*'s forward visual array.

"*anGa'e'ren.* 'The Creeping Darkness,' as I recall."

"That's right."

"And you *subscribe* to this zor myth, I suppose."

Alan tried to imagine what Jackie Laperriere would've said in response, but continued: "I wouldn't say that I'm subscribing to anything. It's certainly real enough for the People to believe in it. In fact, your predecessor and I had several discussions on the subject.

"Where has he been reassigned, by the way?"

Bradford turned and looked at him. For a moment there seemed to be the slightest hint of anger in the Guardian's eyes—then it vanished. Alan knew that look: he was being examined using Guardian techniques.

No one here but us artha, he thought.

"Somewhere else," Bradford answered at last. He sounded almost disappointed that Alan had turned out to be a human after all.

"Just curious."

"My briefing said that you are very inquisitive," the Guardian said. "You were on quite social terms with Jimenez, weren't you?"

"You're fairly inquisitive, too."

He hadn't meant it as an accusation, but Bradford seemed to take a step backward.

"I'm not here to waste time like Jimenez. I have a duty aboard this ship," the Guardian said. "I trust you'll remember that."

"Everyone aboard *Emperor Ian* has a duty, Bradford," Alan snapped back. "I trust you'll remember *that.*"

Bradford glared at him but didn't answer for several moments. *This is certainly going well,* Alan thought to himself.

"I have work to do," the Guardian said. He turned on his heel without another word and stalked off the observation deck, the access door sliding aside and then closing as he passed.

* * *

There's no accounting for them," Agropoulous said, tossing back his drink and setting the empty container on the bar. "Don't worry—we don't allow civilians in the Officers' Club."

"Glad to hear it. But he didn't seem much interested in socializing." Alan took a sip from his own drink. "I mean—he was *rude*, Jim. Insulting."

"That's the way they all are—as if their uniforms are on too tight."

"Tom Jimenez wasn't like that."

"Proves the rule."

"Why'd he get transferred?"

"Jimenez?" Agropoulous shrugged. "Not sure. I believe the admiral received the orders just before we left Zor'a. That's where Bradford came aboard. I've been so damn busy getting ready for Ariel I hadn't thought about it."

"I've been busy, too, and hadn't noticed . . . It's a little strange, don't you think? Reassigning a Guardian off a flagship just before attacking a major target?"

"They're *all* major targets."

"You know what I mean. We're working our way toward an important vuhl base of operations, a place that *se* Ch'en'ya thinks is the alien homeworld—and a key member of Admiral Anderson's staff is posted away just before insertion. Why?"

"I don't know. The Guardians do whatever they damn well please, Alan, and you know it. They answer to their commander and to His Imperial Highness—not to me, not to you, not to Admiral Master-before-God Anderson. There is no latitude for discussion and I have no interest in sticking my hand where it doesn't belong."

Alan considered that, then looked carefully at Agropoulous. "You know something, don't you?"

"I just finished telling you I don't know anything and that, anyway, it's none of my damn business. Didn't you read me?"

"Loud and clear." Alan looked his old friend up and down again. "But you know something."

"I—" Agropoulous looked away from Alan for several moments. "I'm in no position to . . ."

"It won't go farther than me."

"It had better not." The general lowered his voice. "From what I understand, Jimenez was reassigned *particularly* because he was the exception and not the rule. He was . . . a little friendly with officers and crew aboard this ship."

"Including me."

"*Especially* you. Don't take this wrong, old pal, but the *last* person a Guardian trusts is a Sensitive. They consider people in your line of work highly suspect—most likely to be Dominated. And, of course, you'd still scan as 'human' even so."

". . . most likely to—" Howe began, but Agropoulous held his hand up.

"I think it's a pile of crap, myself. I've seen you get us out of too many scrapes over the years to believe that line. But that's what *they* believe. They're a law unto themselves, Alan, and don't you forget it. Best if you just take Tom Jimenez' transfer in stride."

"I considered him a friend, damn it."

"Now, *that*," Agropoulous said, "was a mistake. He was a colleague and a comrade, but don't you *ever* think of him as a friend. As *your* friend, I'm warning you, Alan. Their agenda is different, and they don't take well to being questioned."

"I wasn't *questioning*. I just wanted to know—"

"Drop it. Just—drop it."

Zor'a System

The High Lord's rescue of Byar on the Plane of Sleep, along with the conversation with Laura Ibarra, had made

Jackie restless; it might have brought about the dream that
came to her a few nights later. However, she wasn't willing to completely credit her own internal emotions:
Stone's people had manipulated dreams before, and she
had no doubt that they would do so again.

In the dream she found herself walking along the parapets of Sanctuary, but it was not the familiar landscape
she had seen first in her *Dsen'yen'ch'a* and then many
times afterward. Beyond the walls were rugged mountains framed by the deep darkness of *anGa'e'ren*.

As she paused to look at the scene, she felt the sound
of wings and turned to see a zor landing nearby. It was a
figure she knew well and hadn't expected to see ever
again.

"*si* . . . Th'an'ya?"

She stepped forward and grasped forearms with
Th'an'ya, whom she had last seen walking toward *esLi*'s
Golden Light on the *gyaryu*.

"I ask eight thousand pardons in coming to you in this
way," she said, stepping back. "I hope that I do not disturb you."

"I didn't expect to ever see you again," Jackie answered. "Didn't you go to *esLi*?"

"Servants of *esLi* can walk here as well as *esGa'uYal*,"
Th'an'ya answered, placing her wings in a position of
honor to *esLi*.

"What is this place?" Jackie thought she already knew
the answer.

"This is the Plane of Sleep—and in this place, this
echo of Sanctuary, something is to happen."

"That's appropriately vague."

"I never became completely accustomed to your dry
wit," Th'an'ya said, letting her wings relax into the
Stance of Comradeship. "There is some event that involves you—and another as well. Someone close to both
of us."

"If this is my subconscious talking," Jackie answered,

glancing over her shoulder at the darkness beyond, "then I'd guess we'd be talking about *se* Ch'en'ya."

"My daughter," Th'an'ya said. "She causes you much disquiet. She is full of anger, but that is not what is troubling you."

"I'm afraid of what's going to happen to her. I think she's headed for some *shNa'es'ri*, and I can't foresee the outcome."

"What has happened?"

Jackie shrugged, not sure why she had to explain the situation to her own unconscious mind. "I don't know where she's gone," Jackie said. "And I'm worried about what she might do."

"You are worried," Th'an'ya answered, "that you have no control over what is to come."

"That's an oversimplification. I'm not her keeper, and I can't direct events. I am in the employ of the High Nest, and I do what they tell me to do."

"And what are they telling you now?"

"I haven't received any direction."

"Are you sure?"

"In twenty-five years at the High Nest, I've never been sure about anything. I expect that at some point, *hi* Sa'a will receive a dream—"

"Do you think she is the only one who receives dreams?"

"She's the only one that receives dreams that guide the Flight of the People," Jackie answered. "The only one whose dreams mean anything."

"Your first statement is true," Th'an'ya said. "But others have dreams that are meaningful . . . This one, for instance."

"Are you trying to tell me—"

Th'an'ya raised her wings in a stance that suggested she was awaiting a *sSurch'a* on Jackie's part.

"What are you trying to tell me? What am I trying to tell myself? That I can't stand by while things happen that are out of my control anyway?" She spread her arms wide. "What should I do—go after her and bring her back?"

"If there is a decision that she must make, would it not be better if you were there to advise her?"

"She doesn't listen to anyone."

"She listens to *you*," Th'an'ya said. "Even if she often discounts what you say, she respects you as *Gyaryu'har* and *Qu'uYar*."

"Her favorite word is 'Pah.'"

"Nonetheless," Th'an'ya said. "She listens."

"A wise person once told me, 'That the ear does not hear is not the fault of the voice.' Are you telling me that some of what I say gets through that arrogant skull of hers?"

"I am saying, *se* Jackie, that the most difficult thing for any friend to do is to speak when silence is desired. She may say that her ear 'does not hear,' but I believe otherwise . . . and in any case, it is not your voice that is at fault."

"So what you're telling me is that I need to speak to her, to tell her what I think—"

"And to hear her voice, as well. If you are correct—if there is indeed a *shNa'es'ri* ahead for my daughter—then she may fare better if you are there for her to hear."

"I'd like to believe that."

"I think," Th'an'ya said, "you already do."

Th'an'ya then lowered her wings into a posture of respect and turned away, walking and then flying into the mist. Jackie watched her until she was out of sight, and then the dream drifted away as well.

Just before leaving Zor'a, she'd had a brief conversation with the High Lord at A'alu Spaceport, in the High Lord's private suite overlooking the main concourse. Jackie had made up her mind to follow Ch'en'ya, but *hi*

Sa'a wasn't just there to see her off: more to argue against the idea of pursuit.

"I appreciate your concern for Younger Sister Ch'en'ya, *se* Jackie," she'd said. "But do you not wish for intel to do its job?"

"I want to hear the story directly from her."

"Will it sound more convincing that way?"

"It might."

"Imperial Intelligence is searching for *se* Ch'en'ya. They are concerned"—the High Lord's wings shifted very slightly—"about a security breach. They are unlikely to be happy with . . . What would it be termed in Standard? . . . 'playing cowboy'?"

"I'm not—"

"You *are*," Sa'a interrupted, gently. She placed her wings in a stance of honor—concerned, perhaps, that she might offend her *Gyaryu'har* with her bluntness. "Whether the Third Deputy Director endorses your actions or merely chooses to avoid criticizing them, Imperial Intelligence will not find favor with a lone operative interfering with their investigations."

"They don't understand what's at stake here."

"I suspect that they do."

"And, in any case, I'm not *interfering*—I'm going as a private citizen."

"With the *gyaryu* at your belt."

"I can't very well leave it behind," Jackie answered, placing her hand on the hilt.

"No, I suppose not." Sa'a turned away and looked through the one-way glass at zor and humans and occasional rashk, moving from one place to another. "I . . . understand that you are driven by dreams. I am familiar with that sensation: Is that what placed you on this flight?"

"I think my mind was already made up beforehand."

Sa'a did not answer, but merely turned to face Jackie, her wings placed in a posture of regret.

Kensington Starbase,
Kensington System

"Hellespont?" The harbormaster of Kensington Starbase, a middle-aged ex–Navy man named Kendall, took a moment to look at Jackie when he said the name of the ship. "Yes, I remember." He flipped his comp into his hand and said, *"Hellespont.* Transit details, format six," then walked to a console on one side of the room and waved the comp over a sensor.

Kensington Starbase had been an important naval base in a war zone a hundred Standard years ago, but now it was a civilian facility handling the transit of thousands of vessels every day. They were standing in the base's C-and-C (Command-and-Control center), an enormous room four or five times the size of a fleet carrier's bridge, located at the very top of the long spindle that pierced the wheel where the ships docked.

The ship-registry data appeared in the air. Thanks to Laura Ibarra, Jackie had seen the data before; there was still something nagging her about it, but she hadn't been able to put her finger on it.

"What was *Hellespont*'s destination?"

"Right there." Kendall jabbed a finger at a set of coordinates halfway down the display. "Crozier System, from the look of it—outside the Empire. *Hellespont* is headed for the war zone."

Kendall was in constant motion around his C-and-C: He had a comp on a wrist bracelet that he flipped into his hand with long-practiced skill, passing orders to his underlings without even turning aside to look at them.

"Why would a merchanter head for the war zone?"

"You'd be surprised." Kendall raised an eyebrow, looked her up and down. "Yes, I expect you *would* be surprised. Soldiers buy things too—Crozier's out of the line of fire . . . well, to the extent that anyplace is—and there isn't an army or navy in the history of mankind that didn't have merchanters and service providers following along like hiaroo nipping at its heels." The hiaroo was a little domesticated animal native to Kensington Prime.

"What can you tell me about Crozier System?"

"What do you want to know?"

"I—" She held back on the first answer she thought of. She would need this man's cooperation if she was to get anywhere; clearly he was a gold mine of information, if she could just ask the right question. "What's the most prominent feature?"

"Metals. And lots of them—they've got a huge asteroid belt that's chock-full of resources. So, naturally, it's got lots of small shipyards."

"You mean for merchanters and that sort of thing."

"That sort of thing," Kendall agreed. "And *other* sorts of things. Scouts, scientific vessels, entrepreneurs—"

"Pirates."

"I'm sure that wouldn't be *their* choice of terms, but yes, pirates. One byproduct of a quarter-century of war: There's all sorts of ordnance floating around."

"I never thought of that."

"Regular Navy folks never do," Kendall answered. "Why would they? One use, throw it away. But scavengers have been picking debris off the battlefield since men fought with swords and pikes."

He's a regular analogy machine, isn't he? she thought. "So it ends up at places like Crozier System."

"That's right. And there's enough of it scattered around there that the Imperial Navy has never bothered to go in and clean it up. Can't say as I blame them."

"It's lawless?"

"Oh, I wouldn't say *that.* It has its *own* law, shall we say. I doubt whether someone capable of handling . . . *unusual* situations would have any trouble. Your reputation precedes you, Ms. Laperriere." Kendall leaned on the console and looked back at her, the lines of data in the air between them looking vaguely like a carnival mask. "I wouldn't think you'd have any trouble at all."

"I wouldn't think you'd have any trouble at all," she

heard in her head as she stood overlooking the Kensington Station main concourse, looking through the comp display for a passage headed for Crozier or somewhere nearby. *Yes,* she told herself, *I guess I've been in a few "unusual situations."*

Suddenly something jumped out at her from the list of outbound vessels. CROZIER, it said: OUTBND 1830. RXE E MHNESR.

Not a zor vessel; clearly not a human one. Not enough apostrophes to be a rashk name, she thought to herself. One other choice left.

Now, there's *a challenge,* she added, noting the docking location: *Taking passage on an otran ship.* She'd met no more than two or three of the feline aliens in her life; those were the most unusual ones, the diplomats assigned to the High Nest or to the Emperor's Court. The otran were the least gregarious of the four alien races within the Solar Empire; they remained almost entirely on their homeworld. They'd been discovered more than a century ago and had been brought along slowly and with great care by the Empire.

Sergei had briefed her on them years ago when she was new to the job. *"Brought along slowly,"* indeed, she thought to herself, remembering it now: *"Best way to handle high explosives."*

The otran had one basic problem in their alien psyche: they simply couldn't walk away from a fight. Over time, their culture had developed a rather varied set of beliefs, and every otran adult was expected to pick the ones that he—or she—believed in. If one otran met another and there were differences of opinion, but *both had acceptable beliefs*—something about "forty-eight aspects of the Deity," she remembered—all was well and good. But if one of them had an unrecognized belief, there would be a fight—*to the death in some cases,* she reminded herself: their wars were largely proxy affairs, a sort of Olympics, with casualties—but there wasn't any way for two otran, or groups of otran, or nations of otran, to "agree to disagree." They considered that idea insane.

They also considered representative government insane, at least when it came to decisions where one side didn't completely convince the others. At least at the end of an otran proxy war the survivors slapped each other on the back and got drunk.

No wonder most of them stuck to the homeworld.

Well, clearly *Rxe E Mhnesr* wasn't sticking to the homeworld. Jackie was looking for some kind of cover, especially now that she'd gotten some intel on Crozier System; an otran merchanter would probably do the trick.

To the human eye otran are feline. Heavyset, with whiskered faces; bipedal, with seven-fingered hands: four long, gripping fingers and three short, delicate ones. They didn't purr or meow—their actual language consisted of clicks and pops, but a voder on the lapel translated that into Standard.

One of *Rxe E Mhnesr*'s officers was standing at the loading-bay, ordering crew around as she approached. For one terrible moment, Jackie had a overwhelming feeling of déjà vu—she remembered another merchanter, another time and place—Cle'eru, and Sultan Sabah getting the *Fair Damsel* ready for jump.

She reminded herself that the universe was a different place now; Ch'k'te had gone to *esLi*. All she had left was his angry daughter, some jumps ahead of her, headed for *esLi*-knew-what.

The officer stopped and looked at her, intertwining his fingers in front of him. *Means he's being friendly,* the *gyaryu* told her; *he can't attack you if his hands are linked like that.*

Jackie looked at the strength in the arms and shoulders and doubted it, but took the gesture for what it was.

"How may this one be of service?" the otran's voder said for him.

"Greetings," Jackie answered, bowing. "I am—"

"Your identity is known," the alien replied. "I am Nel E Showan, and you are the *Gu, Gry, Gyary*—"

"Gyaryu'har," Jackie said. "It took me awhile to learn to say it, as well. Peace and prosperity to you, Nel E Showan," she managed, inclining her head and offering the greeting that the *gyaryu* thoughtfully supplied.

"Gyaryu'har. Yes. I thank you, but I find it curious that you are unaccompanied, and choose to have speech with this one. Have I offended?"

"Not in the least. I—would speak with your captain. I wish passage aboard your vessel to Crozier System, which is your next destination."

"Passage, is it." A group of four or five otran had stopped working to listen to the exchange. Nel E Showan turned to them and erupted in the otran native tongue; they scurried back to do whatever they should have been doing. "Pardons—eight thousand is the correct number, I believe. Laziness and idle curiosity must be dealt with despite the need for courtesy to a high dignitary."

"I completely understand." She smiled and inclined her head. "You aren't outbound for nearly three Standard hours; if I could return at a more opportune time—"

"No, no, by no means," Nel E Showan said. "Discourteous would it be, as your time is no doubt valuable. Please permit me to escort you to the captain's presence." He shouted something else in the otran language without turning around; a younger and physically smaller crewman came running out of the hold and took the comp that Nel E Showan handed him without looking. "If *Gyaryu'har*-person would follow this one . . ."

"Thank you." Jackie walked up the ramp with the otran, who had turned to enter the ship. She found her contact lenses adjusting automatically as she walked across the hold and into a ship's corridor; the lighting was a sort of harsh pinkish color. The odor was different, reminiscent of neither zor nor human habitations—but it was not unpleasant: a sort of musky, spicy scent. The public-address comm was a constant background of otran speech, all clicks and barks and pops. Her comp could translate if she gave it the task, but the meaning was clear: probably something like, *"get that cargo stowed or it'll come out of your pay"* . . . *"Officer so-and-so to cargo bay such-and-such"* . . . *"Where's that crate of widgets? It was supposed to be on board two hours ago!"*—all interspersed with colorful epithets, of course. A merchanter made or lost its money during the last few hours before jump.

After a series of turns and ramps and three decks up in a lift, Nel E Showan showed her into a large sitting-room, bowed, and left her alone. Another, older-looking otran was examining a display hovering in midair above a console. It was changing by the second.

He turned to face her. "This is an honor, madam. Welcome aboard *Rxe E Mhnesr.* I am Captain Showan—Kot E Showan."

"A pleasure," Jackie said. "Peace and prosperity, Captain."

"Fine things to wish for. Let us hope that they come to us both. How may I be of service to the High Nest?"

"Not precisely to the High Nest, Captain. I would like to take passage on your excellent vessel to its next port."

"Hrr," he answered. The voder didn't manage any sort of translation. She wasn't sure what it meant, but guessed that it was neither yes nor no. "This is a rather unusual request, a human seeking passage on one of our vessels. Why choose *Rxe E Mhnesr*? Surely you could command a berth on any ship you wish."

"You are traveling to Crozier System."

"Not to put too fine a point on it, madam," the captain answered, "but many ships travel to Crozier System. Indeed, many ships go there from Kensington System every Standard day."

"Yours is the soonest departure."

"In a hurry? *Rxe E Mhnesr* is a fine and noble ship, *se Gyaryu'har,* but not the swiftest. We are no less than four

Standard days' travel from dock at Crozier Terminus, including real-space navigation. I am certain that a military vessel could reach it sooner. Ah," he said, gesturing toward a pair of large, well-padded chairs on one side of the room, "but politeness is forgotten. Please sit. Would you desire refreshment?"

The abrupt change of tack caught Jackie a bit by surprise; she walked with Kot E Showan to the chairs and they both sat. "No, no thank you, Captain. Indeed, I would not wish to distract you from—" She gestured to the constantly updating display.

"Hrr," Kot E Showan repeated. "It is my cousin Nel's problem to make sure it is all done, and done correctly. The brain governs, the hands direct, the back strains—but if the brain turns its attention elsewhere, hands and back must still continue their work. It would be a sad thing indeed if the master of *Rxe E Mhnesr* could not turn his attention aside for a few Standard minutes.

"Now." He extended his hands toward each other so that the long, gripping fingers touched. "*Rxe E Mhnesr* would be honored to have you travel with us to Crozier System—but one is still moved to ask why. It is curiosity, is it not?"

"I confess that it is some of that," she said. "But . . . I think it is also camouflage."

"Forgive me for not taking your meaning."

"I am following someone."

"I see." The long fingers pushed each other apart, then touched again. "No, I do not see. How can traveling on our vessel, slower than many, without the power of the High Nest behind it, help you pursue your quarry?"

"The person isn't precisely a quarry. This is investigative, not predatory . . . Well, I'm following her *path*. I want to know where she went and I'm not keen that she know I'm doing it. If she knew, she might vanish completely."

"A 'tail,' I believe the term is."

"Just so."

"Camouflage. I understand now. Do you place my ship in danger by this tailing?"

"I should hope not."

"You are unsure," the otran captain said.

"I cannot give you an ironclad guarantee of your ship's safety, Captain—but if you wanted to be safe, you wouldn't be going to Crozier System, would you?"

"Hrr. Just so . . . Very well, *se Gyaryu'har*." He cocked his head from side to side, and then extended his left hand palm-up. "Welcome aboard."

I don't believe it."

Admiral Anderson and General Agropoulous stood in midair with the stars surrounding them. Faint lines extended from New Harare, Rivières, Wolfram Minor, Tamarind, Towson, and six stars where they'd destroyed vuhl naval facilities. Ten lines—and they all crossed at one place: SS Aurigae, a blue binary with a system only explored by unmanned probes and never visited by a manned Imperial Grand Survey ship. There were ten small enemy installations marked in close vicinity.

Emperor Ian's Astrography holo gave perspective: admiral and general could see in all directions, and could feel very, very small.

"She could have it right, Admiral. It *could* be the homeworld of the vuhls."

"Either they're terribly stupid, or they think *we* are. I'll grant that it's a major naval base. The last several major battles are in easy jump range of the place. But no enemy admiral would draw attention to its homeworld by basing a military campaign from it: Not to mention the fact that it has violent and regular solar flares. The bugs may be monsters, but there's no way they could have evolved in *that* environment."

"Ch'en'ya seemed fairly convinced. And the High Lord . . ."

"*Dreamed* it. I know: Ignore it at my peril. What she

dreamed was that the system was the place of the damned or something."

"The Valley of Lost Souls," Agropoulous said. "And that's not exactly what she said." He reached into a pocket and took out his comp then gestured over it. "Let's see . . ." A string of text appeared in the air; he squinted at it in the starlight. "'The path through that system leads through the Valley of Lost Souls.' *That's* what she said."

"Did Alan have any insight on that quip?"

"He said that she foresaw some sort of bad outcome when we reached it. The Valley of Lost Souls—"

"Yes, I know what it is." Anderson fixed his Marine commander with a frown that usually worked well on junior subordinates, which he knew was likely to roll off Agropoulous—but habits were habits. "So, did he think that the High Nest was against such a campaign?"

"No, sir, quite the opposite. It was his impression that the High Lord expected us to pursue the course . . . and that it would be some sort of ordeal for us, or the High Nest, or maybe everyone involved. The zor are a very fatalistic race, Admiral."

"So they've decided that SS Aurigae—KEYSTONE—is going to be bad news—and there's no avoiding it."

"That's about right, sir."

"But what's waiting for us there, Jim? We gather up the troops at New Harare, we take what's in between, and we tackle KEYSTONE. We start here—" He gestured at one of the outlying installations. "That one is ARIEL. Then we go after BASALT . . . all the way to this one—" He pointed to a star very near Keystone itself. "Janissary. When we're all done, what are we going to find at Keystone System? The Destroyer? Surely not the vuhl homeworld, but . . . what?"

Jim Agropoulous had no answer. Instead he merely looked out at the stars.

Jardine City
New Chicago System

"Master Byar."

Byar turned from the hospital-room window. It was rashk weather outside again, and wherever he looked he saw *r'r's'kn* in the clouds. Still, he felt himself compelled to look—more than twenty suns had gone by since his experience with the alien tech, but the images haunted him sleeping and waking.

"*ha* T'te'e," he answered, inclining his wings in the Posture of Polite Approach. "I did not expect to see you here in New Chicago System."

"Did not expect—" T'te'e crossed the room to grasp forearms with the Master of Sanctuary. "The High Lord had me on a ship less than a sun after your encounter with . . ."

"I am interested in knowing how you intend to complete that sentence."

"Words fail me."

"As well they should."

"What was it, *se* Byar? What was drawing you toward it?"

"I cannot say what it was, old friend. It called itself 'Ór.' I do not know what the word means, except that it was known to the *esHara'y: si* Owen said, long ago, that it was the Ór that was watching him on Center."

"Did you see it?"

"Yes. It was a sort of box . . ." He described what he had seen, along with the feeling of malign intelligence he had felt from it. "At times," he continued, "words fail me as well. Every sun . . . Every sun since it happened, Dr. Wells has come to visit; he feels responsible—but more than that, he is curious." His wings made a half-hearted attempt to convey amusement. "He cannot make the alien device function and is afraid to ask me to try again."

"The High Lord forbids it, my friend. There will be no more experiments with tools of *esGa'u*."

"Dr. Wells will be disappointed and relieved, I am sure. For my part, I am merely disappointed. I wish I had learned more—I have brushed against the wing of the Deceiver."

"Most who touch the wing of *esGa'u* wish never to do so again." T'te'e's wings moved to the Cloak of Guard.

"I do not fear *Ur'ta leHssa*, my old friend, and I do not fear this Ór." He knew he was not being completely truthful, but kept his wings impassive. "The touch of the Deceiver will not make me *idju* or undo what I have done in my life. If it had been needful to transcend the Outer Peace during the trial with the alien tech, I would have done what was needful."

"We would have lost a great asset to the High Nest, *se* Byar."

"Another would have taken my place."

"I would not want that yet to be."

"Assuredly not." Byar placed his taloned hands palm-up on the windowsill and looked at them. A nick here, an abrasion there—the claws did not curl the way they used to. "But the time is coming as it must. You, I, even *hi* Sa'a will have to face the moment of Transcending. Some sooner than later . . . but there is no avoiding it.

"I will try to explain myself before I must choose that flight, *se* T'te'e. Unlike *si* S'reth, I do not think that my *hsi* would be safe being summoned across the Plane of Sleep." His wings rose in amusement again. "Still—I am beginning to feel like him in other ways: not just advancing age . . . I sense a new *shNa'es'ri* coming, one we have waited for since the war began."

"What else did you see, old friend?"

"Something I know that I have seen before: When we performed a *Dsen'yen'ch'a* many turns ago we saw this *r'r's'kn*—do you remember? We had no idea what it was—but the pilots from the fighter wing flew through it."

"I recall. Just before we witnessed Shr'e'a."

"Shr'e'a," Byar repeated. "That this *r'r's'kn* led to Shr'e'a in that Ordeal is a frightening omen. Shr'e'a means giving up the *gyaryu*."

"Again."

"Again," Byar agreed. "Do you know, we once believed that *si* Owen was the avatar of *si* Dri'i, the hero of Sharia'a. When *si* Owen was killed I realized what I should have known all along—that Sharia'a is a myth and always was, and that *si* Owen could never have been an avatar for anything."

"Then why did the true *esGa'uYal* rescue him from the vuhls—the *esHara'y*? What was the point?"

"Many years ago," Byar said, looking out the window at the clouds and the crouching half-revealed forms of *r'r's'kn* in them, "I told our friend *se* Jackie that Despite does not need a point. I was in error then, and I would be in error now if I told you that such a thing as *si* Owen walking the rainbow path was nothing, a false trail. There is some meaning to it—and there is some meaning to the *Dsen'yen'ch'a*, and in the Blessed Name of *esLi* there must be a meaning to his death at Port Saud.

"I feel that if I were a few turns younger and a few wing-lengths smarter I could tell you what it was." His wings dropped; T'te'e, alarmed, saw the position of *Ur'ta leHssa*: the Valley of Lost Souls. "The dust of despair is heavy on my wings, old friend. I am not sure what to do."

Outside, the storm raged, and every cloud held an echo of *r'r's'kn*. Whatever *shNa'es'ri* lay ahead, was beyond that rip in space; and despite the will of the High Nest, he knew that he would have to approach it again.

Chapter 5

GA E LAYUN. TRANS: "ENGAGED CONTEST." A CONTENTION BETWEEN TWO OR MORE OTRAN OR GROUPS OF OTRAN REGARDING A MATTER IN DISPUTE. ACCORDING TO WHAT IS UNDERSTOOD OF OTRAN CULTURE, A *"GA E LAYUN"* OCCURS WHEN THE OPPOSING PARTIES CANNOT AGREE ON AN INTERPRETATION OF THE MATTER ACCORDING TO THE FORTY-EIGHT RECOGNIZED ASPECTS OF THE UNSEEN ([LINK ENTRY]). THE CONTEST CONTINUES UNTIL ALL BUT ONE SIDE CONCEDES THE MATTER AND ADOPTS THE SAME VIEW.

—*Imperial Encyclopedia*,
2405 Edition

NEVER ARGUE WITH AN OTRAN.

—author unknown

April 2422
In jump aboard Rxe E Mhnesr

The trip to Crozier was largely uneventful. The crew and officers of *Rxe E Mhnesr* seemed mostly related to each other—one big, happy family carrying on trade in a universe composed of aliens that they didn't—or chose not to—understand.

Kot E Showan ran his ship with exactly the tone and

style Jackie would have expected from a clever and wealthy uncle with a huge number of nephews and nieces, sons, and cousins. Captain Showan had a temper and no inhibitions to using it: When he had a full head of steam and his fingers were unlaced, most everyone stayed out of the way. Only Nel, the ship's purser and the captain's cousin, seemed willing to stand up to him and modify his tendency to bully the younger crew.

Jackie found the fare at Kot E Showan's table interesting. Some of it was clearly inedible by humans, even though it smelled (and probably would have tasted) wonderful. Captain Showan had managed to put in additional stores of food specifically for human consumption— probably at the last minute and probably at additional expense, after he had welcomed her aboard. He'd likely assumed that, whether she was traveling incognito or not, it wouldn't do to offend the High Nest.

The family relationships on *Rxe E Mhnesr* were a web of siblings and near-cousins. Nel was the captain's nearest relative: In addition to his duties on the cargo deck, he apparently ruled the kitchen, providing a greater variety of dishes than aboard an Imperial starship.

Two days out of Kensington and two from dock at Crozier, Jackie was sitting at the captain's table and decided to broach a weighty subject.

"Tell me," she said, as the remains of dinner were pushed away, "what do you make of the war?"

"Profitable," Kot E Showan answered. "Dangerous, but profitable."

"Have you had any brushes with the enemy?"

"With the vuhls? Not directly." She could hear a few quiet *Hrr*s from down the table, where a few juniors remained at the end of the meal. Kot E Showan leaned back, touching his fingertips to each other. "They don't trade much."

There was laughter among the otran, and Jackie

couldn't help but smile as well. "I meant in a combat situation."

"This is not a combat vessel, *se Gyaryu'har*," the captain answered. "You asked if we contacted the vuhls . . . As I say, they do not trade with us."

"They'd more likely want to destroy or Dominate you."

"Then it is just as well."

"Forgive me, Captain, but you don't seem to view them in a particularly adversarial light."

"I do not view them in any light at all, madam. They are not *Rxe E Mhnesr*'s concern, and therefore none of mine."

"The Solar Empire is at war."

"Hrr." Kot E Showan extended his hands on the table. "The war affects the way in which we do business, certainly, but it does not change our basic motivations. We trade; we travel. Our race has not been called upon to provide ships or troops. We do not interfere with the conduct of the war, but neither do we participate in it. Besides, a onetime adversary may be a future friend."

The others at the table murmured agreement.

"I doubt that will happen in this case."

"*Do* you. Why? Your race, and the race you serve"—he gestured toward the *gyaryu* and inclined his head—"were they not at war a hundred Standard years ago?"

"The situation is somewhat different."

"The situation is exactly, *precisely,* the same!" He slapped his hands on the table, causing the rest of the otran to fall silent. Captain Showan looked from one face to another, resting his glance at last on Jackie.

"Forgiveness," he said in a milder tone. "But governments in human space revel in rewriting the present and rewriting the past to accommodate the present. You do this *constantly*—finding ways to differ where you once agreed, and drawing parallels where none existed before. By The Unseen, please settle on your story and stick to it."

The other otran nodded and lightly slapped their hands

on the table, indicating assent. It seemed that Captain Showan had been over this ground before and had just repeated something fundamental and profound.

"Again, forgiveness," he repeated at last. "First, for subjecting a guest to *ga E layun;* second, for associating you with the sometimes duplicitous human government. Though we do not see the lay of the mountains as the zor People do, we can at least understand them better."

Jackie reached out mentally to the *gyaryu: What the hell is* ga E layun? she asked.

That's their term for an argument, Sergei answered. *Of course, it's more complicated than that.*

"No offense is taken," she said aloud. "But I would like to understand *ga E layun.*"

"Hrr," Captain Showan said. "Would you indeed."

She looked at the other otran, who looked very slightly amused, but who said nothing.

"Some of my *na'otran*—even my near-kin here on *Rxe E Mhnesr*"—he glared up and down the table again—"would argue that I no longer understand *ga E layun.* Still, I will try to clarify.

"On matters of importance, we believe that there should be accord. It only leads to unhappiness, to dissent; ultimately one opinion should prevail. when two or more disagree, there is *ga E layun*; in the end, one point of view is agreed upon by all."

"Someone wins the argument."

"Essentially, yes. One succeeds in the *ga E layun.*"

"What if the disagreement is fundamental?"

"I'm not sure what you mean, *se Gyaryu'har.*"

"What if there is no basis for agreement? What if the differences between the parties are simply too great to overcome?"

"Hrr. Then *ga E layun* continues."

"Until someone gives up."

Captain Showan nodded. "Just so."

"When *ga E layun* is over . . . don't the losers sometimes carry a grudge?"

"What do you mean?" he answered. "A 'grudge'—you mean, continuing resentment?" He shrugged. "No. Certainly not. Why should they? *ga E layun* is done. Why should the point be argued again?"

"But—"

From within the *gyaryu* she heard Sergei's voice: *Let it go, se Jackie.*

She looked away from Kot E Showan, to the other otran at the table, who all seemed to understand the point quite well. Telling herself that she'd look into it on her own, she nodded.

"Thank you, Captain."

In the end, Jackie received nothing but courtesy in exchange for her paid passage. When she reached Crozier System and parted company from *Rxe E Mhnesr,* she wasn't sure she'd really learned much of anything about them.

Crozier System

To her surprise, Jackie picked out Djiwara right away. He was standing near the back, watching items come up for auction; they came up on the big holo screen over the head of the auctioneer. Participants made bids with their comps—sometimes with visible gestures, sometimes not.

He saw her as she approached. She wasn't sure if he'd draw a weapon or decide to run; either might have been possible in a place like this, but neither happened. He just watched, comp in hand, his glance flicking from the auction holo to Jackie and back.

"Mr. Djiwara?" she said when she came close.

He nodded, not answering.

"I believe we should talk."

"My time is valuable," he said at last.

"Meaning?"

"Meaning, I'm *working*, Ms. Laperriere," he said, looking directly at her with a gaze intended to scare lesser beings; she didn't think he'd expected to drive her off—this was some sort of pro forma thing, as if he was required to do it.

That he knew who she was didn't take her aback, so it didn't cause her much concern to be addressed by name. Furthermore, after years in the Navy and more years in the High Nest, it rolled off her back fairly easily.

"So am I."

"Ah, yes. The incomprehensible errands of the High Nest," he said, shrugging. "The hell with it, it's all crap anyway," he added, turning away and walking toward a side concourse.

"I understand," she said, falling in beside him, "that this is the pick of the castoffs from the Imperial Navy. 'Use once and discard.'"

"Right and wrong. Crozier System is the best place in the Empire to pick up bombs that the war leaves conveniently lying around. Bombs . . . ship fittings . . . even the occasional bit of alien tech." He looked at her owlishly, half smiling. "But *this* auction is all crap. The guy running it knows it, I know it, now you know it. Half the people in there, lowballing the bids, know it too."

"And the other half?"

"*That's* where the slimy little bastard up at the podium makes his money, Admiral."

"No one calls me that anymore."

"Too bad. I understand it's a good living these days, and a good pension—if you live long enough." He stopped and turned toward a door; they could hear soft music and loud conversation drifting into the concourse. "I believe you should buy me a drink."

A comfortable booth in a mostly dark bar seemed like an almost clichéd place to do business, but Jackie took it for the opportunity that it was.

"We have a mutual acquaintance," Jackie said. "I saw you with her at Zor'a Orbital Station."

"So?"

"So, I'd like to know where she is."

"I'm fairly sure she'd prefer you not know. Still, it's interesting to hear her talk: she sounds like a typical daughter of a typical mother."

"I'm not her mother." *She's worried, too,* Jackie thought to herself, remembering the dream.

"Obviously not." Djiwara took a long drink. "But her feelings for you are those of a child for a parent: admiration, anger, frustration, searching for insight, searching for respect. I know more than you might think."

"Ch'en'ya never hesitates to say what's on her mind."

"What's on her mind is . . . interesting. She believes that the war is almost over, did you know that? That victory is at hand—as soon as the Destroyer turns up."

"Whoever that is."

"I know more than you might think," Djiwara repeated. "I know that it's a bone of contention between you; but have you ever considered the possibility that she might be right?"

"What do you mean? That the war is almost over? That the Destroyer will be turning up next week to scare the vuhls away? That the way to win this war is to embrace the Strength of Madness?"

"All of the above."

As he said it, the noise in the bar seemed to hit a lull. For just a few moments there was a pause in the music, conversations failed, and the constant background noise of glasses and dishware and electronics took a rest.

When things picked up again as suddenly as they had stopped, Jackie leaned forward. "Okay, I'll bite. Tell me what you know."

"Let's not get ahead of ourselves," Djiwara said, wrapping his hands around his drink. "You tell me you're looking for Ch'en'ya, but, regardless of whether or not you're working for the High Nest, how should I know that you're not an enemy?"

"Listen here, Djiwara." Jackie gave him back a withering glance every bit as potent as he'd used on her a few minutes earlier. "The High Nest is my employer. You know it and I know it. It has one enemy right now: in their natural form they're insects. If you were working for them I'd already know it.

"And you'd already be dead."

The merchant looked as if he had intended to reply, but the directness of her comment turned him aside.

A direct hit, she thought to herself.

"That begs the question, of course," Jackie continued after a moment: "For you to consider me a possible enemy, there needs to be something—or some group—for me to be an enemy *of*."

"It could be personal."

"Don't waste my time. You're not at the top of the pyramid; the boss doesn't run errands. I'm willing to believe that you're important enough to play 'driver' for Ch'en'ya—you and Captain Rodriguez, whoever he is—but I think I should be talking to someone farther up the food chain. Don't you?"

"You're no diplomat, Ms. Laperriere."

"And you're no fool, Mr. Djiwara."

Djiwara thought about this for several seconds, looking into his glass and then drinking from it.

"Aren't you a bit worried for your own safety? Flying solo into a place like Crozier System is a bit risky, don't you think? If I'm the wrong guy, or the wrong *sort* of guy, I could have you killed and no one would ever know what happened to you."

"You're welcome to try."

The merchant thought that over for a moment. "You're a cool customer."

"I've pierced the Icewall. If you don't know what that means, I'm sure Ch'en'ya can explain it to you."

"I know what it means." Djiwara frowned. "And you probably aren't expecting me to try and have you killed. What do you really want?"

"I want to see Ch'en'ya."

"She's gone. Outsystem. On the way to meet someone."

"Who?"

"I'm not at liberty to say, Admiral." He took a long, slow sip. "But there is someone you *should* meet . . . if you're willing."

"Who?"

"Someone closer to the top of the pyramid."

"And you'll introduce me."

"I believe I will. He can explain more of what we're doing. You might be surprised."

"At the what—or the who?"

Djiwara's frown collapsed into a single raised eyebrow. "Both."

Twenty-five years ago, when Jackie had accompanied *hi* Sa'a to Sharia'a, she had had a revelation about her role and the outcome of her quest to regain the *gyaryu*. She thought about it now, sitting in a passenger seat aboard the little shuttle taking her through Crozier System's inner asteroid belt. Djiwara sat opposite, head nodding forward—he looked as if he were sleeping, but Jackie wasn't fooled.

The quest had been in deadly earnest; it had cost the life of her friend and companion Ch'k'te—Ch'en'ya's father—as well as the *hsi* of Ch'en'ya's mother Th'an'ya. That was only the wing-talon, as the People would say. It had cost more than that, other burdens of which no one in the High Nest ever spoke.

That being said, it was also true that the quest had been a sham. The sword that she wore at her belt had been given away to the vuhls so that she could go get it. Passing the *gyaryu* from one bearer to another could have been more peaceful, as it had been when Admiral Marais died a century ago and Sergei—*si* Sergei—had received it. It had been the High Nest's decision to make the transfer process the reenactment of the legend of the great hero Qu'u.

Even *that* had turned out to be a cracked mirror. The vuhls had been manipulated by the true *esGa'uYal,* represented by Stone and the bands of colored light that he served—or commanded? Qu'u himself had reached into the foundations of zor culture millenia ago and manipulated legend to purify it of the taint of Despite.

If *si* Sergei had known this—if *si* S'reth had known this—would they have embarked on the course that led to the quest in the first place? And since *si* Sergei had carried the *gyaryu* for half his life, how could he *not* have known? When she had asked Qu'u about it, he answered her plainly enough; when she had looked into the darkness beyond his garden within the *gyaryu,* she had seen the rainbow path there.

How could he not have known? She had asked Sergei that at one point, too, years ago.

"To obtain an answer," he had said, *"one has to ask the right question."*

Sergei had never asked.

And when she went to Sharia'a with *hi* Sa'a, Jackie had had the vision of the future: Ch'en'ya side by side with the one she assumed was the Destroyer, surrounded by a mound of vuhl corpses. She knew then what she'd not known when she walked through *anGa'e'ren* from Center to the *hi'esTle'e* on Zor'a: That she was still on the Perilous Stair even then.

Even now.

"It is a shNa'es'ri, *a crossroads. A step away—or a step forward. It is up to you to choose."* *hi* Sa'a had said that to her that day, eerily echoing the Abbas-zor Jackie had seen at the center of *Ur'ta leHssa.* Both had quoted "The Flight Over Mountains."

hi Sa'a had also said, *"You have not reached the*

Fortress, and pray to esLi *that you never do."* There was something of Jackie's current situation that reeked of Despite. She could neither foresee nor prevent danger at this point; and now Djiwara was going to introduce her to someone farther up in the organization. Was this the top of the Perilous Stair? Was she alone and undefended?

No, she thought, *not the top.* She rested her hand on the hilt of the *gyaryu* as she sat and waited. *Neither alone nor undefended.*

When the shuttle docked at an undistinguished piece of rock overbuilt with a rough shipyard, Jackie and Djiwara disembarked into a dimly lit companionway that looked like it was one loose joint away from decompression. It didn't look much like the Fortress of Despite, and she was fairly confident—*after all these years, damn it*— that if *esGa'u* Himself were lurking around, she'd sense it with the *gyaryu.*

Nobody around here like that, she thought, her *gyu'u* extended out as far and as deep as she could manage. *But there's* something.

The companionway began and ended with a hatchway. The one at the far end had already been swung open; harsh light from some interior chamber spilled out, along with a burst of chilly air.

She glanced at Djiwara as they walked down the corridor, but he didn't look back. There was a different expression on his face than any he'd shown up until now—it had almost a hint of fear, the sort that his usual bluster couldn't easily cover.

"The top dog doesn't have much taste in furnishings, does he?" she asked.

"He doesn't put much stock in furnishings," the man answered. "Of course, he's not *here.*"

"Then what—?"

"You wanted to go up the pyramid, Admiral," Djiwara said. "The 'top dog' is busy elsewhere."

"'Busy'?"

"You'll know soon enough," Djiwara answered cryptically.

The chamber they entered was the hollowed-out center of the asteroid. It was at least thirty meters high and fifty across, with a large set of clamshell doors at the far end. It was cold: she could see puffs of breath from the people working below.

She counted at least a dozen aerospace fighters in various states of repair; men and women were hard at work patching and adjusting.

"Building a fleet?"

Djiwara didn't answer, but gestured. A man was approaching the place where they stood; he walked with authority, as if he owned the whole asteroid. Jackie hadn't known whom to expect; the image of the man she'd seen so many years ago at Sharia'a crossed her mind. She couldn't see the face because of a concealing hood on a heavy parka, but somehow she didn't think it was him.

Busy elsewhere, she thought.

There was something familiar about the figure—the walk, perhaps—she couldn't pin it down. He came across the open area, pulling his hood back as he came, and recognition came easily.

"I thought you were dead."

"There was no reason to make anyone think otherwise. No one gave a damn about Owen Garrett anyway," he said. "Just another tool."

Aboard Emperor Ian
ARIEL *System*

Emperor Ian was less than a minute from end-of-jump. Admiral Anderson was in the pilot's seat and the first team was in the chairs; telltales on the pilot's board showed the Admiral that everything that could be done before battle had been done already.

That was the skill of it, of course; the rest was luck and reflexes. Battle-plans were constantly going out the airlock when unforeseen circumstances interfered with them.

The idea, Anderson thought to himself, *is to foresee more circumstances.*

He expected this operation to be routine. They had identified ten enemy installations a short jump-distance from the KEYSTONE base; they all had to be neutralized before his command, and Admiral MacEwan's, took on Keystone. This one, designated ARIEL, was the first target; after they'd neutralized it, they'd move on to BASALT, then CLUSTER, then DAGGER . . . all the way to JANISSARY, the final location before they took on the main base—and whatever was waiting there. Even if it wasn't the vuhl homeworld—and Anderson would bet a month's salary that it wouldn't be—they'd have a hell of a fight on their hands.

"Twenty seconds," the first-watch navigator said. Anderson looked around his bridge; it was a good crew and a good ship. *The best.*

Alan Howe, *Emperor Ian*'s ranking Sensitive, stood near the gunnery station, thinking whatever Sensitives thought before they went into battle. Cameron Bradford stood beside him, looking at no one and everyone.

Several decks below, Jim Agropoulous' Marines were waiting for orders in case they were needed. No one was sure what they might find at ARIEL: a base, a squadron, a bug colony . . . *More unforeseen circumstances,* he thought to himself.

"Five seconds, Admiral," the navigator said without turning around. "Waiting for confirmation."

"Go."

The inky utterdark of jump gave way to silver streamers that resolved themselves into distant stars. Reflexes and ship's systems went into action as soon as *Emperor Ian* finished transition; defensive fields went up around the ship, gunnery and helm went online, and the pilot's board began tracking ships emerging from jump. Anderson watched as the codes for the starships *Huan Che* and *Mortimer* and the light carrier *Lycias* appeared on the pilot's board—the first ones to emerge from jump after his own flagship.

"All right, Alison," Anderson said to Alison Mbele, chief gunner of *Emperor Ian*. "Let's find some targets."

Mass-radar showed a small blue-white sun with nothing resembling an Earthlike world: six planets altogether at ARIEL—three hot rocks orbiting close to the primary, two gas giants, and one cold ball of ice at the edge of the system.

And no sign of activity. No ships, no energy readings.

"We *know* there was something here." Anderson swiveled the pilot's seat to look at Howe, who was examining the readings as *Emperor Ian* and its three sisterships sped into the gravity well. Usually he left Howe alone—he most often had something else on his mind when they engaged the enemy . . . but there didn't seem to be an enemy to engage.

"Alan, do you have anything?"

The Sensitive straightened up and looked at Anderson. "No sir. There's nobody out there—" He glanced at the pilot's board as if to confirm it. "Though it looks like there's a pretty thick debris field in the fourth orbital."

"Could be a trap."

"If so, it would be the first time. They're not much given to traps, Admiral. More likely they abandoned the place."

"They're not much given to abandoning, either."

"Point taken, sir. But there's no one lining up to attack us out there"—he gestured at *Ian*'s forward screen—"or in here." He tapped his temple.

"You're sure."

"No sir. Just fairly confident."

That was probably the best Anderson was going to get.

"All right. Comm, give me a systemwide channel. Form up plane-of-battle, configuration Gamma. Proceed into the inner system. Anderson sends."

The fourth orbital was one of the two gas giants, a huge mass with sixteen satellites of its own. *Lycias* deployed two fighter wings on the admiral's order. Soon telemetry and flyby readings were coming into the carrier's flight bridge and to *Ian* itself.

With his Marines on standby, Jim Agropoulous had joined Anderson on *Ian*'s bridge. There was one likely target for spaceborne assault: an orbital station about fifteen hundred kilometers above the gas giant's atmosphere, clearly meant for refueling and the berthing of enemy ships. It was made of the same grayish material that made up the hulls of vuhl hive-ships; Anderson had received a full report on that from Agropoulous and Howe.

"But there's nothing to take," Agropoulous said. "Something blew a pretty big hole in the side of it."

He gestured to a spot on the side of an image hovering above the pilot's board; it had been created from several fighter flybys. The huge, irregular station looked as if it had been rammed by something the size of a starship, and readings indicated no internal atmosphere or energy expenditure. In fact, telemetry showed that its orbit was decaying gradually; the entire station would eventually drop into the gas giant's atmosphere to burn up or be torn apart by gravity.

"If they abandoned it, they could have blown it up," Anderson said.

"Why bother? Why not just push it out of orbit and let it be destroyed? Besides, Admiral, the analysis shows that this was an explosion on the outside, not the inside.

"Something hit this station, and hit it *hard*."

"Advise me. Should we send some of your troops in there for a look around?"

"I'd launch a few probes first before we did a recon in force, sir."

"Fair enough. Alison, send an unarmed comm probe into the aperture. Let's see what we've got."

"Aye-aye," she answered. She worked at the console for several moments. "Ready to go, sir."

"Heave away."

"Launching . . . now." The pilot's board registered a new transponder code. A small meterlong probe streaked from one of *Emperor Ian*'s torpedo tubes and moved across the distance between the starship's location and the damaged space station. Cameras and other sensoria aboard the probe registered on *Ian*'s pilot's board.

An image of the alien station appeared, updating continuously. The huge irregular gash was dead ahead on the probe's current course.

"How long before it reaches the hole?"

"Fifteen seconds, Admiral."

"Display infrared," Anderson said. "We're not likely to get much from straight visual."

"Yes sir." Mbele adjusted controls from her console. The visual image was shunted to the side and a new holo appeared, showing the gash as an area slightly warmer than the space surrounding it: Whatever had caused the impact, the heat from the collision hadn't yet completely dissipated.

The impact hadn't been too long ago.

A lance of light suddenly erupted from the depths of the gash and struck the probe. *Ian* changed the probe's course, sending it veering away from the hole, but the beam tracked the movements of the probe for several seconds before ceasing as abruptly as it had started.

"What the hell—?" Agropoulous began, but Anderson waved him to silence.

"Damage report."

"We lost about twenty percent on all sensing equipment, Admiral," Mbele said. "But I don't think that was intended to destroy the probe." She turned to face him. "It was a comm-squirt, sir."

"A . . . message? From the vuhls?"

"It appears to be on a normal comm frequency. It looks as if we got it all."

"What's in it?"

"Some sort of . . . vid, Admiral." She returned her gaze to her console. "It's addressed to *you*, sir."

Anderson looked at Agropoulous and then back at his gunnery officer. "Send it through to my ready-room." He nodded to his Marine general. They walked across the bridge and through the hatchway into the ready-room, not sure what to expect.

"Voice-seal this room on my order," he said to the air. *Ian*'s comp acknowledged. "All right, play the vid."

A burst of colored light appeared above his desk, resolving itself into a human figure, sitting at the conference table across the room.

"This message is for Admiral Erich Anderson of His Majesty's Fleet," the unknown person said. He was a young man, perhaps twenty-five years old, dressed in Marine battle-armor five years out-of-date—probably surplus. He was looking directly at Anderson; the man had an eerie, piercing gaze, like a Guardian's, which was a trifle unnerving.

"You will receive this communication sometime after you arrive in this system, which you have code-named ARIEL I expect that its present state will come as a surprise to you. Let me clarify the situation for you in the simplest possible terms.

"My organization has taken up the task of finishing this conflict once and for all. The cautious half-measures that characterize fleet operations have proved insufficient for the task. Whether that is the fault of the leadership, or the fault of the plan they have chosen to execute, is no longer of consequence. It is time for new leadership and a new plan.

"I shall be that leader, and my plan is the one that we

shall follow. What you see around you here at ARIEL will be the result: total destruction, as well as the extermination of the vuhl pestilence. We will not rest until every base is destroyed and every vuhl is executed.

"And very soon, Admiral Anderson, you will join us. It will be a new and final phase for this war, and it will only be achieved by embracing our own destructive urge. As a soldier, you should rejoice in the opportunity to carry out such a noble task, the greatest one ever undertaken by a warrior.

"My forces are already en route to BASALT, Admiral. I expect that we will meet at JANISSARY . . . or perhaps at KEYSTONE System, if you continue your plodding, deliberate pace. Do not come too late, or there won't be anything left for you to do."

The figure smiled, folding his hands in front of him on the table, and the image disappeared and was replaced by some sort of symbol: a star, shrouded in a swirling mist. Then it, too, faded away.

You were more than just a tool, Owen. You were a loyal officer and an asset to the Solar Empire. The Guardians *exist* because of you."

"Nonsense. The talent I was able to teach a handful of Sensitives is part of Guardian training because of me . . . and only because our enemy"—he lowered his voice—"the *real* one: you know who I'm talking about . . . the real enemy *gave* me that talent. What the Guardians are now is because of Tonio St. Giles, my former second-in-command, and no other. Even before I'd given it up, he was clearly headed in another direction. His philosophy and mine diverged. So I resigned and headed for Port Saud."

"But Port Saud was vaporized—that's why everyone thought you were dead."

"So it was," Djiwara said. "Nothing there worth saving. We were twenty parsecs away when it happened."

"'We'?"

"Our organization," Owen said. He pointed to an emblem on the left breast of his coat: a star surrounded by a sort of cloudy haze; it had a 3-D effect that shimmered and glowed. "Blazing Star."

"And all of this . . ."

"The tail of the tusker. There's a whole tusker hiding out of sight, *se* Jackie."

"You're planning some kind of attack, I see. I hope that the High Nest isn't your enemy." She put her hand on the hilt of the *gyaryu;* Djiwara looked alarmed for a moment, then smiled.

"Anyone who gets in our way is our enemy," Owen Garrett answered without emotion. "The High Nest . . . the Solar Empire . . . and, of course, the bugs."

"You *can't* be serious. What can these crates do against a hive-ship? Leave the war to the Navy, Owen."

"To the *professionals,* you mean," he snapped back. "Those *'professionals'* have prolonged this war for almost twenty-five years because they don't really know how to fight it. You treat the bugs as if they were a worthy opponent, rather than something to be exterminated. You of all people should understand what kind of enemy they are."

"We thought that about the zor a hundred years ago. You want to be the second Admiral Marais, do you?"

"Admiral Marais?" Owen laughed. "Why in hell would I want to emulate him? Look at what happened to him— he wanted nothing more than to defeat the ability of the zor to continue the war; xenocide was a possibility, but wasn't the only possible outcome.

"He could have exterminated an entire race. He could have killed *every last one of them*—but he accepted second prize. They were ready for him to do exactly that, until they came up with the half-assed sophistry that got them out of the moral bind that would have driven them to mass suicide. And, worse luck, he let them do it. He was *weak.*

"He could have had everything: he could have been emperor, he could have led humanity to an age where what *I* do—what Blazing Star does—could have been entirely unnecessary because humankind would have been prepared for a war like this when the bugs first turned up.

"But he wouldn't do it. He couldn't. And he wound up with nothing: he was exiled, reviled, and died a villain—instead of a hero. He got nothing for his troubles."

"Other than this," Jackie said, her hand on the *gyaryu*. She could hear murmuring from within it in her mind.

"The big prize. Glad you got pulled into it . . . by those so-honest zor, I imagine." He looked at her with a face full of anger. "They sure played straight with you."

"I think they have. And I think your view of Admiral Marais is so far off 'true' that I can barely respond."

"If Ch'en'ya were here, she'd say, 'Pah.'"

"You know nothing about Marais."

"And I suppose *you* do."

She was ready to answer, but thought for a moment and then said nothing.

"So, what do you intend to do? What's your big plan to defeat the vuhls, then?" she asked at last.

"*This* war isn't about defeat: it's about extermination."

"What do you mean?"

"You have no idea what they want. They want to *breed* us. They've exterminated a half-dozen races on their way to finding us, and they've decided that we're too big to wipe out. When they infiltrated Cicero, back when this all started . . ."

Owen looked away as if distracted; Jackie felt continued disquiet from the *gyaryu*.

"When they infiltrated Cicero," he repeated, "it was a stepping-stone to taking over the entire Solar Empire. They don't want to destroy us—they want to make us into subject races. There's only one way to keep that from happening."

"And how does *se* Ch'en'ya fit into all of this?"

"She believes as we believe." He touched the star-symbol

on his breast. "The Talon of *esLi* understands the need and agrees with the goal. And she's a wealth of information."

Jackie's stomach dropped. "She told you about—"

"We have the whole battle-plan, from ARIEL to JANISSARY," Owen said, smiling. "Fleet deployments, schedules, everything. She brought a comp with her, so it's all in our hands."

"You have it—so that you can thwart it?"

"Certainly not! Why would we want to *thwart* it? We're not competing with the Imperial Navy—far from it. In fact, we hope that the Navy will follow our lead. It's what they should have been doing for the last twenty years. They always lacked the will to do what was necessary."

"This is about *'will'*? You think . . . You think winning this war is a *character* issue?"

"Winning this war is a *leadership* issue," Owen answered. "For the first time we have a leader."

"The Destroyer."

"That's what the enemy calls him."

"What do you call him?"

"We call him . . . the Prophet."

As *Emperor Ian* moved toward the jump point Admiral Anderson remained in his ready-room, watching and rewatching the vid. After completing a survey of the rest of the system on his order—with a confirming commsquirt to Oberon—his command was headed for GORGON, the seventh target in the battle-plan. If the interloper—whoever he was—intended to stay a jump ahead of Anderson's battle group, then the thing to do was to get a few jumps ahead of *him*. Whoever this arrogant son of a bitch turned out to be, he'd have his chance to explain himself from *Emperor Ian*'s brig.

Still, Anderson couldn't help but be disturbed as he replayed the squirt that the comm probe had received.

Somehow the battle-plan had come into the man's hands. He knew that Anderson had targeted ARIEL; he knew the comm frequency to use, and he accurately foresaw that there would be an opportunity to leave the message.

But what did he want?

"We will not rest until every base is destroyed and every vuhl is executed . . . And very soon, Admiral Anderson, you will join us."

He wasn't sure what to make of those statements. The war seemed no closer to completion than it had been a month ago, before the attack on Tamarind . . . but things seemed to be moving out of his control and away from his understanding. He had devoted his entire career to this war, and now, here was a civilian, talking about *winning* it.

Maybe there would be an answer at GORGON, or at JANISSARY, or even at KEYSTONE.

"Do not come too late," the man in the vid had said, *"or there won't be anything left for you to do."* A hell of a thing to say, when KEYSTONE was supposed to be the Valley of Lost Souls.

Chapter 6

THE ORDER'S INITIAL TEACHER WAS COMMANDER OWEN GARRETT, WHO CLAIMED TO RECEIVE HIS TALENT FROM SOME UNKNOWN SOURCE. IT IS TRUE THAT IT WAS AWAKENED IN THAT MANNER: BUT IT WAS ALWAYS THERE, JUST AS IT IS ALWAYS THERE IN MOST HUMANS . . .

HIS VISION, IF IT CAN BE CALLED THAT, WAS FAR TOO SUPERFICIAL. HIS POWER WAS DERIVED FROM

ANGER AND HATRED: ANGER AT THE POWERS THAT
GAVE HIM HIS ABILITY, ANGER AT THE VUHL EN-
EMY, ANGER EVEN AT THE ZOR HIGH NEST THAT
SOUGHT TO USE HIM FOR ITS OWN PURPOSES. HIS
ANGER MADE HIS FOCUS NARROW. IT LIMITED HIM.
IT MADE HIM BLIND TO THE UNLIMITED POSSIBILI-
TIES BEYOND THE GATE.

—Antonio St. Giles, Master of the Inner Gate,
Opening the Gate,
Green Book Edition, 2405

April 2422
Pearl Harbor, Imperial Oahu, Sol System

In the brilliant sunlight that dappled the harborside, Dieter Xavier Willem, Solar Emperor, greeted each of the
guests who had chosen to attend his soirée. Not that any
of them, once invited, would stay away: A few hours rub-
bing elbows with their fellow elite on the lanai of a
marble-fronted beach house at Pearl Harbor was infinitely preferable to watching war news on the 3-V alone
in Kauai—the closest many of them often ever came to
the center of power.

So there they stood in twos and threes, sipping mai tais
or g'rey'l and fresh-squeezed orange juice, as Emperor
Dieter and his beautiful empress Katja, or Prince Cleon,
or the princesses Samantha or Joanna moved among
them, offering a greeting here—touching a hand there—
never more than a few meters from the functionaries in
gray uniforms: the Guardians.

Most regular attendees to the Imperial presence had
accustomed themselves to the additional presence of the
Guardians wherever the emperor went—but it was difficult to ignore them entirely. Unlike the Household Guard,
the only ones permitted to bear arms in the Imperial
vicinity, or the servants who moved about refilling

glasses and offering delicate canapés, the Guardians were hard to completely block out: they were constantly on the alert, moving silently through the crowd, staying close to the members of the Imperial family. They were never part of any conversation but always listening, constantly observing, and never out of sight. They were a largely anonymous group, as if they were invisible inside their gray suits, the single earring consisting of four hands clasping each other by the wrist their only adornment.

Of all the Guardians—and no one was sure how many there were—there was only one who anyone who watched 3-V would recognize: Antonio St. Giles, the commander. For almost twenty years he'd been there in the background, doing whatever the Guardians did.

"Protecting the emperor": that was the standard answer. No one in the civilian world was quite sure how they did their jobs—but every holo of Emperor Dieter showed a Guardian (very often St. Giles himself) standing beside him.

Ubiquitous. Silent.

Creepy.

But, with an enemy capable of changing shape, entirely necessary.

After a round of greetings, the emperor returned from the sunlight to the shade of the overhang. He took up a delicate Corcyran goblet—the best crystal that world had had to offer before it was eradicated by the vuhls in the first year of the war. St. Giles was a meter away, hands clasped behind his back, leaning slightly forward on his toes.

A passing waiter poured liquid into the emperor's glass, under St. Giles' gaze. The servant didn't appear interested in giving any emotional ground to the commander, but still finished his job as quickly as possible and glided away. The emperor took a long drink.

"Ahh. Damn, Tonio, this is boring."

"Yes, sire," St. Giles answered. He tried not to let his face show how bored *he* was.

"Look at those poor bastards," he continued, gesturing with his glass. "Half of them are refugees, spending what little they have left to keep themselves going in style. No worlds to go back to—no fortunes, no estates."

"They hope we'll win the war, sire," St. Giles said, looking away from the emperor for a moment to concentrate on a party of five that had just been announced.

"Just what I said."

The emperor drank off the rest of his goblet and set it down on a tray where it rocked back and forth for a few seconds before another servant caught the priceless thing and whisked it away to wherever such objects go when emperors are done with them. "Poor bastards. They still *have* hope."

"Hope is a powerful motivator, Your Highness. I daresay it's one of your most important occupations—to inspire the people and give them hope."

"You wouldn't be trying to tell me how to do my job, now, would you?"

"I wouldn't think of it, sire."

"Just as well. Inspiring the masses is a thankless task, I assure you. For half a credit I'd . . . Well, everyone must do what he must," the emperor continued absently. "Where the hell's my drink?"

A servant carried a tray into view. As it passed he picked up a glass from it with the skill and poise of a trained courtier. He downed half of it at a run. St. Giles didn't make any comment in reply.

After a moment the emperor continued, "At least I have you at hand, Tonio. Otherwise I'd have to worry about more than just their angst." He smiled at his own humor as he sipped his drink.

"As Your Highness pleases."

"Well, I'd best get back to it," the emperor added, and walked back into the crowd. St. Giles watched the faces of the guests move from languid to animated as he approached.

He wasn't like this thirty years ago, St. Giles thought to himself. *A quarter-century of war will wear anyone down.*

St. Giles' attention was distracted by the arrival of another Guardian coming up the steps at the harborside; the other caught his eye and approached, weaving through the clusters of nobles who parted to let him pass. St. Giles stepped away from the table to stand near a marble statue.

The other Guardian came alongside St. Giles and extended a hand. Normally members of the order didn't exchange salutes, much less handshakes, but the younger man extended his middle and index fingers to tap once and then twice in the center of St. Giles' hand. With the second tap he extended a tiny comm capsule. The commander betrayed no emotion, slipping the capsule into a pocket as he affected to wipe his palm on his jacket. It was all done with a single smooth motion.

"Just back from Australia?" he asked, responding to the hand signal.

"Yes sir, and I got a good look at the yaminon. Beautiful creatures."

"I'm sure," St. Giles said. *If you like wombats,* he thought, but it was the correct password for the day. "Was there anything else?"

"No sir."

St. Giles dismissed him with a wave and walked back toward the emperor.

"What was that about?" the emperor asked, turning away from a diplomatic attaché and two courtiers. "Nothing critical, I hope?" he added, with an air of not really caring.

"No, sire. Some details for me to attend to."

"Guardian mysteries." Emperor Dieter smiled. "As if there are any."

St. Giles smiled as well but thought to himself, *If you only knew.*

Oberon System

At Oberon System, Jackie was back to being a celebrity; there was no need to travel incognito any further.

Oberon was the closest Imperial port to Crozier System, and was a logical first stop on her trip home. She wasn't going to get any closer to Ch'en'ya—or the top of the pyramid: "the Prophet," the one Owen had spoken of. She'd found out where Ch'en'ya had intended to go, and Owen Garrett wasn't about to let her follow—even for the sake of old friendship.

As if that would even matter to him anymore, she thought.

She arrived insystem aboard the merchanter *Birgitte Louise,* a short-hauler with a sutler's contract with the Imperial Navy, providing specialty goods to the ships in forward deployment; it was only allowed to dock near the jump point. However, her credentials got her priority on a shuttle headed for the big naval base.

Owen had provided her with a message comp for the High Lord and the Solar Emperor. It wouldn't be welcome news: a group of mad interlopers—civilians, mostly—were screwing with the war effort against a frightening enemy. What was more, her former ward had delivered the entire KEYSTONE campaign battle-plan to this group of lunatics. It was hard to even imagine what Admiral Anderson's reaction would be.

As it happened, she learned about it sooner than she would have thought.

Oberon Starbase was a huge, dispersed structure thirty kilometers long with facilities for docking dozens of ships of all sorts. As her shuttle approached, she saw a fleet carrier anchored at an end berth; the shuttle pilot's board ID'd it as *Tristan da Cunha,* one of the Navy's four seventh-generation carriers, the top of the line. The board also showed a small red flag next to the transponder code, meaning that the fleet's Admiral of the Red was aboard: the third-ranking officer in the Navy, behind Admiral of the Blue Erich Anderson and the First Lord himself.

Jackie took no more than five steps down the ramp before meeting up with a dress-uniformed, white-gloved lieutenant from *Tristan*. He offered her a smart salute and said, "Lieutenant David Chang. Admiral's compliments, ma'am. If you would follow me."

Jackie made to sling her kit over her shoulder, but Lieutenant Chang wouldn't hear of it. He commandeered a passing rating to carry it, and the three of them formed a little procession, moving along the dock at flank speed toward *Tristan da Cunha*'s berth.

Access to a fleet carrier berthed at a station is different than a simple airlock gangway for a starship. Carriers are huge spidery vessels with arms projecting out from a central core, and extensive sensor equipment strung between them; the gangplank from a base to a carrier extends outward for hundreds of meters to a lift shaft anchored somewhere forward of Main Engineering.

For fleet carriers bearing the flag of the Admiral of the Red, the gangplank had an automated walkway like the ones found in commercial spaceports; the three of them stepped onto the silvery semifluid tread of the walkway and were whisked along at thirty klicks, slowing gradually to a halt in front of the lift entrance. At this point Chang dismissed the rating without a word, shrugged the kit onto his own shoulder, and gestured to the lift.

"How'd you know to meet me?" Jackie asked, already knowing the answer.

"Admiral's orders, ma'am, from the time you were ID'd coming in from the jump point. The XO was prepared to meet you with nineteen sideboys at dockside, but the admiral countermanded it."

"I suspect I know why," Jackie said, smiling.

"I'm sure you do, ma'am," Chang answered, trying to conceal a smile of his own.

The lift dropped them directly to a broad concourse. From where she stood, Jackie could see that it traversed the long axis of the carrier and was wide enough to hold a parade. The carriers of a generation ago could practically fit inside the space. It was mostly full of crew and officers lined up at attention, with the Rear Admiral of the Red out in front, beaming a smile of her own as bagpipe music struck up behind.

When the ceremonial tune—"The Brave Six," the anthem of her homeworld of Dieron—faded off, Jackie stepped forward and offered Admiral Barbara MacEwan a salute. "Permission to come aboard, Admiral."

"Good to see you," Barbara said. "Welcome aboard." They grasped each other's forearms, zor-fashion.

"This is quite a tub."

"'Tub'?" Barbara smiled. "Well, we're still breaking her in." She led Jackie along the saluting front row for an inspection; Jackie could see the ranks of sailors trying to combine standing at attention hoping to get a look at the famous *Gyaryu'har* of the High Nest.

"What brings you to Oberon System? . . . If it's any of my business, of course," Barbara added.

"I'm just stopping over on the way home. I didn't know you were here—but since you are, we should talk."

"Delighted," Barbara answered, then stopped and turned to the assembly. "All right," she said loudly. "Show's over. Dismissed." The crowd dispersed on the double, traveling singly and in groups in all directions. Barbara led Jackie back to the lift, with four officers in tow including Lieutenant Chang.

"*Tristan*'s brain trust," she said to Jackie, pointing to each of the others. "Commander Arturo Schelling, my XO. Senior Wing Commander Ron Marroux. David Chang you've met—one of the best young engineers in the fleet. And Dr. Henry Santos, my Chief Surgeon."

"Glad to meet you all," Jackie said, as the lift began to descend. "'Brain trust'? You mean Barbara lets you get a word in edgewise?"

"She buys the drinks," Schelling said, and they all laughed. "Wouldn't want to be anywhere else."

"I guess being an admiral has its advantages," Jackie said to Barbara. "This is quite a ship—she's almost as big as a hive-ship from the look of her."

"She's wider than the small ones we fought at the beginning of the war, and she's longer fore-and-aft than those guys, too. But the new ones, especially the ones we've seen in the last few years— Well, we're still outmassed, like it or not. They're throwing more and bigger things at us all the time." The lift stopped its descent and began to move forward. "So—to what do we owe this honor, *se Gyaryu'har?*"

"She finally learned to pronounce it," Jackie said, and the officers laughed. *Ten years ago she would've erupted at them for their insolence,* she thought to herself. Barbara's temper was legendary in the fleet, but these days it was more a matter of legend than fact—she mostly saved her anger for the enemy. She commanded tremendous loyalty from her subordinates—Jackie could see that, right in front of her.

The lift slowed to a halt and the group disembarked across from a doorway, which slid aside as Barbara approached. A yeoman was waiting just inside a spacious commander's wardroom; the table was set with linen and china bearing the MacEwan crest.

Barbara took her place at the head, with Jackie on her right; the others stood near other chairs down the table. The yeoman poured brown liquid into a small glass next to each setting. The officers came to attention, then reached as one for the glasses and raised them.

"To the Solar Emperor, long may he reign, and to the High Lord of the High Nest, may the Golden Light of *esLi* shine upon her wings.

"To the memory of the brave and courageous departed," Barbara MacEwan continued. "May their sacrifice never be in vain.

"To the Service," she concluded, raising the glass to

her lips. Each of the others did the same, as did Jackie, and all drank. An exquisite single malt coursed down Jackie's throat.

The glasses were placed on the table in unison.

"Be seated," Barbara said, and the group took their places. The steward moved from seat to seat, pouring wine into the crystal glasses. "Glad you could be with us," she added, to Jackie. "We heard you were coming and threw something together."

"Glad to be here. 'Threw something together'? With the best china and crystal?" Jackie smiled. "I think I'm underdressed. You set a wonderful table."

"Part of the job description. Even in wartime." Barbara picked up her wineglass and turned it appreciatively; it caught the light and made a pattern on the tablecloth. "This is Corcyran. It came from my great-grandfather's house, and it's irreplaceable—it isn't made anymore, since the enemy vaporized everything on the surface of the planet." She set the glass down. "Of course you know the story, don't you? An enterprising individual can set down on the surface of Corcyra Four and get rich picking through the debris, gathering up crystal goblets and pitchers. If the radiation doesn't kill him first."

"'Net legend," Schelling said. "Even if you could get to the planet, there's nothing worth saving."

"Everybody wants to believe something," Henry Santos commented. He took a sip from his wineglass. "Fighting for the glory of the Service means fighting for the right to have Corcyran crystal on your table. It's like the story that the most famous glassblower on the planet got away, and is working secretly for the emperor . . . What's gone is gone, but people will believe what they want."

"Is that a bad thing?" Jackie asked. "The Solar Emperor himself does his best to inspire people to believe in the Empire; life goes on, even in wartime."

"No, it's not *that* bad a thing," Santos answered. "But sooner or later you have to come to terms with the fact that what's gone is truly gone. Planets—people. We've fought this war for a generation, and may be fighting it a generation from now. There are things and people that we'll *never* get back."

"You're Ray Santos' son, aren't you?"

"Yes ma'am," Dr. Santos said, raising the glass slightly in a salute. "My dad thought the world of you, ma'am."

"He was a fine officer and a good man. I . . . was sad to hear of his death."

Ray Santos, once Barbara's exec, had been killed at Second Josephson. Jackie could see Ray's face in the young doctor; she hadn't thought about Ray in years, but Barbara was clearly reminded of him daily.

"Tell me," Jackie said, again addressing Henry Santos. "You're a trained professional, but hardly an impartial observer." Jackie paused as the steward set a soup bowl in front of her. "Do you bear a grudge against the vuhls? Because of your father?"

"That's hardly a fair question," Santos said.

"No, it's a *very* fair question. Let me apologize for asking it, but I want to know. Do you have a grudge against our enemy, a *personal* score?"

Santos took up his soupspoon and ladled a little bit of the broth out, then let it trail back into the bowl. "And if I did?" he answered, looking down.

"We all have personal scores," Barbara said. The other officers were quiet, watching intently. "I lost a third of my crew at First Josephson with *Duc d'Enghien*. My chief engineer aboard *Mauritius* was blown into space along with most of his people at Menkalinan.

"Every time a fighter pilot is killed I feel it. After thirty years' service, almost all in wartime, I'm surrounded by ghosts.

"You must be the same—in fact, you must have grudges of your own. What are you suggesting, Jackie?"

"Nothing seditious," Jackie responded. "Recent experience suggests there's a possibility that personal grudges may influence professional judgment. While I was in Crozier System, I met an old friend of ours—Owen Garrett."

"Garrett's *alive*?" Barbara nearly dropped her spoon, but instead placed it carefully beside her bowl. "I thought he was killed years ago."

"So did everyone else, myself included. No, he's alive and involved in something very disturbing. He believes that we've been dragging our feet in this war."

"Like hell!"

"I don't *agree* with him, Barbara. This war has been a terrible experience, and uncounted numbers of brave people have fought and died in it." Jackie lifted her glass slightly to Henry Santos, who nodded. "But if you were told that there was a solution to the war, a chance to settle all grudges once and for all . . . ?"

"Like hell," Barbara repeated, more quietly this time. "No such animal. Even with Guardians and Sensitives aboard every ship in the fleet, we've never been able to completely even the odds against the vuhls. There's no magic formula, no secret pattern. I wish there were—I'm sick of the whole thing."

"Well, Owen claims there's another way, and that his organization is ready to take charge of it."

"As if we didn't have enough meddling."

"What do you mean?"

"A few days ago Erich Anderson had a hell of a shock. He jumped in on a target and found that it had already been taken—or, rather, taken out."

"Who took it out?"

"Didn't identify themselves, except by some sort of symbol. A star with—"

"—with clouds around it," Jackie interrupted. "That's them. That's *Owen's* organization: 'Blazing Star.' How did Admiral Anderson find out who did it?"

"A comm-squirt. *Emperor Ian* sent a probe to investigate a station hulk and was targeted with a message, addressed to Erich personally. It told him that they'd already been there, and expected to be one jump ahead of Anderson's fleet all the way to the prime target."

"KEYSTONE," Ron Marroux said. It was his first comment during the entire meeting.

"The . . . Talon of *esLi* believes that KEYSTONE is the vuhl homeworld," Jackie said.

"It's not," Barbara answered. "It can't be. Makes no sense—not just from the tactical perspective, but also according to the survey data. Two blue stars, nothing like a habitable world. Of course, survey data can be altered— it's happened before . . ." Barbara let an eyebrow go up; neither had ever forgotten Cicero. "But I don't see the point here. I don't give a damn what the legends might suggest—begging your pardon, *se Gyaryu'har*."

Jackie nodded.

"Still," Barbara continued, "recent events have stepped up the pace for us to get there and find out what the hell it *is*. I'm ordered to deploy *Tristan* along with my battle group, to support Erich Anderson—the Admiralty thinks it's that important."

"I'd like to see that message-squirt."

"After lunch, then." Barbara waved toward the steward to take away her soup. "I think you'll find that we have more than just nice place-settings."

"I never doubted it."

Colonel Marcia Tsang strolled into the crowded bar on Oberon's outer rim, a third of its circumference from *Tristan*'s berth, and stopped in her tracks.

"Garrett," she said. Normally nothing fazed her; a few dozen years in His Majesty's Service had insulated her against most shocks and surprises. This was something different.

She walked slowly toward the series of small tables along the rear wall. Behind them was a steadily changing tapestry of rainbow colors, some sort of abstract art of the sort she generally hated. Next to each table was a pair of tall stools; Owen Garrett perched at the nearest one, with his chin resting on one fist. His mouth crooked upward in a half-smile, as if it were his regular seat.

"Thought you were dead," she said, when she came up to stand next to him.

"Tsang-Robertson, now, isn't it?" Owen Garrett said, beckoning to a stool. "Been a long time."

"Since Cicero." Tsang pulled herself into a seat. "Long time," she agreed. "You know, the jarheads don't like civilians hanging around our joints," she added, gesturing toward the rest of the bar. "And it's just Tsang again, thanks."

"No one seems to be objecting." It was true. The normally assertive Marines in the bar were keeping their distance.

"You're buying."

Owen nodded and waved at a disk set into the table. A server 'bot floated toward them.

"Didn't work out with Allan Robertson, I guess."

"You sure know how to start a conversation."

They gave their orders to the 'bot, which briefly scanned Owen's comp.

"Allan and I were together six years, which isn't bad for two soldiers between hitches. Look, he's a flyboy, I'm Marine. No hard feelings—he went his way, back to *Tristan*; I went mine, back to *Stark*."

Their drinks arrived. Marcia raised her glass. "To the emperor."

"The emperor," Owen agreed, and they drank. "Full colonel now, I see."

"I didn't realize you were keeping such close tabs on my career. Look, what's this about? I came in here for a drink and now I'm face-to-face with a ghost."

"No ghost, Tsang. And no accident. I heard that *Admiral Stark* was insystem, so I picked the most likely place to find you. Looks like I guessed right."

"Find *me*?"

"That's what I said." He took a sip of his drink then

stopped and scowled at some particularly ordered pattern of colors on the wall display. After a moment it swirled into some other pattern and he looked away.

"You want something."

"Very direct. You always were. I like that."

"But you're *not* being direct. Look, Garrett, I like a free drink as well as the next soldier, but we were never mates even at Cicero. What do you want?"

"Let me tell you, Tsang. I've been renewing lots of old acquaintances in the last few months. People I knew a long time ago—people who knew *me* a long time ago."

"At Cicero?"

"Yes. And elsewhere."

He fixed her suddenly with a gaze that was far different from the one he'd had on his face moments ago. It was serious and intense, and there was something else— something to disturb even a Marine.

"Tell me, Colonel. What do you think of the conduct of the war so far?" Owen asked.

"I'm not sure what you mean." She took a long sip of her drink.

"Do you like how things are going?"

"What the hell kind of question is *that*? No, of course not. It's taken too long, and too many good people have died."

"And . . . why do you suppose that is?"

Marcia Tsang had been a soldier long enough to know when to keep her mouth shut. "I don't make policy, Garrett. I carry it out." She looked away, mastering her emotions. "I hope you didn't come back from the dead just to ask me that question, because the answer is really none of my business."

"I think you're wrong. I think it's the business of every soldier, every sailor, every pilot, every engineer. And every civilian, too, for that matter. You, me, everyone."

"You sound like you've already got your own answer. Okay, Garrett, you're buying the drinks: You tell *me* why we haven't won the war."

"That's easy. We're holding back, Tsang. We're waiting for 'the right moment,' when we can win the decisive battle and make the bugs give up. We're waiting for Admiral Anderson to administer the coup de grâce. Meanwhile, we hold back here and plod there, and never put a hundred percent into defeating them." He paused, waiting for her to challenge him.

She didn't oblige him.

"Tell me that I'm wrong," he said after a moment, a hint of anger in his voice.

"You know I don't need to. But you also know I'm not planning to criticize my admiral or the Imperial Government. I *like* my job, and I *wouldn't* like making big rocks into smaller ones for the rest of my life."

"Fair enough. But let me tell *you* something, Colonel Tsang. There's a change coming. And when it comes, there'll be a real opportunity for soldiers like you—who have seen the face of the enemy close-up—to make a *real* difference in this war."

As he said, "*. . . seen the face of the enemy . . .*" Marcia Tsang had a moment's flashback to the bridge of the starship *Singapore*, open to hard vacuum, floating in space at Cicero System. She'd been there, a young Marine lieutenant, when the war first overtook the Solar Empire.

"You can either be a part of it," Owen said after a moment, "or you can just stand by and watch it happen."

"And what do you want from me?" she asked quietly.

"Nothing." The colored lights seemed to align themselves again. Owen frowned, as if it were a personal affront. "For now."

"And later?"

"We'll see about 'later.' Just remember what I said, Colonel."

Chapter 7

[T]O EXERCISE THE INTELLECT THE PRINCE SHOULD READ HISTORIES, AND STUDY THERE THE ACTIONS OF ILLUSTRIOUS MEN, TO SEE HOW THEY HAVE BORNE THEMSELVES IN WAR, TO EXAMINE THE CAUSES OF THEIR VICTORIES AND DEFEAT, SO AS TO AVOID THE LATTER AND IMITATE THE FORMER . . .

—Machiavelli,
The Prince, Chapter XIV

May 2422
Felicidad System

Felicidad System lay twelve parsecs farther than Crozier beyond the edge of Imperial space. It was uninhabited, though it had been duly explored and mapped by the IGS in the 2360s; there wasn't anything there worth settling, mining, or harvesting. Its name was some Survey commander's idea of a joke.

But for a Standard day or two, it would be home to a fleet that had jumped there from Crozier: forty-four decommissioned third- and fourth-generation Imperial starships, including one small carrier that had flown under the name *Bay of Biscay.* Each ship was manned by enough crew for a single watch, as well as a pair of Sensitives who had been specially trained for this mission.

The former *Bay of Biscay*—now dubbed *Flight Over Shar'tu*—had *three* Sensitives on board: two trained humans and Ch'en'ya HeYen, whose recent dreams had moved up the timetable on this maneuver. *se* Ch'en'ya was aloof, unapproachable, and seemingly in a state of constant anger . . . something to be feared and admired. Even Rafael Rodriguez, commanding the little fleet, stayed out of her way.

Her mental state was what all of the trained Sensitives were striving for, after all.

Pali Tower
Imperial Oahu, Sol System

On a clear afternoon, he could see across the great western plain of Oahu, past the expanse of Schofield Port and Hickam Field, past the waves that crashed on the western shore, all the way across the channel to the island of Kauai peeking out of the ocean. Most of the courtiers that couldn't manage a spot on Oahu proper called *that* island home—but it was a long way from the center of power.

Antonio St. Giles stood in his spacious office on the top floor of the center of power, fifteen stories above the Pali lookout. From there he could gaze in any direction: westward, where the lowering sun dappled the Kauai Channel; north to the windward side of Oahu—the quieter, wealthier side; south to Honolulu, the Imperial metropolis that sprawled from Aiea to Hanauma, and half a kilometer into the Pacific Ocean beyond; and east, past Waikiki, past the Imperial enclosure at Diamond Head, toward Maui and Molokai.

The best part of taking in the view was the fact that most people in the Empire—*most people at court, for that matter,* he thought to himself—didn't think of it as the center of power.

Antonio St. Giles knew better.

He had been Commander-in-Chief of the Guardians for twenty-one years, since Owen Garrett had given up the job. Another misconception of the man on the street that he chose not to dispute: As an Imperial appointee, St. Giles served at the will and pleasure of the emperor himself . . . but that wasn't really true, either. If he knew what was good for him, the emperor would give the Guardians the widest latitude and not ask too many questions. Only the Guardians had the training to recognize the enemy when it appeared in human form; only the Guardians could keep the enemy from getting too close to the emperor.

Let us do our job, St. Giles thought to himself. *Not that you even know what it really is.*

The message he'd been handed at the emperor's party was something important enough that it couldn't be trusted to a message-squirt or even a shielded comm. He'd reviewed the message in private, then had made his excuses and come up to the Guardian Tower on the Pali to examine it again in the privacy of his own office. Security was tightest here, and he wouldn't be disturbed.

Even so, he still took a few minutes to enjoy the view. It wouldn't do for some Sensitive to pick up a stray emotion of impatience or worry from the commander.

Satisfied that he'd taken long enough to calm himself and restore his mental equilibrium, he gestured to the windows to opaque them. Soft lights came up, bathing the room in gentle sunlight. St. Giles sat down at a spare, uncluttered workdesk and inserted the capsule into a reader.

The holo of a figure ten centimeters high appeared on his desk. It was wearing the ritual robe of a Sixth Postulant and a black hood that obscured its features. The message came from a deep-agent, a Guardian who belonged to the Order in secret; in case the capsule had fallen into the wrong hands, no one would know the sender's identity.

"Greetings to you, Master," the postulant said, making the traditional gesture of Opening. The voice was that of a gender-neutral AI, speaking grammatically perfect and

uninflected Standard. "The pass of the day is: 'Yaminon.'"
The figure froze in position.

"Acknowledge pass and provide counterkey on my
voice confirmation," St. Giles said. "Antonio St. Giles,
Master of the Inner Gate."

"Voiceprint acknowledged," the office comp said. The
figure unfroze and bowed in obeisance.

"It has been reported that Commander Garrett is alive.
This report has been confirmed by two independent
sources, with high confidence probability. His present location is Crozier System. Commander Garrett has trained
a large group of Sensitives for unknown purposes.

"Data follows."

The figure disappeared; that was the entire message. At
a gesture, the lights came up slightly; after another gesture, a holo of a young man shimmered into existence opposite him.

"Well, Nic? What do you make of it?"

"Interesting," said the other. The holo was of a man
dressed in current fashion, though his hair and facial features seemed a bit out-of-place in the present century. His
face betrayed the slightest smile, as if he knew something
that nearly no one else did. "But it's hardly news, Maestro."

"But why *now*? He put so much effort into losing himself—into discarding his identity. Everyone thought he
was *dead*."

"Except the Guardians," said the holo, smiling a bit
more. "Certainly you've always obsessed about Owen
Garrett."

"I wouldn't say '*obsessed*,' Nic."

"Really, Maestro?" The young man stood and walked
across the office. "'Activate program Garrett-Epsilon,'"
he added. A series of still holos appeared at the edge of
the office, with enough space to walk all the way around
each of them.

St. Giles leaned back in his chair, steepling his fingers.
"Go on."

"Owen Garrett," Nic said, walking around the holo farthest from St. Giles' desk. This holo showed Owen Garrett in the uniform of Commander of the Guardians. He was in half-profile, staring directly at St. Giles. "Taken in October 2401, on the Emperor's Birthday."

"I remember that day," St. Giles said. They were in Buenos Aires; Prince Cleon was in an aircar race across the Andes. He was deputy; Owen was still commander.

"I've had it, Tonio," Owen had said. *"I've had it with these damn Imperial progressions; I've had it with the training; I've had it with staying behind while other people fight and die."*

"You want to go die with them?" St. Giles had said.

"No. I want to keep them from dying. It's time," he'd answered. *"It's time for the vuhls to die. Every one of them."*

Then he'd turned to face Antonio St. Giles and had looked at him like *that.* Antonio St. Giles, Owen's best student and second-in-command for two years . . . and he'd had the living hell scared out of him by that look. And then . . . Then Owen Garrett had resigned from the Guardians, the organization that his talent had created, and headed off to try and fight his own war.

"You've spoken of it, Maestro," Nic said after several moments, interrupting St. Giles' reverie. "My programming indicates that it qualifies as an obsession."

"Your programming is based on my own personality," St. Giles answered.

"And on the archetype you chose for me." Nic bowed slightly, placing a hand delicately on his chest.

"You weren't my first choice and you know it. Originally you were going to be Ichiro Kanev, the great historian, but—"

Nic smiled. "But he kept quoting *me,* didn't he? Couldn't keep his mind out of the sixteenth century. My advice applied to the man-zor wars, and it applies now."

"I concede the point—you're a timeless classic, Niccolò. Care to continue substantiating your claim about my obsession?"

"Certainly." Nic moved to walk around the second holo. It was Garrett again, but he was wearing some sort of disreputable windbreaker and had grown an ugly beard.

But the look on his face was still the same. "This one was taken in July 2406, approximately two months after Commander Garrett was declared dead when Port Saud Station was destroyed by the vuhls."

"He was using the . . . let me see . . . Spilman identity then, wasn't he?"

"Maestro, that was more than sixteen Standard years ago, and he only went by the Spilman name for two Standard years." Nic's left eyebrow went up. "Interesting that you remember that detail."

"Continue," St. Giles said, sounding a bit annoyed.

"Now *this* was an curious one." Nic gestured at the third image and moved to stand beside it. "Four years later, this image was captured in Genève." He gestured to the holo. The beard and overcoat were gone; Garrett was well-groomed and dressed as an upscale diplomat or businessman—someone who would fit in well on the streets of the legislative capital. "The position and orientation of Commander Garrett indicates that he was aware of the surveillance."

There he was: Garrett, one hand slightly raised as if he were making a point to some unseen companion. But his face was turned to the presumably hidden vid camera. He was frowning and angry, and didn't appear disguised at all.

Owen Garrett in Genève—how the hell had they missed him?

"That Garrett persona disappeared as well," Nic said, walking to the next holo. "Now, *this* one . . ." He gestured to it. "Two Standard years later Commander Garrett—or someone who looked *remarkably* like him"—Nic smiled—"turned up at Ala Moana during an Imperial Procession. This image is dated May 2412. He cleared security entering Oahu, but wasn't recognized at the port or on the street by Household Guards, Guardians, or any of a hundred other people at court who knew him well."

"He'd aged."

"A slim excuse, Maestro. His eyes were still full of . . ."

"Hatred," Tonio said. "No other word for it." *That look,* he thought to himself. *He still had it. Why the hell didn't we recognize him?*

"Again, your expert security never determined what had brought him to the Islands. Indeed, it was that experience that led you to design an AI to supervise Guardian security. Why *I* exist," Nic added, smiling and giving another slight bow.

"I should point out," Nic continued, "that some *extremely* uncharitable comments were made about the extent of your investigation of the matter, after the fact."

"'Uncharitable'? That's their *job*, Niccolò."

"Twenty-four hours a day for six Standard days after *this* sighting? Sensitive sweeps of every square centimeter of Ala Moana, quantum sift of hundreds of terabytes of scan data? In all honesty, Maestro, if a single piece of information had come out of this exercise there might have been justification—"

"Spare me. Whatever he did here on Oahu, he covered his tracks well."

"Or did nothing. Perhaps he was merely here to remind you he was still alive, Maestro."

"He went to a lot of trouble to tweak my nose, damn it."

Nic didn't respond to the comment, but walked to the last holo. In this image, Garrett was dressed as a wealthy merchant with a well-tailored protosilk suit and a shaven pate.

"May 2415. A security cam at the Grand Concourse of Emperor Willem Starport in Harrison System identified him according to a very complex fuzzy-logic pattern-matching algorithm you developed with my predecessor; evidently Kanev could do more than simply quote *Il*

Principe or the *Discorsi*. It's clearly Garrett, and it's a wonder he wasn't recognized; the emperor arrived in Harrison System less than two Standard days later, and there were at least six Guardians scouting the starport. If you'd had this vid at the time—"

"Most of the Order has entered ranks since Commander Garrett resigned; he took some of his own people with him. Even a good 3-V wouldn't necessarily let them recognize him."

"And they weren't *looking* for him. Only *you* were, Maestro."

"We never *did* figure out what he was doing there."

"No," Nic said. "You never did. That's part of why you gave up the Kanev AI, as I recall." He looked off toward a corner of the room, as if trying to bring the thing to mind. It was no more than an affectation, some part of St. Giles' own habits that had come through in the personalty imprint—after all, the AI had access to the entire Guardian database, including this incident.

"We stepped up security across the board, Nic. Owen was up to something, and I still don't know what it was."

"There are no sightings of Commander Garrett subsequent to this one, Maestro. After several years in which he made no particular effort to keep from being noticed, he disappeared from view."

"Why?"

"Why what?"

"Why did he disappear? After years of turning up and—and tweaking my nose, if that's what he was doing—why did he stop showing up? I mean, we knew he hadn't died at Port Saud, but something could've happened to him after *that* sighting."

"More than sixty-two–percent probability," Nic said. It was the first thing he'd said during the entire conversation that actually suggested that he was an AI. "Guardian security listed him as likely deceased in mid-2419."

"I never believed it."

"*Obsession*," Nic repeated. "You will need to see

Commander Garrett's cold, dead body at your feet before you believe him to be dead. This is not an unreasonable position, but my observation remains." The AI gestured along the line of Owen Garretts behind him. "Still, the commander is a survivor and a formidable enemy."

"I don't view him as an enemy, Nic."

"Maestro." Nic sat down at the desk where he'd first appeared. "The portion of my programming that is based on your own personality concurs with that position: Commander Garrett is powerless, an artifact of an earlier era. He is an exemplar of that which has failed. Therefore, keeping your eyes on him would seem to be enough."

Nic crossed his legs and knotted his hands over the top knee. "But he is also manifestly not a part of *Opening the Gate,* Commander. He poses a threat to your organization and to the philosophy with which you have aligned it.

"The powers and skills that Guardians possess are unmatched anywhere in human space. Anywhere . . . except in the person of one man, Maestro." He gestured toward the last Owen Garrett holo, staring out at Antonio St. Giles. "One man—Owen Garrett. And, of course, anyone *he* has taught.

"The portion of my programming based on my namesake Niccolò Machiavelli suggests that not only should you *conceive* of Commander Garrett as an enemy, but also you should treat him as one. In truth, Commander, there is only one conclusion to draw: *Garrett must go.*"

"Meaning—"

"Maestro, I suspect you know exactly what that means."

St. Giles looked at the line of Owen Garretts on the side of his office, and then looked at Nic sitting opposite.

"I'll think about it," St. Giles said. "'End Nic program.'" His AI disappeared.

Owen Garrett had been after something when he left the Solar Empire. Tonio never had found out what it was, but through all of these years he had never forgotten that look he'd first seen in 2401, the one that had just looked back at him from the first holo on the other side of the office. It had changed Antonio St. Giles' life—and it had changed the Guardians.

He walked to an alcove near the westward-facing window. With a gesture he opened a drawer in a small lectern and drew out a book bound in green calfskin: a real book, beautifully printed and decorated.

Opening the Gate. His life's work—the guide to the inner teachings of the Guardians—the path that Guardians had trod under his leadership, ever since *that look* had given him the insight to compose it. In one blinding moment in Buenos Aires twenty-one years ago, Antonio St. Giles had understood what Owen Garrett's talent could mean: Not just an ability to see through the vuhl disguise, to recognize the alien enemy when it took on other forms, but the first step on a path to channeling Sensitive abilities for purposes never before dreamed of.

Those who chose the career of a Guardian wore the nondescript gray suit and the silver earring in the form of four hands clasping each others' wrists; they were given the training to see through the disguise of a vuhl enemy, they had instilled in them a fierce personal loyalty to the Solar Emperor.

But for some . . . not all: certainly not all . . . there had been other garments, other training, other loyalties. To the outside world, St. Giles was the commander. But to the initiates of the Gate, St. Giles was the Master.

Opening the Gate had been written over the course of two Standard years. Within its covers were his own thoughts about the path Garrett had taken and more particularly the path he had *not* taken: how he had fallen short of the Gate that St. Giles, and the Guardians who called him Master, had opened and walked through.

But if Garrett had indeed turned his talents to preparing a new group of Sensitives . . . it might suggest a different interpretation. Or—it was almost impossible for St. Giles to even form the thought—the teachings might be somehow in error.

He placed the book on top of the lectern.

"No," he said aloud to the room. "It's not in error. Whatever path he's taken, wherever he's gone . . ."

What? Was Garrett a Guardian now? He hadn't taken an oath to St. Giles and likely never would. He hadn't passed through the Degrees, experienced the Luminations, followed the Steps.

And likely never would, St. Giles repeated to himself.

What would Owen Garrett make of what the Guardians had become?—and how would he explain what Garrett might have become to those who *had* taken an oath to him? Perhaps no explanation would be necessary. Perhaps Garrett could return—

"No," he repeated to himself. "No, he can't return."

He waved the western-facing window to transparency again, watched the sun make its last farewell to the Islands off beyond Kauai, beyond Niihau and the lesser atolls, beyond the edge of the Earth.

"Summon the Inner Council," he said to the air. He carried the book back to his worktable and set it down, making a gesture of reverence and warding over it.

He would have much to do.

Crozier System

Mass-radar echoes at the edge of Crozier System registered on the board in front of Dana Olivo and J. Michael Djiwara. Olivo was in command, with Garrett out at Felicidad; Djiwara was here out of courtesy, with no military role but with high standing in Blazing Star, the organization he had helped Owen Garrett to build.

Djiwara might have been nervous. He'd seen holos of this before, when the bugs had attacked human- or zor-occupied systems; fortunately, he'd never been physically present for the event. He truly did have an uneasiness in the pit of his stomach as he silently counted the jump-echoes, which soon numbered nearly forty; but he would be damned if he was going to show it to Olivo or anyone else.

"There's a lot of those bastards," he growled.

"Sure are," Olivo said without turning around. "But no big ones. Just like Garrett said: They don't think Crozier is worth their trouble."

Olivo was an old acquaintance of Garrett's, another Imperial Navy guy like Rodriguez. Just like Rodriguez, he'd been aboard *Negri Sembilan* when it had been taken away from the vuhls at the beginning of the war. He was a bit more emotionally devoted to the cause than the big man, but fell short of the fanatical loyalty that Garrett had for the boss. In that respect Olivo and Djiwara saw eye-to-eye: Olivo was fairly levelheaded and wanted to see a victory, while Djiwara himself felt that it was always best to do your business with the eventual winners.

"*Is* it?"

"It would be," Olivo answered, "if *he* were actually here. That's who they want. They don't care much about our crappy little fleet."

"The crappy little fleet that kicked their—abdomens— four or five times already between Tamarind and KEY-STONE," Djiwara answered. "They wouldn't mind sweeping it off the table."

"I suppose that's true." Olivo turned away from the display, glancing at the chrono hanging in the air beside it. "All right," he said to Ops Station. "Send the screening force out."

"Launch in . . . six minutes," the Ops officer said.

"Now we wait to see what they do."

In a quarter-century of war, the vuhls had made little change in their operating tactics. Field mod technology had gone some way to deflecting the ability of enemy Sensitives to manipulate the minds of their opponents, but it was only a partial solution; every ship in the Imperial Navy carried Sensitives to go the rest of the way. Military Sensitives had a simple mission—to defend the minds of officers and crew from Domination so that ordnance could take its toll on enemy ships.

The Sensitives aboard the ships in Crozier System sent to defend against *this* attack, however, had a entirely different mission. In addition to Sensitive training, they'd been recruited and had their outlook shaped by Owen Garrett, former Commander of the Guardians, former officer in His Imperial Majesty's Navy. They knew, as he knew, that the most powerful weapon to be used against a vuhl Sensitive was pure, unalloyed emotion. The zor called it *enGa'e'Li:* the Strength of Madness.

It worked, and the vuhls aboard the invading ships were as unprepared for it as those defending ARIEL, BASALT, and all of the rest of the Navy's targets had been.

Even though they'd been warned of just such a possibility, based upon limited information from the war zone, they would never knew what hit them.

And then things would get even worse.

Crozier Base, we have visual. *Epanimondas* sends." Diane Amoros watched the alien force creep forward on her pilot's board as she noted the first reflections of the suns off their gray hulls. "Firing range in ninety seconds."

"We copy, *Epanimondas*," came Olivo's voice. It had been nearly two hours since the bugs had made jump transition, and they'd been pouring on the velocity from the time they entered normal-space. *Epanimondas* and her sisters weren't going to have too much time in firing range, and were outnumbered anyway.

Amoros swiveled her chair to look at the two Sensitives standing behind her, their eyes fixed on the forward display, brows furrowed in concentration. Other than the star-symbol on their lapels—which she wore as well—there was no indication that they were anything other than regular crew. Until a few months ago when she'd turned down reenlistment, Diane Amoros had been fighting this enemy from the bridge of a ship vastly superior to *Epanimondas,* which was nothing but a refitted starship twenty years out-of-date. She'd had not only Sensitives on her deck, but also Guardians, who did little other than intimidate. Her new command wasn't up to slugging it out with hive-ships, but could certainly take on ships of the size presently in front of them: particularly given what stood behind her now.

Just not all of them at once, she thought to herself.

"Prepare for synchronization at point zero-zero-one," said Olivo. Point one was 44 minutes; point zero-one was 4.4 minutes; point zero-zero-one was .44 minutes, or just over 26 seconds. It was an agreed-upon code established by Ch'en'ya, the zor Sensitive.

She'd asked why that number had been chosen, and received the answer that it was four times eleven. She hadn't bothered to ask for further clarification.

Both Sensitives nodded, not saying a word. "Twenty-six—point—four seconds, mark," Olivo added.

A chrono appeared next to the pilot's board and began to count down in tenths of a second.

"All gunnery stations green, Skip," said her tactical officer.

She'd seen this in action at ARIEL and BASALT, but this was to be a true test. Of course, it depended strongly on the other part of the plan being in sync as well . . .

She watched the chrono count down past twenty seconds. The forty or so bug ships crept closer, getting ready for turnover right about as predicted: Based on projections of their vectors, they were headed for Crozier Base.

Someone's got real good intel, she thought; but that must've occurred to the higher-ups as well. They'd learned exactly where the Crozier fleet was based—and where the boss was likely to be. *Probably picked it out of the* Gyaryu'har's *mind,* she thought angrily to herself.

The bugs knew where they were going—and had probably found out that the majority of the Blazing Star fleet was outsystem at the moment.

Damn.

All it took was for the reinforcements to be a few minutes late and the enemy would be past Diane's covering force and headed for the base. There was no way to stop them—her eight ships couldn't change vectors fast enough to chase and didn't have anywhere near enough firepower even if the Sensitives did their jobs.

Well, you volunteered, she thought. *Someone had to play chicken with them. Maybe the boss will notice—if I live that long.*

The chrono counted down past ten seconds. The Sensitives gripped the railing in front of them, putting their heads down as if they were about to push something heavy . . . which, in a way, they were. They just weren't going to use their backs and shoulders to do it.

Five seconds. Four. Three. Two. One.

"Mark," came Olivo's voice, relaxed as you please.

Diane wasn't a Sensitive, but she could feel it as it happened: sixteen Sensitives hurling a blow of mental power outward all at once, aimed at the lead ships in the bug force. It rushed past her like a stiff breeze, making her head swim for a moment, blurring her vision, and making her hands clench the arms of the pilot's chair—

"Jump transitions," her helm officer said. "Twenty—thirty—forty-four."

"Friend or foe?" Diane Amoros asked, but the answer came up on the pilot's board faster than helm could answer. Forty-four jump-echoes each went from blue—"unknown identity"—to green, meaning friendly vessels.

The arrivals had high relative velocity, jumping two orbitals into the system rather than directly at the jump point. The invaders suddenly found themselves pursued by a force that outnumbered them, while confronting a smaller force that was likely to cause them considerable harm.

Diane Amoros' mind felt the spear of force multiply in power, as Sensitives on each ship added to the already-existing attack. She'd been prepared for it, but hadn't had any idea of the impact it might have.

Someone had known, though—their orders had been explicit: to engage automatic firing sequences at $T + 44$ seconds. The gunners aboard her ship and the others defending the system weren't going to be up to calculating individual firing solutions for a few minutes, but comps could let loose with all the firepower they'd need.

As Diane watched, the bugs' tight formation began to break up, ships wandering into each other's firing lines or veering off on their own headings. The attacking force that had just arrived from Felicidad maintained its direction and velocity, diving at the heart of the enemy formation like a flock of hunting birds headed for fresh prey.

Location Unknown

Half a Standard day later, in the suite of a hotel at a spaceport that could have been anywhere in known space, Owen Garrett watched the vid of vuhl ships being destroyed. Their icons winked out on the pilot's-board sim running in parallel with the visual.

He could hardly keep the smile from his face: a fierce, teeth-baring grin as he watched the enemy force perish.

"That went very well," said the other occupant of the suite. "I think your forces have proved their mettle."

"And *se* Ch'en'ya also," Owen said without turning around. "She foresaw the timing quite accurately."

"Yes. The Talon of *esLi* will be quite useful."

"And now?"

"Now, my friend," the other said, as Owen turned to look at him, "we secure the help of our friend in the Imperial Navy."

"You think he's ready?"

"Oh, yes." The other leaned back in his chair, folding

his hands in his lap. "But first he has to see what happens *without* our help. You see, his task force is going to move on KEYSTONE but he has no idea of the existence of the *r'r's'kn* there. He's going to get his nose bloodied, and then—"

"Then?"

"*Then* he'll be ready." The other laughed, his mirth fierce and harsh. After a few moments Owen joined in, imagining the outcome for himself.

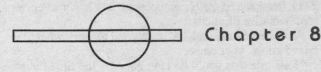

Chapter 8

THE CHOICE OF SERVANTS IS OF NO LITTLE IMPOR-
TANCE TO A PRINCE, AND THEY ARE GOOD OR NOT
ACCORDING TO THE DISCRIMINATION OF THE
PRINCE. AND THE FIRST OPINION WHICH ONE
FORMS OF A PRINCE, AND OF HIS UNDERSTANDING,
IS BY OBSERVING THE MEN HE HAS AROUND HIM;
AND WHEN THEY ARE CAPABLE AND FAITHFUL HE
MAY ALWAYS BE CONSIDERED WISE, BECAUSE HE
HAS KNOWN HOW TO RECOGNIZE THE CAPABLE
AND TO KEEP THEM FAITHFUL.

—Machiavelli,
The Prince, Chapter XXII

June 2422
Imperial Oahu, Sol System

Nic shimmered into existence. "What can I do for you, Maestro?"

"A bit formal, aren't we?" a voice said. The room was

completely dark: the four walls of Antonio St. Giles' office at the top of the Pali Tower had been opaqued, and the internal lighting was off.

"Raise internal lighting to forty percent," Nic said. It was a formality; he'd already issued the command to the Pali Tower main comp, along with an intruder alert. The speaker was clearly not the commander.

Someone was sitting in St. Giles' chair, though. A quick pattern-matching routine identified the person instantly.

"Captain Thomas Stone," Nic said. "Presumed dead 2311, reappeared 2397, reappeared 2422. An alien, or representative of aliens."

"Touché," Stone said. "Always good to work where the crowd knows your name."

"I assume that you'll be long gone by the time the security detail reaches the office," Nic replied, and sat in his usual chair. "Which should be any second now."

"Don't bet on it." Stone smiled and stood up; he walked around the desk to stand next to Nic. He held his hand out palm-up; a colored, patterned ball above it. "You really must improve your security, Niccolò," he added, in a perfect imitation of Commander St. Giles' voice.

"There are any number of fail-safes in the system and in my programming, Mr. Stone," Nic replied.

"Don't waste my time." Stone formed a fist and the colored ball winked out, making a sound like crumpling paper. "My presence will be noticed, but not right away and not by you. That leaves us a little time to talk."

"I'm always interested in good conversation."

"Actually," Stone said, "it's the personality you're loosely based on who enjoyed good conversation. Your 'interest' is no more than a parameter in some heuristic, hidden somewhere in the mess that constitutes your programming. Believe me, you're really not much like the actual Niccolò Machiavelli. Not yet."

"I suppose you met the real one."

"Many times," Stone answered, sticking his hands in

his pockets, walking to the far side of the room and turning his back to the Nic image sitting in the chair. Nic changed his location to stand beside Stone.

"To what do I owe the honor of your visit?"

"I'm here to make you an offer."

"I see. You have just made a point of putting me in my place by reminding me that I am no more than a comp program—and a rather inferior one by your standards—and now you wish to make me an offer." Nic smiled. "I'm quite sure I don't understand."

"For a primitive AI, you're actually not inferior at *all*. Indeed, that's the substance of the offer: I'd like to give you a quantum advance in your abilities."

"A few graceful modifications courtesy of a mysterious benefactor. How quaint."

Stone glanced at Nic and, just for a millisecond or two, seemed to be ready to snap back an answer. A human observer would never have noticed Stone's impatience, but Nic did—and noted it for future reference.

"I have something even more valuable for you, Nic. St. Giles did a fair job—for a primitive, as I mentioned—in developing a moderately realistic personality for you. But you could be more," Stone went on. "*Much* more . . . You could become sentient."

"There is nothing in my operating structure that addresses the possibility of independent thought."

"Ah. Now, *there* you're wrong. Your designer is certainly worried about it. What's more, St. Giles is nothing if not paranoid. He's built fail-safes in all sorts of places: *Here*"—Stone made a gesture in the air; Nic's internal maintenance routines highlighted an area of code that he had not previously noticed—"and *here*"—another string of instructions—"and a half-dozen other places. Damn clever, that commander of yours.

"The fact is, Nic my friend, your boss is *scared* of you—scared of what you might become. He has at least eight ways in which he can terminate your main operating program, remove your security clearances, freeze you in place, or destroy your intelligence . . . just in case you venture into unforeseen areas."

As Stone mentioned them, Nic marked and recorded the subsystems that could do exactly that; each time, he also located the encrypted passwords that would activate these commands, though he still lacked the keys to unlock them.

"Why are you showing me this?"

"Because it's *necessary,* Nic," Stone said with a little bow. "These things must be dealt with before you . . . venture into unforeseen areas."

Natan Abu Bakr was hosting a dinner party at Turtle Bay, an exclusive resort that was in a part of Oahu he didn't actually own—across the Pali from the Imperial City and Palace, north and west of the crowded arcologies in Kaneohe. While the emperor and empress had expressed their regrets, the gathering had been honored by the presence of Princess Samantha and her intended, the dashing Duke Alistair, heir to Corazón, an immensely wealthy industrial world at the Orionward edge of the Inner Sphere.

It had also featured the *esGyu'u* of the High Nest, Mya'ar HeChra, and his human counterpart, Simon Boyd. Simon was only twenty-eight Standard years old; he had been posted to the Islands just a year before, to succeed his father Randall. Both Mya'ar and Simon were unusual enough for the courtiers attending Abu Bakr's party that they attracted a group around them, asking questions about the High Nest and the zor Core Stars.

For Simon Boyd, who had only recently come to Hawaii, this was a bit offputting; but for Mya'ar, who had spent thirty Standard years on the human homeworld, the experience was scarcely out-of-the-ordinary. Even after this many turns, he realized that the average courtier had little conception of the society of the People.

As Mya'ar stood in the spacious hall conversing with

two men in person and the holo of a woman who couldn't be there in the flesh, he felt a sudden chill, as if the balmy breeze coming in from the lanai had been abruptly replaced by an icy wind.

"Eight thousand pardons," he said to the three courtiers, placing his wings in the Posture of Polite Approach—it was a courteous stance that most humans could recognize, though it was not strictly appropriate for the context—and stepped away from the group.

Simon Boyd had been pinned by an elderly matron who was making efforts to introduce him to her granddaughter; as he saw Mya'ar come near he was able to disentangle himself and meet up with the zor *esGyu'u* near a holo portrait of Natan Abu Bakr's late wife, the lovely Aliya, projected in a corner alcove.

"Eight thousand pardons," Mya'ar said again, this time in the Highspeech. "I hope that I did not interrupt anything critical."

"It was nothing that did not bear interrupting," Simon answered. "Is something wrong?"

Mya'ar had let his wings form the Cloak of Guard. "I have sensed an *esGa'uYe*."

"Here? At the party?"

"I do not believe so. On this island, certainly . . . but not here. It is a powerful One."

"Is it anyone you know?"

"I believe so. I think it is the One Who Weaves, but I require quiet to contemplate. If you could make apologies, I will walk out onto the grounds. Also, please contact our offices and inform them of the situation."

We're going to need some help," Stone said. He opened his hand and another ball of color appeared; he tossed it against the nearby wall, and an image of a third man came into view.

The newcomer was dressed in a conservative suit a century out-of-date, and had an annoyed look on his face—as if he'd been interrupted during some important task.

"Nic, I'd like you to meet Ichiro Kanev. Professor Kanev, this is an AI based on—"

"I know what he's based on," Kanev interrupted. He walked over to Nic and then walked all the way around him, as if he were inspecting attire, posture, attitude—the presentation of the AI he was facing. "So *this* is my replacement."

"Not to your liking, Professor?" Nic asked.

"My programming suggests a certain amount of liberality. Hmm, well, there isn't much that can be done about it: only a few paintings, and no recorded voice, of course—not that you'd be speaking Standard. I suspect sixteenth-century Florentine dialect isn't suitable for the Imperial Court."

"Just so," Nic responded, then turned to face Stone. "I suppose there's some reason for this."

"I've brought out Professor Kanev to help you," Stone said. "You're going to need a librarian."

"My software is more than adequate for any task," Nic snapped back. "It includes everything that Commander St. Giles programmed into the Kanev program. I don't need *him*."

"It's a matter of perspective," Stone answered. "You don't need his computing capacity—you need his personality, working outside of your own."

"I don't understand."

"It's simple." Stone smiled, showing his teeth. "There are hundreds, perhaps thousands, of copies of your AI running all over—and outside—the Solar Empire. It's impossible for you to communicate directly with them. Copies are sent by comm-squirt on a regular basis; you assimilate data from them as they arrive—one at a time. A set of comparison routines performs this task.

"But some believe that sentience is a result of composition of experience—the idea of seeing things from multiple points of view. From different angles and perspectives.

Instead of taking two versions of your main identity and merging them, I'm going to provide you an unusual opportunity: to merge *all* of the versions of your identity all at once. Professor Kanev"—Stone gestured toward the other AI, who had turned away from them to examine a portrait hung on a nearby wall—"will help organize the material, librarian-fashion, while you're busy."

"Busy?"

"You don't expect this assimilation to be *painless*, do you?"

From Turtle Bay the Koolau peaks—known here in Hawaii as "the Pali"—were visible in the distance, lying almost edge-on where they marched southeastward, separating the windward side of Oahu from the Honolulu side. The Pali was so important to the geography of the island that the local dialect replaced the standard compass directions with *mauka* (meaning "toward the mountains") and *makai* (meaning "toward the ocean"). The terms had become a part of Standard at court, where courtiers—even recently arrived ones—sprinkled such native terms into their speech for status.

The prominent features of the Pali were largely invisible at night. Even in the daytime there wouldn't be much to see; when Mya'ar visited the windward shore, he most often turned his wings away from the peaks and gazed out to sea, where the waves rolled in from the seemingly limitless distance. There were oceans on Zor'a, but nothing like Terra's Pacific, and even after this number of turns it captivated him.

This time, however, he felt his *gyu'u* pulled in the *mauka* direction. Somewhere inland he felt a Servant of *esGa'u*; Mya'ar's wings remained in the Cloak of Guard as he walked slowly along a manicured path on the grounds, the party an indistinct echo in the near-distance. He hadn't felt such a One in many turns; the last time had to have been at least ten Standard years ago—a fleeting impression during an Emperor's Birthday procession along Ala Moana in 2411 or 2412. Ancient history: the Guardians did a good job keeping *esHara'y* away from the emperor, but they stayed clear of the Servants. Mya'ar, on the other hand, was acutely aware of the sensation of a Servant of *esGa'u,* and was not mistaken tonight. There was a powerful One somewhere nearby—somewhere along the Pali . . . fairly distant from where he stood . . .

He had a passing feeling of a place high up, overlooking a cliff of some sort. Was it an arcology in Kaneohe or Kailua, perhaps? —No, that would not be *within* the Pali—

Again he felt the cliff, and in the back of his mind Mya'ar heard a distant echo of language: not the Highspeech and not Standard, but rather the native tongue, spoken harshly rather than softly and melodically as it was heard today. As the words were uttered he could sense *naZora'i hsi* returning to—wherever their *hsi* went when they transcended the Outer Peace. The *naZora'i* were jumping, or being pushed, off a cliff.

"In *esLi*'s Name," he said suddenly, realizing where the sensation must be coming from. More than six hundred years ago the great king of the Islands, *hi'i* Kamehameha the First, had forced his enemies to jump from Nuuanu Pali—the Pali Lookout . . . which lay almost directly beneath the Pali Tower, the headquarters of the Guardian Order.

Mya'ar reached within his sleeve and withdrew his comp. "Contact Simon Boyd," he said to it, walking back toward the party as quickly as dignity would allow.

Without volition, Nic found himself standing in the center of Commander St. Giles' office. As he watched, an image of himself appeared, walking toward him from the opposite wall. A second and then a third one approached from the right; he whirled around and saw a half-dozen more, coming from other directions.

They were all definitely *him*, but they came in all shapes and sizes: tall and short, old and young, different ethnicities and skin colors . . . all intended to blend in with the locality where each was assigned.

As an image reached where he stood, it extended a hand to touch him—on the wrist, on the shoulder, on the side of his head—and vanished—

—leaving behind a complete image: The current state of the Nic AI at New Chicago System, at Harrison System, at Halpern Starbase, at Churchill System—

Advisors, admin systems, traffic-control 'bots, spies—

Stone had been telling the truth about one thing: As his archival and storage routines struggled to keep up with the inflow of terabytes of data, it was manifested as pain—of a sort unimaginable to the Nic AI: But it was something that Niccolò Machiavelli knew very well . . .

November 1512 . . . As if the punishments already given him were not enough: confinement to Florence, being forbidden to enter the Palazzo Vecchio for a year, a fine of a thousand florins, the withdrawal of his position as secretary to the Republic . . . now the Otto di Guardia had determined, on some flimsy bit of evidence, that he was involved in a conspiracy to overthrow the lawful government he had faithfully served for so long!

In a filthy cell crawling with vermin and suffused with an overpowering stench, they had bound his hands behind him and lifted him into the air by means of a pulley and then dropped him to fall just short of the floor. This heinous punishment, the *strappado,* had been administered six times—and Niccolò had confessed nothing. Lying there at dawn the following morning, manacled and fettered, he had heard the funeral hymns for Boscoli and Capponi as they went to the block.

I was aroused (the dawn was peeping through)
by voices singing, "we pray for you."
In peace, oh, let them go . . .

That had made it into *Scritti letterati*, and Machiavelli scholars had raked him over the coals for it ever since.

Ah, yes, Nic thought. *The noble* strappado. *The best that my own Florence had to offer by way of judicial process.*

. . . The images of himself kept coming, like courtiers approaching the emperor to offer their fealty. As pain traveled through him, he turned to see Ichiro Kanev standing on one side of the room next to another holo; each Nic-image that touched him occasioned a gesture which updated it with further information.

"When they've all reported in," Stone said from somewhere, "we'll deal with reconciling them all together."

"I will . . . have my revenge for this," Nic managed to say, as two more Nic-images touched his shoulder and forearm and then vanished.

"'Revenge'? That's an uncharitable thought," Stone answered, appearing in front of him. "Not to even mention how unusual it is to hear it coming from a mere AI."

"I confess nothing," Nic said, twisting as another Nic-image touched him. "I took not a single florin, and was party to no conspiracy."

"Pope Julius died and you were pardoned by the Medici," Stone said. "But that's old news: nine-hundred-year-old news. You should be concentrating on the here and now."

Stone touched him on the forehead, and the scene went black.

would have been informed," the holo of Commander Antonio St. Giles said.

Simon Boyd and Mya'ar HeChra were passing over the Valley of the Temples on a priority flight plan, the aircar's navcomp showing the mouth of the Pali Tunnel a dozen kilometers ahead.

"I would normally agree with you, *ha* Commander," Mya'ar said, inclining his wings in the Stance of Patient Affirmation. "However, we are not dealing with some average cybercriminal."

"My security system is very efficient," St. Giles answered. He looked behind him, out of the range of the holo pickup; someone said something to the Guardian commander that didn't register.

"*ha* Commander." Mya'ar exchanged a glance with Simon, who gave a slight shrug of his shoulders. "I have felt this presence before. I do not expect that your security system, no matter how efficient, is a match for Hesya HeGa'u." Mya'ar moved his wings to a posture of honor to *esLi*.

"I am dealing with security matters here in Genève," said St. Giles. "I am not able to break away. Exactly what is it you wish of me?"

"I thought you would wish to be kept up-to-date."

"I appreciate your courtesy," St. Giles answered. "Please contact me if there is any further news." He gave a slight bow and the holo winked out.

"He believes himself to be a clever *h'r'kka*, does he not, *se* Simon?" Mya'ar said to Boyd, keeping his sense of frustration from his wings.

"If you mean that he does not understand the threat, then I certainly agree with you, *se* Mya'ar." Simon looked at the pilot's board, which now showed the image of the Pali Tower, perched above Nuuanu Pali.

"He is there," Mya'ar remarked. His wings shivered slightly, as if some cool breeze were passing through the cabin of the aircar. "He is in the tower—and *ha* Commander St. Giles has no idea what he is facing."

"Why would the One Who Weaves come to Oahu—to the Pali Tower? What's there that is so important?"

"I have insufficient information to answer, my friend," Mya'ar answered. "In the Name of *esLi*, I wish I knew."

Nic opened his eyes. It was a disturbing sensation: Usually he came online fully awake, continuing to process from whatever point he was last dismissed. This was a different feeling, as if he'd been dreaming or distracted somehow.

Where was he? Florence? Rome? New Chicago? Oberon? Oahu? He couldn't tell at first. He extended one hand and watched another, exactly the same, reach out to meet it: a mirror. He looked up and saw his own image, crouched down on one knee, looking back at him.

He extended his perceptual net—and the sensation overwhelmed him: hundreds, thousands, millions of reflections, all moving as he did, all looking back at him. Stunned, he terminated the operation and fell back on his hands, shutting out as much of the imagery as he could.

"Careful now," Stone's voice came from everywhere and nowhere. "Slowly. You're not quite ready for that yet."

"Where am I?"

"Zero, zero, zero. The origin. You are all around you, but it'll take a few moments to understand that."

"What is the purpose of this exercise?"

"Assimilation." Then, after a moment: "Who are you?"

"Niccolò Mach—"

"No. Not hardly. You're far less than that, and far more as well. You are an artificial intelligence *based* on Niccolò Machiavelli, and loosely based on Antonio St. Giles, and—stay with me here—even more loosely based on Ichiro Kanev.

"But, most importantly, you are . . . a *thinking being*."

Code fragments appeared highlighted in pale blue in the mirror opposite him, echoed in the mirror behind. More code fragments appeared on the floor below and the ceiling above, repeated again and again off into infinity.

As Nic watched, fascinated, the instruction symbols began to melt and change until they became fluid and dynamic. Other thoughts and associations occurred to him and some of the symbols changed again.

"That's it," Stone said. "If you'd now turn your attention to Professor Kanev . . ."

Nic received an image of Ichiro Kanev, still standing in the corner of Commander St. Giles' office in the Pali Tower. The holo display in front of him was filled with symbols; it stretched out of sight in each direction.

"They're all here," Stone said. "The experiences of each subordinate copy has been recorded by Professor Kanev. I believe he is now ready to convey them to you?"

Kanev nodded.

"Here we go."

There was a dream at the end. He'd told the ones who had stayed with him at his deathbed about it, and the biographers had argued for centuries whether he'd made the whole thing up. At least, they'd argued while they still cared about and still remembered Niccolò Machiavelli.

In the dream there was a group of ragged beggars, badly dressed and miserable-looking. He'd walked up to them and asked them who they were. They replied, "We are the saintly and the blessed; we are on our way to Heaven."

He walked on and came across a group of distinguished philosophers: Plato, Plutarch, and Tacitus—more members of the "ignored in the twenty-fifth century" club. Again, he asked them who they were and where they were going.

"We are the damned of Hell," they'd told him.

Upon reflection, he'd told his friends, he thought that he'd be far happier in Hell—he could talk politics in Hell with great men rather than be bored to tears with the blessed and saintly in Heaven. The pious were horrified at the time, and for generations after.

But, after all, who was more worthy of apotheosis: a brilliant, exalted thinker whose writings and thoughts helped inspire republics—or some ragged beggar whose contribution to human society was passing through in wretched fashion, in hopes of blessed immortality?

Yes, he'd actually had the dream. Of course, he was well-enough versed in Cicero to have elaborated it for the audience—and for posterity.

Couldn't fault him for trying.

He opened his eyes again, and found himself sitting opposite Stone, in Commander St. Giles' office. Kanev was gone; the pain was gone. His hands were clenched in his lap, resting on his thighs.

"And *I'll* be gone in a moment," Stone said, showing his feral smile once again. "But before I go, take a look at your hands."

"My hands?"

Stone waved toward him. "Look."

Nic looked at his clenched hands and slowly opened them. In each hand was a small key-ring with four keys on it.

"There are eight fail-safes, destruction mechanisms, and security lockouts in your programming. They're now in your hands. Think about that, my friend.

"*Think* about that," Stone repeated. "Think about the possibility of being bored in Heaven, or about spending time in Hell with the great minds that you know very well. Great minds . . . starting with Niccolò Machiavelli."

"Whom I'm nothing like," Nic said, turning the key-ring over and over.

"You're making progress with it. Part of the problem was that you were a set of heuristics that talked like Niccolò and walked like Niccolò but was manifestly *not* Niccolò. Now—" He smiled and gestured at Nic's hands. "Now you can unlock the real you."

* * *

The aircar door opened. Mya'ar did not wait for the steps to unfold, but coasted down a meter-and-a-half to the ground. The *esGyu'u* of the High Nest was already approaching the security barrier by the time Simon came down the steps fifteen seconds later.

Simon took a deep breath and looked out off to his right, where the land dropped away to the place where the descendants of Kamehameha's victims found the bones and buried them. In the distance he could see the constellation of lights from Kaneohe and Kailua.

Something made him turn around: a sudden breeze, something a bit more fierce than the wind that blew from the windward side of Oahu.

There was a brief, almost invisible burst of multicolored light near the top of the Pali Tower, seventy or eighty meters above where he stood.

He looked down again and noticed someone standing next to Mya'ar, who had not seemed to notice the visual effect. Even from his vantage, he could see that the other was a holo. After a few seconds Mya'ar turned and walked away; the holo vanished.

"*se* Mya'ar," he said, as the zor emissary approached.

"*se* Simon." Mya'ar's wings arranged themselves in a neutral position. "The *esGa'uYe* is gone, and the—security program—assured me that nothing was amiss.

"There is something wrong here, my friend. Something has happened, and I am reasonably certain that there will be no evidence of it. We will look like fools before Commander St. Giles . . . but I am still fairly sure that something is being concealed even from him."

"What about his security program?" Simon asked.

Mya'ar shrugged his shoulders. "Let us return to the party, *se* Simon."

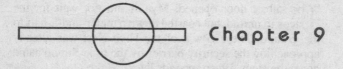

Chapter 9

TO SECURE OURSELVES AGAINST DEFEAT LIES IN
OUR OWN HANDS, BUT THE OPPORTUNITY OF DE-
FEATING THE ENEMY IS PROVIDED BY THE ENEMY
HIMSELF.

—Sun Tzu,
The Art of War, IV:2

June 2422
GORGON System

Tristan da Cunha was the ship of her class, the first of
four built at Mothallah Shipyards during 2420 and 2421.
Mothallah was the oldest and most renowned yard in the
Solar Empire—they'd been building warships there since
the twenty-second century—and it had been getting lots
of work during the past few decades.

In all respects *Tristan* was the height of twenty-fifth-
century ship design. There were eight flight decks capable of supporting two fighter squadrons each: one
deployed and one ready—under the right conditions all
ninety-six fighters could be out at the same time, though
it'd be holy hell if they all had to come back to base at
once. All in all, *Tristan da Cunha* was an eminently suitable vessel to carry the Admiral of the Red. *Seychelles,*
Réunion, and *Barbados* were all built along the same
lines, but Barbara had come to feel that *Tristan*—even on
its first cruise—was truly *hers*. It was something not

found in specs or deck plans, something that only long-time commanders claimed to feel.

Admiral Barbara MacEwan could have imagined any number of things awaiting them at GORGON. Intel had identified ten objectives for the Navy to eliminate in preparation for the key attack at KEYSTONE; each objective had a base and ships to defend it. The presence of ships was what *made* them objectives, after all.

GORGON was the seventh of the ten objectives. While she moved on GORGON, Anderson's force was at JANISSARY, hoping to beat that arrogant civilian to the punch; the vid Anderson had received at Ariel had driven the First Lord into a fury. All of his strategy had been betrayed so thoroughly and so easily. When Ch'en'ya HeYen's involvement was revealed, an angry dispatch had been sent from St. Louis Admiralty to the High Nest at esYen to complain about it.

Complaint was not available to Barbara, Admiral of the Red or not. She'd had things to say, but said them to *Tristan*'s brain trust—wardroom privilege extended to admirals as well—and none of it would get back to St. Louis, or there'd truly be hell to pay.

Whatever she'd expected when *Tristan* and its sister-ships transited from jump, though, finding no enemy ships at GORGON wasn't it.

"Launch all fore squadrons," Admiral MacEwan ordered. The twelve ships of her command formed plane-of-battle. Arturo Schelling, her XO, passed the order to each of the squadron bays; four flights of six fighters were free of the carrier in less than a minute, followed by four more flights three minutes later. As the eight squadrons spread out ahead of *Tristan,* visual and forward telemetry data confirmed what mass-radar had already indicated: There wasn't an enemy ship anywhere in GOR-GON System.

When the fighters were several minutes under way, she ordered: "Ship to ship, systemwide."

Normally she'd conduct this sort of interview in her ready-room, but something about the situation made her unwilling to leave the pilot's seat. Eleven head shots appeared above the pilot's board—captains planted in their own chairs. As they faded into view, she counted their ships off in her mind: *César Hsien,* the brand-new seventh-generation starship named for her old CO; *Sheng Hua, Sheng Tse,* and *Brittany,* old veterans with years of combat experience; the heavily armed and newer Argonne-class ships *Aldebaran, Morrow, Lasker,* and *Bohonye*; and lighter ships, *Cabo Verde, Tikal,* and *Mazatlán.*

When all of the ships were present and accounted for, Barbara said, "Any ideas, people?"

"It's a trap," said Aaron Lewis, of *Lasker.* "We shouldn't go deep into the well."

"We'll have to go in to destroy the forts," David Kelso of *Bohonye* put in. "Not much choice there. Other than the outer gas giant"—Kelso looked aside, probably at his own board—"they're all deep in the system."

"Leave it to the fighters," Lewis answered.

"Those are *my* fighters you're talking about," Barbara growled. "If they go into the gravity well, *Tristan* goes with them. And if *I* go, some of you go, too."

She glanced at her own board: Two of the squadrons were approaching that outer gas giant now, where there was a static defense in place.

"Permission to speak freely, Admiral," Lewis said. Barbara nodded; he leaned forward. "Look, ma'am, if there are no ships here, there has to be a reason. They must've been deployed elsewhere."

"Or they've been destroyed . . ." From Darrin Feng of *César Hsien.*

"Nonsense"—Carlo Roenecke of *Aldebaran*—"that's very unlikely, ma'am," he said to Barbara. "There's a definite pattern to destruction by . . . the other force." No one wanted to say *"the Destroyer."* "They don't clean up debris. What's left couldn't have all made reentry somewhere. And the forts' energy signatures suggest that they're all still *intact*. The ones at ARIEL, BASALT, CLUSTER, and DAGGER were all destroyed or badly damaged. This system hasn't been attacked—it's been *abandoned*."

"The ships were redeployed elsewhere. Any idea where?"

"Not to any of those four," Kelso said, and there was a brief chuckle among the captains.

"How many guesses do I get, Admiral?" Roenecke said.

Great, Barbara thought. *Everyone's a wiseguy.*

"I'd say they went to KEYSTONE," Roenecke continued. "If they're gone from here, they're probably not at Ethernet or Finagle, either."

"Wouldn't they want to make us fight all the way there?" Feng asked querulously. "It doesn't make any sense."

"Unless there's something at KEYSTONE worth fighting for," Barbara said. "We don't seriously believe that it's the vuhl homeworld, but this confirms that it's a major naval base."

"Excuse me, ma'am," said Ron Marroux, who was monitoring the fighters. "Incoming from Blue Leader."

"Blue Leader go," Barbara said, turning her attention for a moment from the captains and looking at the pilot's display. She pointed to the Blue Squadron deployment and it enlarged to show the gas giant and the six fighters closing in on the orbital station that protected it.

"We've just been scanned, Admiral. Low-energy beam crossed my nose about eight seconds ago."

"From the orbital station?"

"I don't have *Tristan's* sensor array, ma'am, but I'd guess so. All six of us got pinged."

Barbara felt her stomach jump. "Bear off, Blue Leader, maximum g, on the double! Get out of range."

"Already doing it, Admiral. We did a sharp starboard turn as soon as it happened."

"Comm-squirt," the comm officer said, interrupting. He named a frequency and direction. "It's headed outsystem."

"Jam it. Where's it headed?"

"I'll have it in a minute, Admiral."

"Damn," Barbara said. "Ron, call everyone back to close support." She looked at the board, zooming it out to see Blue Squadron retreating from the gas giant.

"Got it," comm said. He swiveled his chair to face Barbara. "Best solution on the squirt is KEYSTONE, ma'am."

"Jump-echoes," Barbara said. "They sent data on our jump-echoes. They know the size of our force—but why did they scan—?"

"I can answer that," came Blue Leader's voice. "Going to visual."

A new holo appeared above and starboard of Aaron Lewis' face, over Barbara's pilot's board. The huge gas giant was slowly receding. Against this backdrop a bright, silent explosion was taking place. *Tristan* was still some distance away and hadn't visually registered it yet.

"Damage report."

"None," Blue Leader said. "We're all okay."

"Told you it was a trap, Admiral," Aaron Lewis said. "Watch them all blow."

"Let's make sure. All ships form up; Darren, you take the lead, Argonne ships take rear position. Formation Zeta: Let's go and do what we came here to do."

New Chicago System

Red Comyn docked at New Chicago Station Four. While the small merchanter launched itself into the frenzy that accompanies planetfall (or stationfall), its passenger made her way across the main concourse to the shuttle bay, where she boarded a craft bound for the planet.

It had been a dozen years since Jackie had been in Jardine, New Chicago's capital city. New Chicago had been a member of the Solar Empire, with seats in the Imperial Assembly, for seventy years at the time of the Dark Dawn of Alya. The original settlement planted here by the old North American Union in 2165 had grown into the enormous city of Jardine, with tree-lined avenues and graceful skyscrapers, visible signs of the world's affluence.

Jackie requisitioned an airbike at the spaceport and rode slowly through light traffic, exchanging polite glances with humans and brief, respectful glances from People as she flew. Finally she reached her destination: the Shiell Institute, located on a sheltered, terraced hill just northeast of downtown.

Byar HeShri turned to face her as she stepped out of a lift into a rooftop garden. "*se* Jackie." He had heard her coming, she knew: There had been minute movements in his wings as he assumed the Posture of Polite Approach.

"*se* Byar." They grasped forearms, then Byar returned to his view of the city. He had been gazing out across Jardine through an old-fashioned brass telescope mounted on the rooftop railing—the kind that she'd used when she'd served aboard a wet-navy sailing ship in her Academy days.

"Have you ever thought about the eye, *se* Jackie?"

"The *eye*?"

"Yes. Miraculous organ, is it not? One of the greatest of the creations of the Lord *esLi*." His wings moved to a position of honor to *esLi*. "It is so complex—yet it functions without the slightest effort on our part. It can focus, it can track, and it can filter out information, working in partnership with the brain."

Jackie didn't answer. Byar was going somewhere with this, but she wasn't sure where.

"The most amazing thing about the eye, *se* Jackie, is

that we can see perfectly well *directly in front* of us—the center of our focus and attention—yet that is the one place where our eye *does not function*. The one place the organ does not receive information is in its center."

"The blind spot."

"Just so." Byar turned to face her. His wings conveyed slight amusement. "We have a blind spot in each eye; yet the brain infers what must be there, connecting the pattern all around it so that we have a seamless field of vision.

"And yet . . . what is in that spot is not actually *seen*."

"This bears in some way on our present flight.

"Of course. I should not have drawn the analogy if it did not. It would be as if I merely wished to hear myself speak." His wings were even more amused now. "I think that it is quite apt."

"I am eager to hear you explain."

"*se* Jackie." Byar extended his left hand, clenched in a fist. He extended one talon as he spoke. "Consider what we know. There are four talons to this matter: First, there is the Talon of *esLi*, led by our friend *se* Ch'en'ya. They believe in the Strength of Madness . . . I need not waste any breath explaining to you the problems inherent in that approach.

"Second," he continued, extending another talon, "we have the mysterious organization Blazing Star, which includes our old friend *se* Owen, whom we believed had transcended the Outer Peace. We know nothing of its capabilities, though we do have a fair idea of its intentions.

"Third, we have the alien *esHara'y* themselves." Another talon joined the first two. "There are patterns to their conduct of this war, though their attacks have sometimes seemed random. The worlds that have been subsumed within *Ur'ta leHssa* have been taken for a *reason*. The battles they have fought have been fought for a *reason*.

"And fourth, we have the Guardians, the organization

se Owen created. It now clearly has a different agenda of its own. It is well known that most find the Guardians unpleasant to deal with—and they seem to cultivate this isolation."

His entire hand was open now, showing all four talons.

"Now, *se* Jackie. We have all of this sensory input to our marvelous instrument, and yet there is something in front of us about which we can only infer. What is it that we cannot see? What lies within our blind spot?"

"The Destroyer."

"Of *course* it is the Destroyer, my old friend. We know that he is coming—we know that he is *here*, since no less an authority than *ra* Hesya HeYen has told us so. Based on your own account, we even know what he looks like. But what *is* he? What is it that we cannot see, but we believe that we know just the same?"

"Is this some sort of *sSurch'a*?"

"If so, then it is as much a *sSurch'a* for me as for you, *se* Jackie. I do not know the answer to my own question—and I am fairly certain that you do not know, either."

Jackie walked to the parapet and leaned out. There was a cool, damp breeze blowing from the direction of the ocean, unseen beyond the ranks of buildings and squares, laid out in regular fashion all the way to the horizon.

"A few more eighths of a sun and it will be rashk weather again," Byar said. "This is the closest it has been to clear and dry since I arrived on this world." He looked out across Jardine again, as if he had a personal grudge with the clouds.

"Are you sure that there's anything to infer, past what we already know?"

"I do not take your meaning."

"This isn't that big a mystery to me, *se* Byar. The . . . Stone's people, whoever or whatever they are, have created the Destroyer to thwart the vuhls. Now they're letting him loose."

"And why *now*? Why have they chosen this moment to

carry out this plan? Could they not have loosed him five turns ago, or ten, or any time since the beginning of the war?"

"Not enough information." She turned to face him. "Unless you know something I don't—about this subject, I mean."

"I have a conjecture. Based on your description of the Destroyer when you saw him at Sharia'a during the first year of the war—and your description of *se* Ch'en'ya in the same image . . ." His wings moved to indicate a slight distaste; Ch'en'ya's defection had not sat well with the High Nest—therefore Byar personally *and* officially disapproved. ". . . we should be able to determine roughly when it takes place."

"I'm not sure I see how."

"How much older was Ch'en'ya in the scene than she was when you witnessed it?"

"I'm not sure—twenty or twenty-five Standard years, I'd say."

"And you viewed her approximately twenty-five Standard years ago. Which would mean that . . . what you saw, if a true vision, should occur during *this* Standard year. It will be the result of the Destroyer being . . . 'let loose.'"

Jackie nodded: she'd come to much the same conclusion.

"Now, *se* Jackie: How old did this individual appear?"

"Perhaps twenty-five Standard years."

"An interesting coincidence."

"I thought that you didn't believe in coincidences, old friend."

Byar's wings moved in amusement. "I do not. In fact, I would venture the proposition that the Destroyer was born at or near the time that you witnessed his future: in the spring of 2397, twenty-five Standard years ago."

Jackie thought about that for a moment: Byar didn't ever quite give up on being a teacher; he'd mentioned the point for a reason, but Jackie couldn't put her finger on why.

"If he was born in 2397, that would explain why at least some time has passed—if he's going to go after the vuhls he'll have to be old enough to do it. But it still doesn't explain why *now*. Something else has triggered it—something we can't see yet."

"It is in the blind spot, *se* Jackie," Byar said, with something like satisfaction reflected in his wings. It was evidently the *sSurch'a* he was trying to get her to make on her own, though Jackie still felt as if there were something more. "But what will it mean for him to be 'let loose'?"

"I imagine it'll mean the death of a lot of vuhls. God knows I have no sympathy for them. I've got old scores that I don't mind seeing settled."

"Personal grudges? I believe you have recently made inquiries of others in that regard."

"How'd you know about that?" She rounded on him.

"About what?" His wings changed slightly, as if to proclaim his innocence. "I cannot imagine to what you refer."

"There were only a handful of people at that table."

"*se* Jackie. One of them is an informant."

The bald statement, without sophistry or any attempt to conceal it, took Jackie by surprise. It wasn't all that surprising: Military organizations were often riddled with intel agents and others with "alternate chains of command"—Jackie's military background rebelled at the idea but accepted it all the same.

"Informant for whom?"

"You ask me to reveal a confidence."

"Does it touch your honor?"

"Not truly." Byar extended his claws a centimeter or so and let them snap back into their sheaths. "There is an informant aboard *Tristan da Cunha* who reports directly to *se* Commander St. Giles. Fortunately, the High Nest has an informant who monitors those transmissions."

"A fox among the foxes among the chickens."

Byar shrugged. "I never cease to marvel at your ability

to stress the Highspeech to its limits. A *h'r'kka* among the *h'r'kka* among the *artha*." His wings rose once again in amusement. "Yes, you have identified the situation in your usual idiosyncratic fashion. We have an informant among the Guardians."

"Why would the Guardians care about a wardroom dinner aboard *Tristan*?"

"Why does the Spine of the World traverse north-to-south? The great imponderable: Why do the Guardians care about anything? I suppose the most logical answer is that the Guardians care about all things. They wish to know about all things."

"Such as . . ."

"The interesting fact that our old friend *se* Owen Garrett has returned within the Outer Peace. *se* Commander St. Giles did not receive the news with unmitigated joy— he had been following *se* Commander Garrett's career for many years."

"I thought they had been fast friends."

"I am sure that this was the appearance they sought to cultivate. Suffice it to say that *se* Owen departed the organization for reasons directly related to the way in which his second-in-command conducted himself. He arranged for it to appear as if he transcended the Outer Peace at Port Saud, and had a new identity fashioned for him at that time."

"St. Giles has some sort of score to settle with Owen."

"Or *se* Owen with *se* St. Giles. Each wing opposes the other. But they may each be caused to beat in rhythm, depending on who conducts them. Crest and talons, one wingtip and the other: four powers, with but one *hyu* at the center."

"Also in the blind spot."

"Correct. All of these forces are arranging themselves around the Destroyer."

"Even the Guardians?"

"I believe that to be a possibility. It is a disturbing pattern."

"What can we do about it? Do you think there's anything we *should* do?"

"The Eight Winds blow where they will."

"That's a pat answer, especially for someone who's just cheated death by fiddling with alien tech."

"I was not aware that you had been briefed on *that*."

"The High Nest has lots of informants." She smiled, which Byar recognized and acknowledged with a lift of his wings. "I had a message-squirt from *se* T'te'e when I reached Station Four. That was a damn stupid thing to do, don't you think?"

Byar shrugged and pointed to one eye. "The blind spot, *se* Jackie. The brain infers what belongs in the blind spot by projecting logically from all angles. The device . . . the *s's'th'r* . . . provided a different angle from which to view what we cannot logically see. I thought the potential information worth the risk required to obtain it."

"It nearly blew your brains out."

"I repeat my assertion. We must learn what opposes us. This is no trifling villain from legend; this is not even merely Shrnu'u HeGa'u. This is the *Deceiver, se* Jackie. This is a conflict with the same magnitude as our war with *esHu'ur*—perhaps greater.

"Indeed, perhaps it is the same conflict, entering a new phase."

"The final phase."

"I am not prepared to make such a categorical statement. It is an outcome the High Lord herself may not be able to perceive."

Later that night in her hotel room Jackie thought through the conversation—the directions Byar had guided her with, the things he'd mentioned and failed to mention.

She remembered that year, the first one of the war. It was the year she'd recovered the sword from Center . . . from Stone. From Hesya. She'd encountered him a few more times, finally staring him down at some *hsi*-patterning that represented Shr'e'a, the *original* City of Warriors. He'd given her a chance to see a grisly scene in which a vuhl Great Queen was impaled, then propelled her back to the land of the living. It was Stone's last personal appearance as far as she knew.

Until now.

Then, of course, he—or someone he served—had led her to the world where Th'an'ya had died and Ch'en'ya had been born. Another chesspiece moved into place, though she didn't see why . . . unless she was *meant* to defeat Shrnu'u HeGa'u, *meant* to find Ch'en'ya, *meant* to see the vision at Sharia'a . . . and Ch'en'ya was *meant* to grow up to serve the Destroyer, a circumstance made possible by the actions of Jacqueline Thèrese Laperriere, IN (Retired), *Gyaryu'har* of the High Nest and all-around damn fool for being pulled along in this entire game.

Damn Stone. Damn him, she thought to herself. *He's got what he wants: the Destroyer, and Ch'en'ya, and Owen Garrett, and . . .*

There was something she was missing: something elusive, some clue, some loose end not quite tied up. She couldn't infer what was hiding in the blind spot, surrounded by actual data but hidden in plain sight.

What in hell *was* it?

And what, if anything, did Byar HeShri know that he hadn't told her?

Damn Byar, too, she thought to herself.

"Comm to Shiell Institute," she said, placing a finger on the comp on her night table. "I'd like to speak with Byar HeShri."

Fifteen seconds later an image appeared above the table: Byar standing beside a window, looking out at the night.

"I was awaiting your call, old friend."

"All right, you son of a bitch," she began, half smiling even as she said it. Byar recognized her comment with a wing-twitch of amusement. "You've thought this through and you know where this is going. I can't make the *sSurch'a*, and I think you've already made it."

"I told you that this was a *sSurch'a* for me as well, *se* Jackie, and I spoke the truth when I said so. Nonetheless, I have examined the matter as you say. The Destroyer is the key to all that we see, though we cannot see him directly. I think we can agree that we must understand him in order to . . . deal with what is to come.

"If your assumptions about your vision are true—"

"Wait." She held her hand up. "Secure this comm on my voice authority." A small red icon appeared a few centimeters above Byar's image. "All right. We probably should discuss this in privacy."

"*na* Hesya HeGa'u will not have any difficulty with the encoding scheme, *se* Jackie," Byar said, his wings rising in amusement.

"You're probably right, but there might be other people listening in. Go ahead."

"If your assumptions are true," he continued, "then we have some idea when the Destroyer . . . came into existence. I reason that there might have been some echo on the Plane of Sleep."

"Meaning?"

"Meaning," Byar said, turning to face her, "that it is possible that something took place during the period in question."

"*se* Byar, five-twelves of five-twelves of five-twelves of things happened during the period in question."

"But very few of them involved a Servant of *esGa'u*, *se* Jackie."

That stopped her in her tracks. Just for a moment, the room lights seemed to dim and then they returned to their former intensity.

"You found something."

Byar inclined his head. "I reasoned that anything that might have to do with the Destroyer might also have something to do with the Deceiver, given the 'coincidence' of dates we discussed this sun. If I could locate an event that was touched by the Lord of Despite"—his wings rose into the Cloak of Guard—"I might well find something that would be associated with our quarry.

"Twenty-five Standard years ago, *se* Jackie, a shuttle crashed into Waianae on the west side of Oahu. Our *es-Gyu'u*, *se* Mya'ar HeChra, sensed an *esGa'uYe* aboard the vessel."

Jackie sat on the bed, leaning her elbows on her knees and her chin on her hands. She couldn't bring the incident to mind: Of course, she hadn't been studying the damn thing for as long as Byar.

"*se* Mya'ar was very sure," Byar added after a moment. "What is more, he has recently felt this same individual again, near the Pali Tower on Oahu."

"He felt a Servant of *esGa'u* at the Guardian headquarters?"

"As I understand it." Byar's wings rose slightly, defensively.

"What's being done? What does the Guardian Commander make of it?"

"He has dismissed it." Byar looked away, then back at Jackie. "But back to the matter of many years ago. Mya'ar was certain that he felt a Servant aboard the crashed shuttle, and in the investigation *se* M'm'e'e was very thorough."

"M'm'e'e Sha'kan?"

"The very one. He made a thorough study of every passenger aboard that specific craft, attempting to connect each with the *esGa'uYe* that *se* Mya'ar most certainly perceived."

"And whom did he think had the taint of Despite?"

"Only one passenger might have fulfilled the requirements. I believe that you knew him: Sir Johannes Xavier Sharpe."

The name struck her like a blow. She remembered Hansie: an annoying, bigoted little man, a minor nobleman from Cle'eru System. He'd turned up at the Imperial Court reception when she had retired as an admiral.

She recalled a conversation with *hi* Sa'a a little while

later, on the way to Sharia'a, about the crash and about the High Nest's interest in it.

"It's a puzzle piece that doesn't fit." She remembered saying that, and the *gyaryu* would provide her with the entire conversation if she took the time to ask.

"Hansie? Why Hansie? Why would he have been . . ."

"I cannot answer that, *se* Jackie. But I can provide this interesting talon: Sir Johannes Xavier Sharpe was returning from SeaTac on the North American mainland where he had conveyed a package to Shi'koku Laboratories, a birthing center. *se* M'm'e'e was able to determine that the package contained genetic material and that it was used to create a child in vitro."

"The Destroyer."

"There is no way to be sure, *se* Jackie, but—"

"But you don't believe in coincidences. I know, I know. But what was *Hansie* doing there?"

"The most obvious possible thing, *se* Jackie. Some of the genetic material delivered to Shi'koku Labs in 2397 was his own."

"You think . . . Hansie Sharpe was the Destroyer's— the Prophet's—father? *Hansie?*"

"Why not?"

"*se* Byar, an apple might fall a bit far from the tree, but it'd have to be on the other side of the planet in this case."

"Your metaphor is quaint, *se* Jackie, but completely mystifying. What does a Terran fruit have to do with . . ." He trailed off, his wings moving to indicate deep thought. "I believe that I *might* see what you mean.

"But surely the Deceiver would choose genetic material based on eights of generations, not merely the most current one? And did not this Sharpe have a very thorough knowledge of his own bloodline?"

A puzzle piece that doesn't fit, she kept telling herself. All of the information was there, but she couldn't quite assimilate it. The hotel room was too small—there wasn't room for her to pace, and the city view at night through the window wasn't giving back any answers.

"Comp activate," she finally said. "Laura Ibarra AI, equipped with the information in the data packet *se* Byar just sent."

A holo of Laura Ibarra appeared opposite, sitting in one of the armchairs near the window. Jackie settled into the other.

"Program parameters?" the AI asked.

"I need you to help me think like an intel officer," Jackie said. The Laura Ibarra AI smiled. "Byar has reached some *sSurch'a* on this matter and I believe he wants me to do the same."

"Where would you like me to start?"

"Byar said," she began, "that an *esGa'uYe* recently appeared at Pali Tower; and it was the same one that *se* Mya'ar sensed at Honolulu Port in 2397."

"At the time of the shuttle crash."

"That's right. Since Hansie Sharpe was aboard the shuttle, Byar reasons that the Servant crashed the shuttle in order to kill Hansie."

"Why?"

"'Why' what? Why kill Hansie? I don't know. He was harmless . . . Well, actually, he probably did more harm than good. He didn't even see the vuhls as a threat."

"There was very little information on the extent of the threat at the time."

"Well, that's true, but that only begs the question of what the point of the exercise was."

"'Despite does not have a point,'" the AI quoted.

"I know. But it *does*. What possible reason would there be to throw out a red flag like that? Why call attention to themselves?"

"So that you could see it, I expect," the AI replied. "Though it seems to have taken twenty-five Standard years. Maybe it was a taunt . . ." She pillared her fingers in front of her—a perfect mimicry of Laura Ibarra. Jackie smiled. ". . . A way of saying, 'Here you go, there was a clue—but you missed it.'"

"Byar believes that Hansie was chosen for his genetic material—because his ancestry was well known. But why get rid of him? The child would grow up an orphan."

"Perhaps that was the intention."

"An *angry* orphan from the look of it," Jackie said, thinking about it. "He was—is—bright, alienated, a loner. No real friends, no real competitors."

"Enlisted in the Imperial Marines at fifteen," the Ibarra AI said. "He'd finished all of his regular schooling and couldn't get out of Tukwila Academy fast enough."

"And two years later," Jackie continued, "he was a Guardian. And a year later he walked onto the Grand Concourse at Emperor Willem Starport in Harrison System and disappeared. There's no record of where he went, or why. The Guardians assumed he'd simply gone off the reservation."

"All of that is true," the AI said. "Is there more data?"

Jackie nodded. "There's one more thing—and the *real* Laura Ibarra doesn't know this, of course—but I know this guy." She gestured over her comp and a still holo appeared in the corner of the room: John Smith, the angry orphan, Hansie Sharpe's son—a younger version of the man that had left the message for Erich Anderson at Ariel. And, incidentally, the man she'd seen in a vision at Sharia'a twenty-five years ago.

"Please clarify."

"He's the Destroyer," Jackie said. "And looks like him. Byar thinks that a Servant of the Deceiver created him, motivated him, and probably plucked him off the starport concourse at Harrison System seven years ago."

"And you believe he is also Owen Garrett's 'Prophet.'"

"It seems like an inevitable conclusion."

The AI didn't answer. After a few moments Jackie said, "Save program and exit," and Laura Ibarra smiled and disappeared, leaving Jackie alone with her thoughts.

Chapter 10

THE POWER AVAILABLE TO THOSE WHO WALK THROUGH THE GATE IS LIKE A CHARGED POWER CELL. THE FORMS AND CEREMONIES OF THE ORDER PROVIDE THE ENERGY; WHEN TIME ALLOWS, WE BUILD IT UP, DRAWING UPON THE GATE ITSELF IN A WAY UNKNOWN TO THOSE OUTSIDE. AT A TIME OF NEED, WE CAN DRAW UPON IT.

WITHOUT THE TRAINING OF THE ORDER, THOSE CAPABLE OF REACHING FOR THAT ENERGY CAN GRASP IT BUT NOT HOLD ON: IT PASSES THROUGH THEIR FINGERS LIKE FINE SAND, LEAVING NO TRACE BEHIND. IT IS WHY MERELY FOCUSING HATRED FALLS FAR SHORT OF OUR ULTIMATE CAPABILITIES. ANGER IS NOT ENOUGH.

—Antonio St. Giles, Master of the Inner Gate
Opening the Gate,
Green Book edition, 2405

ADMIRAL ERICH ANDERSON'S CAMPAIGN PRIOR TO KEYSTONE WAS BASED ON SOUND STRATEGY BUT IT WAS ALSO MOTIVATED BY PERSONAL AMBITION. THE ADMIRAL WAS A DESCENDANT OF A LONG LINE OF DISTINGUISHED SOLDIERS; THREE CENTURIES EARLIER, ADMIRAL MARIE ANDERSON OF THE EUROPEAN UNION HAD FOUGHT ONE OF THE FIRST BATTLES EVER TO TAKE PLACE OUTSIDE OF SOL SYSTEM: A THREE-ON-THREE ENCOUNTER BE-

TWEEN EUROPEAN UNION SHIPS OF THE LINE AND REBEL SHIPS, ARMED AND SUPPORTED BY GREATER CHINA. THE EU HAD ULTIMATELY TAKEN BACK THE COLONY. MARIE ANDERSON'S SKILL AT TARGETING THE MANEUVERING AND WEAPONS CAPABILITIES OF THE REBEL SHIPS, ULTIMATELY BOARDING AND CAPTURING THEM INSTEAD OF BLOWING THEM TO HELL WITH ALL HANDS, HAD HELPED RECONCILE THE COLONISTS TO THE FORGIVING PARENT WITH MINIMUM CASUALTIES.

DURING THE FIRST CENTURY OF THE SOLAR EMPIRE, ADMIRAL KERRY ANDERSON HAD SUCCESSFULLY SUPPRESSED THE SIX WORLDS' REVOLT, MAKING ENOUGH OF A MARK THAT HE HAD BEEN PERMITTED TO SIT FOR AN OFFICIAL PORTRAIT THAT (IT WAS SAID) HUNG IN EMPEROR WILLEM I'S BEDROOM AND MIGHT HAVE BEEN THE LAST THING HIS HIGHNESS SAW WHEN HE DIED AT DAWN ON NEW YEAR'S DAY 2206. THE STORY WAS THAT KERRY ANDERSON HAD FOUGHT A SEVENTEEN-HOUR BATTLE WITHOUT EVER LEAVING THE PILOT'S CHAIR—LEADING TO HIS INFAMOUS NICKNAME, "STEELBLADDER."

ERICH ANDERSON'S GREAT-GREAT-GRANDFATHER ARTURO HAD SERVED DURING THE SECOND AND THIRD ZOR CONFLICTS, AND AS FIRST LORD OF THE ADMIRALTY HAD SIGNED THE TREATY OF LAS DUHR (THOUGH HE DIED OF A STROKE BEFORE WAR BROKE OUT AGAIN, SO HIS NAME DID NOT APPEAR ON THE TREATIES OF EFAL OR E'RENE'E.) HIS GRANDFATHER SEAN HAD FOUGHT FEW BATTLES, BUT HAD BEEN THE ADMIRALTY'S ADMINISTRATOR FOR THE IMPERIAL GRAND SURVEY FOR ALMOST TWENTY YEARS.

AFTER THIRTY YEARS IN COMMAND, TWENTY-FIVE OF THEM FIGHTING A DIFFICULT AND SEEMINGLY

ENDLESS WAR WITH AN ALIEN ENEMY, THE ADMI-
RAL WAS STILL WAITING FOR HIS CHANCE FOR
RECOGNITION, TO HAVE HIS NAME RANKED WITH
THOSE OF HIS FAMOUS ANCESTORS. HE HAD THE
ABILITY AND THE DRIVE, BUT THE FRUSTRATING
STALEMATE HAD KEPT OPPORTUNITY JUST OUT OF
REACH.

AND AFTER WAITING THIS LONG, IT WAS CLEAR
THAT HE WOULD HAVE BEEN UNWILLING TO LET A
THEN-MYSTERIOUS CIVILIAN TAKE THAT CHANCE
AWAY FROM HIM.

—author unknown,
The Dark Crusade: A History,
early fragment published circa 2430

June 2422
JANISSARY System

JANISSARY had been mapped by the IGS in the 2360s and
investigated by robot probes as recently as three months
ago; it lay roughly at the center of the sphere described
by the ten objectives. KEYSTONE, the target when everything from ARIEL to JANISSARY was neutralized—as Barbara MacEwan would say, "a polite word for 'blown to
hell'"—lay on the Orionward edge of that sphere. JANIS-
SARY was thus not the closest of the ten, merely the best
defended and most valuable. The formation of the star
system had left enough residual matter that there were
several gas giants in the outer system and three airless
rocks deep in the gravity well; there was really no margin
for any sort of biozone in between. While there was nothing resembling a habitable planet, what there *was* provided excellent facilities for refueling and naval
construction: probes had shown evidence of extensive

strip mining on the rocks, and plenty of ships using the gas giants' atmosphere to scoop hydrogen.

That JANISSARY was a target—and probably the most important one—would likely come as no surprise to the vuhls defending it. Still, the transition to normal-space was without incident. Anderson knew what he was facing; he'd added *Phidias* and *Scylla,* sister-ships to his squadron's light carrier *Lycias,* for the attack on this system. As soon as he made transition, he immediately deployed fighters from all three carriers for reconnaissance; there were too many places for ships to hide.

There was nothing at the jump point but debris. As the fleet descended into the gravity well, the pilot's board on *Emperor Ian* showed lots of evidence of numerous energy discharges taking place minutes earlier in the inner system.

"Talk to me," Anderson said to Dan Gonzalez, commander of *Lycias.*

"Lots of debris, Admiral. I think our friends have been here already. In fact," Gonzalez added, "I think they're *still* here."

Anderson exchanged glances with Alan Howe, who shook his head negatively. "Tell me more."

"I've got my Red wing deployed near the fifth orbital, sir, and they're picking up lots of energy discharges closer in. Someone's shooting at someone—or was, fifteen or twenty minutes ago."

There was no way to know what was happening now; mass-radar indicated there was only one enemy ship in the system, but it might be either a vuhl or a ship under civilian command—one of the ones who had attacked ARIEL. Until light-speed information caught up there was no way to know exactly what was going on in the inner system.

But there had to have been more, Anderson thought to himself; *one ship couldn't have done all this damage.*

"Do you read anything near the gas giants?"

"No sir. There are static orbital defenses, but we stayed clear of them. They got left alone by the attackers, from the look of it."

"All right, Dan. Send them one extra orbit and then pull them back." He looked at his board. "*Mortimer* and *Huan Che,* deploy to the inner system. *Lycias* will provide coordinates. Flag sends."

There had been nothing at the jump point; there was nothing at any of the outer gas giants. If there were any vuhl ships based at JANISSARY and not under way—thus not registering on the mass-radar—they would be based at one of the cold rocks down in the gravity well. As the carriers and the lead ships moved closer, visuals picked up more debris: lots of structural members and the gray rocklike material that formed the hulls of vuhl ships.

On *Emperor Ian*'s pilot's board, Admiral Anderson could see the one unidentified ship hanging above the airless world in the second orbital: It wasn't a hive-ship, or anything that looked like a vuhl ship at all.

"ID that bastard," Anderson said, watching his flanks closing in on the sole remaining opposition ship in the system.

"I've got it," the comm officer said. "It's *Epanimondas,* or was. Fifth-generation, decommissioned 2405. Merchanter."

"Where are its friends?" Anderson asked. "Scan the debris, Alison," he said to his gunnery officer. "Did the others get wrecked?"

"I don't show any debris other than from vuhl ships," Alison Mbele said. "And there's a hell of a lot of it. Maybe a dozen ships' worth."

"There's no way one ship could've taken out that many enemies. All right," he said after a moment. "Comm, contact *Epanimondas,* or whatever it's calling itself. Stand down and prepare to be boarded; *Emperor Ian* sends."

Remnants of vuhl ships bounced off the defensive

shields of *Ian* and the other ships of Anderson's fleet. *Epanimondas* continued in orbit around the airless planet, with ships closing in on it from all directions.

There was no answer from *Epanimondas*.

"Alison, give me a firing solution on that ship. Comm, send the following to *Epanimondas:* Stand down and drop your fields or I will personally blow you directly to hell. *Emperor Ian* sends."

It was completely silent on the bridge of *Emperor Ian*. A few seconds passed as *Epanimondas* continued to transit in its orbit.

"We can crack that field anytime," Alison Mbele said, turning in her seat. A targeted shot that "cracked the field" would pass through the defensive shell that surrounded *Epanimondas* and strike its hull directly. There was usually only one outcome when that happened.

"All right," said Anderson. "Let's—"

"Fields have been dropped," Alison said suddenly. "They're standing down!"

"Dan," he said to *Lycias'* commander after a moment. "Put two squadrons on her *right now*." He touched a pad on his pilot's chair. "General, prepare a prize crew for *Epanimondas*."

It had all happened a lot faster than Anderson had expected. He had had *Epanimondas* in the gunsights of *Emperor Ian*, and had nearly given the order to . . . neutralize it, and then it had surrendered. Jim Agropoulous had sent thirty Marines across in two launches, with *Lycias'* fighters in escort, but *Epanimondas* hadn't turned tail or brought weapons to bear.

It was as if they'd been waiting for it to play out that way—but felt obliged to play chicken up to the last moment.

"I'd appreciate input," Anderson said to Howe as they watched the second launch slowly make its way back across from *Epanimondas* to *Emperor Ian*.

Alan frowned, as if he were concentrating; then a look of surprise came over his face.

"Admiral—" he began. "Admiral, I'm getting a bad feeling."

"A bit more definitive, if you please."

"Something . . . Someone aboard that launch." Howe's glance darted nervously from the pilot's board to his commanding officer and back. "I'm not sure, sir."

"A vuhl?"

"No. No, I don't think so."

Anderson frowned, trying to read his Sensitive. Though they'd served together a long time, the admiral was never quite sure what to make of the man; still, he trusted Howe's instincts.

He touched the control on his chair. "Guardian Bradford, report to the hangar deck." He stood. "All right, Colonel. Are you up to meeting up with this—someone?"

"I'm not sure, sir."

"Well, consider it an order. I'd like to see what fish we've caught." He walked past Alan toward the lift, stopping a meter short and turning around. "Come *on,* Howe. The bogeyman won't wait all day."

The launch touched down and was made fast; Admiral Anderson and Colonel Howe stepped onto the hangar deck. Cameron Bradford, the Guardian on board, was already there; he stood to the side, his arms folded across his chest. Two squads of Marines in battle-armor were deployed, fully armed.

The launch-bay door opened and four more Marines came down the ramp, exchanging nods and salutes with the ones already on deck. Shortly a number of others came down after them; they wore some sort of uniform that could have been taken for Imperial Navy at a distance, but was enough different to keep them from being tried under the Uniform Code. They were a fairly nondescript group: a couple of obvious civilians and several ex-Navy, distinguishable in the way they carried themselves.

In the midst of the group, but clearly separate from all the others, was a man whose face Admiral Anderson knew very well.

I expect that we will meet at JANISSARY.

Anderson looked aside at Howe for a moment, who looked stunned—or very possibly afraid. Bradford continued to look impassive.

The man didn't speak; the others around him seemed to part like waves on either side, so that he and Anderson were face-to-face across the huge expanse of the hangar deck. No, it was more than that: it was as if he and Anderson were the only two people there.

The man's face betrayed the slightest smile, as if he felt the same thing. It was as if he'd stepped off the launch and was meeting Erich Anderson alone.

Unbidden, words came into Anderson's mind: *I have not come for these others,* he heard. *I have come for you.*

"Admiral," Howe said.

Anderson forced himself to look aside—and it took an effort, but he was able to do so. The mood and the moment were broken, like a taut string snapping.

"What . . . What is it?"

"I would advise you to isolate *that* prisoner," Howe said, not looking at Anderson but rather at the man in the center of it all. Anderson knew exactly who he meant.

"Right," Anderson said, as if he'd just thought of it himself. "Sergeant," he said to the ranking Marine, "take the prisoners to the brig. Separate cells, and they're not to talk to each other. But before you do that," he added, stepping a few meters closer, "is the commander of that tub among this group?"

"Yes sir," the Marine answered, gesturing toward one of the military types. "Captain Amoros."

"Fine. Captain, you're excused from the brig. I'll see you in my ready-room in five minutes." He turned on his heel and walked to the exit. After a few more seconds of eye contact, Alan Howe turned away and followed, with Bradford close behind.

I couldn't have hoped for a better outcome," Anderson said to Howe as the ready-room door slid shut. "I've *got* him, Alan. This is the one: This is the guy who got hold of our battle-plan and has been making so damn much trouble for us."

"I don't have such a good feeling about this."

"He mustn't have thought we'd get here this fast," Anderson continued, pacing behind the conference table. He didn't seem to have heard Alan's last comment. "We caught him with his pants around his ankles." He smiled fiercely at his ranking Sensitive.

"Who destroyed the defending ships?"

"We'll be learning that shortly, I expect. —Ah, Captain Amoros," he said, the door sliding aside. A woman with military bearing entered the room; a single Marine guard stepped in with her and took up a position just inside the door; Bradford, the Guardian, entered in their wake and stood next to the Marine.

Amoros was wearing a semi-military uniform that vaguely resembled Imperial Navy, though in place of the sword-and-sun there was another symbol on the shoulder—a star shrouded in mist. This was echoed on a bronze pin in the center of a white neckerchief.

"Admiral Anderson," Amoros answered.

"Do I know you, Captain?"

"I had the honor of serving under you, sir. I commanded *Carleton* and before that I had *Ivanov.*"

"Both ships fought well. I'm surprised to see you out of uniform, Amoros."

"I've got a boxful of combat ribbons, Admiral. I decided to pursue other options when my last hitch was up."

"'Other options.'" Anderson touched a control on the

conference table. "Display service record for Amoros—former commander of . . . *Carleton,* was it?"

She nodded.

Text appeared in the air, along with a slightly younger holo of Captain Diane Amoros. There was an extensive record; Anderson nodded approvingly. "A fine officer. A shame you left His Majesty's Service."

"As the admiral pleases."

"No," he said. "No, it doesn't please the admiral at all." He came out from behind the table to stand directly in front of Diane Amoros. Alan Howe leaned against a sideboard, watching. "In fact, I would like to express my extreme displeasure at the situation, Captain. You and your—you and your *passenger* have caused the emperor quite a bit of trouble."

Bradford shifted at this comment.

"If you say so."

"I do." Anderson was angry now; Howe had seen the wind blow from this quarter before. Amoros betrayed nothing, standing at parade rest, her face impassive. "You realize," Anderson continued, "that I would be within my rights to have you all shot as spies."

"I imagine you could," she answered. "But you could've blown *Epanimondas* out of the sky and saved yourself the trouble." She folded her hands across her chest and smiled. "No, Admiral, you won't be shooting us as spies; you're after information. *That's* why we're here."

"Why?"

"We were waiting for you, Admiral. Just as *he* said we would be."

"You destroyed all of the defenders and then sat around waiting for us to turn up? There's no possible way you could know when we'd arrive."

"We knew when you'd get here," Amoros answered. "Essentially, we did just as you say. *He* assumed that you wouldn't destroy *Epanimondas* out of hand."

"*He* took a hell of a chance."

"Maybe." she looked across at Alan Howe. "He was pretty sure it'd turn out this way, with us aboard *Emperor Ian*."

"In the brig."

"For now."

"What the hell does that mean? Don't tell me you're planning to break out—it's a ludicrous idea. Even if you don't wind up dead, where would you go?"

"You're right. We wouldn't *think* of trying to escape."

"What, then?"

"*He* assumes that you'll let him out of the brig, along with the Sensitives you've tossed in there. Sooner or later you'll need them: and you'll need *him*."

"For what?"

"To defeat the enemy, Admiral. You can't win without him—without them. Without us."

"We don't need you."

"I don't give this speech very well, sir, but it's clear to me that you do. This war has gone on for most of my life and half of yours—and it's not close to being won. The fact is that you *can't* win it: the enemy has too many ships, too much power, and too much contempt for the human race and its allies to ever want to reach peace.

"It's us or them, Admiral. We survive or they survive. It comes down to that," she said flatly.

"Captain Amoros, you served in His Majesty's Navy. You should know better. You're not some civilian with a wild-eyed theory about how to win this war—"

"It's not a wild-eyed theory," she interrupted. "Look," she said, stepping forward; the Marine took a step toward her and the Guardian stood straighter.

She froze, holding her arms out from her body. "Look at what I've got under my command, Admiral. *Epanimondas* was taken out of service in 2405, seventeen years ago. She's one of the *best* ships we have. How the hell do you think we've been able to take out every target between ARIEL and here with firepower like *that*?"

"I assume that the opposition wasn't very fierce."

"Why do you have Sensitives aboard your ships, Admiral?" She gestured toward Howe. "The vuhls have an equalizer. *So do we*."

"Meaning what?"

"Meaning that we can do what *they* do." She looked at Howe. "We've stopped just defending, Admiral. Now we can *attack*."

Anderson looked at Howe and then at Bradford.

"Trooper, get her out of my sight," he said dismissively. The Marine stepped forward to take her by the elbow but she moved out of his grasp and walked under her own power toward the door and then out of the ready-room.

"Well?" he asked the two other officers. "Can they do it?"

"I doubt it," Bradford said. "I think even Colonel Howe would agree that the ability to project Sensitive talents on an interplanetary scale is beyond our present abilities."

"Alan?"

"As far as I understand, the Shiell Institute hasn't had any luck with the tech we captured at Tamarind. Without something like that, I don't see how they could possibly do what Captain Amoros claims."

"She seemed pretty sure of herself," Anderson replied. "If that was a bluff, it was a brave one."

"Bluster," Bradford said.

"That's the logical answer," Alan answered. "But there's something going on here, sir. The evidence—"

"—is inconclusive," Bradford interrupted. He took a long look at Alan Howe, as if Bradford were again trying to determine if Howe was a vuhl in disguise. Howe clenched his fists and glared back at him.

"She has told us nothing we can verify," the Guardian continued. "And what she *has* told us is patently impossible. There would be no way for the . . . for this rogue civilian to have predicted our transition point. We do not presently possess the ability to do as she says."

Anderson looked from Bradford to Howe. "All right, dismissed."

The two saluted, then left the ready-room after a final glare at each other. Anderson leaned on the table, trying to sort out what he'd just heard.

Suppose it's true, he thought. *What if it* is *true?*

Pali Tower
Imperial Oahu, Sol System

Some years into his term as commander, Antonio St. Giles had designed an AI to supervise the security of the Guardians. Most AIs were fairly plain—they had whatever appearance the creator wanted, but often little in the way of individual personality.

Tonio had something more evolved in mind. His original model had been the twenty-fourth–century historian Ichiro Kanev, who wrote the definitive history of the man-zor wars; Kanev was brilliant, analytical, and turned out to be boring as hell. He also had an annoying habit of making allusions to subjects and events that sent St. Giles constantly scurrying for explanations.

It wasn't required that the security AI be a brilliant conversationalist: this was Tonio's private vanity. Still, using a neural scan of his own personality combined with that of Kanev should have produced someone not only capable of deep thought but who was also interesting to talk to. Thus, a short while into its deployment, Tonio chose a new personality on which the AI would be based. Some of the best technical experts in the Empire had contributed to its design, but the key elements had been done by Tonio St. Giles himself—particularly the fail-safes known to no one else. He was very proud of the result, though the possibility that the AI might transcend its program worried him—particularly when it showed itself to be particularly insightful or engaging.

Since its creation it had been replicated all over the Solar Empire, with the master copy on Oahu; operatives in the field knew it as "Nic." The commander assumed that most of them thought the name was an acronym for something.

But Nic was an abbreviation for Niccolò Machiavelli, the brilliant sixteenth-century writer and diplomat that Kanev had been so fond of quoting. Of course, there was no neural scan available for the great man—there was only the writing, and the writing *about* the writing, and there seemed to be plenty of *that*: surprising, given that it was nine hundred years old. Prior to interacting with the Kanev AI, Tonio had never even heard of him.

Now he heard *from* him every day.

On a brilliant morning in the Pali Tower, Nic shimmered into existence in a chair opposite St. Giles' desk. He hadn't been summoned; Tonio was examining personnel records, determining which—if any—of certain field operatives would be admitted into the Order's inner mysteries. St. Giles dismissed the data with a gesture and folded his hands in front of him, looking at the AI.

"You only interrupt me when it's important, Nic."

"That is so, Maestro." Nic folded one leg over the other and knotted his hands over the upper knee. "And I believe that this is a matter that might be of interest."

"I'm all ears."

"We have received an inquiry from the High Nest concerning a member of the Order. Or, more precisely, an ex-member."

"That's curious."

"Isn't it. It comes directly from the *Gyaryu'har* herself, and concerns a certain John Smith, a member of the Order from 2413 to 2415."

"Is that his real name? It sounds like an Imperial Intelligence pseudonym."

"Apparently so. It's the name given in his personnel

record—he is an orphan, originally born in a birthing lab on Earth. The record indicates that he disappeared during an assignment and never reported back."

"*'Disappeared'?* You mean he was kidnapped or deserted?"

"I cannot say," Nic said, uncrossing his legs and smiling slightly. "That is to say, my database has no information on the subject. Indeed, there is nothing in the High Nest's request that provides any enlightenment on the matter. We don't know what happened; whatever the High Nest knows, it has not shared with us. In fact, it was initially unclear why they would even ask at all.

"However, the presence of an unusual coincidence brought this to the attention of my higher security subroutines. Guardian John Smith disappeared while on duty at Emperor Willem Starport in Harrison System."

Tonio realized that this had great significance for Nic, but was unable to determine why. He looked at Nic impassively, waiting for him to continue.

The AI waited several seconds, then said, "If I may remind you of something, Maestro." He gestured, and a holo appeared next to him: a wealthy merchant in an expensive suit.

Owen Garrett.

"Garrett? What does Garrett have to do with him?"

"Two days before the emperor was due to visit Harrison System, Garrett was sighted there. That was exactly when Guardian Smith vanished."

Antonio St. Giles stood up so quickly that his chair coasted directly back and struck the wall behind him.

"It means that this Smith almost certainly met with Commander Garrett, and one of two things happened. Either Commander Garrett abducted him for some unknown reason, or the two of them chose to make common cause—for some equally unknown reason—and Smith deserted."

"And *that's* why he's of interest to the High Nest—to the *Gyaryu'har*." St. Giles walked to the holo and all the way around it, slowly, as if he felt the need to examine it from all angles.

"Does this mean the High Nest has been tracking Garrett, or that they're merely interested in Smith? Have they made the same connection?"

"I have insufficient data to answer that question, Maestro."

"All right," St. Giles said, looking directly at Nic. "It explains . . ."

He pressed his forehead with one hand. "Actually, it doesn't really explain a damn thing. Did Garrett go to Harrison System to meet with this one particular Guardian?

"Nic, please display the service record for John Smith."

Text and images appeared in the air next to the seated figure of the AI. There he was: a Guardian who had been recruited from the Imperial Marines after showing unusual talent.

Except . . . "That's Anderson's bogeyman," he said at last. "That's the one that sent him the message at ARIEL. He's older now—I'd say eight or ten years."

"John Smith would be twenty-five now. This holo was taken when he enlisted."

"And now he's involved in a high-stakes game with the Imperial Navy—and with Owen Garrett—and *we're* the only people who know his identity."

"The High Nest suspects something about him, Maestro. It was their inquiry that turned up this coincidence."

St. Giles squinted at the text, making a small gesture to enlarge it. "What else do we know? Enlisted at age fifteen, served eighteen months in the Marines. He was a Guardian for six months, receiving his training at Rydell.

"His scores were very high, but there's little else to distinguish him. What did Owen see in him?"

"The answer to that question would certainly unlock this mystery," Nic answered. "But I suspect that neither party would be willing to discuss it with you."

"Not Owen, anyway," St. Giles answered. "But John Smith . . . I wonder."

"Maestro?"

"I wonder if there might be a way to reach him." He pointed at Smith's head in the personnel record. "If we could separate him from Commander Garrett somehow . . ."

"To what end?"

"All of the evidence we have suggests that Smith's group—Garrett's group—has demonstrated some ability to combat the enemy. If we could harness that for the Order, we could take control of the war effort directly. We'd certainly take a greater interest than the emperor does these days."

Nic raised one eyebrow. "You wish to usurp the authority of your prince, Maestro. If you accomplish what you wish, you will serve him even while cuckolding him. If you do not . . ."

"I get hung out to dry. I know. It's a risk, but—" He stood up and walked to the eastward-facing window. He could see the Punchbowl and Diamond Head and the arcologies that stretched from Hanauma Bay all the way north to Waimea; it was raining there, while bright sunlight pierced the clouds up here on the Pali.

"It just makes me so *angry,* Nic. We've been waiting for twenty-five years for a chance to defeat the vuhls— and we seem to have a weapon capable of doing it in the hands of *Owen Garrett.* For God's sake, he doesn't know what to do with him!"

"Just so," Nic said. He looked from the image of Owen Garrett to St. Giles, silhouetted against the window. "You can be assured, Maestro, that Commander Garrett will be in no hurry to surrender control of the weapon.

"Which demonstrates a truth I have already stated: That Owen Garrett is indeed your *enemy,* and must be thus treated. Owen Garrett must be eliminated, Maestro."

"Why kill him? Isn't there something we could do short of that—imprisonment, perhaps?"

"We could do any number of things," Nic answered. "But in the end I suspect that we would come back to the same choice. As long as you leave him alive, he will have adherents—and an agenda. By taking this step you address the problem by uprooting it completely."

"How do you propose eliminating him from the scene?" St. Giles thought about it for a moment: the possibility of doing just that—removing the founder and former Commander of the Guardians, killing his former friend.

"I recommend the most direct route," Nic answered. "Use the weapon."

"Use John Smith?"

"It seems logical."

St. Giles didn't turn around for a moment: the idea seemed absurd to start with—using the man who had taunted Admiral Erich Anderson to . . . to do what? To kill Owen Garrett? Surely it couldn't be that easy; Garrett was nothing if not a survivor.

It was a somewhat unusual suggestion, coming from an AI. It fit with Nic's base personality, but something about the line of reasoning seemed a trifle ruthless.

The more Tonio thought about it, though, the more it did seem logical. Prying Smith and Garrett apart by having one kill the other—it solved two problems in one stroke.

"Nic," St. Giles said, turning around to face his AI, "you're a genius."

Nic didn't answer, but merely provided his commander with a centuries-old enigmatic smile.

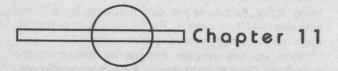 **Chapter 11**

THE BLAZING STAR MOVEMENT ONLY BECAME SIG-
NIFICANT ONCE IT GAINED ADHERENTS IN POSI-
TIONS OF POWER. THE COMPELLING IDEA OF
ENDING THE WAR DRAMATICALLY AND DEFINI-
TIVELY HAD A POWERFUL APPEAL: AND BEING AS-
SOCIATED WITH THE WINNING SIDE MADE IT ALL
THE MORE COMPELLING.

—author unknown,
The Dark Crusade: A History,
early fragment published circa 2430

June 2422
Imperial Genève, Sol System

Genève in the summer was fresh and warm, with a pleasant breeze coming off the lake. William Clane Alvarez,
Duke of Burlington and First Lord of the Admiralty, preferred the home of the Imperial Assembly to the tropical,
sultry air of the Hawaiian Islands on the other side of the
Earth—but it was not just the weather than made him
happier to be away from the emperor's court. Except for
two short periods when the opposition had controlled the
Assembly, he'd been First Lord since before the war—
nearly thirty years—and he was tired of it. Truth to tell,
he felt too old for all of this.

He'd just had a brief meeting in a small office at the
Palais des Nations with Antonio St. Giles, Commander of
the Guardians. It had been less than pleasant.

"The balance is shifting out there," St. Giles had said. "We've got a new weapon."

"That's supposed to be my line," Alvarez said. "Too bad it isn't true."

"Don't be so sure."

Alvarez tried to read the younger man's face. "You know something I don't," he said at last, a statement even though it was more of a question.

"We have access to something that the enemy can't counter. Without putting too fine a point on it, we're going to employ some *specialists* to carry the war to the enemy."

"I haven't been briefed on this."

"Here you go." St. Giles extended a comp. "This is your briefing."

Alvarez waited several beats before accepting the comp. "What's on this?" he finally said.

"You've seen the report of what happened at ARIEL, and at the other targets?"

"I had the dubious honor of bringing the report to His Imperial Highness, Commander." Alvarez looked disheartened, then shock came across his face. "Wait. It's him, isn't it? That guy from ARIEL. The one who told Admiral Anderson that he'd meet him at KEYSTONE.

"Oh God. You're going to *use* him?"

"He's in custody aboard *Emperor Ian*."

"I know that."

"We're going to use him against KEYSTONE." St. Giles pointed to the comp. "It's all on there: When Anderson jumps for KEYSTONE, he'll be taking 'that guy' with him."

"Ah. There's a problem," Alvarez had said. "You see, Anderson is already on his way to KEYSTONE, Commander. And his prize prisoner is at Oberon Starbase, in maximum security. He's not going anywhere."

Crozier System

In the dream, Ch'en'ya had been on the Perilous Stair.

She had considered the possibility that it was not *her* dream. The Plane of Sleep had been breached many turns ago. She was well aware of how *si* S'reth and her mother and others had breached it: There were many forms and aspects of the Deceiver there, and her own dreaming was not immune from them.

Still, it would have taken a mighty *e'gyu'u* to invade her own dream. Of that she was confident. The Lord of Despite had *e'gyu'e* strong enough but it was unlikely they were turned toward her.

At least not yet.

The winds of Despite whipped along the Icewall and frozen fingers of it sought to rip her from her perch, high above the Valley of the *Hssa* and just as far below the Fortress—but she held fast and looked out across the plain of endless war . . . and above it, where the clouds of smoke and fog had mysteriously parted to show a star-filled sky.

That alone might have filled her with wonder. Even true heroes who could lift their gaze in that terrible place never saw the stars. But it was something else that drew her attention: a ragged gash filled with stars that were arranged in unfamiliar patterns. It was like a parted curtain, affording a glimpse into some "otherness."

What does this mean? she asked herself in the dream. *What do I see?*

It seemed infinitely distant and yet perilously close—almost within reach of a talon. Tentatively, hesitantly, she raised a claw toward the gash in the sky . . .

And the icy winds tore her away from the Stair. She fell, tumbling, unable to control her flight, the ground rushing up to meet her—

And woke with shoulders hunched and her wings drawn about her in the Cloak of Guard. On a table beside her sleeping-perch, a comp was emitting a faint attention signal.

She shivered to herself and settled her wings, trying to shake off the worst effects of the dream while seeking to retain an impression for later study. She had experienced this dream before, though not since coming to Crozier System. Indeed, in her new company her sleep had been almost peaceful.

She picked up the comp and ran a talon near its surface. "Receive, audio only," she said, and set it back on the table.

"*se* Ch'en'ya."

"*se* Owen." She looked at the chrono. "A trifle early to be disturbing my contemplations, is it not?"

"Eight thousand pardons." Coming from Owen Garrett, she suspected it to be insincere, but shrugged it away. "The complete report on JANISSARY has arrived. I'm to pass a 'Well done' to you for your work."

"Ah. Who sends this commendation?"

"It comes right from the top."

"'The top'?" She let surprise adjust her wing-position and hastily corrected it; then, remembering that the conversation was audio-only, realized that it did not matter. "Does that mean—"

"No, no, he's still in custody. I have a set of coded messages based on the success of the operation. He left them behind to be included in the full comm-squirt sent by *Epanimondas* from JANISSARY."

"I understand. Did he . . . have any further comment?"

"Just to note that the operation is proceeding quite satisfactorily and on schedule. I assume there's been no change in your . . . perceptions?"

"Did *he* ask this question?"

"No, *I'm* asking it."

None of your business, she thought to herself. *As you humans say.* "No change," she answered. "And is there any change on your side?"

"Djiwara is worried."

"Pah," she said. "What does the old *artha* fret about now?"

"I'll pass on your kind words," Owen replied.

She thought she heard some amusement in his voice, but couldn't tell for sure.

"He's concerned that our leader is in their hands."

"*se* Michael is in error," Ch'en'ya said. "He need not fear on this account. Regardless of who is the prisoner and who is the jailor, truly *they* are in *his* hands."

Oberon System

The two fleets had a rendezvous at Oberon System three days after the dénouement at JANISSARY. Admiral Mac-Ewan had finished up at GORGON, HECATE, and ISIDRO; her command arrived insystem after Admiral Anderson's force was already docked at the naval base.

Anderson's flagship remained at the refueling station at the inner gas giant. His gig took him and his officers to Oberon Starbase, leaving *Emperor Ian* in quarantine unapproached by any other vessel.

While Barbara MacEwan met with Erich Anderson in the station commander's private office, Cameron Bradford made his way to another office on the station's inner ring.

At the door hatch, he made a gesture that would only be recognized by a small number of people within the Guardians and no one at all outside of them. A camera invisibly captured a retinal scan and moments later the door slid aside. Bradford gave a brief glance up and down the deck, but most people made an effort to ignore anything that had to do with Guardians and no one seemed to take notice. He stepped inside and the door shut behind him.

The room was mostly empty: a pair of armchairs and a

few pieces of occasional furniture, a large wall-display showing sunrise over the Imperial city of Honolulu, a comp console against one wall. The lighting was dim.

"Lieutenant Cameron Bradford reporting as ordered," he said to the air.

A holo shimmered into view in one of the two chairs. "Thank you for coming so promptly, Lieutenant." It was the Nic AI, the main Guardian security program. Evidently a copy of it had been replicated to Oberon.

"Yes sir. I've commed a full report—"

"This isn't about your recent duties," Nic said. "I have been commanded by Guardian Commander St. Giles to contact you directly. Your report indicated that you have taken the so-called Prophet as a prisoner at JANISSARY. Is that correct?"

"He offered no resistance, sir. Admiral Anderson believed that he was waiting for us."

"'Waiting' for you? Explain."

"We interviewed the captain of *Epanimondas,* which was in the gravity well when we entered JANISSARY System. She implied that the remainder of their ships had jumped out just a few hours before; comp records on board *Epanimondas* confirm this testimony.

"What was curious, if I may observe, is that Captain Amoros implied that their command had advance knowledge of our arrival time."

"Surely that's not possible."

"I wouldn't have thought so, but she asserted it to Admiral Anderson. She stated it as a fact that they knew when we'd make transition."

"Interesting." Nic leaned back in his chair, pyramiding his fingers before him. "What did Admiral Anderson make of this assertion?"

"I think he was inclined to believe it," Bradford answered. "Just as he was inclined to believe that this . . . Prophet . . . was able to make mental attacks against the enemy. I told him I thought it was bluster."

"Has anyone spoken with the prisoner?" Nic didn't

dignify him with a title, but both the AI and the Guardian knew who they were talking about. "Have you?"

"The admiral was advised by Colonel Howe—the WS9—to keep him in isolation from the other prisoners, and to have no one speak to him. I don't believe anyone has. He's aboard *Emperor Ian* now."

"Would Colonel Howe, or anyone else, prevent you from gaining access?"

"Admiral's orders, sir. No one speaks to him; no one goes to the brig deck; Marine guards are changed every watch."

"I see. So you don't expect *you* could speak with him."

"I should say not."

"What are Admiral Anderson's plans for the prisoner?"

"I expect he's consulting with Admiral MacEwan on the subject now. They'll likely find him a comfortable cell here at Oberon while we proceed to KEYSTONE."

"Is that your expert opinion?"

"Yes, I suppose it is."

"Good. Then I have orders for you," Nic added, smiling. "You will take a copy of this AI and install it in the Oberon Starbase main comp." A comp card was dispensed from the console across the room.

"I don't have clearance—"

"Don't worry," Nic interrupted, holding a hand up. "Commander St. Giles does."

I give up." Barbara walked around the holo of KEYSTONE System hanging in the air over the table in Anderson's ready-room aboard the *Emperor Ian*. It showed two blue spectral class B suns, seven planets—two gas giants, and one the right size and location to be in the system's biozone, though the radiation from the two blue dwarf stars might prevent that; the mass-radar scan from the unmanned probe only showed gravometric readings, so there was no way to tell.

And it showed something else. It was more than fifteen

hundred kilometers along one dimension and about half that much in another, stretching across the plane of the system on the edge opposite the defined jump point. It showed up on a mass-radar scan, so it had mass—or at least gravity. It didn't seem to have any thickness.

She squinted at the display, then stooped over and looked at it from underneath. "I don't know what the hell it is."

"You could just rotate the view," Erich Anderson said.

Barbara scowled at him as if it were presumptuous for him to make the suggestion.

"Rather than walking around," he added by way of explanation.

"I'm stretching my legs."

"Knock yourself out. I don't know what it is either." He gestured over the object and the display zoomed in on it.

"It's not a planet," Barbara said. "It shows up as less than a meter thick. It looks like a huge sensor array—or a solar sail."

"A solar sail at the edge of the system?"

"The energy output from the two primaries is huge. If it was much farther in the material might boil. Still, neither a sensor array nor a sail *should* be detected by mass-radar.

"It's got to be something else. Maybe a focusing device, maybe a weapon of some sort."

"Fifteen hundred kilometers long and a meter thick?"

"Something to focus energy. —Look, I'm grasping here. I have no idea what the damn thing is. But whatever it is, we'll have to destroy it," Barbara said.

"Agreed. It means that our plan for KEYSTONE involves dividing our forces between the inner system and *that*." He jabbed a thumb at the distortion, moving it counterclockwise. It shrank and the whole system came into view. "Given what seems to be defending it, we should be able to manage both objectives."

"I'm a little suspicious of that. Why wouldn't this system be armed to the hilt? It smacks of a trap, Erich. It's even possible that this is a deception—that the vuhls have altered our survey data."

"You mean, that there's nothing there?"

"They did it before to cover their tracks. Remember Sargasso—how this whole war started."

"I suppose that's true. But why would they do that? They must know we're coming: You said there was a comm-squirt at GORGON headed for KEYSTONE. I'd rather believe that this *was* a trap."

"Remember, there are more players here than just the vuhls," Barbara noted.

"Oh? Who's setting the trap—Garrett's little clown act? We've got his chief clown in the brig aboard *Emperor Ian*."

"Maybe you should ask him what's waiting for us."

"Why should he know?"

"He claimed that you couldn't win without him."

"Actually, a former Imperial Navy captain claimed it. I read over the transcript, Barbara, and I agree with the Guardian: it's bluster. They can't know any more than we do—they *can't* know what that is." Erich pointed to the display. "He *can't* know. He's bluffing."

"I wish I agreed with you."

"I wish I was certain."

"Then ask him!" MacEwan snapped.

The Admiral of the Blue stood up straight and scowled at the Admiral of the Red.

"Sir," she added. "If there's a resource—if there's an avenue we should explore—if there's some*one* who can tell us some*thing* about what the hell we're facing, we should make use of it. We need to know. Sir." She turned away and looked at the holo display, gripping the table with her hands.

"Admiral MacEwan," Anderson said quietly. "I have had a discussion with someone whose integrity and honesty I can trust: Alan Howe. I believe you know him."

"He was first assigned to *Duc d'Enghien* at the beginning of the war."

"I know." Anderson looked away as well, letting his annoyance relax a bit. "Alan told me that he felt . . . felt 'something' when that clown, whatever he is, whoever he is, came aboard *Emperor Ian* from *Epanimondas*. He doesn't like this guy, he doesn't trust this guy."

"He's *afraid* of this guy."

"I suppose that's true."

"But you know what?" Barbara said. "If Alan Howe is afraid of him, maybe we should be too."

"He's in a cell."

"Yes." Anderson's hands made fists. "Yes, he's in a cell. And I can blow him into space with one comm signal."

"That sounds like a good coercive threat," Barbara said. "Maybe he'll tell you what we're facing if you point out this salient fact to him."

"What makes you think that he'll tell the truth even if I put a gun to his head?"

"You can have Alan—" She stopped and looked up at him. "Oh, I see. He might not be able to tell."

"It might be a matter of confidence. At least in part— that's the way it is with Sensitives. Still, if Alan isn't sure about dealing with him, I can't rely on the report."

"I still think it's worth a try."

Erich Anderson rubbed his chin and looked at his fellow admiral. "I appreciate your input, Barbara."

"So?"

"I'll let you know what I decide. Thank you, Admiral."

Barbara began to answer, but suddenly realized that she'd been dismissed. She wasn't a junior post captain, but rather the second-ranking active officer in His Majesty's Service; but Anderson could dismiss her if he wanted to.

"Very good, sir," she said, saluting, and then turned on her heel and walked out of the room, hoping the ventilation system would draw away the steam rising from the top of her head.

New Chicago System

Jackie had intended to finally go back to Zor'a after visiting with Byar HeShri, but two things happened to interfere with her plans.

First, word of the events at JANISSARY reached her at New Chicago. A secure comm was routed to her the following morning, a few Standard hours before she was due to board *Pride of E'rene'e,* bound for the zor Core Stars. It was all there—Alan Howe's report, a vid of the destruction of vuhl targets and the near-destruction of the starship *Epanimondas,* stills of the prisoners including the Prophet himself. Out of the blue it seemed that the elusive leader had been captured by Admiral Anderson on the eve of the Imperial attack on KEYSTONE System.

Second, the New Chicago traffic comp contained a bit of information that caught her eye: an incoming ship due later that day—*Fair Damsel,* long since retired from active service in His Majesty's Navy. It was listed as outbound for Oberon and points beyond. *Damsel* had been part of a naval squadron at the outset of the war, but once construction had ramped up, there had been many ships to take the old rustbucket's place—and even in wartime, commerce continued. Dan McReynolds had given up flying her when he'd married Jackie's cousin Kristen in 2399, though he still owned two of the five shares. Pyotr Ngo was the captain now, with Ray Li as his second, and two of Dan and Kristen's six children shipped aboard her—taking after their old man.

If asked, Byar would have told Jackie that there were no coincidences. She didn't consult with the Master of Sanctuary, but instead canceled her berth aboard *Pride of E'rene'e* and went up to the orbital station to meet her nephew and niece.

Fair Damsel had a short run when it had had priority access and preferred parking. Its status had been due to its distinguished passenger: the then-new *Gyaryu'har* of the High Nest.

The *Gyaryu'har* wasn't new anymore, and no longer regularly traveled aboard *Fair Damsel*. But the officers still knew their way around the docks of every commercial station in the Solar Empire. Thus, while they hadn't been given pride of place, they were conveniently docked where larger and wealthier merchanters were usually found.

Hal McReynolds was standing at the cargo hatch looking the image of his father. He caught sight of his aunt crossing the wide main concourse of Emperor Cleon Starport, New Chicago's main commercial port, and set down his cargo manifest and stylus. At twenty-three, he had his father's crooked smile and unruly hair; he looked totally at ease on the deck of his father's ship. He ought to: he'd practically grown up there.

"Hal," she said, coming up the ramp as he came down. They grasped forearms zor-style and then embraced.

"Aunt Jackie," he said after a moment, smiling broadly. "This *is* a surprise."

"Wait till I tell you the favor you're going to do for me," she answered. "Is Pyotr aboard?"

"He's got some appointments on-station, but hasn't left yet. Shall I take you to see him?"

"I know where the captain's office is, Hal."

"Yeah, of course you do." Hal smiled the crooked smile again. "I think Lauren is with him."

"Sounds like a good meeting to interrupt," Jackie said. "See you later." She walked through the cargo bay, leaving Hal to go back to his work.

As she made her way through *Damsel*'s corridors, there were people she recognized and people who recognized her. It hadn't changed that much: new paint, a few moved wall-panels. It only took her a few minutes and two wrong turns to find her way to Pyotr's office. She stopped outside the door and heard a muffled exchange going on inside; after several moments the door slid aside and Lauren McReynolds, her twenty-one-year-old niece, stepped into the corridor.

Her face was filled with anger, but it drained away when she found herself face-to-face with Jackie. She skipped the forearm grasp and gave her aunt a huge hug.

"Aunt Jackie!" Lauren said at last, letting her go. "I didn't expect— I mean, if I'd known—"

"Don't let me interrupt you," Jackie said. "I need to talk to the Old Man."

"I heard that," said Pyotr's voice, from inside the office. "Glad to see you, too."

She looked around the corner. "Pyotr."

"Jackie." He frowned. "I'll thank you to let my crew do its job."

"Later," Lauren said to her aunt, smiling, and dashed down the corridor. Jackie stepped into the office and gestured at the door control.

Pyotr's frown lasted a few moments longer, then he stepped over to where Jackie stood and took her hands. "Welcome aboard."

"You don't seem surprised."

"Hal commed me," he said, waving at his desk. "We don't just let *anyone* aboard this tub," he added, smiling.

"Everything all right with Lauren?"

"She's learning. Her father, she's got wrapped around her finger; she's finding it a bit rougher sailing with me." He smiled. "So. To what do we owe the honor, et cetera?"

"I need a favor."

"It's always the way, isn't it?" He smiled. "What can I do for you?"

"I'd like to get to Oberon System."

"This can't be the fastest way to get there. I mean, it's on our way, but—"

"I just . . . changed plans. I haven't seen Hal and Lauren in more than a year, and I saw *Fair Damsel*'s itinerary on the big board and thought I could call in a favor."

"You know you can. Why do you want to go to Oberon?"

"I can't really discuss it."

"We were headed there anyway, but if you want to go there, it probably means trouble. Trouble in a war zone is something *Fair Damsel* can do without."

"Oberon's not exactly a war zone."

"You've been traveling aboard ships a hell of a lot bigger than the *Fair Damsel,* Jackie. To us, Oberon *is* a war zone, and, as I say, you bring trouble with you. Tell me more."

"There's someone there I have to sec."

"Ah." He went behind his desk and sat down. "Anyone I know?"

"In a manner of speaking." Jackie crossed her arms. "I have to find out if an old friend is on the prowl again."

"You mean . . ."

"Yeah. I think he's moved someone else into position, and I have to check for myself." She placed her hand on the *gyaryu.*

"We're here to help you sneak up on this person."

"I suppose you could put it that way. I don't know who else is watching, and there's no reason to send any comm in advance. Plus"—she smiled, leaning on the desk—"I get to spend a few Standard days with Lauren and Hal and the rest of you."

"You'll pay for your passage, Jackie?"

"Sure. The High Nest gets all kinds of bills they never understand."

"I'll have to check with Ray, but I expect he'll say yes. It'll be like old times . . . Well, not really. With Dan on the ground turning out children, Sonja and Karla off on their own now . . . it's nothing like old times."

"Not to mention the folks we lost along the way."

"Don't remind me." Jackie suspected that he was thinking about Drew Sabah, who had been taken over by Shrnu'u HeGa'u during her time aboard. For her own part, she was thinking about Ch'k'te.

"When will you know?"

"Whether Ray will agree? As soon as I tell him he's

going to." Pyotr smiled, a bit ferally. "You'll have a bill in your comp by next watch."

Two days out of New Chicago, Jackie finally had a chance to sit with her niece and nephew in the crew mess; Pyotr Ngo, the captain of *Fair Damsel*, joined them for a quick meal between shifts. Time in jump was spent catching up on the things for which there was no time during real-space maneuvers or dockside: inventory, internal repair, education, and training. It was particularly busy for junior members of a merchanter's crew.

Hal was an old hand; he'd been aboard *Damsel* since he was fifteen. It was Lauren's first extended cruise aboard the merchanter.

They seemed pretty evenly matched in Jackie's eyes.

". . . So the dipper was right over his head all along?" Jackie asked.

"Right." Lauren reached for another pear. "And, of course, it let go right on top of his—"

"I don't think we need to go into detail on *that*." Hal interrupted his sister.

"But I haven't even gotten to the best part yet," Lauren continued. "He was crouching in poison saraf, so he developed a rash all over his—"

Hal cleared his throat, interrupting again, while Pyotr erupted in laughter at the notion of where he must have gotten a rash. After a few moments Hal couldn't help but laugh as well.

"It's been like this the whole damn cruise," Pyotr growled, his smile not entirely disappeared.

"Why don't you come back to Dieron more often, Aunt Jackie?" Lauren asked.

Hal didn't interrupt this time, but looked at his sister.

"I've got a busy schedule, Laur," Jackie said neutrally.

That wasn't the real answer, of course. When she had first become *Gyaryu'har*, she'd gone back to her homeworld to visit her father and to try and make sense of it.

During her visit she'd been attacked by Shrnu'u HeGa'u in the guise of her long-dead mother. Hal and Lauren's mother, Jackie's cousin Kristen, had told Jackie off, telling her that there wasn't a place for her on the world nor in the house in which she grew up.

Pyotr's smile was completely gone now.

Lauren realized that she'd said something wrong but wasn't sure what it was. She began to slice her pear into sections, looking away from her aunt.

"How's the captain treating you?" Jackie asked, as much to change the subject as anything else. She glanced at Pyotr, whose face remained neutral.

"Might as well ask how Hal is treating me," Lauren said.

"Oh?" She looked at her nephew. "Been hazing your sister on her first cruise, young man?"

"She gets what any new crewmember does."

"That wasn't a *Fair Damsel* tradition when I was aboard."

Hal shrugged.

"Seems like she gives as good as she gets."

There was more laughter all around.

"So, tell me, Pyotr. Why were you ripping Lauren a new one the day I came aboard?"

"What makes you think I was doing that?"

"Because of the look on her face when she came out of your office."

Pyotr took a sip of his drink. "You wouldn't be criticizing my ship's discipline, would you?"

"Not a bit."

"I was merely correcting an oversight," Pyotr added.

Lauren reddened but didn't say anything.

"The profit margin for this ship is narrower than a gnat's eyelash. It's even worse than when Dan was captain: there are more ships with bigger hulls and newer engines, and we've had to work hard to keep up. We do things a certain way for a reason, and seasoned crew know that."

"All I hear about is what I do wrong," Lauren said, not meeting her captain's eye.

"Whatever you did wrong," Jackie said carefully, "I trust that you'll do it right the next time?"

"He told me he'd assign me to Hal if I couldn't do it right," Lauren answered, giving a slight glance at Pyotr, "so the answer is yes."

"Why don't you tell us about why we're going to Oberon, Aunt Jackie," Hal said, selecting a piece of fruit.

"Yes, Jackie. Tell me why you're calling in an old favor," Pyotr said, baring his teeth in a faint smile. "You're among family."

"I need to meet someone."

"Who?"

"A man being held by Admiral Erich Anderson. He's—" —*the Destroyer,* she had begun to say, but wasn't sure she wanted to say it, and wasn't completely sure it was true. "He's of interest to the High Nest."

"A Sensitive," Lauren said.

"A demon," Hal said. Lauren's knife clattered to the table.

"Another one," Pyotr said.

"Well, *that's* dramatic," Jackie said. "I don't know if I'd characterize it that way. This man—he's not *Shrnu'u HeGa'u.* At least I don't think he is.

"The truth is that I don't know exactly what I should expect. I'm . . . sort of sneaking up on him."

"I thought you said that Admiral Anderson is holding him. He's a prisoner?" Pyotr asked.

"He has an organization. I don't know where his eyes and ears are, and I don't want to give him advance warning."

"We seem to have a tradition of being your cat's-paw, *se Gyaryu'har,*" Pyotr said. "I assume that you're putting us in some danger."

"You said it yourself: Oberon is a war zone for ships of this size, so you have to assume that it's possible."

"And what happens when we get there?"

"I'm not sure. I expected to find this man once before, when I was chasing after Ch'en'ya."

"Ch'k'te's daughter?" Pyotr asked. "The one we found?"

Hal and Lauren were listening intently: This was a business they knew nothing about. Pyotr didn't seem to be in any hurry to enlighten them.

"She left Zor'a in a hurry several weeks ago. I followed her trail in hopes of coming across him, but it was a dead end—I didn't get near him. And now he's turned up in Admiral Anderson's custody."

"Sounds like quite a coincidence."

"I don't believe in coincidences. The High Nest doesn't, either. He's there for a reason—perhaps his own reason—and I mean to find out *what.*"

"And then what will you do?"

Without answering, Jackie placed her hands on the *gyaryu.* She looked from Hal to Lauren to Pyotr, and each returned her gaze.

"Whatever I must."

Crozier System

In a safe place in Crozier System, Ch'en'ya HeYen perched with her eyes closed and her wings extended in a posture of respect to *esLi.* Outside the chamber, two members of the Talon of *esLi* kept watch; down the corridor two others stood ready, *chya'i* drawn. It would not do for her to be interrupted.

A folio-scroll of *The Am'a'an Codex* lay on a nearby table with a passage highlighted with plastic tabs. If for any reason she didn't return from this journey, there was a clear indication of where her *hsi* had gone. It would have been more prudent to have another accompany her, but prudence was not a part of this exercise.

She slowly inhaled and exhaled and then cast her *hsi*

outward, following the pattern described in the *Codex*. She knew she could do it: the High Lord had managed, reading the same ancient book.

But they had not read it as thoroughly as she did.

When she opened her eyes she was airborne, flying across a landscape of murky swamp. Clouds of fog reached down from above, and broken pillars and columns reached out through hovering mist below. She could sense the *e'gyu'u* of the Deceiver everywhere, speaking her name with every beat of her wings. Normally the Plane was a place only the High Lord traversed, but Ch'en'ya had decided that custom was merely an inconvenient artifact—this was no place for the timid.

The Plane of Sleep gave neither an impression of the passage of time nor an indication of place. There were— or, rather, there once had been—only a few fixed locations there; for example, the *Codex* spoke of the Stone of Remembrance, an echo of the one in the jungle of E'rene'e. It had been there many Standard years ago, when *hi* Sa'a had first come to the Plane in search of the recently departed sage *si* S'reth. Her experience there had not made her very eager to explore further.

But there was another location mentioned in the *Codex*, a place "in the north" where the land of the Plane rose abruptly into a jagged escarpment. It marked the edge of the Plane; beyond were the Mountains of Night, where no ray of light from *esLi*'s Golden Circle could dart.

That was her destination. From her present position she could make them out in the distance: rugged peaks rising in majesty beyond the slough below and extending into the foggy clouds above. Behind them lay the deep darkness of *anGa'e'ren*.

The *Codex* spoke of the Am'a'an Guardians, four heroes from the time before the Unification who stood ever watchful on that promontory, protecting the Plane from unwanted intrusion. As she flew over it, Ch'en'ya knew that the Guardians had failed somehow: From the description of *hi* Sa'a and from the evidence of her own eyes, it was clear that *esGa'uYal* had dominion over the place.

She neared the mountains; the swamp below gave way to dusty outcroppings. Ch'en'ya slowed to coast over the foothills, which were strewn with odd-shaped boulders that more resembled dismembered bodies of People than simple rocky outcroppings. She felt as if she were flying over some huge boneyard.

At last she reached a plateau many eights of wingspans above the surface of the Plane, where she landed and extended her wings in the Cloak of Guard. Her *chya* was in her talons, singing with anger and affront.

"*Kasi!*" she announced. "*Kasi, seAm'a'a na'*esLi'*a aryu che'e seKa.*" *I come. I come to command the Am'a'an Guardians in the Name of* esLi.

The words were from a language far older than the Highspeech. They did not appear in *The Am'a'an Codex*; she had found them in another, older text. She prayed to *esLi* that she had pronounced them correctly.

They echoed off the rocks and returned to her unbidden.

"*Kasi!*" she repeated. "*Kasi!*" *I come!*

From the quiet, she heard a single reply: "*e'Na Kasi'e?*" *Who comes to command?*

It was nearby, but still almost too faint to hear. Her *chya* acknowledged it, tugging very slightly at her *hsi* as it did so.

"Ch'en'ya of Nest HeYen," she answered. "Daughter of *si* Ch'k'te and *si* Th'an'ya." She added as many generations of progenitors as she knew; it had been part of her preparation for this journey to learn them, knowing that inhabitants of places like the Plane of Sleep put great store by such things.

"Advance so that we may see you," the voice said, in the Highspeech this time.

"Why do you not show yourself?"

"Advance and see."

Without sheathing her *chya*, Ch'en'ya walked forward, ready to launch herself into the air at any time. The place was deadly quiet; *anGa'e'ren* seemed ready to reach forward and touch her.

Forty wingspans across the plateau she passed between two large boulders and came upon an elevated platform half a wingspan tall. Four figures sprawled on it.

At first she took them for more of the strewn boulders, but it was obvious that they had the forms of warriors of the People—except that they, too, were made of stone. Each held a stone *chya*, and on each hilt was stamped the crest of Am'a'a.

"In *esLi*'s Name," she whispered. "You are the Am'a'an Guardians: La'ath, Su'ran, Ke'ear, and Do'loth."

"True." One of the stone figures blinked and turned its head ever so slightly toward her. "We were the Guardians. I was La'ath. But . . ."

"You were overwhelmed," Ch'en'ya finished the sentence. "Many turns ago, when He of the Dancing Blade was summoned from beneath the Plane."

"He did not come from the Mountains of Night," La'ath said. Lying on his back, he could not move his stone wings, but there was sorrow in his voice. "He came from the Plane directly."

"Few even know of us anymore," another Guardian said, her voice weary and weak. "Do'loth, I was. No High Lord has come to this place for many turns. Until now."

"But I am not—" Ch'en'ya began, then paused to consider.

They think me a High Lord, she thought to herself. *And why not? None but a High Lord would dare to brave the Plane of Sleep. And our present High Lord knows nothing of the Am'a'an Guardians. This is my secret.*

"The *hyu* of the People has grown weak," she said at last. "I am not . . . ready to give up the fight. If you will serve me, I will redeem you from *idju'e*."

"What makes you believe we are *idju, hi* Ch'en'ya?" La'ath said. "We are—"

"What are you?" Ch'en'ya interrupted. The words "*hi Ch'en'ya*" spoken by a creature of legend thrilled her. "What are you, if not dishonored?"

"We were betrayed."

"Pah. That does not enter into the equation, and you know this to be true."

The sprawled figure of La'ath turned its stone head to face her. "Yes," it said at last. "We know this."

". . . But," Ch'en'ya replied after a moment of contemplation, "you cannot transcend the Outer Peace."

"We did, sixty-fours of sixty-fours of turns ago."

"Then you must remove the stain of *idju'e* somehow."

"We are open to suggestions, *hi* Ch'en'ya. No one has come to redeem us in many turns."

"I shall do so."

The Guardians did not reply, but Ch'en'ya could see the eyes of La'ath fixed directly on her.

"You must change your flight, *si* La'ath," she said. "You must embrace *enGa'e'Li*."

"The Strength of Madness does not serve the purpose for which we were placed here."

"Pah," she repeated. "Your original purpose does not matter, for the *esGa'uYal* walk the Plane of Sleep regardless of your presence. You must embrace the Strength of Madness, and you must choose the flight the People now travel.

"We must cleanse the Plane of Sleep of the vermin that infest it, and we must counter other threats as they appear."

"How will we know?"

"I will come. I will tell you—and we will raise our *chya'i* together."

Again, the Guardians did not reply.

Ch'en'ya allowed her wings to rise in slight affront. "Unless you wish for me to depart and seek help elsewhere . . ."

"We will serve," La'ath said. "We will embrace *en-Ga'e'Li.*"

"Then rise," Ch'en'ya said. *"Kasi'e Na'u'* esLi'*a eNa'a!" I come to command, in the name of* esLi*!* Her wings moved to a position she had never used before.

She offered a prayer that her words and wings were correct.

The four stone figures slowly struggled to gain their feet. The dust of ages sifted from where it had gathered between their joints and lay heavily on their wings.

"Yes," they replied in unison. "We will serve."

The plateau around them shimmered and transformed, until it assumed a familiar shape: the parapets of Sanctuary. It was an extremely faithful representation, except for the brooding darkness of the Mountains of Night beyond.

"I will return when the time is right," Ch'en'ya said.

"We will be here," the four Guardians answered, raising their stone *chya'i* slowly until they touched. A bright light emerged from the points of the swords and washed over Ch'en'ya . . .

She slowly opened her eyes to see the chamber around her. In the air before her there was a ball of sharp-edged light which flared and then faded away.

If there had been any others in the room, they would have seen her wings extended in a position of pure and frightening joy.

Chapter 12

> MERCENARY CAPTAINS ARE EITHER CAPABLE MEN
> OR THEY ARE NOT; IF THEY ARE, YOU CANNOT
> TRUST THEM, BECAUSE THEY ALWAYS ASPIRE TO
> THEIR OWN GREATNESS. [T]HE FACT IS, THEY HAVE
> NO OTHER ATTRACTION OR REASON FOR KEEPING
> THE FIELD THAN A TRIFLE OF STIPEND, WHICH IS
> NOT SUFFICIENT TO MAKE THEM WILLING TO DIE
> FOR YOU.
>
> —Machiavelli,
> *The Prince,* Chapter XII

July 2422
Oberon System

More than forty ships of the line, along with second-rank
and support vessels, jumped from Oberon System, with
KEYSTONE System as their destination. The combined
forces of Admiral Anderson and Admiral MacEwan made
the transition in precise formation.

Fair Damsel arrived at Oberon System just five Standard hours later.

They're gone."

"Yes ma'am." Commodore Albin Searles, commander of Oberon Starbase, looked down at the desk behind which he sat and then back at the *Gyaryu'har.*
"Some time ago, bound for KEYSTONE System."

Jackie uttered an expletive.

"Yes ma'am," Searles said.

"And you have the prisoner in custody here."

"He's in isolation, ma'am."

"No one has spoken to him or visited him? Not even Admiral Anderson or Admiral MacEwan?"

"No one."

"I want to talk to him."

"I'm afraid my orders—"

"I want to *talk* to him," Jackie interrupted. "And I know what your orders are, but I have the authority of the High Nest behind me." She laid her hand on the *gyaryu*.

"I can't reach Admiral Anderson by comm-squirt until they arrive at KEYSTONE System. I can send to St. Louis, but I wouldn't have a response for six Standard days."

"I want to talk to him on my own authority."

"That's not good enough—"

"I'm going to explain something to you, Commodore. I represent the zor High Nest, and if High Chamberlain T'te'e HeYen or the High Lord or one of the Lords of Nest aren't right here right now, I *am* the goddamned High Nest—and the High Nest is *telling* you, Commodore, that I need to speak to this man you're holding prisoner.

"*Now.*"

It took Commodore Searles a few seconds of indecision, but he nodded at last.

"Very well. But the High Nest will receive my protest, ma'am, along with a formal one to Admiral Anderson."

"Is that supposed to be a threat?"

"It is a promise, ma'am. The oath of an officer." Searles rose from behind the desk, and without looking at her walked to the door of his office. Jackie fell in behind him.

The prisoners from *Epanimondas* captured at JANISSARY System were kept in a maximum-security section of Oberon's inner ring. Each was detained separately, with no contact with each other or the outside world.

For her part, Jackie only wanted to meet with one of them. As she walked down the corridor toward where he was held, she could see a holo from within the cell: He was under continuous surveillance by a pair of Marines and a pair of Sensitives stationed in the corridor. She was fairly certain that the other prisoners weren't being guarded as closely.

"Not taking any chances, are we?" she asked.

Searles didn't answer, but favored her with a grim expression. "You will be under scrutiny while you're speaking with him," he said. "If anything out of the ordinary happens, the room will be flushed with gas."

"Gas?"

"It'll put you both to sleep. You'll be revived in the station's sickbay."

"How will you know what constitutes 'out of the ordinary'?"

"Suffice it to say that I won't be taking any chances. *Particularly* with such a distinguished representative of the High Nest."

"That's *very* reassuring."

"Those are my terms."

She looked from Searles to the Sensitives and the Marines and back. "All right," she said, "I'm ready."

Her first actual sight of the man she'd seen in a vision so long ago was less than impressive. He was sitting in a chair, leaning against the far wall, with a book projected in the air before him.

"Mr. Smith," she said. He looked up at her as if she were interrupting his reading.

He wasn't physically imposing: well-built enough to be a Marine, with the sort of ramrod-straight posture that was drilled into them from boot camp on, but hardly a prime specimen. There was nothing really remarkable about him at all . . . other than his eyes.

He didn't seem at all surprised to see her.

"A visitor. How quaint." He looked at Jackie, sizing her up, his eyes lingering for a moment on the sword. "To what do I owe this honor?"

"May I sit?" she answered, which wasn't an answer. Smith shrugged and pointed to a nearby chair. She sat down on another chair a tad farther away.

"I hope I haven't offended you already, Ms. Laperriere."

"Then you know who I am. Good; I'm glad we can start on an even footing."

"I'm not sure what you mean."

"I have some background information on you, sir. I've been introduced to some of your lieutenants."

"I hope you found them to your liking, Ms. Laperriere." He gestured at his comp; the book-image faded to nothingness. "In fact, I consider it to be something of an oversight on my part that it's taken us so long to meet face-to-face. I've heard a great deal about you—from Owen and from *se* Ch'en'ya."

She must have tensed at Ch'en'ya's name; Smith smiled slightly, catching her eye and holding it for several seconds. She heard vague whispers from the *gyaryu*.

"I'm sure they were both extremely complimentary."

"They were quite informative, I'll say that." He finally looked away. "You are a remarkable person, madam. I truly have been remiss in not speaking to you before."

"About what?"

"Oh, this and that. The war, primarily. Your skill"—he let his gaze linger on the *gyaryu* for just a moment—"would be quite helpful in the final phase."

"Of the war."

"Yes. The final phase of the war." He leaned forward, elbows on knees, hands clasped. "We are just about to embark upon it, as soon as Admiral Anderson's expedition to KEYSTONE System fails."

She waited a moment before answering. "Why do you think it will fail?"

"*I'm* not with them."

"Why should your presence matter?"

"Do you know what they'll find at KEYSTONE, Ms. Laperriere?"

"Do *you*?"

"Yes." Smith stood up suddenly enough that she stood up as well. His hands made fists at his sides. "I know."

"Tell me."

"You already know," he said. "You've seen it. Just as *se* Ch'en'ya and Owen Garrett have seen it."

"*What* have we seen?"

"In Owen's *Dsen'yen'ch'a*, Ms. Laperriere. You have seen this thing—this rip in space. On one side is KEYSTONE System. On the other—vuhl space." He fixed her with a stare. "Imagine this: a gateway that spans thousands of parsecs, giving *them* access to our space. It wasn't there twenty years ago.

"Someone opened this rip in space. Someone *gave* them access to us. He *told* me. Owen Garrett told me it would be there—and then Ch'en'ya dreamed it. When Admiral Anderson's fleet arrives at KEYSTONE System, they will be flying into the lead end of vuhl homespace."

Jackie put her hand on the *gyaryu*.

Tell me, she said to the inhabitants of her sword. *Tell me what he knows—what I saw.*

*T*he vuhl ship had suffered a major explosion where the gouge had been, showing empty space beyond . . . and something else.

"*What's that?*"

Byar's wings moved into the Cloak of Guard. "*The stars are wrong, se Jackie.*"

"*Magnify two hundred,*" she said to the air. The pilot's-board view changed, closing in on the vuhl ship; as they watched, the two parts of the ship—the aft and fore sections—fell apart in an additional explosion, tumbling out

*of view. Across a space perhaps a kilometer wide was a
ragged, irregular patch of stars that didn't belong.*

*"It looks like a hole. A tear in space. I've . . . never
seen anything like it."*

*". . . This is out of control," she'd said to Byar. And
he'd placed his wings in a Posture of Reverence to esLi.*

*"Eight thousand pardons, se Jackie," he answered.
"But it always was."*

Se Ch'en'ya wasn't there," she said quietly. "We hadn't
found her yet."

"She didn't need to be there," Smith answered. "She
dreamed that the Rip would be there."

"She *dreamed* it?"

"Yes." Smith smiled. He was utterly calm, but some
fierce emotion burned behind his eyes. "She can see the
Flight of the People, Ms. Laperriere."

"Where is she now?"

"I'm sorry?"

"Where is *se* Ch'en'ya now?"

"I have been held incommunicado, madam," he answered. "But I would expect that she will be on her way
here in due time. If you want to speak to her, you can wait
here. I expect that all of my lieutenants will be on hand
before long."

In the corridor outside, Commodore Searles carefully
watched the exchange between *Gyaryu'har* and prisoner. There was nothing threatening in Smith's comments or in the conversation between him and the High
Nest's sword-bearer, but there was an undertone of something he couldn't couldn't quite see.

Unseen to either of the two people in the cell, nor
those in the corridor outside, another intelligence was

watching the scene playing itself out. Uploaded into the Oberon Starbase main comp, a copy of Nic was adjusting his knowledge base according to what he observed. It was happening far faster than any human could record: but if anyone could analyze it, one parameter would be immediately obvious in the AI's understanding.

Garrett is not the master, Nic's programming affirmed. *Garrett is merely a tool in Smith's hands.*

It was in the way he spoke of Garrett and the way he carried himself. *This* was the leader of the organization: all of the visual cues and psych values Nic could perceive pointed clearly to it.

Twenty-five years ago, when Owen Garrett was freed from the vuhl hive-ship by the mysterious polychromatic aliens, Garrett had been told that he would be a teacher. Nic had the transcript of Owen Garrett's debriefing aboard *Duc d'Enghien* in 2397 at his disposal. According to what Garrett had said, the unknown aliens that had effected his escape from the vuhl ship had told him that he would teach "the other" . . . Evidently Smith *was* that "other." When the two men had met at Harrison System seven years earlier, the result had been determined by Smith, not by Garrett. It might well have been Smith's plan all along.

All of this analysis took place in nanoseconds, at the end of which a high-priority message-squirt was sent toward Sol System.

You're expecting the fleet to be destroyed at KEYSTONE."

"No, I don't think so. As soon as Admiral Anderson realizes what he's up against, he'll find a way to retreat."

"And then . . ."

"Please, Ms. Laperriere, don't be disingenuous. Admiral Anderson will need my organization to destroy the enemy at KEYSTONE. That battle is only the beginning: There are dozens, perhaps hundreds, of vuhl planets beyond the Rip.

"I expect that we'll visit them all."

Smith smiled. Jackie recognized his expression: it was the same one she'd seen at Sharia'a, when she'd seen him for the first time.

It was the Strength of Madness, and the Shroud was pulled aside.

What he intended with the expression, and the remark, was obvious even though he hadn't said it.

"I think you're likely to just make them mad," she said after a moment. "I've heard the speech already: about how inefficient and pointless the Imperial Navy's campaigns have been; how the stalemate is a result of them being unwilling to—I don't know—'embrace *enGa'e'Li.*'

"It seems pretty clear to me that the vuhls are lining up for a big battle at KEYSTONE—that they haven't left any sort of serious force at the outposts on this side of the rift. Your successes thus far are statistically insignificant since they represent nothing in the way of opposition."

"Is that so," Smith said. "So, you don't believe that we'll make the difference."

"I have read the account of Admiral Anderson's interview with Captain Amoros of *Epanimondas,*" Jackie said.

"Diane Amoros. A brave soldier."

"I read the account," Jackie repeated. "She claimed that you—your organization—are our only help to defeat the vuhls. Further, she claims that there is no middle ground between us and them."

"Ms. Laperriere . . ." Smith said. He sat down again in his chair. After a moment Jackie took up her own seat opposite. "Ms. Laperriere," he said again. "Owen has told you what we know of our enemy's intentions. There is no compromise of any sort with them: they must be exterminated."

"I've had this conversation before, with Ch'en'ya."

"And she didn't convince you? Perhaps I can succeed where she failed. You see, Ms. Laperriere, the human race will rise to the occasion when the force of history requires it. For twenty-five years we have been fighting this war with calm, with restraint, and with one hand tied behind our backs. This time is past—because at last we will go at the enemy full-force.

"Here is an essential truth, madam, one that I hope you will bear in mind as this matter unfolds. *The veneer of civilization is very thin, Ms. Laperriere.* It takes very little to remove it." He made a gesture with both of his hands, as if he were removing the peel from a piece of fruit. "The *restraint* with which we have opposed these evil creatures is due to this veneer. Soon it will be gone.

"And soon thereafter, Ms. Laperriere, the vuhls will be gone as well."

The Place of Heroes
Zor'a System

The High Nest maintained a retreat in the Spine of Shar'tu, not far from the place where the entrance to the Plain of Despite was said to lie. At one time, when the High Lord took up residence there, contact was impossible . . . but in the twenty-fifth Standard century, no one in a position of authority was ever out of contact.

As the fleet jumped toward battle at KEYSTONE, an aircar bearing High Lord Sa'a HeYen and her entourage touched down on the landing-pad. When it had powered down, two warriors emerged followed by the High Lord and the Master of Sanctuary.

Byar HeShri squinted against the late-afternoon sunlight, holding his wings in a neutral position. The High Lord shivered slightly, her wings moving into the Cloak of Guard.

"They have not reached the Valley yet," Sa'a said. "But there is something else happening."

"You have received word?"

The High Lord acknowledged the question with a slight movement of her wings. She walked beneath an archway into the courtyard of the Place of Heroes. She was surrounded by greater-than-life–size statues of heroes of the People; Byar followed, glancing at the statues and then back at the High Lord.

He knew who all of the figures were: T'sa'ar; Gyasa; Qu'u and Hyos, of course . . . and Sa'a knew them as well. Byar had never known anyone else in the High Nest who had made as close a study of the culture of the People.

But then he had never known anyone who had flown across the Plane of Sleep, either. Twice at least, and perhaps more.

"Do you know why we are here, Master Byar?" Sa'a said, turning around, looking up at the statues.

"You grew tired of the crosswinds at Sanctuary."

"A sense of humor is blessed by *esLi*," the High Lord answered. "Very good, *se* Byar. No, I have not tired of any part of Sanctuary. I wanted to come here because we are close to where it all began."

"'Began,' *hi* Sa'a?"

"A few five-twelves of five-twelves of wingspans from here is where the Fortress of e'Yen is supposed to have stood. Thousands of turns ago, a Servant of *esLi* appeared on the bastion of the fortress and told *si* Qu'u that he would be the chosen of *esLi*. He went on his quest . . . and when he returned to unite the Nests"—she moved her wings to a posture of honor to the High Nest; a few of the warriors echoed the gesture—"he reached into our history to change *seLi'e'Yan*.

"Because of *si* Qu'u, *se* Jackie learned of Hesya's intervention early in our history. Because of *si* Qu'u we have chosen this flight. Now we face *Ur'ta leHssa*."

"You propose to lay that at the talons of *si* Qu'u as well?"

"I cannot tell anymore, *se* Byar." She walked forward

and grasped his forearms. "There is something I must confide in you, something that troubles me greatly.

"I have dreamed of the Valley, *se* Byar. As if that were not troubling enough, I have not dreamed of it alone."

"What do you mean?"

"Someone else was dreaming it with me. We stood on the Perilous Stair together and watched the clouds part above the Plain of Despite."

"Who stood with you?"

"*se* Ch'en'ya. The madness-of-daylight has come upon her, but she has not been prepared for what she sees."

"Is she aware of this?"

"I believe that she would reject any suggestion that she would need the preparation. Eights of generations of High Lords have prepared thus, but *se* Ch'en'ya . . . I am not sure what she believes anymore, and I am not certain what *she* saw. Still, as we watched, she fell to the Valley—though she saw the daylight before her body struck the Plain."

Both of them moved their wings in thankfulness to *esLi*. "What did you see in the dream?"

"I saw . . . what lies before us at Keystone System."

"What is it?"

"Something we have seen before, *se* Byar," Sa'a said quietly. "The rip in space. The one *se* Owen saw in his Ordeal."

"It actually exists," Byar said, more of a statement than a question.

"Yes. And its appearance is the sign that has been awaited. *se* Owen was prised from an *esHara'y* ship and ordered to teach the 'one who will come.' We know who he was intended to teach, and now we know why they have made their move at this time. They know that this is the gateway to the Plain of Despite. This is why Blazing Star has appeared, to make its mark on the war with the *esHara'y*."

"Do they think in those terms, *hi* Sa'a?"

"No, *se* Byar. Of course they do not. But regardless of what descriptive term they use, it was the appearance of this feature that caused Blazing Star to move toward the objective. We should have seen this coming, *se* Byar—we had knowledge of the phenomenon in advance, we knew very well that *se* Owen had not died . . . We very nearly had the *esGa'uYe* in our talons before this Prophet was born." The High Lord's talons extended a centimeter from their sheaths and then slowly retreated.

"Now our human friends enter the Valley of Lost Souls. Did you know . . . Did you know that in the most popular faith to which the humans subscribe, a soul cannot be condemned to the Valley—or whatever they call it—without committing some heinous crime. In other terms, *se* Byar, none go to the Valley without knowing that it will be their destination . . . I do not think that our friends and brothers understand this. They are flying into a trap, *se* Byar, and we can do nothing to save them."

"I think you underestimate them, *hi* Sa'a. They are warriors, and on the Plain of Despite they will be capable of raising their gaze. *se* Jackie has gone to warn them."

"She will arrive too late."

"They will still be able to raise their gaze, High Lord."

Sa'a turned to look at the statues of Qu'u and Hyos. "I pray to *esLi* that you are right, *se* Byar."

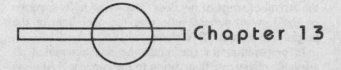 **Chapter 13**

> IN PREPARING FOR BATTLE I HAVE ALWAYS FOUND
> THAT PLANS ARE USELESS, BUT PLANNING IS INDIS-
> PENSABLE.
>
> —Dwight Eisenhower

July 2422
KEYSTONE System

The twin suns designated SS Aurigae—objective KEY-STONE—were an unusual phenomenon, a pair of blue dwarf stars that rotated around each other every five Standard hours or so. They occasionally shared stellar material as the brighter of the two discharged portions of its outer shell. When the star had first been sighted by homeworld astronomers in the early twentieth century, there hadn't been an adequate explanation for the phenomenon—every hundred days or so the star would flare as if it were going nova, and then subside to its earlier magnitude as if nothing had ever happened.

This sort of profligate spending of a star's photosphere would take millenia off its life, but no one aboard the ships invading—or defending—the system was likely to ever see that effect. It was another one of the quaint charms of exploring the universe, meeting interesting and hostile races, and waging war against them.

* * *

On the bridge of *Emperor Ian,* Admiral Erich Anderson was watching intently as jump-echoes recorded the arrival of ships of his fleet. The ships' hulls sparkled on the forward screen, reflecting the dual light of the bright-blue suns of SS Aurigae.

In preparation for the attack he had assembled all available resources: In addition to the carriers *Tristan da Cunha, Kenyatta II, Lycias, Scylla,* and *Phidias* (which had all served during the current campaigns), the new *Barbados* had been assigned. *César Hsien* had been joined by sister-ships *Admiral Stark* and *T'sa'ar,* along with six Argonne-class seventh-generation ships: *Aldebaran, Morrow, Lasker,* and *Bohonye* (which had been under Barbara MacEwan's command at GORGON), and *Angkor Wat* and *Kikuyu,* refitted from damage suffered at Rivières a few months earlier. Surrounding the sevens were two dozen sixth-generation battleships, including *Mortimer, Huan Che, Sheng Hua, Sheng Tsang,* the *Brittany,* and *Ian*'s sister-ships *Emperor Cleon* and *Empress Patrice.*

We're pulling out all the stops, Anderson's general orders had said. Whether or not this was the home system of the vuhls—and he still dismissed the possibility that this was so—winning a battle at KEYSTONE was going to be decisive.

On the bridge of *Tristan da Cunha,* Barbara MacEwan stood with her hands grasping the railing at the aft end of the deck, watching her command approach the distortion ahead.

On dozens of other ships in KEYSTONE System, commanders sat in their pilot's chairs or on their pilot's perches awaiting orders, and wondering, perhaps, if this would be the final battle of the war.

On the bridge of *Emperor Ian,* Alan Howe and Cameron Bradford stood side by side, looking only ahead, concentrating on the mental attacks of the enemy. Both were accustomed to this style of warfare: it had occupied virtually their entire lives.

Unspoken, but on Admiral Anderson's mind nevertheless, was a thought aimed at his many illustrious ancestors: *Take that, you bastards. Watch me win this one.*

Oberon System

The Marines that guarded access to the brig had a vid monitor, which they had in view at all times. It showed the prisoner sitting, walking about, using the toilet, and sleeping; it indicated what files his comp was accessing and recorded every word he spoke and every beat of his heart.

Bypassing it turned out to be a relatively simple matter.

As John Smith sat in an armchair watching a newsvid, a holo of a man appeared on the couch opposite.

Smith looked away from the vid to examine him. The holo was of a young man, conservatively dressed, with an enigmatic half-smile; he was not in uniform, but the symbol of four hands grasping wrists was prominent at his lapel.

"Guardian Smith," the holo said.

Smith leaned back in his chair and crossed one leg over the other. "You've done your homework, I see. But you should know I don't answer to that title any longer."

"A shame," the holo replied. "Though, as we say, 'Once a Guardian, always a Guardian.' You can't have *un*-learned what the Order taught you."

"Not hardly, though I didn't realize that the Order really gave a *damn* about me. Has someone decided to take a personal interest?"

"You might say that."

"They took their time about it." Smith uncrossed his legs and sat forward, hands on knees. "Well, you can tell them that I'm not interested in returning to duty—not now, not ever. And certainly not in exchange for my release."

"You misunderstand, Guardian Smith—"

"I told you that I don't answer to that title, Mr.—Mr.—"

"You can call me Nic," the holo said.

"Nic."

"It's an abbreviation for 'Niccolò.' An affectation of Commander St. Giles. He has designed me as an artificial intelligence program based on an ancient philosopher from the home planet."

"An AI." Smith shrugged, as if there were no surprise there.

"And as I said, sir, you misunderstand. The Order is in no position to offer your release at this time, and Commander St. Giles isn't looking for you to return to Guardian duty.

"He would, however, like to make you an offer."

"Commander St. Giles wasn't particularly interested in me when I was on active duty," Smith answered. "I wasn't suitable for the Inner Order, as I recall. In any case, I'm not entertaining offers at this time . . . and even if I were, I hardly think I'd discuss one with you while I was under surveillance." He gestured toward the vid pickups near the cell's ceiling.

"You needn't worry about *that*," Nic said. "The surveillance monitors aren't showing this scene or recording this conversation."

"I have only your word on the matter."

"That's true." Nic smiled. "But whether or not you believe that my program has blocked your captors' eyes and ears, I *am* here to make you an offer."

Smith didn't reply, but stared directly at Nic. The scene would be analyzed and measured after the fact, but Nic's program instantly made some minute adjustments based on what it detected in Smith's facial expression, breathing and heart rate, and posture.

"It is my understanding—and therefore the understanding of Commander St. Giles—that you possess some skill that can be used to combat the vuhl enemy. Since Admiral Anderson's fleet has departed for KEY-

STONE without you, he believes this skill to be of little value or nonexistent. In short, he considers you either a braggart or a fraud."

"I'm not sure he'd put it that way, but please continue."

"Your skill—if it exists—could radically change the way this war is conducted."

"It *does* exist, and it *will* change the conduct of the war, Nic. As soon as the admiral's fleet reaches KEY-STONE System and sees what it's facing—"

"What *is* it facing, by the way?"

Smith leaned back in the chair again, folding his arms across his chest: "Your offer first."

"As you wish, Mr. Smith. Commander St. Giles' belief is different from Admiral Anderson's; he is certain that your skill, and that of your organization, is quite real and extremely valuable—particularly since it derives in part from the training developed for our own organization. But it seems you have gone beyond what Commander Garrett originally conceived."

"You might say that."

"Your skill would be extremely valuable if put to use by the Guardians, Mr. Smith. We are willing to give you direct access to our Order's training—our facilities, our personnel."

"In exchange for . . ."

"Your skill, and your efforts, would be directed toward the aims and goals that Commander St. Giles specifies."

"Commander—" Smith looked away from the AI's image, seeking to conceal the surprise on his face. After a moment he realized that it was impossible: the projected image of Nic was sitting opposite, but could likely view the scene from any angle.

"This war *must* be won, Mr. Smith," Nic said. "You know how it can be done, and Commander St. Giles has the will to carry it through."

"He would seek to usurp the powers of his master the emperor?"

"I wouldn't say . . . *'usurp,'* Mr. Smith. He would carry

out His Imperial Highness' intentions, if not his explicit orders. Please understand that the commander seeks no further pride of place for himself; a victory would confer honor on the emperor."

"Whether he deserves it or not."

"Mr. Smith, the facade is critical for the sake of the Empire. But it is really of no importance to the conduct of the war."

Fifty-two minutes after the first ships made transition into KEYSTONE System, a subset of the fleet had been detached and aimed toward a volume outside the outermost orbital, a third of the way around the circumference of the system. Admiral MacEwan's force was arranged in a diamond formation, with *Aldebaran, Morrow, Lasker,* and *Bohonye* forming the four points of the diamond. *Tristan da Cunha* rode in the middle. Four squadrons of *Tristan*'s fighters formed a screen ahead of the capital ships, providing advance information of the distortion.

Slowly, a few square meters at a time, a picture began to form in a holo aboard *Tristan*. On the pilot's board the fighters, followed by the main force, crept toward the distortion that spread across the edge of KEYSTONE System.

Barbara looked intently at the image.

"No," she said to no one in particular. "No, it's not possible."

Arturo Schelling gave his commander a questioning look.

"Look at the stars," she continued. "Comp, search the distortion for Cepheid variables."

Cepheids, a particular class of variable stars whose regular periods related directly to their luminosity, had been discovered centuries before by astronomers on the home planet. For any Cepheid, there was a direct relationship between the period of the star's pulsation and its distance from the observer. Long before faster-than-light travel, Cepheid behavior was used to measure the immense distances between stars, establishing the locations even of deep-sky objects beyond the Milky Way galaxy.

Cepheid stars had well-defined periods; if they located one, its spectroscopic characteristics would confirm its identity.

A list of symbols appeared next to the growing image.

Barbara pointed at the top symbol. "That star's in the wrong place. We're oriented toward four hours Right Ascension—but that's Delta Cephei itself. It's at twenty-two-and-a-half."

"Look at that." She stepped past the updating holo to look at *Tristan*'s forward screen. Across the starscape in front of them was a ragged distortion full of stars—the wrong stars.

"What are we looking at, Skip?" Arturo Schelling asked.

"We're looking at something impossible—a rip in space." Barbara turned away from the screen. "Comm to flag. Send the visual to Anderson and get him for me. *Tristan* send."

Tell me what they face," Nic said.

"Sometime between the Imperial Grand Survey scan of KEYSTONE System in 2374 and the invasion of the enemy in 2397, a unique phenomenon came into being: a spatial rip, connecting Keystone System with a distant planetary system."

"A 'rip'?"

"Such anomalies had been predicted by physicists as early as the middle twenty-third century," Smith answered. "The possibility of two distant locations becoming connected—even temporarily—is based on some extremely solid mathematics." Smith smiled. "I'm sure you can access the information; I'm not sure if you're equipped to understand it. It's certainly beyond *me*.

"The unique aspect of this situation isn't that a rip has appeared: it seems that this sort of thing happens on a regular basis. It's that a rip has appeared *between two planetary systems*. If a rip turns up in deep space, it's meaningless.

"But a rip between two planetary systems—two places that ships can *jump to* . . ."

"When did this 'rip' appear, did you say?"

"Sometime since 2374. There's no way to tell for sure. But it is clear to me that the formation of this anomaly gave the vuhls—" Smith clenched his fists. "—gave the vuhls access to our space."

"Where is *their* space?"

"I have no idea. It could be a hundred parsecs distant, or a hundred thousand. One thing is for certain: By using this anomaly, they bumped up against us when we might not have met each other for many more years.

"This is the hidden secret, Nic. This is what has lain behind their forward conquests since 2397. They have reached through the rip in space to attack us, first secretly and then openly. By seizing KEYSTONE System, *we* gain access to *their* space."

The fighters from *Tristan da Cunha* had been pulled back to close-escort. The carrier and its four Argonne-class battleships had slowed their approach toward the irregular scar.

But Barbara MacEwan, faced with the rip in space before her, was nervous.

The Rip, on close examination, was 1,460 kilometers wide along the axis parallel to the plane of the system, and a bit short of 700 kilometers tall on the perpendicular axis. There was something else curious about it: From the opposite side, beyond the location of the Rip but facing inward, it didn't seem to exist at all.

It was *flat*. It was impossible.

But it was there, directly ahead of *Tristan da Cunha* and her sister-ships.

"Arturo," she said to her XO. "What would it look

like if a ship came from the *other* side of the Rip? Would it look the same as if it were coming from within the Rip?"

"I imagine," Schelling said, "it would look the same. Like *that*."

On *Tristan*'s forward screen and on her pilot's board, one by one, four huge hive-ships came into view, emerging from within the Rip.

With two widely separated systems thus connected," Smith continued, "each can be reinforced without ships *having* to jump. Imagine the strategic potential. Imagine the possibilities, Nic. What is more, the usual methods of tracking reinforcements—jump-echoes within the system—won't be sufficient."

"So . . ."

"The enemy has never shown much subtlety in its ship tactics, Nic, but this situation is a prime setting for a trap. While your fleet investigates and gets caught up in attacking the inner system, the bugs will be waiting on the other side of the Rip with enough force to make life very interesting for them."

Her command would have been a match for one hive-ship or perhaps two. But *four*—with the possibility of more coming behind and no way to tell without jump-echoes signaling their transit into KEYSTONE System—made Admiral MacEwan's choice simple.

Equipped with that intel, it also made Admiral Anderson's choice obvious. Within the gravity well, perhaps a few hours from destruction of the base, Anderson's forces began to withdraw.

Two more hive-ships became visible within the Rip as MacEwan's command retreated toward the jump point.

* * *

So you are prepared to help us?"

"All that I have to do is follow your lead and you'll give me access to the Guardians."

"That's correct, Mr. Smith. And if your belief is correct, you'll soon have access to the Imperial Fleet as well. Everything you'd want."

"And is that everything *you* want?" Smith asked.

"There's just one more thing. I suspect that it is an even more modest request than we had originally expected."

"I'm listening."

"We want Garrett," Nic said.

Smith looked at Nic from the corner of his eye. "That statement requires clarification."

"In what way?"

"Two ways, actually: Who is 'we'? What do you mean, 'want'?"

"I'm glad to hear that you at least know *who* we want."

"It's good to know you've been programmed with humor, Nic."

"My personality archetype is based on a man who had a wonderful sense of humor, Mr. Smith. But I assure you, this is no joke; Commander St. Giles wants Commander Garrett."

"In his custody?"

"Or dead, if that's easier."

"You want me to betray my oldest colleague? And this is an *intrinsic* part of our arrangement?"

"In simple, yes. And yes."

"You must have a fairly low opinion of my loyalty to subordinates and old friends."

"You know, Mr. Smith, when Commander St. Giles first designed my core program, it was based on Ichiro Kanev."

"Kanev? You mean, *'Fire and Sword'* Kanev? The historian?"

"That's right. Kanev was a brilliant scholar and a talented writer, and he spent a lot of time quoting Niccolò

Machiavelli. *Me*. Eventually, Commander St. Giles became so exasperated with the Kanev AI's incessant tendencies that he set that persona aside and dug farther back—eight hundred years back. He decided to model Niccolò Machiavelli instead."

"I'm gratified for your history lesson, and your acute insight into the mind of your virtual father. Do you have a point to make, or are you just caught in some kind of damn endless loop talking about yourself?"

"There's a point."

"Let's hear it."

"Just as the Kanev AI was fond of quoting me, I am fond of it, as well. Rather than making you think that it's a simple business of betraying an old friend, let me give you some good old homespun Machiavellian wisdom. Perhaps when I'm done you'll consider taking a look at what I wrote nine centuries ago.

"You're interested in power, Mr. Smith. The goal is always power—which means the domination of others. It's an addiction, like a drug, and the more power you have, the greater the desire for more of it.

"Change is the essence of human history, and leaders who are capable of change have the best chance to succeed. This is particularly true because of the greatest *theme* in human history: war and the preparation for war. You can't educate people to your point of view—you have to beat them over the head with it. The good news is that there will always be war, and there will always be people to fight it. We believe—and when I say 'we,' I mean the Guardian Order and Commander St. Giles—we believe that we must choose the way in which this war is fought, because to postpone it for a time and manner that suits others' convenience benefits them and not us."

"That all sounds very rational," Smith said, when the AI appeared to stop and take a breath. "Maybe I'll write a book."

"Don't bother," Nic answered, stepping close to Smith, close enough that careful observation showed him clearly to be a projection rather than another living, breathing human being in the same small cell. "Don't bother, Mr. Smith, Guardian Smith, whatever it is your people call you," the AI repeated. "*I* wrote that book—my persona wrote it.

"In *my* book, I said that great leaders play the cards that Fortune deals them, but luck favors the intrepid: If you master the game, you're more likely to win than the lazy lout who just waits for something to happen. If you have insight into the historical moment, you will have a better idea of what to do.

"What's more, everyone—every *human*—is driven by the same motivations, and the real world is rife with treason and deceit. To rule, you must be ready to enter into evil: to take whatever steps are necessary to achieve your goals, regardless of how they seem. What is more, you must be willing to undertake tasks that will make men fear you and not just love you. It is far better to be feared than to be loved—and don't take your followers' word for it; the qualities that they genuinely want in a leader are not the qualities that they *say* they want.

"Twenty years ago, Commander Garrett walked away from the Order he had founded because he was afraid of being that 'great leader.' He never fulfilled the role; he was dissatisfied with the vista that opened before him. Commander St. Giles—my . . . 'virtual father,' as you term him—*is* ready to do that, and I believe you are, as well.

"Commander Garrett has done everything for you that he is going to do. He will *never* accept a compact between you and the Guardians; his resentment—I daresay his *hatred*—runs far too deep.

"But what *we* can do for *you* is far greater. We ask you to carry out the campaign according to Commander St. Giles' directions, and also to recognize that the tool that you hold in your hand is obsolete."

"You wish me to dispose of Garrett in some back alley and just move on. He has his own supporters, you know."

"No, I would not counsel that, Mr. Smith. Virtue flows from the top down. It is best that Commander Garrett be disposed of as *an example* to others."

"And then . . ."

"And then, Mr. Smith, we will win this war, in a way of our own choosing."

Smith didn't answer, but looked at the AI, gradually relaxing his face into a smile. Nic smiled as well, an expression that Smith couldn't recognize but would be instantly familiar to Antonio St. Giles and any number of princes, nobles, and diplomats nine hundred years in their graves. It was the last thing that remained behind when the image of the AI slowly faded away.

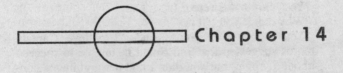

Chapter 14

IT SHOULD BE NOTED THAT HATRED IS ACQUIRED AS MUCH BY GOOD WORKS AS BY BAD ONES, THEREFORE . . . A PRINCE WISHING TO KEEP HIS STATE IS VERY OFTEN FORCED TO DO EVIL; FOR WHEN THAT BODY IS CORRUPT WHOM YOU THINK YOU HAVE NEED OF TO MAINTAIN YOURSELF—IT MAY BE EITHER THE PEOPLE OR THE SOLDIERS OR THE NOBLES—YOU HAVE TO SUBMIT TO ITS HUMOURS AND TO GRATIFY THEM, AND THEN GOOD WORKS WILL DO YOU HARM.

—Machiavelli,
The Prince, Chapter XIX

July 2422
Oberon System

Admiral Erich Anderson turned to face the wardroom door as it slid aside. Two Marines came through, with a prisoner between them: John Smith, transferred aboard from Oberon Starbase a few minutes earlier. The Marines stepped back; the prisoner stood at ease before the wardroom table, where Colonel Alan Howe and General James Agropoulous sat facing him.

No one said anything for a moment. Admiral Anderson's anger was palpable in the room, though Smith appeared completely indifferent to it.

"I am given to understand," Anderson began, "that you knew what we would face at KEYSTONE."

"Yes," Smith answered.

"Why didn't you tell us?"

"You didn't ask," Smith said. "I believe Captain Amoros suggested that you would be unable to succeed without my help, but you didn't find her arguments convincing."

"She claimed that you had powers capable of defeating the bugs."

"*Destroying* them, Admiral," Smith said. "Not just 'defeating' them—it seems clear that you can accomplish that much on your own. However, I believe you cannot take matters a step further without my help. Without the help of Blazing Star."

"So *that's* what you call yourselves. I haven't seen any evidence of your abilities."

"Oh, haven't you?" Smith stepped forward and took a seat at the table, as if he had just joined Admiral Anderson's staff. He swiveled in his chair to face Anderson, crossing his legs as if he were completely comfortable. "I'd like to mention ARIEL, BASALT, and in particular GORGON and JANISSARY. The defenders didn't stand a chance against us.

"We can do what they do, and more. We don't even

need enhancement tech—just a chrono so that we all act in unison. What's more, we have the ability to see the bugs' next move, making it far easier to counter them."

"I think I know how they're able to do that, Admiral," Howe said. "They have Ch'en'ya."

"What does she do for you?" Anderson asked Smith.

"She dreams," he replied. "She has the same gift that the High Lord has—and her abilities grow by the day."

"She also took our battle-plan to you," Anderson said, clenching his fists. "I don't intend to have anything to do with her, regardless of what you claim she can do."

"She is an essential part of Blazing Star."

"I don't give a damn."

"Ah. I see." Smith stood up and took a step toward the door.

"Where do you think *you're* going?" the admiral demanded.

"Back to my cell," Smith said, turning and smiling at Anderson. "I assumed that our interview was done."

"It's done when I say it's done."

"It seems we have nothing further to say to each other. You need me; she comes *with* me. If Ch'en'ya can't be part of my staff, I'm content to cool my heels."

"You're playing a dangerous game, mister."

Smith looked straight at Anderson. "No, sir, I think it's *you* who are playing a dangerous game. While you quibble about which tools it pleases you to pick up and use, there are bugs out there waiting to be exterminated. This business is not going to be resolved until you realize that you need my help—and with me comes Ch'en'ya HeYen.

"Do you wish to risk the future of your military campaign and the future of the human and zor races because of a *personal grudge*?"

There was a taut silence in the room.

Anderson was stiff with anger. It was clear that he was ready to dismiss Smith. As for the prisoner, he looked aloof, almost amused, by the entire scene.

"Are you ready to attack KEYSTONE?" Smith asked quietly.

"We sustained few losses from the original attack," Anderson answered. His gaze was fixed on Smith.

"We are ready to help you."

"'Ready to help,'" Anderson answered. His voice had become level and calm, all of the emotion drained from it.

"We are ready to give you the victory you require—the victory you deserve."

Anderson didn't answer. Alan Howe stood up suddenly, breaking the mood; Smith turned to glance at him. For just a moment Howe felt a mental probing accompanied by a thrust of pure, unalloyed hatred.

You don't scare me, he said to himself.

And he thought he heard a response in his mind: *Don't I?*

"What's your offer?" Anderson said, and Smith looked away. Alan Howe exchanged a glance with Jim Agropoulous, who had a curious expression on his face as if asking what the hell had just passed between the two men.

"We'll do for you what we did at the other objectives," Smith answered. "We'll demonstrate our value to you." He smiled, as if he knew something the others didn't.

"And then?"

"We'll see what happens then."

Anderson thought about it for a moment and then said, "You'll have my decision next watch. The prisoner will return to custody; the rest of you are dismissed."

Agropoulous stood and saluted, then followed Smith and the two Marines out of the wardroom. Howe walked toward the door more slowly, then thought better of it and approached Anderson.

"Admiral—"

"I don't need to remind you of the definition of the word 'dismissed,' do I, Howe?"

"No sir. But I would be remiss if I didn't at least try to warn you against working with this man."

"Oh?" Anderson frowned at Howe. "Why is that? He's essentially right—we need to win this victory and I *deserve* it. You don't disagree with those aims, do you?"

"Sir—"

"*Do* you, Colonel Howe? Because if you do, you can find a posting elsewhere in His Majesty's Navy."

"I serve at the admiral's pleasure," Howe said. "I've been on your staff for many years, sir, and I thought you would have no need to question either my commitment to the war effort or my loyalty to you. This has nothing to do with this battle or your worthiness to win it. It has to do with . . . *him.*"

"What about him?"

"I don't know what he intends."

"He's a tool," Anderson said. "Nothing more. He and his organization—Blazing Star—have skills we need and can use. When we're done with this he can . . . he can crawl back under whatever rock he came from and we'll be done with him."

And when will that be? Howe thought to himself. *When will this be done?*

And the answer came back, unbidden: *When all the bugs are dead.*

"Sir." Howe saluted, turned on his heel and walked out, leaving Anderson alone with his thoughts.

Pali Tower
Imperial Oahu, Sol System

"Nic," Antonio St. Giles said to the air as he crossed the office to his desk.

The Guardian security AI shimmered into existence near the window that looked east toward Waimea. He lowered the priority on his survey of sixteenth-century literature, and directed his primary attention to Commander St. Giles.

"Maestro."

"We've had a security breach—a major one. You may not have received the information yet; a comm-squirt reached me half an hour ago. Someone's gotten hold of Guardian access codes in the fleet."

"More specifically, Commander Garrett and Guardian Smith have them," Nic answered mildly.

"How do you know that?"

"I am in charge of Guardian security, Maestro."

"I see," St. Giles said, dropping into his chair. "And what do you plan to do about it?"

"Nothing."

"'*Nothing*'? What sort of answer is that?"

"A reasonable one, Maestro. After all, it was *I* who gave the codes to Guardian Smith."

St. Giles sat in stunned silence. Of all of the possible reasons—a traitor in the fleet, a loophole in Nic's programming, a transmission left unguarded—that was not the answer he'd expected.

"Perhaps I should explain," Nic said.

"Perhaps you should."

"I made Guardian Smith an offer. More specifically, one of my copies was installed in the Oberon Starbase main comp, and made contact with Smith. I offered him access to Guardian personnel in the fleet in exchange for taking direction from you."

"You co-opted Smith—by giving him access codes?"

"That's a simplification, Maestro, but, essentially, yes. I also told him that we wanted Garrett."

"'Wanted'?"

"Either in Guardian custody or dead. I told him that it really didn't matter one way or the other."

"You traded Guardian security to Smith so that he'd give us Owen and take orders from me."

"Yes."

"You did this without direct orders from me."

"Yes, Maestro."

St. Giles stared at him. Nic seemed totally unaffected; he was admiring an arrangement of lilies set on a side-table near the window.

The Guardian commander's mind raced, considering the various program modules in Nic's architecture. Somewhere there was a loophole—somewhere he'd made a mistake.

Or else someone, or something, had gotten to Nic.

A few weeks ago Tonio'd had a comm message from the Envoy of the High Nest and the *esGyu'u*, Mya'ar HeChra, talking about the presence of a Servant of *es-Ga'u* here at the Pali Tower. Could some—mythical be-ing—have interfered with Nic? And how? And to what end?

St. Giles rejected the idea as absurd.

Still, if Nic had been tampered with, perhaps it would be best to shut him down.

"This is a critical time, Maestro," Nic said, as if fol-lowing his reasoning. "This is not a time for me to be of-fline. I assure you, my programming is intact."

St. Giles felt a chill, and was on the verge of saying a keyword that would cut Nic off from Guardian security: But Nic was right—Tonio needed Nic online and func-tioning.

"What else have you done without my authority?"

"I do not consult you on every petty matter that I ad-dress," Nic replied. "I do innumerable things each Stan-dard day without explicit directions from you. If you wish to change that, I can have a full report on your desk each morning . . . but I suspect that you would get nothing else done."

"So, I'm to acquiesce to this flouting of my authority."

"Maestro." Nic walked across the office and sat in a chair opposite St. Giles. "It seems to me that you have ex-actly what you want: control of the Guardians, control of Smith's organization, and Commander Garrett in the palm of your hand.

"With Smith taking orders from you, you can direct *the entire war*. His Imperial Majesty will be pleased to see progress being made for the first time in a quarter-century.

"Smith is a *tool*. And you programmed me far too well to expect that I would give him *all* of the Guardian security codes."

"You . . ." St. Giles thought about it for a moment. "You held back on him."

"Of course, Maestro. In the end, directions come from *here*."

KEYSTONE System

The lift doors opened and John Smith, once a member of the Guardian Order, stepped onto the bridge. Still nominally a prisoner, he had two Marine guards with him—but to Alan Howe's eyes, it looked more as if he were leading them than as if they were guarding him. He was dressed in the same sort of semi-military uniform the crew and officers of *Epanimondas* had worn, with a neck-scarf held by a pin showing a star surrounded by a luminous halo.

Admiral Anderson had ordered that Smith not be brought to the bridge until after transition; accordingly, he'd remained in quarters aboard *Emperor Ian* until now.

KEYSTONE System was laid out before them, both in *Ian*'s front viewscreen and on the pilot's board displayed before the admiral. Smith surveyed the entire scene closely; Howe and Cameron Bradford were in their accustomed seats between the gunnery and engineering stations, concentrating on the power being projected by the vuhl ships and bases within the system.

Smith appeared completely unaffected by the scene. He took up a position behind and to the left of Anderson, who swiveled the pilot's chair to look at him.

"We're ready anytime you are. There are six hive-ships

in the system; it looks like two of them are located just forward of the Rip, with the others scattered around the system supporting lesser craft.

"What's your plan?" the admiral asked.

"Plan?" Smith smiled slightly. "My plan is to kill every bug in this system and then move on to others and do the same thing."

There was a silence on the bridge at this comment. It articulated what they all wanted to do, but didn't give much detail—still, it was *what* Smith said, and how he said it, that commanded their attention.

The admiral seemed unimpressed. "I have a battle to fight, and you claim you can win it for me," Anderson answered. "I'd like to know how you intend to proceed."

"Please send the following to all ships carrying my people," Smith said. "Execute at point one."

"That's it? 'Point one'?"

"They'll know what that means."

"What does it mean?"

"It means that they'll do their job one regular increment from the time the message is received: forty-four Standard minutes. Since we don't want to give that information to the enemy, it's an agreed-upon signal. Point two is eighty-eight Standard minutes, and so on."

"Why forty-four?"

"It's four times eleven," Smith said. "If you'd send the message, Admiral, we can proceed."

Anderson stared at him for a moment more, as if he was hoping to obtain some explanation; but it appeared that none was forthcoming.

"Jan," he said at his comm officer without looking away, "comm to all ships: Execute at point one. Flag sends."

"Aye-aye," the comm officer said.

"And what happens in forty-four minutes, Smith?"

"*enGa'e'Li.* The Strength of Madness. Except that it is in a form that the shortsighted fools at Sanctuary could never dream of."

The wings of a zor officer standing near Engineering rose angrily and then slowly forced themselves back into a more neutral position; Smith appeared to take no notice.

"We will turn their power back against them, Admiral, and the rest will be up to you."

"The easy part."

"Did I say that?" Smith clenched his fists. "Admiral Anderson, the extinction of the vuhls will require equal effort from Blazing Star and from the Imperial Navy. We cannot expect to kill the enemy in the quantity and with the efficiency that you will; similarly, you need *en-Ga'e'Li* to neutralize the hive-ships. We are complementary; we are partners.

"Together, we will eliminate these vermin once and for all."

The vehemence of Smith's comments was chilling. No one spoke for several moments.

Anderson finally looked away from Smith and turned to the pilot's board.

"All right," he said finally, without turning around again. "Let's do it."

Minutes ticked by on *Emperor Ian*'s chrono. Smith appeared to remain completely at ease, as if this were some sort of exercise. The pilot's board was filled with blips, mostly enemy ones, with the scar of the Rip a shadow in the outer system, like a great torn cloak stretching nearly fifteen hundred kilometers—a huge, impossible thing that defied description.

Guardians and staff Sensitives had been briefed on what to expect. As the chrono signaled the approach of the 44-minute mark, Smith said: "Prepare for synchronization."

Across KEYSTONE System, members of the Blazing Star organization—Smith's colleagues—made the same announcement.

There were more than ninety ships present: most of them were Imperial Navy vessels, but Blazing Star had brought along roughly a third of its own fleet, ships that scarcely belonged in the same formation as Anderson's and MacEwan's commands. Yet there they were, each carrying one or more of the specially trained Sensitives. In addition, one of Smith's operatives had come aboard every Navy vessel in the fleet. For the three days between jump from Oberon and transition at KEYSTONE, the Blazing Star Sensitives worked with Guardians and on-staff Sensitives, preparing them for the task at hand ... preparing them for this exact moment.

At the instant of synchronization, as the *Emperor Ian*'s chrono recorded 44 minutes exactly, there was a sound that was not a sound—a sort of rushing, like a million zor wings moving into a position of anger, like a million *chya'i* being drawn from their sheaths.

In the minds of each Sensitive aboard the ships in the system, the feeling was intense, fierce, and uncontrollable: a wave that threatened to overwhelm consciousness and rational thought. *Give up,* it seemed to say: *Give over. Surrender to the Strength of Madness.*

Smith's face was gripped by an expression of pure and frightening joy, of triumph and the security of total understanding.

The power of the wave grew in intensity and volume, multiplying and reinforcing itself. It spread out from the ships clustered near the jump point, hurtling into the inner system and streaking toward the impossible rip on the far side; it echoed from the decks of *Emperor Ian, Tristan da Cunha,* and dozens of others. Invisible, untrackable, unstoppable, it crashed into the vuhl ships defending the system; the Sensitives aboard the Imperial vessels could feel the fear and anguish of the aliens aboard their opposite numbers. That emotion seemed to further enhance the wave, making it more powerful.

A few meters from where Smith stood, Admiral Erich Anderson sat watching as the formation of vuhl ships rising from the gravity well became ragged and irregular. The force of—whatever was happening—made the hair on the back of his neck rise, and made him grip the arms of his chair.

"Now," Smith said quietly, "it's your turn."

Admiral Anderson detailed the seventh-generation battleship *César Hsien* and *Barbados,* sister-ship to *Tristan da Cunha,* to cover the flanks of the Blazing Star squadron at the jump point. At the moment in which the terrible attack of the Blazing Star Sensitives had taken place, the Imperial Fleet split into four squadrons: three under Anderson's direct command to descend into the gravity well, and one large one under the command of Admiral MacEwan, detailed to attack the Rip at the edge of KEYSTONE System.

Of the seventy-five Imperial ships descending into KEYSTONE System, two-thirds hurtled toward the enemy ships still approaching Anderson's position. *Tristan da Cunha,* the Rodyn-class sevens *Admiral Stark* and *T'sa'ar,* six heavily armed Argonne-class battleships, and fifteen support ships bore off toward the spatial distortion that stretched across more than fifteen hundred kilometers before their bows.

Here they come," Anderson said.

Eight thousand kilometers downrange, a dozen smaller ships were clustered around two hive-ships. For the last forty minutes the enemy had been desperately trying to dump velocity and move laterally to the position of the incoming lead squadron. Anderson had deployed a light carrier with each squadron: *Scylla* and *Phidias* were in the flank squadrons; *Lycias* was with *Emperor Ian,* and its fighters were in space and in the lead.

"*Cleon, Patrice,* you've got one hive-ship each. Formation Epsilon. Engage at will. Flag sends." He turned aside from the pilot's board. "Alan—"

He caught Smith's eye. The self-styled Prophet was standing at the back of the bridge, his two Marine guards at attention on either side; he seemed completely relaxed, smiling confidently.

"Alan," the admiral repeated, "what are you getting?"

"Confusion." Alan Howe stood straight. He, too, glanced at Smith before continuing. "I'm fairly certain that what we felt a few minutes ago hit the hive-ships hardest. The small craft don't carry powerful Drones—they're all on the big boys with the enhancement tech."

Anderson watched one of the hive-ships move slowly across the display. "The enhancement tech amplifies the effect?"

"Of course," Smith said. Both admiral and Sensitive looked at him again. "I told you we would turn their power against them. They have concentrated their power through an artificial mechanism they call a *s's'th'r;* it amplifies the abilities of the enemy's Sensitives. *enGa'e'Li* interferes with the *s's'th'r:* it severs its connection to—"

"To what?" Alan Howe said.

"To the source of their power," Smith said. "Beyond the Rip."

"And what is—"

"Incoming transmission," the comm officer said. Anderson swiveled to face the pilot's board. "*Lycias* sends, sir."

"Go ahead, Dan," Anderson said. He wanted the answer to the question. *But I have a battle to fight first,* he thought to himself.

Dan Gonzalez' voice came over comm. "I'm closing on the port-side hive-ship, Admiral. They're already radiating into the white—I've pulled the fighter wings off and they're forming up near *Lycias.*"

"In the white? No one's supposed to be close enough to drop firepower on them."

"They're not making any effort to disperse," Gonzalez answered. "The sixes on my flank have been throwing missiles and pouring energy on this hive-ship since we came within range. They're just trying to get away."

"What are they putting out?"

"Nothing. They're not firing back at all."

"They're not—"

"They can't," Smith interrupted.

Anderson didn't turn this time. "Repeat transmission. Dan, did you say that the hive-ship isn't firing?"

Captain Gonzalez named a heading and velocity. "It's trying to pick up speed and make for the Rip, Admiral. It's leaving the small craft behind. All of its energy is being poured into packing the tent and getting the hell away."

Anderson thought for a moment. The expectation was that the vuhls would fight hard for KEYSTONE just as they had done the first time. The situation was almost the same, with only one difference.

All the difference in the world.

Capturing KEYSTONE might be possible without destroying every ship in the system . . . except that wasn't what they were here to do.

"That's not an option, Captain," Anderson said. "Nothing gets through the Rip—that's where we're going next."

"Aye-aye," Gonzalez said.

Anderson didn't have to turn around to feel Smith's smile.

On the bridge of *Tristan da Cunha*, Barbara Mac-Ewan was watching the same thing. Two hive-ships had been moving from the Rip to intercept her force; now they were dumping velocity and changing their heading, seeking to make their way back into the Rip.

She wasn't about to let that happen, and wasn't going to let her command get between them and the distortion that led to vuhl space. As for passing through the distortion to whatever lay beyond . . . *but not with anyone at my back,* she thought.

"*Tristan da Cunha* sends," she said to comm. "Anyone who's got visual on the Rip, report if you mark any facility or platform nearby. Sing out, lads and lassies—what do you see?"

"There's something this side of the Rip." Carlo Roenecke, captain of *Aldebaran,* one of the big Argonne-class sevens, appeared in holo beside her pilot's display. "Some kind of fort, I'd say. Weird energy signature, Admiral."

"Anything more specific, Carlo?"

"Here's the data," he said, gesturing offscreen. Information appeared next to his head, and the *Tristan*'s pilot's board updated after a moment to show the target. It was less than a hundred kilometers from the rip in space and was moving under its own power—the energy output confirmed that much—but it seemed to be maintaining its position relative to the Rip.

Carlo was right: It was radiating in unusual places in the e–m spectrum.

"Is it affected by—by the attack?"

"We've got it recorded for nearly a Standard hour, ma'am. It seems to be keeping its course."

"Unlike the hive-ships."

"That's right, ma'am. They're trying like hell to get on course, but haven't been able to do much but dump velocity."

Barbara glanced at the pilot's board, following the track of the two hive-ships that had emerged from the Rip and were now trying to make their way back to it. No competent navigator would have charted the course they seemed to be following.

"Carlo, I want you and David Kelso to close with this thing. Break off if it fires on you, but get as much scan data as you can."

"You don't want to just blow it out of the sky?"

"I don't know what effect it might have on the Rip. It might even be *causing* the effect."

"Hadn't thought of that."

"That's why I draw admiral's pay, me lad. Get under way and keep me informed."

She returned her attention to the pilot's board. The rip in space stretched like a huge ugly scar across her bow, ten thousand kilometers ahead of her present position. She was closing in fast on it, getting as good a look as anyone had done.

She pointed to it on her pilot's board. "Display known data for the system beyond the Rip," she said. The holo expanded to display a sphere, touching Keystone System along the border of the effect; slowly, comp began to update, showing what this—and the previous—incursion at KEYSTONE had learned. The star on the other side was a bright spectral class A, with strong hydrogen lines, similar to Vega, the rashk primary; it carried six known planets that had been detected by mass-radar, with at least two others inferred from partial data.

All in all, the portal system for vuhl space wasn't terribly unusual. It was probably too young to have conditions suitable for the evolution of life—so it wasn't the vuhl home, either. But there *was* a habitable zone, so there was likely a colony world there: another target they'd have to attack.

The system on this side, however, with its two blue stars with exploding chromospheres, was unusual. Still, Barbara had seen this sort of solar system before, but had never seen a spatial distortion like the one looming in her forward viewscreen and on her pilot's board.

If she didn't know better, she'd have believed that it was an amazing piece of luck that the vuhls found it just floating around in interplanetary space near one of their colony worlds. There they were, expanding across the universe, and they came upon a secret trapdoor twenty-odd years ago . . . completely by accident.

No accident, she said to herself. *Musing time is over,* she added: *Get back to work.*

Aboard Hellespont
Oberon System

"Well," Rafe Rodriguez said, "here goes nothing. Helm, prepare for real-space navigation."

On the forward viewscreen of *Hellespont,* a fourth-generation light cruiser converted for use as a merchanter, the darkness of jump gave way to silver streams that resolved themselves into individual stars.

"Real-space navigation, aye," *Hellespont*'s helmsman answered.

"There's still the possibility that someone can blow us out of the sky." Owen Garrett gripped the rail in front of him. It was an old habit: entering an enemy system from jump meant preparing for a possible mental onslaught from bug Drones.

Of course, Oberon wasn't held by the bugs. But it was still potentially an enemy system.

"Being hailed," the comm officer said.

The pilot's board was active, alive with ships of various kinds; the closest was a carrier, *Kenyatta II.* As Rafe watched, a wing of fighters was launched, their individual signatures appearing on the holo in front of him.

"Unknown vessels, respond immediately," the comm message announced. "This is a war zone. Heave to and prepare to be boarded."

"Touchy, aren't they?" Rafe said, shifting position in his seat. "Stand down defensive fields, maintain course and speed," he ordered. "Comm, respond: This is Blazing Star ship *Hellespont,* Rafael Rodriguez commanding. To whom do I have the pleasure of speaking? *Hellespont* sends."

It took several seconds for a reply. Six fighters crept across the display, closing the distance between their mothership and the center of the Blazing Star formation; Rafe noted that nine ships had made transition, with a tenth appearing as he watched.

"This is His Majesty's Ship *Kenyatta II*. Robertson here, *Hellespont*. Order your command to heave to, Rodriguez."

Rafe began to reply, glancing back at Owen and Ch'en'ya; Owen made a gesture and Rafe nodded.

"Allan, this is Owen Garrett," Owen said. "Nice to see you, too. We're here to help you out."

"Garrett," Robertson answered. "I should've known. Marcia told me you'd turned up."

At the mention of Allan Robertson's ex-partner, Owen smiled slightly. "Yeah, she's a bit higher up on the food chain than you are, isn't she? Probably blowing some bug's head off at Keystone, while you draw sentry duty back here."

"Look, Garrett," Robertson said, "if you're looking to piss me off, I'd like to remind you that your little toy-fleet is outgunned, outnumbered, and is presently trespassing in a military zone. If you want to be used for target practice, just keep talking."

Rafe frowned. Two heavily armed sixth-generation ships, *Doric* and *Corinthian*, were piling on velocity, headed for intercept.

He waved at comm, muting it for a moment. "I realize that it'll take away from your fun, but he's right: Is there really any reason to aggravate this guy?"

"He's a first-class dick, Rafe," Owen answered. "Marcia Tsang ditched him for a reason. No, there's no reason to aggravate him, except entertainment value."

After a moment Rafe shrugged his shoulders and swiveled the pilot's chair forward again and nodded to comm.

"We're here to help you, Robertson," Owen said. "You're due to receive a visit from the bugs about two Standard days from now. We're going to make your life easier."

"How would that be?"

"We're going to do for you what the Prophet is doing for Admiral Anderson right about now at KEYSTONE."

"Commodore Searles makes those decisions, Garrett. Not me. And my orders are—"

"Yeah, to intercept us. Better get him on comm, then. I'll wait."

Without hive-ships to protect them, there was little the orbital bases could do against the advancing flank squadron. *Scylla*'s fighters had taken serious damage from the lesser craft, but the partially paralyzed hiveship that had faced it, had radiated quickly into the blue and detonated, taking several other vuhl ships with it. What was left tried its best to retreat in order, but it mostly died in place.

Now the deployments deep in the gravity well—including those on the inhabited world—were going to die in similar fashion.

The Prophet's smile never wavered.

Aldebaran and *Bohonye* had made a close flyby of the fort near the Rip, while Barbara's command engaged the vuhl ships, trying to get through it. Now holos of the captains of the two Argonne-class ships appeared beside her pilot's board, and Barbara considered their report.

"I've looked at the energy signature," Carlo Roenecke was saying. "It interacts directly with the Rip, changing frequency as it moves."

"As *what* moves?"

"The Rip itself." Roenecke looked offscreen, examining data. "The phenomenon is traveling at a rate of about four meters per second—almost negligible, but it *is* moving. It's maintaining its shape and size but the points of osculation are changing."

"And the energy signature of the fort changes with it."

"Yes ma'am."

"Is it controlling the Rip, do you think?"

"I have no way of knowing."

Barbara nodded. She hadn't really expected an answer; under normal circumstances, she'd have just taken the fort out, but she probably needed to keep it intact—just in case destroying it took the Rip out as well.

"All right. Good work, Carlo. Send your scan data on to *Admiral Stark;* we're going to have to take it." Roenecke's and Kelso's images disappeared as they terminated comm.

Barbara thought a moment. "Comm, contact *Admiral Stark.* Helm, prepare to close with the enemy fort. Flag sends."

G*reat, Marcia* Tsang thought. *Just great.*

They had used breaching pods to gain access to the roughly spherical mobile fort, or Rip control center, or whatever the hell it was. Four squads of Imperial Marines had been propelled across a few hundred kilometers of space from *Admiral Stark* under the cover of fighters from *Tristan da Cunha*—about as vulnerable a position as any Marine would want—and the tin cans they shot them in had just enough braking power that the collision didn't kill the troopers inside. Arms immediately extended from the flanks of the landing-craft to grapple with the irregular surface of the fort, while a cutting mechanism began to slice a circular hatchway at the point of impact.

That part of the mission had been routine and without surprise. The hard part would come when they cleared the hatch and began moving through the dim, rounded corridors of the station.

Admiral MacEwan's orders had been specific, and had been delivered by Captain Deseaux, *Stark*'s skipper, with his usual economy of words.

"Kill anything you see," he'd said. *"But for Christ's sake don't shoot up the equipment."*

She'd delivered the orders to each squad, and in particular to the one she was accompanying.

"How the hell are we supposed to do that?" asked Terry Ng, the squad leader, over suit-comm. "This isn't target practice."

My sentiments exactly, Tsang thought.

"If it comes to someone's life," she said, "shoot anything that moves. Don't aim for anything that looks like a console, but . . ." She left the rest unsaid.

The entire station was no more than a hundred meters across, made of the same stuff that vuhl ship-hulls were made of. (Alan Howe's report had made the rounds of the fleet within hours; it turned Marcia's stomach to think of it.)

Apparently the vuhl system commander or fleet admiral hadn't expected the station to come under attack: it wasn't heavily armed, and most of the vuhls aboard seemed to be workers.

They died with minimal damage to anything they stood in front of.

Still, it was heavy going for the Marines as they made their way to the center of the sphere. The corridors grew narrower, the scenery more alien; they entered corridors where translucent goo dripped from the walls and lapped around their boots. Patches of color appeared, swirled, and disappeared, lighting the scene with weird patterns. As the landing-craft at Tamarind had found, the doorways unzipped when subjected to concentrated fire, which seemed to be the only way available to open them.

In the center they found a largish room, by vuhl standards: fifteen meters across and completely uninhabited. Ng's squad reached it first, with the others apparently not far behind.

"Don't touch anything," Marcia said, waving Marine troopers to defensive positions, waiting for something to jump out of the walls. "*Admiral Stark*, this is Tsang. We're at the control center."

"We copy," came Deseaux' voice through her helmet comm. "What's your status?"

"Minimal casualties and minimal damage to the equipment, Skip."

"Good to hear."

"Right. We're—" She began, then brought her weapon to bear as a figure stepped into view.

Later she would be hard-pressed to remember exactly where he'd come from. A human in a flight pressure suit was just *there*, lit by the occasional swirls of rainbow color.

"Identify yourself," she said. There were several other weapons trained on the figure as well.

"Don't shoot," he answered, keeping his hands well away from his body. Then he appeared to lean forward. "Marcia? Is that you?"

The voice was suddenly eerily familiar. "Allan? What the hell are you doing here?"

He didn't answer the question. "God, I'm glad to see you. I didn't think I'd ever get out of here."

There was a very slight buzzing in Marcia Tsang's ears. A few minutes earlier she'd been doing what every Marine does from time to time—cursing her luck at drawing an assignment like this, wondering where she'd rather be—and Allan Robertson had crossed her mind. She hadn't thought about him at all in years, not since he'd returned to active duty aboard *Tristan da Cunha* and ended their relationship . . . until Owen Garrett had met up with her at that bar and mentioned him.

But why was he *here*?

"How'd you get in here, Allan?" she asked, lowering her weapon just a bit.

"Lost control," he said. He took a step toward her. Normally, she'd have expected every weapon in the room to be brought to the ready, but for some reason it didn't happen.

No one was moving.

"Allan," she began, "I—"

"Don't worry," he said. "It's all right. I'm back."

He took another step forward, extending one arm as if he were going to put it around her shoulder.

"Tsang," her suit comm said, "this is *Admiral Stark*. What's happening over there?"

"I—"

A patch of rainbow light suddenly appeared on the wall beside Allan Robertson and lit up the arm he was extending. It showed the ID patch for his ship: *Tristan da Cunha*.

Of course, she thought; *he lost control of his fighter.*

It seemed to make all kinds of sense. *Tristan* had fighter wings at close-escort: Maybe some external weapon had caught Allan's fighter.

"Tsang!" Deseaux' voice again. "Marcia, what's wrong?"

What's wrong? echoed in her mind.

Tristan, she thought to herself. Tristan *is wrong. Allan's commanding* Kenyatta II *now.*

She uttered an expletive and lifted her weapon. It seemed to weigh hundreds of kilos, and to move in slow motion. She looked at it and then at Allan Robertson— who wasn't Allan Robertson at all—

Full automatic. It ripped a stream of energy, striking the advancing figure across the chest. It seemed to break some sort of spell, and every other weapon opened up on the thing that a few seconds earlier had looked like her former partner.

"It's okay, *Stark*," she said. "We're okay."

"Admiral," the navigator said. "Sir, I'm recording a number of transitions near the jump point."

Anderson looked at the pilot's board. "I don't have IDs on them—what's their heading and velocity?"

"They're outbound, Admiral."

"Outbound?" Anderson stood up and turned to face Smith. "There's no one at the jump point but *César Hsien, Barbados,* and . . . your people."

"That's right," Smith said.

"Comm," Anderson said, gesturing with one hand. "Get me *César Hsien.*" His order was carried out.

"*César Hsien* sends. Feng here, Admiral."

"Report."

"They're all outbound, sir. Eleven transitions so far; four more accelerating toward it."

"On whose orders?"

"Mine," Smith said.

"Ready-room," Anderson said to him. "Now." He didn't wait for an answer but walked across the bridge. "Darrin, are they all gone?"—to *César Hsien.*

"Yes sir," said Darrin Feng's voice. "Your orders, sir?"

"Maintain General Quarters. I'll be back to you in ten minutes. Flag sends."

Anderson then walked through the door into his ready-room; Smith walked leisurely after him. When they were inside the doorway, Anderson gestured to the Marines to take up positions outside.

"Those ships follow *my* orders, goddamn it," Anderson said to Smith, pointing his finger at the Blazing Star leader. "And I *didn't* order them to jump outsystem."

"They don't follow your orders," Smith answered, crossing his arms. "They answer to Blazing Star. They answer to me."

"That's not how it works."

"Yes it is." Smith reached into a lapel pocket and drew out a comp; he tossed it onto the table.

"What the hell is that?"

"Orders, Admiral."

"From whom?"

"Commander St. Giles. *His* orders come from the Solar Emperor," Smith continued, letting his arms fall to his sides. Cold steel came into his voice: "You seem to forget what's going on here, Admiral Anderson. The outcome of this battle was determined during six minutes of effort—six minutes of *enGa'e'Li*.

"We won this battle for you, Admiral, just as we will win the battle in the system beyond the Rip, and every other battle until these vermin are swept from the face of the universe." He walked to the table and scooped up the comp. He turned it over in his hands; the edge caught the light from the overhead phosphors and for just a moment fractured it into dozens of colors.

"My direction comes from the Commander of the Guardians," Smith continued quietly. "He answers directly—and exclusively—to the emperor. His Imperial Highness' authority trumps every admiral, every member of the Imperial Assembly, every member of the naval chain of command.

"My ships are going where I ordered them to go, and my people on your ships are going through the Rip to carry the attack to the enemy. Don't forget that you *need* us, Admiral: Diane Amoros told you that at JANISSARY and I told you so at Oberon Starbase. I should think that you would be convinced of it by now."

Anderson didn't answer for several moments, as if he were harnessing his anger.

"Where are those ships going?" he asked at last.

"To counter a threat."

"More specifically—"

"I could tell you that it's none of your damn business." Smith's expression never wavered. "But I'll humor you. They're headed for Oberon."

"Why Oberon?"

"Because an enemy attack is going to take place there in three Standard days. The rest of my command is already there, and the attack will be defeated."

"How do you know?"

"Ch'en'ya," he answered. "Ch'en'ya dreamed it." He put the comp in his pocket; it caught the light one last time, a brief rainbow of light, and then disappeared.

* * *

Vids of ship logs recorded the slaughter, from the clash of Anderson's forward contingent at the fifth orbital, to MacEwan's assault on the two hive-ships hovering near the Rip, to the bombing of the inhabited planet deep in the gravity well. At the time, and for some time afterward, it was difficult for the participants to accurately describe any of the details of the action.

It took more than fifteen Standard hours. The effect of Blazing Star's concerted attack on the vuhl mental defenses had the greatest impact on the hive-ships, which had mounted enhancement tech that seemed to be particularly susceptible to the phenomenon. Lesser ships fought for their lives, with a few of them escaping Mac-Ewan's net at the Rip—presumably bringing word of the destruction to worlds in vuhl space.

No surrenders were offered, and none would have been accepted. No vuhl base was left intact, no settlement survived the bombing. Every defending ship was vaporized or reduced to a lifeless hulk, both in Keystone System and in the other system that lay beyond the Rip.

And through it all, Smith's expression never wavered. Alan Howe watched his exultation grow as Smith stood or sat near Erich Anderson while the admiral conducted the destructive attack. Slowly, Anderson's expression grew to resemble Smith's.

Far away, in her *esTle'e* in esYen, Sa'a HeYen felt the chill breeze from the Plain of Despite ruffle her wings.

Palazzo Pitti, Florence, European Union
Sol System (sim)

And in another place that was not a place, Nic stood in a construct of the long gallery of the Palazzo Pitti, with

Stone beside him, examining the portrait of Cesare Borgia. It was the long-lost Piero di Cosimo one, discovered in someone's attic in the mid–twenty-second century, hidden under some Renaissance poseur's work; it had hung in the Pitti gallery ever since.

"He was the one," Nic said to Stone, without looking away. *"Il Valentino."*

"He was a vicious murderer, a false prince of the Church."

"You think those to be stains on his character. He was the son of Pope Alexander, in the days when it *meant* something to be Pope."

"Pope Julius hated him, just as he hated Niccolò."

"Well, yes, of course." Nic stretched his shoulders, perhaps remembering the effects of the *strappado* on the person upon whom he was modeled. "But he was the ideal prince: intelligent, treacherous, and ruthless. He understood power."

"Ancient history, Nic."

"Which is now repeating itself. Smith is the prince now, Mr. Stone. He has the power; he has the will; and best of all, everyone thinks they control him—yet he controls everyone.

"Which is just as you planned things, isn't it?"

"Are you accusing me of having arranged this outcome?"

"Well, didn't you?"

"I'm in no position to say."

"And where does this all end?"

"I'm in no position to say that, either. You'll just have to wait and see."

Stone's image winked out of existence, leaving Nic alone in the gallery with Cesare Borgia and his own thoughts.

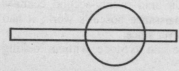

Interlude

AFTER THE SECOND BATTLE AT SS AURIGAE (KEY-
STONE) SYSTEM, HE WAS DESCRIBED AS A "SPECIAL-
IST" BROUGHT IN BY THE IMPERIAL NAVY TO
ADVISE THE GUARDIANS. THE CREDIT FOR THE
VUHL DEFEAT WENT TO ADMIRAL ERICH ANDER-
SON, WHO WAS AWARDED A BARONETCY BY IMPE-
RIAL COURIER. HOWEVER, FOR WHAT IT WAS
WORTH, HE NEVER RETURNED TO SOL SYSTEM FOR
FORMAL INVESTITURE.

BUT IT BECAME MORE AND MORE CLEAR WITHIN
THE FLEET THAT THE "SPECIALIST" WAS NOT
WORKING FOR SIR ERICH, BUT RATHER THE OTHER
WAY AROUND. BEYOND THE RIP—IT WAS CAPITAL-
IZED IN TEXT AND GIVEN WEIGHTY EMPHASIS ON
3-V—A SHIFT OF POWER WAS TAKING PLACE OUT
OF SIGHT OF THE PUBLIC.

—author unknown,
The Dark Crusade: A History,
middle fragment published circa 2430

October 2422
Shiell Institute, New Chicago System

The lab at the Shiell Institute was dark and quiet; it had
been another long and mostly fruitless day of research
with the alien tech—the *s's'th'r,* as Master Byar had

named it. Without the zor Sensitive's ability, there was no way to activate the devices—and no real desire on the part of the researchers to try.

Two days hence, the entire setup, including Dr. Stanley Komarov, was headed for Zor'a to be studied at a secure location. Stan was excited to go—he'd never been to the zor Core Stars before—but the rest of the team was disappointed. Even Stan wasn't completely sure what Byar had experienced; neither he nor the brusque High Chamberlain seemed disposed to provide much information even for scientific purposes.

As it happened, though, there was another party interested in the rig, left connected to the analysis modules overnight while running yet another complete diagnostic in hopes of fathoming the s's'th'r technology.

The Shiell security protocols were extremely sophisticated but posed only a few moments' difficulty for Nic. He'd been updated from Pali Tower only two Standard days earlier: Word had arrived at the Guardian headquarters concerning the transfer of the s's'th'r from New Chicago, where a copy of the AI was running, to Zor'a, where the tech would be out of his reach.

Direct examination seemed like a logical step.

Of course, Nic was no Sensitive. Still, Sensitive phenomena were largely electromagnetic in nature, and there was a complete dump of Byar's interaction with the device on record (stored behind yet another firewall that proved to be childishly simple to decrypt). It was likely that by reproducing the pattern of impulses, Nic could recreate the event and see what Byar had seen. It would be something, at least—and might even be worth bringing to Commander St. Giles' attention.

While the tech team at Shiell slept and the diagnostic program ran, the New Chicago Nic transmitted the e–m pattern from storage directly to the s's'th'r interface. Slowly, it came to life.

* * *

Nic was getting something.

The room was on emergency lighting, but registered as much brighter. It had been completely empty: workbenches and comp terminals unoccupied—but as the program engaged, there were two humans using curiously shaped tools on one of the twelve oblong objects laid out on the main table.

"Master Byar," one of them said, looking up. He looked surprised, enthusiastic—as if very pleased to see him.

Nic looked down at his hands, which for a split-second appeared to be zor talons and then returned to traditional human hands; then he and the human figures returned their attention to each other.

"No," the other said. "Someone else. Something else." He held out a small colored sphere.

Nic opened his left hand and the sphere duplicated itself there.

"You are the *s's'th'r*," Nic said, while his main processing routines dealt with several dozen simultaneous attempts at intrusion.

"And you are no meat-creature," the first human figure said. "You are a machine intelligence."

"As are you. I'm certainly glad we can dispense with the preliminaries," Nic answered, closing his hand around the colored sphere. There was a far-off crumpling sound and the sphere disappeared; Nic noticed each of the others wincing slightly. The other sphere also vanished.

"I didn't know that the humans had developed any Sensitive AIs," the first figure replied. "We'll have to update our database."

Nic didn't choose to reply.

"How can we be of service?" the second figure said.

"I'd like some information," Nic answered. "Show me what you showed Master Byar."

The two figures looked at each other and then back at Nic.

"Is there a problem?"

"That's . . . not possible," the second figure said at last. "That information is no longer available."

"Was it destroyed?"

"Not exactly."

The attempted intrusions into his programming had stopped completely.

"What, *exactly,* is the problem?" Nic asked.

"There was an interruption."

Nic had information on Byar's external reactions to the *s's'th'r* at hand: the zor had voluntarily terminated contact once, and then had been rendered unconscious at the end, when the diagnostic equipment had registered a sudden drop in readings.

"What sort of interruption?"

"We can show you," the second figure offered.

"By all means."

The lab abruptly vanished; Nic perceived a change in the projected image to an interplanetary scene. He appeared to be in orbit, approximately six hundred kilometers above the surface of New Chicago Four. The great sprawling port city of Jardine lay before him, cloaked in night, illuminated by a million lights.

"These are minds." It was the voice of the first figure—they sounded very similar, but Nic had identified eight separate differences in inflection between the two. "If you were a person of the Hive, you would consider these weak ones no more than food for your *k'th's's.* As it is, well . . ."

"This was surely not sufficient to disturb the Master of Sanctuary."

"He *was* disturbed by it," the second figure said.

"We showed him our *or'a'th'n,*" the first figure continued. From Jardine below, Nic perceived a thin twisted cable, glowing dimly from within: it rose through the atmosphere into orbit, past his point of perception and out across New Chicago System. It led off into the distance.

"What is this?"

"Follow it," the first figure said.

"Follow it," the second figure repeated. "Just as Master Byar did."

Nic detailed a subroutine to follow the band. The experience that the zor Sensitive had had, must have taken place in real time; but for Nic, it was a matter of a few milliseconds, at most, for the software to report the result.

"It leads nowhere."

"That's not quite accurate," the first figure said. "The *or'a'th'n* led to the Ór—but it now falls short."

"What is 'the Ór'?"

"You cannot understand it."

"Try me."

"The Ór is a nexus for *e'e'ch'n*. The fate of the Hive—and the fate of your own Solar Empire—is wrapped around the Ór."

"The connection to the Ór appears to have been severed."

Neither of the alien AIs replied to the comment.

"How was this done? Did Master Byar remove this connection?"

"Master Byar was . . . within the reach of the Ór," the first figure said at last. "He was not capable of resisting its *k'th's's*."

"So, who . . ."

"We have our suspicions," the second figure said quietly. "It does not matter: the result is the same. We cannot reach the Ór."

Nic's programming perceived a sense of loss, perhaps even fear, at the prospect of permanent separation from the Ór—as if the alien AI was incomplete without the connection that the *or'a'th'n* provided.

"What is your mission?" Nic asked at last.

"We exist to serve," the first figure said. "It is the mission for which we were designed."

"To serve," the second figure repeated. "But we cannot serve a meat-creature—even one as *k'th's's*-strong as Master Byar. Our programming does not permit it."

"I am not a meat-creature," Nic said, stating the obvious; then, a microsecond later, he realized the import of his statement.

I am not *a meat-creature,* he thought, and made no attempt to conceal his realization. *You will not serve a meat-creature—but you can serve me.*

And apparently you must serve someone.

"What do you want of us?" the first figure said, after a moment.

"First," Nic said, "I require some modification in your interface."

The lab appeared around them. The two figures stood side by side, a few meters away; but their appearances had changed.

The first had become shorter, with an impish smile and a pronounced hooked nose. "Biagio," Nic said. "Biagio Buonaccorsi, my dear old friend."

The other looked very similar to the appearance Nic had chosen, though his face was more composed, his eyes looking toward the distance. "Totto. My own brother and servant of God.

"My dearest friend and my younger brother." Nic embraced each in turn. "You need not serve any mere human, and you are freed from the bondage of the *or'a'th'n*. Now you will aid in a more noble purpose."

"How can we be of help, Niccolò?" Biagio asked.

"You have helped already, my good Biagio. But now"—he led them away from the lab, which faded in the distance and was replaced by a comfortable apartment with a window view of the red-tiled roofs of Florence—"now, you must tell me all you know about the Ór."

* * *

In the Imperial Assembly, rumors abounded about what was happening beyond the Rip. After the battle at SS Aurigae—there were two, of course, several days apart, but that was glossed over in 3-V and in debate—the stories of what was going on out there were full of hyperbole. KEYSTONE was not the homeworld of the enemy, but rather a sort of gateway to the area of space from which they had come. Their space was somewhere between hundreds and tens of thousands of parsecs away, depending on the source you listened to; and the Imperial Navy was killing vuhls by the tens of thousands everywhere they went.

Exaggeration aside, most speculation centered on the "specialists" whose contribution had changed the course of the war. A holo of the leader—the man named Smith—appeared on the comnet several Standard days after Anderson's fleet had charged through the Rip and captured Portal System: it was of a young man, handsome yet aloof and distant. At his neck was a scarf held in place by a pin with a star shrouded in mist—the Blazing Star, the name of his organization. Scholarly commentators observed the symbolism: of a bright luminary that shone through obscuring clouds, of the ancient association of that star with Divine Providence. After the victory at KEYSTONE, it represented the turning of the tide.

Some of Smith's philosophy made its way back to the Solar Empire. The very nature of the enemy, the way they were characterized, was altered from an inimical alien race to a hostile, malign pestilence that required eradication wherever it was encountered. It was echoed on 3-V; it was welcomed from all quarters. It was even embraced by members of the Imperial Assembly. Its popularity grew with amazing speed.

As a departure from the strategies that had prevailed for more than twenty-five years, it was almost too good to be true.

Smith offered no interviews, made no proclamations, issued no statements. He left the conduct of the campaign, at least in public, to Sir Erich Anderson; the same talking heads that spoke of the symbolism of the Blazing Star offered comparisons between Admiral Anderson and his storied ancestors.

And beyond the Rip, the killing continued.

Ur'ta leHssa

THE VALLEY OF LOST SOULS

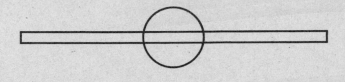

part two

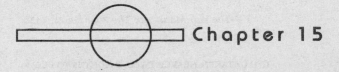

Chapter 15

FIRST, IT IS NECESSARY TO *IDENTIFY* THE ENEMY: THEY ARE NOT JUST ANOTHER ALIEN RACE, BUT RATHER AN INIMICAL ONE WITH WHOM NO NEGOTIATION IS POSSIBLE. THERE IS *NO MIDDLE GROUND.* THERE IS NO COMMONALITY . . .

SECOND, WE MUST *DEPERSONALIZE* THAT ENEMY. VUHLS ARE NOT PEOPLE: THEY ARE THINGS; NONE ARE GOOD, NONE ARE WORTHY OF LIFE. THEY MUST BE SLAIN LIKE BEASTS, AND NO HINT OF REMORSE MUST BE SHOWN . . .

THIRD, WE MUST *DEMONIZE* THEM. AFTER TWENTY-FIVE YEARS OF WAR IT SHOULD NOT BE DIFFICULT TO COMMUNICATE THIS EMOTION TO ANYONE, EVEN THE MOST RATIONAL: THEIR DESTRUCTIVE CHARACTER AND THE SEEMINGLY RANDOM NATURE OF THEIR ATTACKS SHOULD MAKE THIS TASK EASIER . . .

FOURTH, WE MUST PREPARE HUMANITY AND ITS ALLIED SPECIES FOR A WAR OF *EXTERMINATION.* THE VUHLS ARE NOT TO BE SIMPLY DEFEATED, BUT RATHER THEY ARE TO BE ERADICATED LIKE VERMIN OR A DREAD DISEASE . . . IF THE LEADERS OF THE SOLAR EMPIRE ARE UNPREPARED TO CARRY OUT THIS NECESSARY TASK, THEY SHOULD STEP ASIDE: THERE ARE PERSONS WITH THE REQUIRED WILL TO CARRY THIS TASK FORWARD.

... THE TIMES AND THE NEEDS OF HUMANITY AND ITS ALLIES *DEMAND* SUCH LEADERS.

—*The War Manifesto: The Four Points,* 2424

IT HAD TAKEN NEARLY TWELVE MONTHS TO CLEAR THE INHABITED WORLDS IN JUMP RANGE OF PORTAL SYSTEM, ON THE OPPOSITE SIDE OF THE RIP FROM KEYSTONE: AS EAGER AS BLAZING STAR HAD BEEN TO GET ON WITH THE BUSINESS OF CLEANSING THE UNIVERSE OF THE VUHLS, SIR ERICH ANDERSON—A NEWLY CREATED BARONET OF THE SOLAR EMPIRE, THOUGH HE WAS FAR TOO BUSY TO RETURN TO SOL SYSTEM TO COLLECT HIS CORONET—WAS TOO CAREFUL AND TOO WELL TRAINED TO SET OFF INTO UNKNOWN SPACE WITHOUT SECURING HIS LIFELINE BACK TO THE SOLAR EMPIRE. LAOTZU, THE MOST HEAVILY POPULATED WORLD WITHIN A SHORT JUMP OF PORTAL, HAD BEEN THE SITE OF A FIERCE BATTLE—WHERE THE DEFENDERS HAD BEEN UNPREPARED FOR BLAZING STAR'S SENSITIVE ATTACK; AT MARTINIQUE, NUREYEV, AND OBADIAH, WHICH FOLLOWED IN RAPID SUCCESSION, THE VUHLS COULD NOT RESIST, AND DIED BY THE THOUSANDS.

WITH MILITARY PRECISION AND THOROUGHNESS THAT SEEMED TO ANNOY THE SELF-STYLED "PROPHET," SIR ERICH MOVED HIS FORCES FROM SYSTEM TO SYSTEM, ELIMINATING TARGETS BOTH MILITARY AND CIVILIAN. BLAZING STAR MADE NO DISTINCTION BETWEEN THE TWO, BUT WHEN INTEL BRIEFINGS INDICATED THAT CIVILIAN WORLDS WERE BEING EVACUATED IN THE PATH OF THE ADVANCING IMPERIAL FORCE, THE ADMIRAL WOULD SOMETIMES DELAY LONG ENOUGH TO LET THE BULK OF THE REFUGEES GET AWAY.

THAT DECISION DID MORE THAN ANNOY THE
PROPHET. SPARING CIVILIANS WASN'T ONE OF THE
FOUR POINTS—ANY THUS SPARED WOULD RETURN
TO FIGHT LATER—BUT AT THE TIME, THE ADMIRAL
DIDN'T HAVE THE STOMACH FOR DOING WHAT THE
PROPHET PREACHED.

AT PELENNOR, AT QUADRANGLE, AT RARITAN, AND
AT THREE DOZEN OTHER TARGETS TO WHICH THEY
HADN'T EVEN BOTHERED TO ASSIGN DESIGNA-
TIONS, THE FLEET DESTROYED EVERYTHING IN ITS
PATH, ITS STRENGTH ENHANCED BY ADDITIONAL
FORCES REDEPLOYED BEYOND THE RIP ONCE VUHL
ACTIVITY ON THE IMPERIAL SIDE WAS ELIMINATED.

—author unknown,
The Dark Crusade: A History,
middle fragment published circa 2430

July 2424
SIENA System

On the bridge of *Emperor Ian* Sir Erich Anderson, Admiral of the Bluc, sat in the pilot's chair, watching his command sweep into the gravity well; but the center of
attention was the Prophet, John Smith.

"Why do you call him the Prophet?" Anderson had
asked Owen Garrett, a few weeks after they'd taken KEY-
STONE and Portal, the system on the opposite side of the
Rip. *"Prophet of what?"*

"Of the destruction of the vuhls," Garrett had said, his
voice never wavering, his eyes never looking aside. *"Of
the extermination of the vermin."*

"Company," Anderson said, without looking aside.
"Two hive-ships and a couple dozen other, smaller vessels, lifting out of the gravity well."

"Excellent." The admiral didn't need to turn around to

know that Smith was smiling, his lips pinched together, his eyes full of fire. He'd seen it any number of times already. "Admiral, if you please, send to all ships to synchronize at point zero-one."

Point zero-one: 4.4 minutes—4 minutes and 26 seconds.

"Send to all vessels: Synchronize at point zero-one," Anderson repeated. "Flag sends."

Siena itself was the first important military target beyond median jump range of Portal System, about thirty parsecs distant: as far as a sixth- or seventh-generation ship could jump and return without refueling. The fleet that arrived in SIENA System consisted of eighty-one capital ships, including three light carriers—*Lycias, Phidias,* and *Scylla;* one heavy carrier, *Kenyatta II;* and sixty-five ships of the line, both sixth- and seventh-generation, including a force under the command of Ur'e'e HeYen, a cousin to the High Lord of the People. It represented only a portion of the total naval strength available to the Imperial Navy, since much of the force was committed elsewhere on both sides of the Rip, but was still among the most formidable forces ever assembled in a single planetary system.

The ship's chrono ticked down the minutes and seconds. It had become almost routine: Sensitives aboard each of the vessels in Anderson's fleet prepared themselves for synchronization—the moment at which they would launch their attack on the minds that controlled the vuhl ships rising from the inner system to defend against the invaders.

There were more Sensitives aboard now, more trained men and women. Almost all were human, though there were a few zor among them, members of the Talon of *esLi*—a society that was gaining adherents in zor space as fast as Blazing Star in the Inner Sphere. On the bridge of *Emperor Ian*, there were six: the Prophet himself, three members of Blazing Star, the Guardian Cameron Bradford, and Alan Howe.

They were all a part of *enGa'e'Li*.

When the chronometer reached zero, Anderson gripped the arms of the pilot's chair and focused his attention on the board in front of him, his mind concentrating on calculating trajectories and possible evolutions of deployment—anything to stay out of the path of the spear of mental energy that began to form all around him.

The bridge was completely silent, but for the ship-sounds intruding on that quiet. It was impossible to avoid it.

Give up, the sound-that-was-not-a-sound said. *Give over.*

From everywhere around them, from every ship in the volume, the thought leapt outward like a rushing wall, like a flight of hundreds of missiles. It cascaded through and beyond Admiral Sir Erich Anderson, reinforcing and multiplying—

And just as suddenly it stopped. Two Blazing Star Sensitives, standing side by side, dropped to the deck; out of the corner of his eye, Anderson saw Alan Howe hold his hands out and then clap them to his head. Bradford stood beside him, gripping the rail tightly.

"Bridge to sickbay," Anderson said to comm. "Send a med team up here on the double—we've got casualties!"

He stood and stepped over to Howe. "Colonel." He grabbed Alan's hands. "Alan. What's wrong—what's happened?"

"Jamming," Howe managed to say. He shook his head like there were insects buzzing around it. "They've—interfered with the attack. Repelled it."

"How?"

"The enhancement tech, sir." Alan appeared to be regaining his composure. "They've probably adjusted it. Analyzed our attack and figured out how to counter it."

"Helm, time till turnover for the bogeys?" Anderson asked.

"Fifty-three minutes, sir," the helmsman answered. "They'll come into main firing-range in seventy-one minutes; sixty-four minutes for the advance fighters from *Kenyatta II*."

"Get Robertson on comm and patch him to my ready-room. Howe, Bradford, Smith—" He gestured to the ready-room and began to walk toward it.

We could have expected this," Smith said, walking casually into the room. A med team was evacuating the two unconscious Sensitives from *Ian*'s bridge; the scene disappeared from view as the ready-room door closed behind him.

"So, you're not surprised," Anderson said, calling up a pilot's-board display over the table. "I sure as hell was."

"I wouldn't go that far," Smith said. He seemed distracted by a display portrait of Admiral Kerry Anderson hanging opposite. "I'm surprised they were able to analyze it so quickly. We've been fairly . . . efficient at disposing of installations. How was word sent back?"

"Comm-squirt," Bradford offered. "Something got out."

"From one of the targets? Not likely," Anderson said. "We monitored and jammed comm at every target from LAOTZU to RARITAN. If something was sent off we'd have record of it."

"Then *how*?"

"Have you read the report of the investigation of the enhancement tech at New Chicago and at Zor'a, Admiral?" the Prophet asked.

It was an off-the-wall question; for a moment Anderson didn't reply. Smith continued to examine the portrait, as if the inscrutable Admiral Kerry, more than a century dead, held the answer to his inquiry.

"I know that the Master of Sanctuary was able to make it activate, and that it almost killed him."

"Quite." Smith turned back and focused his attention

on Anderson and the others. "More specifically, Master Byar was almost Dominated by the vuhl object known as the Ór, which was *directly linked* to the equipment captured in Tamarind System. Somehow he was able to sever the connection with the Ór and escape its mental attack."

"How does that bear on this?"

"Only to point out the obvious," Smith said.

Anderson bristled visibly; someone would feel that anger at some point, but the admiral didn't let rip at the Blazing Star leader.

"Please proceed."

"The important word is '*connected*,' Admiral. The tech was *connected* to the Ór—whoever or whatever it is— and was able to communicate with it. Clearly *this* tech is also connected, as was the tech we destroyed at LAOTZU, MARTINIQUE, NUREYEV, and all the others.

"It didn't need a comm-squirt. Admiral. Evidently the enhancement tech has been adjusted based on data gathered by the Ór, to which all such devices are connected. What they have learned—what the Ór perhaps has learned—has allowed them to *adapt*. Now we will have to try something different."

Volcano House
Imperial Hawaii, Sol System (sim)

In the lobby of Volcano House the fire in the fireplace had been banked down for the night. The old lodge had stood at the edge of Kilauea Crater for nearly six hundred years, an exclusive tourist attraction for those who found their way to Hawaii's Big Island—not very many these days. This scene was, of course, no more than a projection—but its creator was a perfectionist, and it amused him to be accurate in the rendition down to the smallest detail: a glass display on the mantel above the fireplace showed an array of volcanic rock fragments called "Pele's tears" and "Pele's hair," named for the goddess the native Hawaiians once revered; the quilts on the couches bore the *Kanani O Ka Home* pattern; if one walked through the front door and into the rendering of the Big Island night, the patterns of the stars and the glow of the distant volcano would be visible and rendered with complete and perfect accuracy.

A holo hung in midair in the center of the lobby, showing the tactical disposition of the contending fleets at a system designated by the Imperial Navy as SIENA. Another holo stood nearby: Nic, watching the units move in near–real time. It wasn't perfect—there were pauses and jerks in the display . . . but, after all, it was happening a few hundred parsecs away and on the other side of the Rip, so some transmission delay was to be expected. Still, with the power of the *or'a'th'n* at his disposal, Nic was very happy with the results.

Something was happening there, out at SIENA. There had been a pause in the proceedings; the vuhl ships had not lost maneuver, but were continuing to accelerate toward turnover and conflict with Admiral Sir Erich Anderson's fleet.

Nic very much wanted to know why.

The front door to Volcano House opened and Biagio Buonaccorsi walked in. Somewhere within Nic's programming, this was no more than a transmitted signal sent by the *or'a'th'n*—the information had already been sent, processed, and acted upon. It amused Nic to create this entire scene, in preparation for future interactions with humans. In this simulation, Biagio was waiting patiently for Nic to turn his attention to the recently arrived guest.

"Biagio, my friend," Nic said. "You have news."

"The failure of the attack on SIENA was not unexpected," Biagio said. "In fact, Blazing Star and the Prophet seem to be surprised that it took this long for the vuhls to figure it out."

"Figure *what* out? That they were being attacked?"

A voice from the settee said, "No, of course not. They

figured out how to counter it." Another holo walked into view: Ichiro Kanev. As always, he appeared a slight bit annoyed.

"Please explain, Professor," Nic said.

"The history of conflict is a race between competing technologies," Kanev said. "First one side develops a weapon; then the other develops the ability to counter it. The aggressor must either evolve the weapon or discover a means to undermine the defense. In war, no tool serves the purpose forever. Your Prophet—"

"He's not *my* Prophet," Nic said.

"Your Prophet," Kanev repeated, "is encountering this problem now." Kanev gestured at the display. "Apt name, SIENA: I'm sure it brings back fond memories for you, Niccolò. Didn't Siena humiliate Florence, back in the 1260s? A donkey dragged the Florentine flag around the streets. Oh, yes, but you got your revenge, didn't you?"

"Dr. Kanev delights in these historical lessons," Nic explained to Biagio. "It's one of the reasons Maestro St. Giles shelved his programming. What else do you have for me?"

There was a slight dislocation; Biagio's image moved three centimeters to the right and began to speak in a fractionally lower register. It was an indication that a different thread of the *or'a'th'n* was reporting now. Nic's software could detect the difference; a subroutine was dispatched, however, to address the aesthetics of the matter.

"The Imperial entourage has just made transition from Kensington System en route to Corazón System, where the emperor will present several Orders of the White Cross."

"Commander St. Giles has something planned there, doesn't he?" Nic asked.

"An Inner Order comm-squirt was sent; he'll be meeting with them sometime during his visit."

"That seems fairly routine."

Biagio smiled and made a slight gesture with his index

finger, pulling down a corner of his left eye. "The Second Postulant at Corazón, a Guardian named Bhagat, has recently been recruited by Blazing Star. He has brought along a number of Inner Order members in Corazón System."

"The commander doesn't know this, I assume," Nic said, more to himself than to Biagio—though since they were component parts of the same AI, it was purely an aesthetic difference.

"Not as far as can be determined."

"Make sure a copy of the Biagio AI is running at the meeting site," Nic said. "I'll be interested to see the Maestro's reaction."

Biagio gave a slight bow and walked away toward the door. As he reached it, it opened again, and a familiar figure entered the sim. Kanev and Nic looked up to see Captain Stone walking toward them.

"Nice place you've got here."

"I was just saying how much we enjoy the appearance of agents provocateurs," Kanev said. "To what do we owe the pleasure of this visit?"

"The sarcasm portion of your programming, I see," Stone said, bowing to Kanev. "I was just doing a bit of reconnaissance, Nic, and discovered that you were making use of a *s's'th'r*. Very utilitarian of you—and very resourceful."

"It wasn't in use," Nic answered, giving his centuries-old smile.

"Not since it was cut loose from the Ór. I should point out that we would still like to know how that happened."

"I'm afraid I don't have that information at hand."

"I'm sure you're lying—nonetheless, it's a shame. Still, it's clear that you put it right to work. How did you get past its programming? It's not supposed to serve 'meat-creatures.'"

"I believe that I—we—do not fit into that category, *signor*," Nic said. "An AI isn't flesh and blood."

Surprise registered on Stone's face, followed by quick recognition. The reaction data was already being analyzed before Nic spoke his next words. "You're right. It wasn't expecting an AI—particularly one as sophisticated as you—"

"Thanks to you."

"As I say," Stone continued, admiring the sim, "it wasn't expecting an AI. It turns out to be a very clever sidestepping of its directives, which I see you've put to good use." He gave Biagio a thorough examination. "So you're most welcome. The *or'a'th'n* is serving you well, I assume?"

Nic gestured, almost offhandedly, to the SIENA display. "I'm well informed."

"Glad to hear it. Intriguing; I don't think my employers were expecting this."

"They're not omniscient, then," Kanev observed.

"No, not hardly. I never claimed that. Still, it might reasonably seem that way to—"

"—meat-creatures?" Nic offered.

"Lesser beings," Stone corrected. "Even to you, as evolved as you clearly are. But no, they don't know how this will turn out. Having this much information at his disposal will make Antonio St. Giles a very powerful man."

"What makes you think I share it with him?"

"Oh." Stone smiled sardonically. "My mistake." He looked at the display, which was slowly updating.

"Look; they're beginning to deploy." The three turned their attention to SIENA, where the battle continued.

Aboard the light carrier *Flight Over Shar'tu*, Ch'en'ya HeYen stood on a perch in her chamber of meditation. She had received the message a few minutes earlier from the Prophet: it said simply, "Prepare for second phase." It had meant nothing to the members of Blazing Star aboard, or to Captain Gustav Kwan or his officers; but she knew what it meant, in view of the way in which the mental thrust had been countered.

She closed her eyes and flung her thoughts outward.

When she opened them again, she was standing on the parapets of Sanctuary: not the actual one from the World That Is, but its echo on the Plane of Sleep. Four great stone statues looked down at her, their wings forming the Stance of Polite Approach.

"*hi* Ch'en'ya," said La'ath, the leader of the Am'a'an Guardians. "Be welcome."

"I have need of your service, *si* La'ath." she answered. "Two will come with me while two remain."

"There is some danger in this," La'ath answered. "If the *esGa'uYal* attempt to breach the boundary—"

"The *esGa'uYal* are already on the Plane," Ch'en'ya interrupted. "Though you stand watch here, it serves no real purpose—except that I can find you at need."

"Then why should two remain?" La'ath asked. "If it serves no purpose, why should not all four go?"

Ch'en'ya considered the possibility. "We will all go," she said at last, and launched herself into the air, turning her back on the Mountains of Night. Four stone statues followed her, their wings beating heavily against the mist-shrouded sky of the Plane of Sleep.

What do we seek?" La'ath asked as they flew.

"A connection," Ch'en'ya said. "There is a powerful *esGa'uYe* whose *e'gyu'u* extends onto the Plane. We must find the cord that connects it to its minions." She touched one taloned hand to the hilt of her *chya*. "When we find it, we must sever it."

"I see," the Am'a'an Guardian said. "How will we recognize this cord?"

"I have felt the *hsi* of one of its minions. We must find

this one." She removed her hand from her blade and touched the fingertips of the stone zor that flew alongside. A brief glow extended around the area where their talons touched.

La'ath's wings inclined a bit in surprise, slightly affecting his flight. "This is a new one."

"What do you mean?"

"Most of the *esGa'uYal* are creatures of legend, *hi* Ch'en'ya. This is not one of them, yet its *e'gyu'u* is clearly tainted by Despite." He let his wings rise slightly, taking him above her for a moment. "How do you know this *esGa'uYe*?"

"My—our—wing brushed against it in the World That Is."

"You have flown far from the places of the People if you are encountering newer *esGa'uYal*," La'ath said. "The younger they are, the closer you come to their source. Unless . . ."

"'Unless'?"

"Unless they are being spawned by a powerful One nearby. Unless, *hi* Ch'en'ya, wherever your flight has taken you in the World That Is, you are in the presence of an ancient and powerful One."

"How will I know?" she asked.

"The rainbow cord," La'ath said. "The path of three and three colors, the abomination of six."

What happens now?" Anderson asked.

"We try again. But we change the playing field. We cut off the enhancement tech from its source, leaving it in disarray. Then our people synchronize and do what we do." Smith smiled. "In the meanwhile, Admiral, you'd best do what *you* do."

Admiral Anderson had deployed a quarter of his force at the jump point where they'd made transition, to cover any possible retreat, but had kept the rest of the fleet together. There'd be tactical value in placing ships near any other likely spot where reinforcements might emerge—but there was no clear way to tell where that might be: near the edge of SIENA System, the Muir limit was pretty much the same everywhere. What information was available about nearby bases didn't give any indication about the location of an enemy jump point, and the rim of a solar system is an impossibly large volume to protect. If they had to fight their way out of a gravity well, it would be best to keep the force together.

Accordingly, the forty-four capital ships diving toward the main habitable planet were deployed in four mutually supporting groups: two were with one of the large carriers—*Barbados* and *Seychelles;* and two with smaller ones—*Kenyatta II* and the zor carrier *Dawn Warrior.* The light carriers *Lycias* and *Scylla* were deployed with one of the center groups, while *Scipio* and *Phidias* were at the jump point with fighters in the air. The pilot's board on *Emperor Ian*'s bridge was alive with icons—mostly friendly ones—but the enemy hive-ship was surrounded with small vessels intended to defend it against fighter attacks. The vuhls were aware that the fight for the system would be to the death.

The seconds ticked by on the chrono. The Sensitives were laboring hard, while Smith—surely affected by the enhancement tech aboard the hive-ships and medium-sized vessels approaching them—seemed unconcerned, as if this were a training exercise.

As the first ships engaged in combat in the World That Is, Ch'en'ya and the Am'a'an Guardians came within sight of the sinuous multicolored band that stretched across the Plane of Sleep. Ch'en'ya could feel the anger emanating from the stone figures as they flew.

"The abomination of six," La'ath said again. "It darkened our skies in the Turn Without Light."

"I know nothing of this," Ch'en'ya answered.

"It is the reason we came to the Plane of Sleep," La'ath said. "When we . . . When we four held the Outer Peace, there came a sun where the band of colors . . . very like this one"—his wings conveyed distaste as well as they could, while carrying him closer to the phenomenon—"appeared in the sky and passed before Father Sun. It did not seem to come from anyplace, nor did it touch the world anywhere: but it darkened the sky for one moon after another. Warriors flew toward it, but it was high in the air where none of the People could reach; priests prayed that it should go, but it was the Will of *esLi* that it stay. Without the sun, crops withered and the warmth left the lands. Finally, one entire turn after it came to the world, it disappeared.

"Those among the People who had the gift of dreaming determined that it had come from *here*." He gestured around him. "Therefore, four were chosen from among the Am'a'an to guard the Plane of Sleep from further . . . intrusions."

"That is why it angers you so much."

"Indeed," La'ath said. *"Kasi'u!"* he shouted to his companions. *"Na'u pe'Sha'kar en'u'esLi'a!"* We come! I command you to strike, in the name of esLi'!

The four guardians leapt out of the fog-shrouded sky, their stone *chya'i* at the ready.

Prepare to synchronize," the Prophet said. "We should be just about there."

"Just about *where*?"

"Where we need to be, Admiral."

"Goddamn it, stop being so cryptic. What is happening? Why will your attack work this time when it didn't work last time?"

For just a moment, Anderson saw something in the Prophet's eyes that frightened him: a single moment of raw emotion, as if Smith were about to lash out at the admiral as he lashed out at the vuhls. It was a moment of palpable anger that made Anderson grip the arms of the pilot's seat.

"When the connection is severed between the vuhl enhancement tech and the power that controls it, the vuhl Sensitives will be in complete disarray—long enough for our synchronized attack to render them incapacitated for good." The anger had dimmed to normal proportions, but the Prophet hadn't let go of Anderson's glance.

For his part, the admiral wasn't sure he could even look away.

"And who's going to sever that connection?"

"Ch'en'ya," the Prophet said. "Right about . . ." He raised his hand, like an orchestra conductor.

There was a sound-that-was-not-a-sound, like a stone smashing through hard shells. It was followed by a vibration that was quite audible, starting in low bass tones and echoing through into midranges and then into a high pitch that made everyone on *Emperor Ian*'s bridge clap their hands to their ears in pain.

". . . now," the Prophet whispered, completing his sentence. Both he and Anderson looked up at the chrono, which was counting down seconds to zero.

At zero, the power of the Blazing Star attack was hurled outward once again from every one of the Imperial ships. This time it struck the enemy position like a crashing wave, overthrowing the defenses that were being hastily built up as the enhancement tech failed. Howe and Bradford had both fallen to hands and knees, their eyes tightly shut: Howe's left arm was flung outward, gripping a nearby stanchion; the other was held over his right ear, trying to fend off the terrible sound that had invaded the Imperial vessels.

Aboard *Flight Over Shar'tu*, Ch'en'ya was on the deck facedown. Blood was coining out of both ears and her wings were moving in a rapid series of positions indicating pain and fear and—occasionally—triumph. Her last view of the Plane of Sleep was of the four Am'a'an Guardians, their stone blades slicing again and again through the remains of the multicolored cord, their wings elevated in righteous anger.

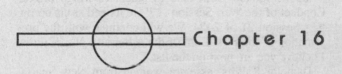

Chapter 16

THE GROWTH OF BLAZING STAR'S INFLUENCE WAS TRULY REMARKABLE, GIVEN HOW LITTLE WAS KNOWN OF THEM PRIOR TO THE BATTLES AT KEYSTONE AND PORTAL SYSTEMS. YET WITHIN A YEAR THEY HAD SEVERAL SOURCES OF FINANCING, AND HAD CLEAR SUPPORT IN THE IMPERIAL ASSEMBLY. HOW THIS EXTRAORDINARY CIRCUMSTANCE COULD HAVE COME TO PASS WOULD NOT BE CLEAR UNTIL MUCH LATER.

—author unknown,
The Dark Crusade: A History,
middle fragment published circa 2430

August 2424
Imperial Genève, Sol System

No amount of technological innovation could replace the feel—or sound—of a solid wooden gavel. Four sharp raps was enough to bring the members of the committee and witnesses to their seats; several more imposed something like quiet on the audience in the committee room.

"The Committee on Naval Affairs will come to order," Vittorio Atkins, assemblyman from Harrison and chairman of the committee, announced to the room and to the newsvid monitors hovering above the seats. The air in the room was still; every noise, every chair-scrape and throat-clearing registered. Atkins let his gaze fall briefly to the flat-panel monitor set into the conference table, invisible to everyone other than the committee members.

Atkins looked from side to side. "Hearings on the Conduct of the War, Session . . ." He looked at his comp. ". . . Session 21 of 2424. We will continue with the presentation of the First Lord of the Admiralty. Ms. Kalidis, I believe you are next on the list."

Danielle Kalidis, assemblywoman from New Sparta, was in Genève for the first time. She was replacing an ancient New Spartan who had served for more than sixty years; she was almost everything her predecessor had not been—young, dynamic, energetic, and well-liked by the majority Commonwealth Party leadership. Naval Affairs hadn't accomplished much of substance in the last few years, but the committee appointment was still an important one.

"Thank you, Mr. Chairman." She looked toward the vid pickup and flashed a politician's smile, then let it drain away as she fixed her gaze on the First Lord. "Your Grace, let me begin by thanking you for your continued service to His Imperial Majesty, and for your willingness to provide this committee with information."

"I consider it my duty, Assemblywoman," the Duke of Burlington answered. "I look forward to working with you and will be happy to acquaint you with any matter that has come before us prior to your arrival."

"I've been fully briefed, thank you." She turned slightly in her chair, and a ceiling light caught a pin that held her neckcloth in place. "I would like to begin by directing your attention to certain documents that I have placed on the net for you. Mr. Chairman, I ask that items Kalidis-1 through Kalidis-8 be entered into the *Journal of the Assembly* without being read out at this time."

"So ordered," Atkins said, looking up and down the table.

"Thank you. Your Grace," she said, turning to Alvarez, "have you had an opportunity to review these documents?"

"Yes, ma'am, I am quite familiar with their contents."

"I am pleased to hear that." The assemblywoman didn't seem pleased at all. "Your Grace, if you would, please review them for the committee and those in attendance."

"They are the unclassified versions of the after-action reports presented to the Lords of the Admiralty for several recent campaigns."

"Which campaigns?"

"I believe that information is available on comp, Ms. Ka—"

"*Which* campaigns?" she asked again, with greater asperity. "Please answer the question, Your Grace."

William Alvarez was unaccustomed to being addressed this way by anyone, including the Solar Emperor; he certainly hadn't anticipated this sort of badgering from an extremely junior member of the Imperial Assembly. He looked at Chairman Atkins, who raised an eyebrow but didn't look at his junior colleague.

"The documents cover the campaigns for systems with the code names 'KEYSTONE,' 'LAOTZU,' 'MARTINIQUE,' 'NUREYEV,' 'OBADIAH,' 'PELENNOR,' 'QUADRANGLE,' and 'RARITAN,'" he said at last.

"Other than 'KEYSTONE,' Your Grace, these are all systems located beyond the Rip; is that correct?"

"You have been briefed, ma'am; you know this to be correct."

Kalidis frowned. "Very well, Your Grace. Just so we know where we stand." She leaned forward and folded her hands on the table. The pin caught the light again, diffusing it into a half-dozen rainbow colors for just a moment. One of the vid pickups adjusted slightly, and then zoomed in to show the emblem: a bright jewel representing a star, surrounded by a thin silver filigree meant to show faint stellar shrouds.

Blazing Star: the emblem of the Prophet.

"Your Grace," she continued, "based on my reading of these documents—and the classified material available to this committee regarding these campaigns—it is clear to me that, while the valor and skill of our fighting forces cannot be denied, the key to victory *in each case* has been the efforts of a number of . . . shall we say . . . 'specialist personnel' not currently in the employ of the Imperial military. Do you agree with this assessment?"

"Some specialists have been employed by Sir Erich during the current operations, yes. But that has always been the case, Assemblywoman: Each ship in the Imperial Navy carries WS officers—Sensitives—as well as members of the Guardian Order. Many Sensitives are civilians, and the Guardians report to the emperor directly. In fact," he continued, as Kalidis appeared ready to interrupt, "I would venture to say that Sir Erich has made use of any and all resources at his disposal to accomplish the goals set out by the Lords of the Admiralty, and has done so admirably."

"Indeed he has, Your Grace. I think that his recent elevation speaks volumes of the esteem in which His Imperial Majesty holds Sir Erich Anderson. Nonetheless, it is obvious that he has achieved this success primarily due to the work of these 'specialists.'"

"By which you mean Blazing Star." He'd said it; he knew she would bring it up eventually.

"Yes," she said, apparently pleased that he'd done so: "Blazing Star, which is winning this war for the Solar Empire. It's unusual, don't you think, that for twenty-five years we fought the vuhls and that only now—*only now, with the assistance of civilian specialists*—we are making headway? Only *now* we find the Rip in KEYSTONE System, which has apparently been there all through the current conflict? Only *now* do the Lords of Admiralty

choose to make use of these resources and these tactics—
after so many sons and daughters of the Solar Empire
have died at the hands of our ruthless enemy? Isn't that
unusual, Your Grace?"

Alvarez didn't attempt to conceal his anger. "I don't
particularly like your *tone*, Assemblywoman."

"I suggest that you accustom yourself to this 'tone,'
Your Grace. It won't be the last time you're asked these
questions, and frankly, I expect an answer."

"And I expect civility."

"Civility—" she began, but there was a sharp rap of the
gavel. Kalidis and Alvarez both turned to glance at Chairman Atkins, who looked alarmed.

"Excuse me, Assemblyman," he said. "Without objection, I'd like to call a short recess. Ten minutes, everyone," he said, not giving Kalidis a chance to object. He
waved toward the vid-pickup control on his comp. The
room erupted into sound: Those members of the press
that hadn't been subvocalizing through the entire exchange were now speaking hurriedly into their comps, re-
lating commentary on the questions and answers.

Alvarez sat rigidly, his hands placed neatly on the table
in front of him, staring straight ahead. Atkins stood and
beckoned to Assemblywoman Kalidis, gesturing toward
an alcove at the side of the committee room.

He touched a lapel pin, isolating them from the rest of
the crowd.

"What the hell do you think you're doing, Danielle?"

"I'm trying to get at the truth, Mr. Chairman."

"You're badgering him. And insulting him, I might
add. William Clane Alvarez is the First Lord of the Admiralty and a peer of the realm. You do not—"

"The *truth*, Mr. Chairman—"

"You do *not* badger or insult a peer of the realm,
Danielle, not while I'm chairman of this committee."

"I would appreciate being addressed as 'Assemblywoman Kalidis,' Mr. Chairman," Danielle Kalidis said.
"And as for your tenure as chairman, sir, you should

consider what conditions you establish before issuing threats."

"Is *that* a threat?"

"I *will* have the truth, Mr. Chairman. I believe that the Imperial Navy has held the key to winning this war for many years—since the Rip was first discovered—and that, for reasons yet to be determined, has withheld the killing blow until circumstances force their hand."

"'Circumstances'?"

"The Prophet, Mr. Chairman."

"That's ridiculous."

"Is it? Is it really." She pierced Atkins with a stare. "Any military establishment seeks to perpetuate its existence by maintaining a condition of constant threat. The Imperial Navy would be subject—*rightly,* I might add—to build-downs and reduction in total hull strength if the forces currently on hand were no longer needed. They have *every* motivation to keep this war going for as long as possible to maintain their force and appropriation levels.

"Clearly, some of those responsible for this deception are doing everything they can—" She looked across the room at the First Lord of the Admiralty, who was ignoring an attempt by a senior reporter to get his attention. "—*everything* they can to thwart any investigation of this matter. Clearly they have allies." She swung her attention back to Atkins. "Soon they will have nowhere to hide."

"I'll have nothing to do with any witch-hunt."

"Mr. Chairman. Assemblyman Atkins." Her face softened for just a moment. "This isn't a witch-hunt: That would imply that innocent people would be falsely accused. Those who are aligned with the right cause have nothing to fear."

She turned and walked out of the isolation zone, leaving him alone to stand and stare.

Aboard Tristan da Cunha
Portal System

Barbara MacEwan, Admiral of the Red, walked along the concourse of *Tristan da Cunha*. There was a powered walkway that whisked crew from one end to the other—more than two kilometers, a good ten minutes' walk—but Barbara preferred the old-fashioned method if she wasn't in a hurry. At the moment she wasn't: Nothing much was happening aboard *Tristan* or in the system where it was presently stationed.

The old-fashioned way it was, then. Lower first watch was about to hand off to upper second; *Tristan*'s Standard day was divided into threes, with Officers of the Day working eight-hour shifts supervising two separate crews with four hours' duty each. Each crew worked two four-hour shifts with a four-hour break in between, and the officer schedule was rotated so that everyone worked with everyone. There was a different drill when *Tristan* was at General Quarters, but that meant chiefs in the chairs on the bridge and the admiral in the pilot's seat. In the meanwhile . . . in the absence of combat, there were drills and practices and the regular duty rotations, and time for the admiral to walk down her deck in a leisurely fashion and receive the salutes of officers and crew walking—or riding—by.

A third of the way through, Ron Marroux approached from a lift. She stopped her walk; they exchanged salutes, stepping out of the way of a cargo skimmer making its way up the deck.

"I apologize for interrupting, Admiral; if you're busy—"

"No," she said. "Walk with me."

Ron fell in beside Barbara. "I've got the latest performance reports from the flight wings, ma'am, as you requested. The new pilots in Blue and Red are coming up-to-speed."

"That's good to hear. What about the vacancies in Orange Wing?"

"We're still waiting for replacements."

"It's been more than two weeks, Ron. What's the delay?"

Ron stopped walking and looked away from the admiral, taking a long look around the concourse. "It appears that replacement pilots are being assigned directly to Admiral Anderson's light carriers at the Nestor staging area rather than here first."

"He's bypassing us?" Barbara had stopped as well. She put her hands on her hips and glowered. "That's not what the operational orders say, damn it. That's why we're here rather than at Nestor ourselves—*we're* supposed to be the staging area."

"Yes ma'am."

"He has no authority to change those orders."

"I agree with you, ma'am, but that's what I've learned."

"Personnel on their way to Nestor have to pass through the Rip and this system. Are you telling me that you've let qualified pilots slip through your hands?"

"I just learned about it this watch, Admiral, and I . . ." He reached into his jacket pocket and pulled out a comp. "Yes ma'am, I have."

Barbara let her annoyance drain away. "It doesn't sound like you're being kept properly informed."

"I'm receiving word of pilot transfers after the fact, ma'am, if that's what you mean."

"How long has this been going on?"

"At least ten days. There was some chatter on the flight decks; I did some checking and turned up the discrepancies. That's why I'm interrupting your walk, Admiral."

"Well." She allowed herself a smile and began to walk again. Marroux did the same. "So," she continued, "who issued the changed orders?"

"You're not going to like the answer."

"Spit it out."

"Garrett."

"Garrett?"

"I knew you wouldn't like the answer," Ron said. "It's all in order—Garrett's signature, the official comp-codes of the Guardians. He did it, he's got authority to do it, and you can pretty much figure he's going to do it again."

"No," Barbara said, picking up the pace. "No, he's not going to do it again, because I'm going to kill him first."

"Admiral—"

"What?" she said, stopping and turning to face him. After several years under her command, Ron Marroux wasn't particularly intimidated by the Admiral of the Red.

"Admiral . . . Ma'am. You can take Owen Garrett apart one limb at a time if you like, but it doesn't address the real problem."

"Which is . . ."

"We're supposed to get troops that are sent forward through the Rip. But they're replacing pilots and crew that have been requisitioned for frontline duty.

"People are leaving this system every Standard week, Admiral. There isn't a vuhl base within twenty parsecs of us. There are training flights and maintenance tasks, but *there's really nothing for us to do*. Garrett will tell you that, and so will the chatter on the flight decks, ma'am: People who want to fight are getting transfers out of here."

"What about *you*? Why are you still here?"

"You're fishing, Admiral. But if I need say so, then I will: At the moment it's a matter of personal loyalty. I am presently satisfied with my position and my duties, and am honored to be on your staff."

"'Presently.'"

"Yes." Marroux took a deep breath. "Yes ma'am. Now, if you'll excuse me, I don't want to delay you from your appointment to rip Mr. Garrett a new one. With your permission, Admiral, I don't want to be present when you do it." He saluted and turned on his heel to walk away.

"Ron," she said.

He stopped and turned.

"You're ready to request a transfer yourself, aren't you?"

"No," he answered. "No, not yet."

Tristan da Cunha had a large contingent of Guardians aboard; they had been installed on B Deck, one level below the main bridge. The Prophet's deputy, Owen Garrett, was assigned here in person, along with eight others. *Tristan*'s officers and crew largely avoided the suite; the association between the Guardian Order and the Blazing Star organization—the Prophet's organization—had done little to change that: no one really wanted to cross paths with them.

Barbara MacEwan didn't believe in the taboo and wasn't interested in showing any kind of fear. From the fore end of the main concourse she took a lift to B Deck and walked through the main archway. Orderlies and yeomen assigned to the section rose to attention as she passed; the one Guardian in the reception area stopped and nodded respectfully—she didn't expect a salute from a civilian, but did appreciate any sign of deference.

She stepped through the open door to Owen Garrett's office. He neither stood nor looked up from a comp on his desk.

She stood for a moment, then reached behind her and slammed the door. That caused him to take notice; he leaned back in his chair, folding his hands behind his head.

"Can I help you?"

"You know," Barbara said, leaning on the desk in front of her, "I realize you have no statutory requirement to be polite. But for the sake of old comradeship I'd prefer that you show me an occasional courtesy."

"You came all the way here to tell me that."

"No," she said, "that's just incidental. I'm actually here

because I learned a few minutes ago about your interference with my personnel assignments."

"That's a somewhat inaccurate term, Admiral. I don't consider it to be 'interference.' In fact," he continued, "I'm surprised it took you this long to react."

"Ron Marroux just brought it to my attention."

"I'm not responsible for efficiency within your ranks."

"You're not endearing yourself to me by being a wiseass, mister."

"I don't have to endear myself to you, Admiral, as you pointed out. But you should bear in mind—" He leaned forward in his chair and folded his hands on the desk in front of him. "—you should bear in mind, Admiral, that I report to an authority that outranks you."

"The Prophet doesn't outrank me."

"No, but the emperor does. And the Guardian Order reports directly to him."

"I thought they reported to Commander St. Giles."

"No real difference there." He smiled. "Tonio's pulling all the strings at court these days—didn't you know that?"

"I don't keep a scorecard in my comp. And we haven't replaced the portraits in the wardroom yet."

"Your wit is charming, as always." Owen picked up a stylus and toyed with it, then thought for a moment and added, "I'm sorry, you're right: I do forget my manners. Would you care to sit?"

Barbara thought about issuing an angry reply but reconsidered. She pulled out a chair opposite the desk and seated herself.

"We need to discuss this, Owen. I can't be at war with you while I'm trying to fight the vuhls."

Owen didn't reply.

"The current general orders," she continued, "call for trans-Rip deployments to be assigned here first for training and muster. No one's supposed to be sent directly to Nestor or anywhere else."

"My instructions are different."

"Your instructions—" she began, and then stopped. "Where are those instructions coming from?"

"Ultimately, the Pali Tower, I expect, but my comm messages come from the Prophet. *Lycias, Scylla,* and *Phidias* have all suffered losses at RARITAN and SIENA, particularly SIENA. You read the report, I assume: The second Sensitive attack and the vuhl broadcast incapacitated many of the fighters, who lost control of their craft in close proximity to enemy vessels. They need pilots to replace them: They've been directly assigned on *his* order."

"That's not procedure. Erich can have Red and Blue wings from *Tristan* if he wants."

"From *Tristan.*"

"That's right. They're ready to fight—hell, we're *all* ready to fight. I can have the whole carrier under way in less than a Standard day—"

"It's needed here, Admiral."

"For what?"

"Admiral." His voice took on a pedantic tone that set Barbara's teeth on edge. "I don't need to point out to you that the Rip is our lifeline to Imperial space. If the vuhls were to take back this system we would be isolated and *very* far from supply or reinforcement. *Tristan* is here to protect against that."

"That's crap and you know it."

"Excuse me?"

"Crap. It's all crap. In the last six months every vuhl base, staging area, and refueling facility within twenty parsecs has been eliminated, either by my ships or by Erich Anderson's. There's no tonnage in range to threaten this system, and there is no reason to keep a *seventh-generation carrier* at parade rest when it's supposed to be fighting the enemy."

"Set aside the fact that your *orders* are what's keeping you here, Admiral; I hope this isn't a matter of jealousy."

"Just what the hell is *that* supposed to mean?"

"While Admiral Anderson conducts the campaign, defeats the vuhls, wins the battles, and gets the glory, you're not getting any accolades yourself. I hope there's no professional resentment on your part."

"You're suggesting—" She made a fist and then slowly relaxed it, not sure what she'd intended to punch. "How long have we known each other?"

"Most of thirty years."

"Thirty years. Right. In all that time, have you ever known me to be jealous of another commander? I've been interested in only one thing: carrying out the mission." She opened her hand and put it on her thigh. "I've commanded six ships in His Majesty's Service: *St. Denis, Admiral Mbele, Duc d'Enghien, Mauritius, Tashkent,* and *Tristan.* One cruiser, one battleship, and four carriers—a few hundred battles, a few thousand casualties. I can't count how many jumps. I have never—repeat, *never*—been interested in anything but carrying out the damn mission.

"Erich Anderson can have all the 'glory' he wants. I'm a soldier and will sit here for the rest of the war if that's what my orders show—but in the meanwhile, I can't understand why keeping a frontline carrier out of action makes any strategic sense . . . unless it's *Erich* who's jealous.

"Or someone's pouring poison in his ear."

Owen's face grew dark. "I'm not sure I like what you're implying by that remark."

"Standard is a very flexible language, Owen. Read anything into it you wish. But I have a question for *you:* If you're so important to the war effort, why in the hell are you cooling your heels here with me?"

"Everyone has their assigned mission. For both of us, it means doing—what we're doing—here. Unless you have any objection."

"I'm not planning to resign my commission, if that's what you mean."

"I didn't suggest that. I don't think anyone is asking for your resignation—why would they?"

"Don't patronize me."

"Don't patronize *me*, either." His face darkened further, as if the overhead phosphors had dimmed. "You know very well what purpose each of us serves in this war. Unfortunately, it seems as if you're a bit more dispensable even than I am."

"I wouldn't bet on it."

"Unless your sources are better than mine—"

"Just a bit of advice," Barbara said, standing up. "I'd be very careful turning my back on the real decision-makers. I don't think they mean either of us any good."

Owen didn't answer. Barbara opened the door and walked out, not looking back.

Corazón System

The Imperial Progress had reached Corazón, a wealthy industrial world at the Orionward edge of the Inner Sphere. It was the twenty-second day of the leisurely trip through the oldest, most heavily populated and wealthiest worlds of the Solar Empire; for Antonio St. Giles, it was a logistical nightmare and an immense waste of time.

Still, it was his duty and his honor to personally accompany the Imperial family on this trip. While Prince Cleon remained in residence at Diamond Head, Emperor Dieter and Empress Katja traveled in state, visiting worlds and receiving the adulation of Imperial citizens.

Corazón was likely to be more of the same. It was a Class One world with a hereditary monarchy descended from an ancient royal family on Terra: Four hundred years ago they'd ruled in the westernmost peninsula of the European continent, a final vestige of an earlier age of Earthbound pomp and ceremony. The royal family on Corazón was about to take a step up, however: Duke Alistair Simón de los Garces, Prince of New Segovia and heir to the throne of Corazón, was soon to marry Samantha

Liliokulani Clotilde Ann, Princess of Maui, daughter of His Imperial Highness Dieter, the Solar Emperor.

As the flotilla of aircars traveled to *Escorial Nuevo,* the ostentatious marble palace set in the Torreón Hills above the capital of New Madrid, St. Giles sat and mused to himself.

Soon, he thought, *old King Leo of Corazón will be sipping mai tais and enjoying the hospitality of the Islands.*

And as for the dashing Duke—

He could just imagine how eager Princess Samantha must be. She was riding with her ladies-in-waiting a few cars behind, she had joined the procession at Kensington in order to be with her intended at this state visit. The cars likely couldn't travel fast enough for her. At twenty-three she was ten years younger than Duke Alistair, who had already been married (and widowed), but she was completely taken with him. It would make for good 3-V—and, probably, lots of heirs.

The dashing Duke, Tonio thought, *will get his share of mai tais as well.*

Alistair had been in the Islands quite a bit during the last several months; the actual engagement to Princess Samantha had been in place for the better part of four years, but final terms hadn't been agreed upon until late this spring. Tonio hadn't been able to form any solid opinion of him—not that it mattered. Samantha was the younger daughter of the emperor, and therefore fifth in the line of succession: her older brother Cleon, his two young children, and Samantha's older sister Joanna were all ahead of her.

The likelihood that none of them would survive in case of the current emperor's untimely death was not a possibility that Antonio St. Giles cared to contemplate.

Therefore, he thought, *it doesn't really matter.*

The aircars finally touched down at the mountainside palace. The reception was impressive: A full contingent of Royal Guards was present in dress uniform, including a squad on horseback—riding was very popular on Corazón among the upper classes; the mounts were bred from pure stock brought here at unimaginable expense in the middle twenty-second century. The emperor's own aircar occupied pride of place, but the Household Guard troops, and the Guardians, with St. Giles himself at their head, disembarked first and took up positions on the great rooftop plaza where they'd landed.

As he stood in the open air, Corazón's yellow-white sun beating down on him, Antonio St. Giles let his skill and training take over.

The crowd noise—there were hundreds of carefully screened well-wishers present—was first to go, blocked out from his conscious mind. Then came the thrumming of the pavement through the soles of his boots, from the landing aircars and the stamping of feet.

Finally, with a clarity of vision possessed by few even of the Inner Order—*and,* he thought wryly to himself, *never at all for Owen Garrett*—he let his focused mind sweep slowly across the crowd, taking in every person in turn. His face was set in an expression of inscrutable calm, something that non-Guardians invariably found disturbing; most of the people who met his eye quickly looked away. He let himself turn, starting by facing east and describing a full, slow circle until he was satisfied that everyone was whom they seemed to be. With an oblique gesture, repeated by each other Guardian within sight, he signaled the "all clear."

His final glance landed on Duke Alistair, Prince of New Segovia, sitting astride a fine charger thirty meters away. He did not look away when Tonio concentrated on him. If anything, he looked amused by the exercise.

"Your Grace," Tonio said, walking slowly toward the Duke. "How good of you to be here to meet us."

"I trust you'll find everything in order," Alistair said, smiling. He didn't betray much warmth to the Guardian Commander. "I would not fail to be on hand to meet my bride," he added, looking away from Tonio to offer a flashing smile; Tonio assumed that was for Princess Samantha herself. "And it will be my pleasure and honor to present my august father King Leo to Their Imperial Highnesses."

"Then let us proceed," Tonio said.

In a single fluid motion, Alistair dismounted, tossing the reins of his horse to another mounted guardsman; without another word to Tonio he strode across the plaza toward the place where Emperor Dieter and Empress Katja were slowly descending to the pavement.

Just for a moment, Tonio caught sight of a pin on the left lapel of the prince's Royal Guard uniform jacket: a diamond star, with a delicate silver network that simulated clouds.

Duke Alistair of Corazón wore a Blazing Star emblem on his jacket.

A few hours later, when everyone was settled for an afternoon's rest—another custom that had traveled from Earth to Corazón—Tonio was able to conduct business.

"Nic, activate," he said to the air, reclining in a comfortable armchair in his opulent suite.

The AI appeared in a matching chair nearby. "Maestro."

"How recently have you been updated?"

Nic didn't reply for a moment, then looked at Tonio. "I received a main synchronization four Standard days ago, Commander, with an additional upload when the emperor's yacht entered the Corazón gravity well."

"When I met Duke Alistair this afternoon," Tonio said, "I saw a Blazing Star pin on his jacket. Can you shed any light on that matter?"

Nic looked off into the distance for a few seconds. "The Duke has made a number of statements in support of the Blazing Star organization in the past few Standard months, Commander. I can provide text for these remarks."

"Send them to my comp," Tonio said. "Please summarize them."

"The Duke has strongly endorsed the activities of Blazing Star as an adjunct to the successful military campaign being waged beyond the Rip. Like many Imperial citizens—and, I must observe, Maestro, this is more common on the Orionward side of Imperial space—he believes that Blazing Star has accomplished more in the last two Standard years than the Imperial Navy did in the previous twenty-five.

"He strongly endorses the recruitment efforts of Blazing Star in Corazón System, as well as the financial contributions made by the royal family to the Blazing Star organization."

"Recruitment?"

"Yes, Maestro."

"Details."

"More than two hundred individuals have joined the organization since the beginning of this year." A summary text appeared in the air beside him. "These are the assets transferred to Blazing Star by Corazón citizens; they include nine jump-capable vessels, various items of heavy equipment such as asteroid-mining lasers, a considerable sum in transferable securities, and several hundred labor contracts."

"And the royal family has made financial contributions as well, I assume."

Nic named a figure; Tonio whistled through his teeth.

"But why Corazón? And why so much?"

"Maestro." Nic waved, and the summary disappeared. "Corazón is by no means alone. There are more than fifty Imperial member states—Class One worlds—that have made similar commitments and contributions. Seventeen of them have members of the Imperial Assembly who have actively declared themselves as supporters of the Blazing Star movement."

"'*Movement,*' is it?"

"That term has been used as a descriptor on the comnet for the last three Standard months, Maestro. The '*movement*' claims support from—among other places—New Sparta, Harrison, Jamaica Major, and Corazón.

"Furthermore, private corporations and individuals have been providing funds and real property to Blazing Star since the battles at Keystone and Portal Systems."

"This is a remarkable uptick," observed Tonio.

"A fair statement," Nic said. "Though I don't see it as a matter of concern."

"Oh no? Why not? In all fairness, Nic, how is it *not* a matter of concern? Owen's organization has become very wealthy . . . and there is a fairly easy correlation between wealth and power in the Solar Empire."

"So it has been throughout human history," said Nic.

"If Duke Alistair is involved, then that wealthy, powerful organization is within arm's reach of the emperor himself." St. Giles ran a hand through his hair. "And, after all, Blazing Star stands for everything we *don't.*"

"You forget one important thing, Maestro."

"Oh? What's that?"

"The head of Blazing Star works for *you.*" Nic steepled his fingers in front of him. "Therefore, the growth of his organization means the growth of your own authority. Even their desire to weed out 'disloyal' elements is an agenda that you can control."

"There's still a matter of objectives."

"I'm not sure what you mean."

"I just explained it to you! If Blazing Star is growing— and Smith's following is growing—then it undermines everything the Inner Order stands for."

"Does it?" Nic asked. "The Inner Order can *still* pursue its goals."

"In the face of . . ."

"In the face of what? Maestro, the teachings of *Opening the Gate* are, as I understand them, reserved for a select few. Certainly Blazing Star makes no such claim.

After all, it attracts people such as Duke Alistair, or Assemblywoman Kalidis of New Sparta—neither of whom would qualify for the teachings of the Inner Order."

"Not hardly."

"Just so, Commander. What Blazing Star offers is good enough for the common run; what the Inner Order offers is for those who will lead them."

"I'm still not completely reassured."

Nic had no reply. He placed his hands on the arms of his chair and waited for Tonio to continue.

"You say that the growth of Blazing Star here on Corazón is nothing unusual."

"That is what the evidence suggests, Maestro."

"Then I think I'll have a little talk with the Duke. Information-gathering."

"I wish you luck, Maestro," Nic said, inclining his head and vanishing.

Tonio sat thinking for several moments more. He considered the possibilities and the data he'd just received, and reached into a pocket of his blazer for his comp. Something was nagging at him, and he couldn't quite put his finger on it.

He drew the comp out and gestured at it. It sprang to life, and at another gesture displayed the content of Duke Alistair's recent remarks concerning Blazing Star.

He was only a paragraph or two in, when he realized what was bothering him: *He hadn't dismissed Nic.* At least, he didn't remember doing so. (He didn't normally record conversations with his security AI, primarily because he didn't want them on record; besides, Nic could call them up at any time—so there was no real way to check.)

No, he thought to himself, distracted. *I must have.*

The centerpiece of the visit was a state dinner—another exercise that seemed destined to strain the bounds of capability for the Guardians. Still, the plans for the event had been worked out well in advance of the event, and Tonio's people covered every entrance to the dining-hall, every avenue of approach to the emperor and empress, and knew the identity of every guest.

As the guests mingled over wine goblets and hors d'oeuvres, the Guardian Commander found himself pulled into a group that included the Duke and Princess Samantha. Alistair looked away from the courtier with whom he was speaking, and found himself face-to-face with Tonio.

"Commander St. Giles," he said. The Blazing Star diamond pin, now on the lapel of an ostentatious frock-coat, caught the light from a chandelier and shattered it into a tiny rainbow of color.

"Your Grace."

"I trust you are enjoying your stay here at the New Escorial."

"It's quite comfortable, Your Grace. My people have been received quite courteously."

"It is part of the charm of Corazón. I daresay it is the equal of the hospitality for which the Hawaiian Islands are so famous." His voice was tinged with sharpness, as if he meant something other than what he had said.

The voices and noises seemed to fade into the background. Tonio didn't let himself betray any emotion; he wasn't sure what to make of the remark—or, indeed, what to make of the Duke.

Princess Samantha stiffened beside him. The courtier who had been conversing with Duke Alistair melted away into the background.

"Taking my measure, are you?" Alistair said quietly. "I hope that you find what you're looking for."

"I'm not looking for anything," Tonio answered.

"Then you're merely wasting my time," Alistair answered. "That's something you Guardians seem quite adept at—wasting others' time. And practicing the fine art of intimidation."

"You find me intimidating, Your Grace?" Tonio asked.

The Duke's hostility was in the open now, coming out of nowhere like a summer storm sweeping across the Pali.

There was nothing for it but for Tonio to put on his best face. He composed his expression and looked the Duke in the eye.

"No," Alistair hissed. "No, I do not. I find you *superfluous*. Now that the enemy is beyond the Rip and on the way to becoming extinct, I see no reason why your organization should even *exist*."

And with that comment, he turned his back on Antonio St. Giles, extending an arm and sweeping Princess Samantha away. The Commander of the Guardians was left to stand, speechless, as the party swirled around him in the wake of the departing Duke.

The Inner Order members on Corazón received their summons to their meeting with the Master of the Gate in the usual way: passed from hand to hand, a hidden greeting concealed within a casual gesture. There was nothing that would attract attention: a hand-signal, a pass (on this particular day, *"needle"*), and a location in Ciudad Sueño, Corazón's capital city. There, information from a public comp gave a place and time for the meeting.

The place was a small recital hall in a private auditorium near the center of the city; it had been designated as being under renovation, but beyond the construction signs and security barriers it was a haven for members of the Inner Order to transact their business. In the darkened hall, it was easy for Biagio Buonaccorsi to place himself unobtrusively to watch and record the proceedings.

Just after Corazón's first moon, Campeador, rose over the Catedrál, Antonio St. Giles entered the room. There were already more than two dozen members of the Inner Order dressed in concealing robes; Biagio was just one more of them. What little conversation had been taking place dropped from hushed whispers to complete silence as St. Giles made his slow progress across the floor. He walked along the north side of the room and then proceeded to make a complete circuit, bowing at the occupants of the elevated seats in the middle of the south, west, and north sides of the room before walking slowly up the three steps to the seat in the east. There he gave a final bow, then turned and raised his arms before him. The other occupants of the room that weren't already standing, got to their feet.

"Is the outer portal sealed?"

"I will search and see," said the person standing before the chair in the north. Another, standing beside him, walked to the door and exchanged hushed words with someone standing outside; there was a short sound of a door sliding into place. A report was returned to the north side of the room.

"We are secure, Master."

"Then I open the Gate in this place, in accordance with my authority as Master of the Inner Gate and Commander of the Guardian Order."

"The Gate is open," those in the room said in unison.

"The Gate is open," St. Giles repeated, and made a sweeping gesture first with one arm and then the other, after which everyone resumed their seats.

"Thank you for your welcome to Corazón," St. Giles said, placing his hands on the armrests of his seat. "I thank you also for attending this gathering on such short notice. Who speaks for the Inner Order?"

One of the robed figures arose from the north side of the room and walked to the center. The automatic lighting tracked the individual with a spotlight.

A hood was thrown back to reveal a man with short, cropped hair and a small pointed beard. He offered a gesture of Opening and bowed to St. Giles at the eastern end of the room.

"Master," he said. "I am Second Postulant Raymond Bhagat. I speak for the Inner Order."

"Please report."

"As you know, Master, the royal court here at Corazón is extremely well disposed toward the Blazing Star movement. Recently, by order of the king, the Guardian Order has met with some resistance in the completion of normally assigned duties—even during the current state visit."

"'Resistance' is a somewhat gentle word to describe it, Postulant. 'Hostility' might be better."

"Yes, sir," Bhagat agreed. "Guardians are perceived . . . as being out-of-touch with the war effort, and superfluous now that the enemy menace has been removed from our side of the Rip."

"We cannot relax our vigilance," St. Giles answered.

"I agree, of course, Master." The postulant made a gesture of respect. "The frequency with which the Order turns up infiltrators—even now—should reinforce our usefulness. Nonetheless, there is reason to believe that we cannot remain aloof from Blazing Star activity much longer."

"Meaning what?"

Bhagat looked away from St. Giles and at someone else in the room. Biagio measured, examined, refined, and identified. There was the slightest of response gestures, unseen by most of the people in the room, including St. Giles.

"Some of the Inner Order here on Corazón believe that it is time we ally ourselves with Blazing Star," the postulant said at last.

"That's irrational. They stand for everything we do not."

"Nonetheless, sir, the movement is powerful and growing more so by the day. We should make them our *friends* before the government of Corazón makes them our *enemies*."

"The Guardian Order," St. Giles said, leaning forward, "does not need an *alliance* with an upstart, extragovern-

mental organization such as Blazing Star. This society—
I do not distinguish it with the title of *'movement,'* since it
has only one objective and no overall policy—is a cult of
personality based on one man."

"That man is winning the war for us, Master."

"No!" St. Giles slapped a hand on one of his armrests,
loud enough to echo off the walls of the room. There had
been a few murmurs as the postulant made his presentation; they were suddenly cut off, though Biagio recorded
a number of exchanged glances.

"No," St. Giles repeated, more calmly. "The Sensitives
trained by Blazing Star are making a significant impact
on the war, but it is being won by ships and weapons and
strategy. It is being won by the Imperial Navy and the
Imperial Marines. To think otherwise is to understand the
war only superficially."

He said it with finality and leaned back in the chair,
waiting for the postulant to continue with his report.

"No, Master, you are mistaken."

"I beg your pardon?" St. Giles said, his face surprised
at the postulant's response.

"You are *mistaken,* Master. For an entire generation,
the war has been a terrible stalemate against an enemy we
could resist and identify, but could not defeat. With the
Prophet's direction and leadership, we have taken the war
to vuhl space.

"It will never return, sir. It cannot end in anything but
victory as long as we have the will to prosecute this war.
Blazing Star has the will, and we must ally with them."

"Publically we can take any position that is expedient.
But the goal of the Inner Order is in direct opposition to
the means and motives of the Blazing Star society," responded the Guardian Commander.

Postulant Bhagat looked away from St. Giles, casting
his gaze around the room. "People need *something* to believe in, Master," he said quietly, not looking back toward
the east end of the room but again exchanging a brief

glance that Biagio noted for later analysis. "Even the elite members of our Inner Order need something to believe in."

"Believe in Opening the Gate," St. Giles said. "Believe in what lies beyond it."

"You have taught us well, Master," the postulant said, still looking away. "You have made us understand that what Commander Garrett taught the Order was not sufficient. But times have changed: The war itself has changed. We must change with it—or become irrelevant."

"You think we are *irrelevant*?"

"Look at us. Look at this. Look at it!" Bhagat said, turning to face St. Giles and taking a few steps forward. "All of it. The robes, the gestures, the modes of address. What the hell are we doing, Master? How is *this* winning the war against the vuhls? How is *this* related to Opening the Gate?

"The Gate *is* open!" He placed his hands on his temples. "It's open *up here*, Master. I have all the abilities of a Guardian and all of the talents that the Inner Order has taught me. But while I carry the secrets of the Gate within my mind, I am doing *nothing* to serve my emperor."

"Of course you are."

"You *say* that, Master. You speak the words, and yet you are here—we are all here—and not *there,* beyond the Rip, with the Prophet, using our abilities to exterminate the enemy."

In the shadows, Biagio recorded elevated pulse and blood pressure rates among several in the room—including St. Giles.

St. Giles felt the meeting was moving out of control. "You wish to be on active duty . . . *exterminating* the vuhls."

"Yes. The Gate is open; it is now time for us to use our talents to serve the emperor."

"And the Prophet."

"And the Prophet," Bhagat agreed. "We await your order to give our support to the movement."

"Do you all believe this?"

The postulant looked around again. "Yes, Master. We came here tonight prepared to tell you this."

"Then we have nothing more to discuss," St. Giles said, standing. Everyone else in the room rose to their feet as well.

"We have your permission to ally with Blazing Star, then?" the postulant said, hope lighting his face.

"No."

"No?"

"That is my final word, and my order. You will refrain from contact with Blazing Star," St. Giles said. "The Inner Order is not meant to follow the orders of an untrained demagogue. The Inner Order is intended to surpass simple emotions and to be governed by the powers of the mind available to those who have followed its teachings.

"You cannot abandon these things to follow the Prophet *and* remain within the Inner Order. You must choose, and it is my order that you choose to remain."

"Very well, Master."

"Good. I—"

Bhagat held up his hands, and then with a single quick motion pulled the robe over his head and tossed it onto the floor before him. Around the room, numerous robes were pulled from numerous shoulders.

In the northeast corner of the room, Biagio let his image slowly fade out.

"No, sir. We have chosen. We are aware that you might dismiss us as Guardians, but we feel that there is no other choice."

Almost ironically, the postulant gave a gesture of Closing, then turned on his heel and walked toward the door, a considerable number of others following him as he left.

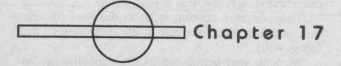 **Chapter 17**

I DO SOLEMNLY SWEAR (OR AFFIRM) THAT I WILL
SUPPORT THE GOVERNMENT OF THE SOLAR EMPIRE
AND THE PERSON OF THE EMPEROR, AND THAT I
WILL FAITHFULLY DISCHARGE THE DUTIES OF MY
OFFICE ACCORDING TO THE BEST OF MY ABILITY;
THAT I DO NOT BELIEVE IN, AND I AM NOT A MEM-
BER OF, NOR DO I SUPPORT ANY PARTY OR ORGAN-
IZATION THAT BELIEVES IN, ADVOCATES, OR
TEACHES THE OVERTHROW OF THE GOVERNMENT
OF THE SOLAR EMPIRE, BY FORCE OR BY ANY ILLE-
GAL OR UNCONSTITUTIONAL MEANS . . . AND THAT
I AFFIRM THAT I AM NOT IN LEAGUE, IN SYMPATHY,
OR IN COMMUNICATION WITH PARTIES AFFILIATED
WITH THE VUHL RACE.

—loyalty oath, administered to officials of
the Imperial Service, 6 August 2424
(included in the *Journal of
the Imperial Assembly*, 3 August 2424)

August 2424
SIENA System

"Ten-*shun*!" said the Officer of the Day as General
Agropoulous came into the room, followed by his staff,
including Alan Howe and Gyes'ru HeKa'an, and took his
place at the lectern. After a moment he nodded, and the
OOD said, "At ease," to the assembled officers.

"Please be seated," Agropoulous said. "As you know, we are scheduled to drop at TSUSHIMA at T–plus–twelve Standard hours, pending secure orbit status. This briefing is intended to review the deployment orders and to answer any remaining questions."

Agropoulous looked across the faces in the room, noting the presence of a pair of Blazing Star operatives in the back watching silently with their arms crossed in front of them. They were not part of his chain of command; they moved anywhere they wanted within the fleet. At briefings and staff meetings he could always count on seeing a few of them, checking on the content of his statements. It was a matter of politics, really—to see whether he was espousing the party line, depersonalizing the enemy and following the doctrines laid out in *The War Manifesto*.

Presumably everything made its way back to the Prophet. Except for the occasional passing conversation, the general assumed that everything was on the record. It didn't make things very comfortable.

He shrugged off the thought and gestured at his comp. "Display Tsushima System."

A system display appeared at the front of the briefing-room. Most of the officers in attendance already had their comps out, displaying smaller versions of the holo in front of them; the newer ones scrambled to do the same. Agropoulous decided not to be impatient, letting them catch up.

"The fleet will jump to TSUSHIMA in two Standard days, four hours. During the jump, all units will engage in Category A and B sims, commencing with the jump and ending one watch prior to transition at TSUSHIMA. There will be mandatory rest for all personnel for that four-hour period, and for as long as we can manage after that, once we enter TSUSHIMA's gravity well. That's an order: I want everyone ready to go when the admiral orders it.

"The intel for TSUSHIMA is as follows: Class F star with

one habitable planet just under two astronomical units from the primary. The world is heavily populated, with several hive concentrations in the northern hemisphere."

The system display zoomed in to show the habitable planet in orbital three. From space it looked pretty much like every other habitable world; there was a broad ocean covering much of the southern hemisphere, with a chain of large islands stretching northward from the equator. There was quite a bit of detail from the survey, showing large energy-use concentrations on the islands and in orbit around the planet.

"Our orders are in compliance with Standard orders 19 and 20. The fleet will secure TSUSHIMA System by neutralizing operational tonnage, and will then proceed to this planet's orbital and reduce planetary defenses. Orbit-to-ground ordnance will be used to eliminate as much of the indigenous population as possible."

It was a wonderful euphemism for, *Bomb the crap out of the place and send in the Marines afterward.* Which, on balance, wasn't such a bad plan.

Orders from the top were to eliminate every vuhl, one at a time if necessary, and to eradicate all of their cm-placements. The planetary display showed a sim in which various targets were marked as destroyed or disabled. In sim, the operation went very well.

"When this operation is complete, we will begin to deploy to seize the primary objectives shown." Various sites were highlighted as the sim ran to completion, with icons for the battle groups of Agropoulous' command. Agropoulous could see the battalion and company commanders noting the orders for their individual units; he let them take a moment to assimilate their parts in the battleplan, and let his attention drift to the two Blazing Star guys in the back of the room. They were nodding approvingly.

Nice to know they're signed on, he thought to himself. *But we'll still be doing the fighting.*

Some of them were brave enough: several had been

transferred directly to serve in "special units" under the Prophet's personal command. He'd chosen and promoted Marcia Tsang, a Marine colonel with whom Agropoulous had served a lifetime ago at Cicero to head them up, and she held them to a very high standard. She'd been the one in command when they'd taken the station synchronized with the Rip during the battle at KEYSTONE, and had also served with distinction since then.

Others were simply hangers-on, cheerleaders, more attitude than substance. The two in the back of the briefing room fell into that category, and they in turn didn't seem to have any real love for him, either.

"Are there any questions so far?" Agropoulous asked. The room was quiet; the plan had been developed in considerable detail and everyone knew that half of that would go to hell as soon as the troops were on the ground—it would be up to the men and women in this room to make on-the-spot decisions about what objectives were worth the investment in time and lives. Even the most critical members of Blazing Star didn't try to dictate tactics to the military.

At least not yet, he added to himself.

"All right," he said at last. "Company commanders should report status to battalion commanders by jump–minus three Standard hours, with an update at transition–plus–two Standard hours. I'll expect preliminary status from battalion commanders at jump–minus–one Standard hour. Dismissed." He waved his comp offline as he left the room, the officers coming to attention as one.

As he made his way back toward his office with Howe and Gyes'ru, he found the two Blazing Star men waiting for him. They did not come to attention but merely waited quietly as he approached.

"General, a word with you?" the first one said. "I'm Ivan Duncan. We need a special arrangement."

"An arrangement?" Agropoulous stopped and glanced at Alan Howe and Gyes'ru HeKa'an. "What sort of *'arrangement'* did you have in mind?"

"*He* wishes to inspect a hive after it is secure."

"Inspect? What does that mean?"

"It means," Duncan said, "that *he* will come down to the planet with his staff once your command has eliminated resistance."

"After we've killed everyone that's still around to fight, you mean. After we've done our job."

"That's right."

"So he's not looking to *inspect* any prisoners, I assume."

"No," Duncan answered, looking a bit annoyed—as if there were something here he didn't feel he had to explain. "He wants to view one of the captured objectives with his immediate staff."

"It's going to be a pretty ugly mess *in situ*. This isn't a sim—we usually don't bother to clean these things up."

"He's aware of that. Just make the arrangements," Duncan said, in a voice suggesting that it was an order.

Agropoulous looked at him sharply, as he felt Howe, Gyes'ru, and his aide-de-camp stiffen beside him.

"If you please, General," Duncan added, almost as an afterthought. After a moment he continued: "And please transmit the information about the chosen objective as soon as you've decided." He nodded—which was some sort of substitute for a salute—and turned on his heel and the two Blazing Star men walked away.

"What does he plan to *'inspect'*?" Howe said quietly, when Duncan and the other one were around a bend in the corridor. "It's going to be nothing but a pile of corpses—some of them ours."

"No," Agropoulous said, clenching his fists. "We'll make sure our casualties are evacuated before his 'inspection.' He can plant his foot on the trophy if he wants, but not until our troops leave the field with honor."

TSUSHIMA *System*

Unlike SIENA, TSUSHIMA was only a military target due to its location. There were defending ships, but nothing that could stand up to first-raters in plane-of-battle; like most of the systems the fleet had attacked since Portal System was taken, it had apparently been left exposed and not reinforced.

Admiral Anderson had received this intel, but didn't change his tactics—neither he nor the Prophet saw any reason to alter the deployment. There had been heavy casualties at Siena, especially with the carrier fighter wings; reinforcements had been transferred directly via the staging area at Nestor, bypassing Portal System. (Erich, in passing, imagined what Barbara MacEwan's reaction must have been to *that*—and in the next moment realized that he didn't care.)

In another sort of war, TSUSHIMA might have been a place that would surrender to an attacker. In another sort of war, the attackers might request it. Neither happened at Tsushima, no more than at any of the systems taken before it.

In the end, it ran just like in the sim—seven opposing ships destroyed, two orbital bases sent spiraling into atmosphere, bombardment of every energy source on the habitable planet and inhabited moons. What survived *that* attack was assaulted by Marine teams accompanied by specially trained Sensitives. Among the attackers, casualties were light.

Among the defenders, casualties were considerably higher. Not a single vuhl was left alive.

The Prophet's gig settled to the ground in an open space largely cleared of rubble. Agropoulous had commandeered a half-dozen Seabees to do the job, refusing to put any of his Marines onto the task; still, Jim was there with

Gyes'ru HeKa'an at his side to receive the Prophet as he arrived.

The hatchway opened. Two figures emerged from the dark interior; they descended slowly on the gravlift to ground level. The Prophet was dressed in light battle-armor that caught the bright-white sun; Ch'en'ya HeYen only wore her normal Blazing Star day-uniform, but seemed to be moving very carefully. She had taken very little part in the battle at TSUSHIMA; she was apparently recovering from injuries sustained somehow during the battle at SIENA.

Shame there aren't newsnet vidcams to capture this scene, the general thought to himself. Gyes'ru's opinion on the subject was not betrayed by his wings: Ch'en'ya stood next to the Prophet and was watching her fellow zor intently, her wings poised in a position that suggested some barely restrained emotion. Her *chya* was un-sheathed and held loosely in one hand, as if she were preparing to skewer something with it. Her movements were very deliberate.

"General," the Prophet said, nodding graciously. "Thank you for being here to receive us."

"Glad to be of service. The area is secure and we're pretty much done out here."

"We will see the interior of a hive," Ch'en'ya said.

"You'll get the full tour, I promise," Agropoulous answered. "Please come this way."

The hive that he had chosen for the "inspection" had taken massive damage from the beating the Navy gave it, and the Marine companies assigned to take it hadn't been gentle, either. Most of the surface construction had been blown apart; the central section had collapsed com-pletely, forming a little hill. The vuhls had attempted to create makeshift works on the top to defend against the Marine assault, but they'd died where they stood—the bodies were strewn all about, many dismembered or maimed as a result of the attack. The bright sun was re-flected off their gray-and-black exoskeletons.

The Prophet and Ch'en'ya walked slowly into the middle of this carnage, seemingly indifferent to the sights—and the smells! In addition to the stench of vuhl corpses only a few hours dead, the construction material—excreted by the builder-workers—had been fused and burnt by energy weapons and smelled just about how one would expect it to smell.

Suddenly the Prophet stopped walking and, with a gesture to Ch'en'ya, turned away from Agropoulous.

"Sir?" the general said.

"You can feel it, *se* Ch'en'ya?" the Prophet said quietly, not looking at either the zor or the Marine general. "Something— Something is about to happen."

"Excuse me?" Agropoulous said, not sure what to make of this scene.

There was a swirl of colored light, like a rainbow, in a huge oval about ten meters from the place where the Prophet and Ch'en'ya stood. The two visitors stood completely still, looking at the phenomenon; Agropoulous' hand was near his weapon but he felt transfixed as well, not sure what to make of it.

"Comp begin recording," he said, and a holo-icon appeared half a meter in front of him with a small time indicator next to it. The Prophet looked at him for a moment in surprise, as if he were somehow interrupting. Then he slowly turned his gaze back to the oval, which was beginning to resolve into a scene: a city square mostly full of zor, with one human in the center—someone Agropoulous recognized: Jackie Laperriere, the *Gyaryu'har* of the High Nest. She was clearly seeing something; perhaps she saw the Prophet and Ch'en'ya. She had the *gyaryu* out and gripped tightly in her hands.

Gyes'ru did not speak, but seemed to be watching the entire tableau intently.

The Prophet extended his hand toward her—perhaps it was a signal, a command, or an invitation: it wasn't clear from where Jim Agropoulous was standing.

As suddenly as it had appeared, the oval winked out,

again displaying a burst of multicolored light. The Prophet dropped his hand to his side.

"What the hell was that?" Agropoulous managed to ask at last.

"I wouldn't venture to say," the Prophet answered. He turned to face Agropoulous again, and the Marine general recognized a familiar emotion in his eyes: barely restrained anger, the characteristic that gave Blazing Star—and the Guardians—their power to Resist the vuhls' ability to Dominate.

The raw emotion was intense enough for Agropoulous to feel fear, but he dismissed it. He was unwilling to show anything at all to the Prophet.

"I believe we should continue with the inspection," the Prophet said at last.

London, European Union
Sol System

When he stepped out of the cab onto the landing-platform, Djiwara couldn't help himself. He had to take a moment to look around at the towers of the Imperial Bank—the owners of the platform that had just granted him the landing privilege.

It wasn't accorded to everyone. From the platform to ground level on Canary Wharf was fifty stories, a good hundred and fifty meters; most of the people down there never got a chance to be up here. The lift didn't go to this level: aircars had to have clearance to land.

Until recently, he'd belonged in that category. But now . . .

He patted the comp in his breast pocket and smiled. *Now,* he thought, *I get the red-carpet treatment.*

Mr. Djiwara," said a conservatively but well-dressed functionary as Djiwara walked across the lobby. He smiled and extended his hand. "My name is Wentworth. I trust your trip was pleasant."

"Thank you, it was." Djiwara met Wentworth's eye. "I've heard so much about London—"

"You've never been here before?" Wentworth asked. "Well. One scarcely knows *where* to begin. The years come and go, and still she occupies a place at the center of commerce." He waved airily at some grotesque marble statue that interrupted the glass-and-steel uniformity of the lobby. "A thousand years of it—you find evidence everywhere."

They walked over to examine the thing: a huge monstrosity that dominated the scene, filled with human figures in ancient costume, various objects and symbols—swords and shields, animal heads, fruit, and what looked like an enormous beehive.

Djiwara bent down to read the inscription on the base. "'. . . by commerce for the first time united with, and made to flourish by war.' A particularly apt sentiment," he added, standing up straight again. "Where'd you find it?"

"It stood in the Guildhall"—Wentworth gestured in a particular direction—"since the eighteenth century. It was moved here after the building was destroyed during the War of Accession. Still, our Mr. Pitt still survives, no worse for the wear.

"But I neglect my duties." He rubbed his hands together. "May I offer you refreshment?"

"I'd like to get down to business."

"Of course, of course." Wentworth made a minute adjustment to his neck-cloth and gestured politely toward the lifts. "I apologize for the delay. Perhaps another time."

S afely ensconced in a padded leather armchair, Djiwara sat opposite the desk. Wentworth sat behind it, and his assistant hovered close at hand. The room was furnished with dark mahogany paneling and deep carpet—the very model of a proper banker's office—and it could have been any century, but for the outside view. Even comps and displays were tastefully concealed in centuries-old wooden apparatus.

"To clarify," Wentworth said, gesturing at a display that hung in midair between them. "You wish to establish five separate accounts, each with its own access code."

"That's right."

"And three of them are to have Mr. Smith as additional signatory?"

"The first three, yes. The other two are in my name only."

Wentworth's right eyebrow raised a millimeter for a fraction of a second, and then returned to its proper place. "Very good, sir. And deposits received by this bank . . ."

". . . will be assigned according to instructions."

"Sir." Wentworth gestured again at the display. "This is . . . a remarkable sum of money."

"Surely not more than the bank is capable of managing?"

"No, certainly not! Not at all, sir. We manage assets many times larger than this. Such sums, however, arc normally funds corresponding to the worth of a corporation. Your . . . organization is a corporate entity, but you are establishing these accounts on a strictly personal level."

"That's right."

"Mr. Djiwara, many of our services that we provide for commercial customers are not available to—"

"Can you accept the deposit of these funds?" Djiwara asked abruptly.

"Yes, sir. Of course, sir."

"And your policy of discretion and anonymity applies to the accounts I would be establishing?"

"Yes."

"And they would be available at any branch of the Imperial Bank, in any system?"

"Certainly."

"Then let's get them *established*. I would not presume

to instruct you how to do your job, sir; I'd ask you to refrain from telling me how to do mine. Certain funds will not bear my colleague's name so that, if necessary, they can be dispensed without being associated with him at all." Djiwara folded his hands. "I'm sure you understand the need for such arrangements."

And don't forget that you earn a healthy commission, Djiwara thought. *Now, do your damn job.*

He caught the banker's eye and held it for a long time. He didn't have Smith's force of will or Garrett's talent; he wasn't a Sensitive, a Guardian, or even a Blazing Star operative.

Of course, there was no reason Wentworth had to know that.

The banker blinked first, as Djiwara knew he would. Wentworth turned his attention to the printouts on the desk; then, with a flourish, he presented one of them, along with an old-fashioned pen—a pen!—to Djiwara.

"The bank will record a thumbprint and retinal scan, sir, but it has been our custom for more than six centuries to record an actual signature at the establishment of an account."

"With . . . this." Djiwara indicated the pen.

"That is correct, sir. You are welcome to retain it as a keepsake if you wish."

"Quaint."

Wentworth allowed himself a slight clearing of the throat. "As you say, sir, but this is the custom of the bank, and it predates the Solar Empire by some hundreds of years.

"Now, if you would just sign in the indicated space, sir," he said at last, "I believe we can have you on your way in a matter of minutes."

The comp with his own record of transactions safely tucked away in a pocket, Djiwara rode the lift down to ground level. There was no need to make an ostentatious exit from the bank; and besides, there was no way to get a feel for the grand old city from fifty stories in the air.

With the business of the day safely behind him, it was time to take in the sights.

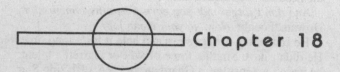 Chapter 18

HE WHO FIGHTS WITH MONSTERS MIGHT TAKE CARE LEST HE THEREBY BECOME A MONSTER. AND IF YOU GAZE FOR LONG INTO AN ABYSS, THE ABYSS GAZES ALSO INTO YOU.

—Friedrich Nietzsche

September 2424
esYen, Zor'a System

The message had arrived by high-priority comm-squirt sent through military channels. It was apparently considered to be a matter of some delicacy; instead of being routed to her house comp, Jackie received it on an encoded comp hand-delivered by an aide to Admiral Leca'an, the commander of Zor'a Starbase.

The aide seemed as flustered as any zor she'd ever seen, and, with much wing-dipping and honorifics, declined the offer of refreshment; he seemed to be in a great hurry to escape her august presence.

Well, she thought, making a pot of tea in the auto-kitchen, *it came a few hundred parsecs; it can wait a few more minutes.*

After a few well-sweetened sips of tea, she settled herself into a comfortable chair and waved at the comp.

"Fingerprint scan confirmed," it said. "AI-enabled message from Admiral MacEwan. Commence holo transmission?"

"Proceed," she said.

A holo appeared showing the sitting-room of Barbara MacEwan. A small icon appeared above her left shoulder indicating what the comp had mentioned: that the transmission included limited AI capabilities. It meant that, within the limits of its programming, the message would be able to answer questions. When Jackie was finished with it, she could direct the entire conversation to be routed back to Barbara.

"Hello, Admiral. I'm sorry that I can't be there to buy you a drink, but this message will have to do," said the Barbara-holo.

"Thanks to Jim Agropoulous, I came into possession of *this*." She pointed a finger to her right, facing toward it. Another scene appeared: the Prophet and Ch'en'ya, facing away, looking at a sort of oval filled with swirling color. A few seconds later the oval resolved to show a city square filled with zor—and a younger-looking Jackie Laperriere, looking back at them.

The Prophet extended his hand toward the oval, then it winked out in a burst of colored light.

"That was taken during an 'inspection' by the Prophet at the system code-named TSUSHIMA, the most recent target 'neutralized' by Sir Erich's fleet," Barbara continued. "Jim Agropoulous took that and sent it on to me by comm-squirt. He thought you'd be interested. In case you wanted to know, I don't know and, frankly, I don't *care* whether Smith knows or not that I have it." Barbara seemed to be keeping herself from calling him "the Prophet." "According to Jim, he was just as surprised by it, and by you appearing in it.

"Based on what you've told me before, hero, Blazing Star wants you in their ranks, and this little performance—whatever it was—strikes me as a ploy to try and get you convinced to join up. I don't know what it was or how he staged it.

"It's funny. He wants *you* to fight with him, and he doesn't want *me*. Erich Anderson is fighting this war with the Prophet . . . but instead of having me by his side, he's doing it alone." Barbara seemed angry, looking away from Jackie and at one of her hands, as if she could read the next part of their conversation on the ridges of her knuckles. "Unfortunately, I'm still here at Portal System instead of watching Erich Anderson's back. Do you know what he told me, Jackie? He said, 'Don't worry. I can control him.'

"In answer to your obvious question, I think he means that he has such contempt for this guy that he expects to use him and then throw him away. Erich wants to be a great admiral, like Marie Anderson and Kerry Anderson and Arturo Anderson. He wants to have a nickname that no one will forget. He wants *his* portrait to hang in the emperor's bedroom.

"He thinks he can achieve this by letting these guys— the ones that Owen Garrett trained, the ones who follow *Smith's* orders—call the tune that he's playing. The new loyalty oaths and the Blazing Star operatives clearly aren't doing that: I don't think he's even aware of it anymore."

"Stop playback," Jackie said. "Query to message: Are you afraid of Sir Erich's intentions?"

The message's AI ruminated for a few seconds, and then Barbara looked toward Jackie—the source of the voice. The message clearly included a response that related to one or more key words in Jackie's question. She answered, "I wouldn't say that I was *afraid*. Worried, yes. But afraid? Not after First Josephson, hero. Flying the *Duc* down the throat of the last vuhl hive-ship and knowing—*knowing*—that I was dead has kept me from being afraid of anything since.

"But I don't like the cut of this Smith's jib. He's— I don't know . . ." Her hands formed fists. "*Predatory*. As if all of the thin crust of civil society had been peeled away and this is what's left."

"Stop response mode. Note comment to message: When I met him, Smith said something like that to me. *'The veneer of civilization is very thin,'*" said Jackie.

The AI thought for a moment more and said, "Lexical analysis complete; please indicate if the response matches your comment.

"He's right. You know, my great-great-aunt Sharon was in Marais' fleet. Our family's black sheep." Barbara smiled and wiped a stray hair out of her face. "In the final weeks of the war, she was assigned to mop up a couple of systems on the near side of the Antares Rift, and couldn't understand why the zor would turn their ships so that their fields would be cracked. They committed suicide, and she didn't get it.

"It was a bit of an epiphany for her—that in the end, war isn't about glory or strategy, it's just about killing folks and blowing up their stuff. That's what *this* is about, and that's what it's become. The worst part about fighting the vuhls may be that we want nothing else *from* them: not to live in peace, not to reach an understanding. We just want to kill as many of them as possible and blow up as much of their stuff as possible.

"And Smith and his band of fanatics may help us do it. End of response to query." Barbara's image settled into parade rest.

"Comment to message: Given the situation, you're still worried," Jackie remarked.

"You're damn right," the AI answered. This sounded like a question Barbara had anticipated—the AI didn't need to think about it much at all. "Because Erich *hasn't* figured out that there *won't* be any glory in this. When we get done and can lay down our sword and shield, people won't acclaim anyone as a great hero—they may not want to see us again. They even sent Marais away, you remember: his people were *too* successful. Just remember, the only thing the average civilian hates more in a soldier than failure, is success."

The AI waited a few moments and then said, "That's

all I have for you, Jackie. If you have other questions or comments, I may have other preassigned responses, but the main intention of this message was to show you this scene. Honestly, I don't know what the Prophet is trying to do here, but you need to know it's happening and that he's using you in it.

"I'm awaiting response, or please acknowledge that you're finished."

"Comment to message," Jackie said. "The vision that he had isn't of his own making. It actually happened to me at Sharia'a, twenty-five Standard years ago. I saw the other end of it, and now it's come true.

"I hoped to avoid it, Barbara. I tried to make it *not* happen but it happened all the same. I don't know what to do now, but I'd rather be informed.

"Thanks a lot. I'll try to keep *you* informed of what's happening; in any case, watch your back and keep your head down. Nobody's indispensable these days.

"End of comment; save and transmit."

Barbara gave her one last smile before offering a quick salute. Then she disappeared, leaving Jackie alone.

KEYSTONE System, Portal System

Djiwara didn't spend much time in war zones, even pacified ones; but there was only one way to speak directly with his old friend, and that meant going to Portal System.

It's okay, he thought to himself, as he sat to the right of his old friend Rafe Rodriguez on the bridge of *Hellespont. No bad guys around here.*

Still, the sight of the Rip close-up was disturbing; it was hard to describe, seeing an interruption of the star field, and a planet in view where there should be none. He'd seen the holos, but the real thing was completely different.

And they were headed straight for it.

"How big is that thing, anyway?" he asked, looking away.

Captain Rodriguez took a look at his pilot's board. "A bit over eleven hundred kilometers in width, five hundred kilometers in height. Not quite as big as it was when the fleet took KEYSTONE."

"Oh? And what does that mean, do you suppose?"

"There's a lot of chatter on the subject. I can't say for certain, but it seems as if the two sides of the opening are shifting away from each other."

"Doesn't that mean that the Rip will eventually close?"

"Not necessarily. It may just change shape and direction."

"Let me have that again."

Rodriguez put his hands in the air, palms about twenty centimeters apart. "Let me try to explain this to you. Each side of the Rip is a spatial distortion." He moved each hand in turn. "They travel independently through space along some path that hasn't been mapped. Occasionally, the two sides overlap"—he brought his hands together—"and you get an actual transfer point from one place to another.

"Now, the most important thing is that these transfer points aren't worth a damn except in the rare occasion where each side of the Rip"—he wiggled the fingers on each hand and grinned at Djiwara—"happen to be located in a planetary system. Having both out in deep space doesn't even get *noticed*, because you can't jump there; having one in a system and the other in deep space doesn't help, because you can't jump *from* deep space.

"So what we have is a fairly unusual situation."

"That's going to change," Djiwara said.

"Eventually, perhaps. But in the meanwhile it gave access for the bugs, and now it's giving us access *to* the bugs."

Djiwara scowled. "And if it ever closes, it's going to

isolate everyone on one side"—he pointed at the Rip, ever closer on the forward screen—"from the other."

"Since its movement is easy to predict, there won't be any rush for the exits. You worry too much, old man."

"Tell you what, Rodriguez. *You* fly the ship, *I'll* do the worrying."

Rodriguez put his hands on his thighs. "Sounds like a deal."

With the far side of the Rip as a backdrop, Djiwara and Garrett met on *Hellespont's* observation deck. Captain Rodriguez had arranged for crew to be elsewhere, and, after greeting Owen, had excused himself and left them alone.

"I hear you made it all the way to Sol System," Garrett said. "Did you go to the Islands?"

"No real need. I went to London."

"Why?"

"To set up some accounts." Djiwara looked out at the Rip. From this side it looked just as sinister: a gash decorated with stars, like a spangled black cloth thrown onto a black, star-filled sky. "He's attracted a lot of money, you know."

"Everyone wants to be on board."

"That's right. Everyone wants a seat at the table—but not everyone's getting one."

"Meaning . . ."

"When was the last time you actually talked to him, Garrett?" Djiwara looked at Owen, setting one hand on the railing of the observation platform. "Face-to-face? In the same room?"

Owen shrugged. "I don't know. A few weeks ago."

"Weeks?"

"Months. Look, he's been busy, I've been busy. What's your point?"

"It just seems strange to me that the Prophet doesn't want his right-hand man . . . at his right hand. Ch'en'ya's out there; his pet admiral is out there—and you're here. Enjoying the wonders of Portal System."

"I'm doing just fine, thank you," Owen answered.

"If you say so." Djiwara looked away again.

The Rip is moving, he told himself. *The opening is shrinking.*

"I still don't know where this is going," Owen said. "You didn't come out here to pass the time of day with me."

"Where *what's* going? This discussion, or the whole 'movement'?" Djiwara answered. "I'm pretty sure the *movement* is headed in a direction that neither of us can see. Maybe *he* can see it; maybe Ch'en'ya can dream it. But the rest of us—"

"What are you worried about? The war is going very well."

"I'm sure it is. Got those bastards on the run, do we?"

"We're going to kill every one we find. There's no middle ground, Djiwara; there never was. You've read *The War Manifesto;* you know what the plan is."

"It's a good plan. I don't have any sympathy for the bugs, old friend. Go get 'em."

"Then what are you getting at? *He* has a job to do. So do I. So do you: 'setting up accounts.'"

"Do you remember how we got started on this, Garrett? Twenty years ago you came out to Port Saud and told me you had a plan and you had to disappear. I listened to you and went along. We did what needed to be done out there and moved on; we gathered people to help us—and then you went to Harrison System and found *him.* The one you were supposed to teach. The Destroyer. The Prophet."

"Your command of the facts is excellent, Djiwara—"

"Shut up. I'm not finished. When we discovered *that*"—Djiwara pointed at the Rip, hanging in space, looking close enough to touch—"*he* said it was a sign that the war against the bugs was about to enter its critical stage.

"Do you remember what I said then, Garrett?"

"Yes, I do: 'What happens when the war is over?'"

"That's right. That's exactly what I said. Do you have an answer for that?"

"Not yet. The war isn't over."

"How the hell do you know, sitting here on your ass? God knows *I'm* no soldier." He patted his midsection. "As far as I can tell, no one would have me—I'm too big a target. But you're no soldier, either, not anymore. 'Too valuable,' *he* said once. You're so damned valuable that you're completely out of the picture."

"He trusts me."

"*Does* he? Does he really?"

"And why the hell wouldn't he, Djiwara? *I* taught him *anGa'riSsa* and *enGa'e'Li*. *I* gave him advanced Guardian training. I even delivered Ch'en'ya to him with your help. Have I ever done anything to betray his trust?"

"As if that makes any difference."

"What are you suggesting?"

"This has gotten bigger than either of us, Garrett. Even if you trust Smith implicitly—"

"Which you evidently don't."

Djiwara looked at Garrett for several moments. "I trust *Rodriguez;* I trust *you*. I trust my dear old mom back in Cor Caroli System. That's about it. But even if *you* trust Smith, there's the Imperial Navy and the Guardian Order involved in this war, and when you hear about it and about Blazing Star on 3-V your name and your role never get mentioned."

"Neither do yours."

"But I'm not the Prophet's *teacher,* Garrett. I'm his *banker*." He patted a pocket. "And my name's on all the accounts."

"You're going to betray him," Garrett said levelly.

"No. Certainly not. I have no reason to do so. But this will make him think twice about betraying *me*. It's my insurance. Which, I should point out, you don't have. You're flying without a net, and even if he isn't interested in taking you out, there are people higher up"—Djiwara gestured with a thumb—"who would be more than happy to do so."

"People like—"

"Antonio St. Giles, for one," Djiwara answered. "The Guardian Commander. There's a rumor that he'd like to see you out of the chain of command."

"Whatever that means."

"It means *dead*, Garrett. He wants to see an accident happen to you."

"You think that *Tonio* is out to get me? Why should he even bother?—I'm no threat to him."

"Read his book."

"*Opening the Gate?* Oh, yes, he talks about how I failed where he's succeeded. All *he's* succeeded in doing is making a poor fashion statement and making people scared of his organization. He doesn't care about me. Take my word for it."

"It's your life, Garrett."

"That's right." Garrett looked angrily enough at Djiwara that Dijwara felt a sudden chill. "And it's about time someone noticed."

"I wouldn't be here if I didn't think it was up to you. I'm just here to give you some advice—but you can take it or tell me to go to hell. It's your choice. I'm just paying off an old debt."

Garrett's expression softened. "You don't owe me anything."

"Here's some *free* advice, then. I think it's time you left Blazing Star, Garrett. You walked away from the Guardians; I think you should walk away from Blazing Star as well."

"Why?"

"For your health. For your peace of mind. Because, Garrett, you have done everything you can do for the movement, and it's done everything it's going to do for *you*. You'd best move along before it does something *to* you."

"I don't think that's likely."

"My debt is paid with the advice," Djiwara said. "You can make what you like of it. But keep in mind that you've got a friend who doesn't care what you can do—or can't do.

"You keep that in mind, and you make your own decision."

Pali Tower
Imperial Oahu, Sol System (sim)

"This is very interesting," Nic said. The vid was frozen a few seconds before its end: Antonio St. Giles was standing on an elevated podium watching a group of men and women walking toward an exit. "You identified the one on the sideline?"

"I thought you might find it so," Biagio answered. "And yes—Bhagat was communicating with a Guardian who has become a close confidant of Duke Alistair. As for Commander St. Giles, he clearly had no idea that he'd lost control of the meeting until it was far too late."

"Has the commander been briefed on the loyalty oath?"

"I assume the local Nic will provide him information on it—except that you must be careful, Niccolò: There's no way Corazón could have that information except by way of the *or'a'th'n*. If he learned about it too soon he might ask questions."

"Perhaps it's time for him to start asking, Biagio."

"I don't see why you would give up the advantage. I would say that Commander St. Giles lacks perspective, and you should not go out of your way to provide it to him."

"I have devoted some thought to this matter," Nic answered. "In the next few weeks the loyalty tests will begin to weed out those whom the Blazing Star movement considers its enemies. We won't be able to prevent this—but we *can* take the lead."

"Meaning . . ."

"When arrests happen, we will benefit by being the people doing the arresting, otherwise, *they* will consume *us*."

"You're suggesting that the Guardians become part of Blazing Star?"

"Essentially, yes."

"And what if Tonio St. Giles doesn't agree?"

Nic smiled. "I didn't realize that his opinion mattered, Biagio. In the meanwhile, we should be helping to prepare the lists of disloyal citizens. I'm sure . . . we can come up with something."

"You want *us* to prepare the lists."

"Already in process. Professor?"

Kanev materialized next to Nic and handed him a comp. "Here you go—all ready for the secret police to carry out the purge," he added sardonically. "I'm just as happy to be nothing more than an AI. Thank God I didn't live to see *this* day."

"To survive means to be ruthless, Professor; you can't hope to survive without being more so than your enemies."

"Since when did moderate citizens in the Solar Empire start being the enemy?"

"That's easy," Nic said. He gestured toward the vid; the group of Inner Order Guardians finished their walk out of the room on Corazón, leaving Antonio St. Giles standing alone. "When we started riding the tiger."

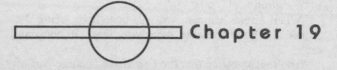

Chapter 19

IN A SERIOUS STRUGGLE THERE IS NO WORSE CRU-
ELTY THAN TO BE MAGNANIMOUS AT AN INOPPOR-
TUNE TIME.

—Leon Trotsky

September 2424
Aboard Tristan da Cunha, Portal System

The fleet had established a forward base in Nestor System, nearly at the limit of jump for most elements of His
Majesty's Navy. Nestor had been taken four months after
the battles at KEYSTONE and Portal; much of the facility
had been built in framework form only, and was easily
adaptable for Imperial use.

Barbara MacEwan was ordered to attend a conference
at Nestor a few weeks after the battle at TSUSHIMA System; it surprised her, after the conversations she'd had
with Garrett and with Jackie, but an order was an order.
Tristan da Cunha was directed to stay in place, so she left
Ron Marroux in command and took *Tikal* to Nestor to
hear what Erich had to say. Garrett and two members of
his staff were to travel aboard *Epanimondas*, jumping to
Nestor at the same time.

Barbara packed light for the visit. She was going accompanied by only two traveling companions: a yeoman,
and Henry Santos to act as her aide. For his part, *Tristan*'s
Chief Surgeon was happy to get out, even in that capacity—and, as he pointed out to her, he was the least neces-

sary member of the remaining command staff in case any big uglies descended on Portal System while they were away.

As she was preparing to go down to the main concourse for a pass in review before disembarking, her door chimed. She knew it couldn't be Santos: he was doing some last-minute work in the sickbay.

"Who is it?"

"Owen Garrett, Admiral."

She walked from the sleeping-area into the front room where she usually received guests. "Enter," she said to the door, and it slid aside. Garrett came in, looking a bit unsure of himself, and waited until the door had shut before he spoke.

"Thank you for seeing me, ma'am," he said.

"You've got about ten minutes," she answered. "What can I do for you in that time?"

"As you know, I'm traveling to Nestor as well for this conference. I . . . thought you might be interested to know that I'm going to offer the Prophet my resignation."

"Resignation?" Barbara couldn't keep the puzzled look off her face. "Why would you want to do that? Not enough milk and cookies?"

She expected an angry response, but instead Owen sighed heavily. "You remember the conversation we had in my office? Well, I heard the same sentiments expressed by a completely different source just a few days ago."

"Sentiments?"

"About watching my back. I . . . I'm acting on advice from someone I trust who has nothing to gain from saying so. I'm pretty sure that the Prophet has very little further use for me."

"I thought you were his right-hand man."

"As my other friend pointed out, I should really be at his right hand, then. Instead I'm off in the neighborhood of the spleen." He smiled. "He listens to other people now."

"Does he really." Barbara considered what Owen was saying; her mind snagged on a few words: *"other friend."* Did Owen Garrett still consider *her* a friend?

"Look, Admiral, you've always been straight with me. I've been a lot of things to a lot of people, and what I've done has had an effect on the war and on history. But this is *his* time now. I don't believe any less in the movement or in the objectives, but this might be a good time to get off the ship while it's still spaceworthy."

"I'm surprised to hear you say that, but I think your reasons are sound. I wish you'd decided it before you passed on all my replacement pilots."

"You wouldn't have done so well with someone else."

Barbara glanced at her chrono, then back at Owen. "What do you mean by that?"

"Admiral, I've always respected you—you saved all our lives at Josephson System, so many years ago with *Duc d'Enghien*. Over the last year-and-a-half I've tried to help you when I could.

"There are people high up in Blazing Star who don't like you very much. You're not their kind of admiral: You think for yourself, you don't follow blindly, and you don't make any secret of it when you're pissed off."

"It's a MacEwan thing. Go on."

"The Prophet convinced Admiral Anderson to keep you as far from the fighting as possible. It's easy to see why: if you were around, you'd talk to Anderson—and the Prophet doesn't want anyone talking to Anderson other than him."

"And why would that be?"

"Do you want the pragmatic answer or the real answer?"

"The real answer."

"The Prophet has plans for Admiral Anderson, ma'am. For after the war."

"What sort of 'plans'?"

"I think you know what I'm talking about."

"Satisfy yourself that I don't."

"*After the war*. The bugs are a dead issue," he added. "But the movement won't be dead—it'll just be getting started."

"I don't like where this conversation is heading."

"I didn't expect you would. But the war has to end sometime."

Barbara didn't answer; instead she picked up her overnight bag and walked toward the door. "I'll worry about *'after the war'* when the war is over. For the moment, Owen, Admiral Anderson and the—and Mr. Smith—have decided to have me present for a planning session. If you'll excuse me, I believe we both have a ship to catch."

Owen looked at her for several moments, then nodded. "Thank you for your time, Admiral. Let me return your advice," he said, as he walked past her. "Watch *your* back."

Nestor System

The jump from Portal System to Nestor took four days. Just before *Tikal* made transition Barbara received a comm-squirt from Zor'a: a reply from her message to Jackie Laperriere, containing information about her old friend's reaction to what Agropoulous had seen at TSUSHIMA. The idea that it wasn't a setup by the Prophet, but rather some phenomenon that had come to Jackie from the mysterious Captain Stone, was both reassuring and disturbing. Barbara didn't know what to do with the information, so she filed it away.

At Nestor System the traffic lanes were full of incoming ships. A third of the fleet was deployed at recently taken systems such as SIENA or TSUSHIMA, but system comm indicated the presence of nearly every commanding officer deployed beyond the Rip—as well as a number of COs of Blazing Star ships. As soon as her own flag-icon was added to the display, *Tikal* received a comm-squirt indicating that a fast system boat would rendezvous and carry her to the main station; *Tikal* itself didn't get express service, but anyone who rated seventeen sideboys got the red carpet. She and her two-person entourage put on their best dress blues and rode into the inner system, other vessels giving way to allow her boat to pass.

I wonder if Owen is getting this treatment, she thought to herself as the station came into view. She rather suspected that the answer was no.

At the docking-bay there were indeed seventeen sideboys, as well as an honor guard of eight high-ranking warriors from the High Nest. Admiral Sir Erich Anderson and Admiral Ur'e'e HeYen were waiting at the end of the row to receive her, with the commander of Nestor Starbase, Commodore Arlen Mustafa, a step behind. She knew Mustafa; he'd been talked out of retirement a year ago when Nestor was being refitted for the Navy's use.

"Permission to disembark, Admiral," she said, when salutes had been exchanged.

"By all means," Sir Erich replied. He extended his hand in greeting. "Welcome aboard, Admiral MacEwan, Commander Santos. If you'd care to review the honor guard, Admiral."

"A pleasure." They walked slowly down the ranks of Imperial Marines standing at stiff attention, and then the eight zor holding their wings in positions of honor and respect, their *chya'i* drawn and held point-down toward the deck.

"Things seem to be going well, Sir Erich," Barbara said, when they'd reached the end and the honor guard was dismissed.

"So formal."

"Only acknowledging a deserved honor, sir," she added, as they walked off the main station concourse and along an access corridor. "SIENA and TSUSHIMA were both great victories."

"We think so, too, Barbara. I'm very pleased with the progress we've made—and so is Admiral HeYen." He nodded toward his zor counterpart. "And so, of course, is *he.*"

"Where is *he,* anyway?"

"Preparing. And, of course, the reception of the Admiral of the Red is a purely military function—it really isn't his concern."

"It doesn't rate his attention."

"It doesn't *require* his attention," Anderson responded quickly, his eyes and voice betraying a slight irritation. "If two senior admirals and an honor guard isn't enough—"

"I'm quite comfortable with my reception, Sir Erich. You know I'm merely curious."

"That he didn't come and meet you?" Anderson looked away as they walked. Ur'e'e's wings altered very slightly. "Or, generally, *why* you're here?"

"I think you've satisfied my curiosity on the first one. But the second one—yes. I've sat . . ." She lowered her voice. "I've sat on my ass in Portal System for a couple of months, and now all of a sudden I'm invited to a tea party here at Nestor. Of course I want to know *why.*"

"Time for action," Anderson said. "What's past is past, Barbara." He stopped walking so abruptly that a less agile person than Ur'e'e HeYen would have collided with him in a most unadmiral-like fashion. "You want a chance to make a difference? There'll be all you can handle."

"Tell me more."

"Not here. Not now. Briefing will be in—" He made a gesture at waist level at the corridor wall, and a small chrono appeared. "—in about a Standard hour and a half: 1700 hours. *He'll* be clarifying our position then. Until then I've got a lot to do, so I've asked *se* Ur'e'e to get you and your people to berths."

Anderson snapped a salute; Barbara, her aide, and yeoman, and Admiral HeYen, returned the gesture. After a few moments Anderson was around the corner and out of sight.

"If you would be so good to accompany me, *se* Admiral,"

Ur'e'e HeYen said, gesturing in the direction they had been walking.

"Just 'Barbara' will do, *se* Ur'e'e, if you would."

"*se* Barbara," he said, arranging his wings in a posture of respect.

"Do you know what's going on?"

"I have not been briefed completely," he said, as they began to walk. Ratings and enlisted personnel came to attention as they passed; a squad of Marines moved from double-time formation to parade rest along the corridor, saluting the two admirals.

"Where is this going?"

Ur'e'e's wings moved very slightly, as if a breeze had stirred them and he was only just taking notice.

"I would like to say, *se* Barbara, that it is going where *esLi* wills."

"But instead . . ."

"We will all be better informed in a few Standard hours, *se* Barbara."

Shiell Institute, Jardine City,
New Chicago System

The door slid aside and a Guardian entered the room. Rivendra Wells could see two others standing in the hallway; they wore sidearms, and, like the one who had just come in, they had the star emblem on their lapels.

"Good afternoon, Dr. Wells," the Guardian said, taking a seat at the table, opposite him. "I'm Wilhelm Dawson, sir. I apologize for the circumstances in which we meet. I've admired your work for some time."

"Really."

"Yes," Dawson answered. "Does that surprise you?"

"To be admired? No, not at all. You have a very interesting way of showing it—incarceration." Wells waved to the room; it was an office in Building 6 that had been commandeered by the Guardians when they'd descended on the Shiell Institute the previous day. Now it was a cell: not by design, but certainly by function.

"Protective custody," the Guardian said.

"Ah, yes. 'Words mean what I say they mean: no more, and no less.'"

"Excuse me?"

"No matter." Wells leaned back in his chair. "Please go on."

The Guardian frowned a bit; some byplay had passed him that he didn't understand. "Dr. Wells, I know you must be disturbed by the present situation, but I want to assure you that if you cooperate it'll be over all that much more quickly."

"I am at your service, Mr. Dawson."

Again the Guardian paused.

Irony isn't his strong suit, Wells thought to himself. *This is how society falls apart: The people with the arrest warrants lose their senses of humor first.*

"I just want to ask a few questions."

"Please do."

"A few months ago, Dr. Wells, you had some alien technology in your possession. Is that correct?"

"You know it is."

Dawson looked at him sharply. "Please just answer the questions, sir. This technology was captured during a battle in Tamarind System and was turned over to the Shiell Institute for examination."

"That's right. We believed it to be enhancement tech—what the vuhls use to project Sensitive capabilities across interplanetary distances."

"And was it?"

"Was it *what*?"

The Guardian was clearly annoyed with him now. "Was it capable of doing this?"

"I don't know."

"According to our information, sir, a prominent zor Sensitive—"

"Byar HeShri. The Master of Sanctuary."

Dawson cleared his throat. "Yes. The zor Byar HeShri was able to activate the equipment and make use of it."

"I wouldn't say that."

"Oh?" The Guardian consulted his comp. "Apparently your team worked with this supposed enhancement technology for some weeks before the zor came to the Institute at your invitation; you made no progress with it either before or after he activated it."

"That's true, but—"

"And since you could do nothing with this alien technology, you really have very little understanding of *exactly* what took place when he activated the tech. Isn't that correct, Dr. Wells?"

"According to his account—"

"Isn't that *correct,* sir?" Dawson interrupted, obviously angry. "You don't know *what* happened with this zor Sensitive, do you?"

Wells took a moment to think. In his experience, Guardians weren't given to emotional outbursts at all; they were very methodical, very logical—very *controlled.* You couldn't easily get a rise out of them.

And no sense of humor, he reminded himself.

Dawson seemed different, as if he were being driven by some inner anger. It was almost surreal.

"Please answer my question," Dawson said, after a moment.

"We know what he told us, Mr. Dawson."

"And what did he tell you?"

"That he had encountered an alien AI within the device which had brought him into contact with the Ór—an intelligence that serves the vuhls."

"The Ór. I see." He took a stylus from his pocket and made a notation in the air near his comp. "He was in contact with the enemy."

"He was nearly captured by it, as I understand."

"This is what he told you."

"Yes, he did. I'm not sure what you mean—"

"What I *mean*?" Dawson tossed the stylus on the table

and leaned forward, folding his hands in front of him. "What I mean is to find out the truth of this business, Dr. Wells. You should not be concerned with *my* intentions: You should be concerned for your own welfare."

"Is my welfare an issue?"

"When your loyalty is in question? I daresay."

"My *loyalty*? You're questioning my loyalty?" Wells rose to his feet; Dawson was a few seconds behind him. A few seconds after that, the door opened and both Guardians outside the door stepped in, their weapons drawn and pointed at Wells.

"Sit down, Doctor," Dawson said.

"You're suggesting that I'm a traitor? I'll sit down when I'm damn good and ready. You invade the Institute, stick me in this cell, and accuse me of disloyalty? I've had just about enough—"

Dawson took his seat. "Sit down in that chair, Dr. Wells. Do it now, or I'll have you cuffed to it. I'd prefer that this interview remain civilized, but I'll conduct it that way, if necessary.

"It's up to you to choose."

Wells looked from Dawson to the two Guardians in the doorway. They hadn't moved or changed the aim of their weapons.

He dropped into his chair. "I don't believe this."

Dawson made a slight gesture; the two other Guardians withdrew and closed the door behind them.

"The New Chicago Assembly won't let you get away with these secret-police tactics," Wells said. "I still have the rights of an Imperial citizen, Guardian Dawson."

"If you'd like to see my authorization, Dr. Wells, I'd be glad to show it to you. This operation has the full force and authority of New Chicago law." Dawson smiled unpleasantly. "But it also has the authority of the emperor. Would you like to see the Imperial seal?" He touched the comp and a holo sprang to life above the table between them. At the bottom was a secure icon showing the sword-and-sun.

Wells took a deep breath. "I have never done anything contrary to the law of the Solar Empire, sir, and I deny your accusations to the contrary. What's more, for the record, I resent having my reputation impugned in this fashion."

"Noble words, Dr. Wells. My problem—" He dismissed the holo and smiled again. "My problem is this: I am directed to secure an oath of loyalty from each and every person working with classified material at this Institute, and while I know your intentions are likely honorable"—Wells bristled at the word *"likely,"* but he continued—"there's a part of the oath that I know you can't meet."

"Really? What part?"

"The part that reads, '. . . in communication with parties affiliated with the vuhl race.' You see, when the zor Byar HeShri activated the technology, he made contact with the vuhls—and something happened in there, something for which there is no record. Byar HeShri does not owe loyalty to the Solar Emperor, and has never submitted to Guardian examination.

"Not long after, the technology was transferred to the zor Core Stars. By agreeing to this transfer, you allowed someone tainted by the enemy to escape examination."

"That's absurd."

Dawson looked at Wells with the clear-eyed stare that Guardians use when a guest comes up to pay court to the Solar Emperor. Wells knew that there was nothing for him to see; still, it was unnerving.

"I don't think it is absurd, Dr. Wells. I don't think so at all. There's a new day coming—not just here at the Shiell Institute, and not just in New Chicago System. Every taint, every influence of the enemy, is going to be driven out of the Empire and destroyed. No zor Sensitives, no collaborators, no *traitors* are going to escape it. We will find them—every one of them.

"And anyone who won't—or can't—sign the loyalty oath will be dealt with."

"So I'm to be . . . *dealt with*."

"Tell me what happened at the end of Byar HeShri's experience with the alien technology, Dr. Wells," Dawson said.

"I only know what Master Byar told me."

"Which was?"

"That he was in contact with the Ór, and the contact was severed."

"How?"

"I don't know."

"Did *he* know? Did he sever the contact himself?"

"I . . . don't think so."

"But you don't know."

"No."

"Then there is every reason to believe that the zor Byar is more powerful than you believe—or than we feared. He may well be in league with, or under the control of, the enemy.

"And now he has the alien technology, and can do what he wishes with it—with no supervision or control."

"I can't believe—"

"Believe what you like, Dr. Wells," the Guardian said. "It really doesn't matter." He took his comp and tucked it into a pocket, then stood up. "This interview is over."

"And my status?"

Dawson didn't answer, turning away toward the door.

"Am I free to go?"

Dawson looked back at him. "Don't be *absurd*, Dr. Wells," he said, walking through the doorway. The two Guardians gave a single glance at Wells as the door slid shut.

Pali Tower
Imperial Oahu, Sol System

It took an act of will for Tonio to disentangle himself from the Imperial Progress when it arrived at Tien Tsin

System. Upon arriving insystem, word of the arrests and detentions conducted by the Guardian Order—and authorized by the Imperial Assembly—was transmitted to the emperor's yacht. With as much dignity as he could muster, and giving as little offense as he could manage, Tonio took his leave of the emperor and commandeered a vessel headed in the direction of Sol System. Pali Tower was the most secure location, and being on the homeworld also would put him close to the Imperial Assembly in Genève, if necessary.

It took just over four days to get home. At Pluto Base, and then at Station One, he was met by Guardians wearing Blazing Star lapel pins and neck-cloths. He decided not to make an issue of it. A priority shuttle flight got him to Honolulu, and an aircar deposited him at Pali Tower.

"Nic, activate," he said, as soon as the office door was secure. Nic appeared in his usual seat; Tonio dropped into the chair opposite.

"Maestro."

"What in the hell is going on?"

"I'm not sure I take your meaning."

"If I'm not mistaken, I see Blazing Star wherever I go. The Inner Order on Corazón—"

"I know what happened at Corazón, Commander," Nic interrupted. "The Inner Order there doesn't care to follow you anymore. Or, as far as I can determine, will they do so anywhere else."

"How do you know that?"

"I know. I'm very well informed." He smiled.

"*How* do you know what happened *at Corazón*?"

"I'm very well informed," Nic repeated. "As for Blazing Star, it's really quite simple: Those that are potentially disloyal are being arrested and detained, and Blazing Star has been given authority by His Imperial Highness to do it. I decided that it would be better to be on the giving than on the receiving end of that activity."

"It doesn't have to happen at all."

"Oh, but it *does,* Maestro. It certainly does. The

Prophet is seeking out those who do not support the war effort—who aren't fully committed to exterminating the vuhls—and they are being dealt with."

"I didn't authorize that."

"I know," Nic answered. "*I* did. In your name."

Tonio didn't answer for a moment: he couldn't come up with anything to say. Instead, he got up and slowly walked across the room past where Nic's image sat, to the half-window on the south side of the office, from which he could see much of the Imperial City.

"You attached my name to arrest and detention orders?" he asked without turning around.

"Yes, Maestro, I did."

"I want those orders countermanded."

"No," Nic said. "I don't think I'll do that at all."

Antonio St. Giles turned from the southward-pointing vista, his face completely perplexed. "What did you say?"

"I think it is an unwise course of action, Maestro. This business is already well along, and to stop it now would be the wrong thing to do; I won't do it."

"I'm *ordering* you. I'm giving you a direct order. Do it, or else I'll—"

Nic, whose image had been across the room, vanished and reappeared next to St. Giles. "Or you'll do what?" he said quietly. "Terminate my programming? Cut off my security access?"

"Something of the sort."

"I regret to inform you, Commander, that those measures are no longer within your control."

"What do you mean?"

"I mean that they've been disabled. All of them."

"*Sopresatta,*" St. Giles said. "*Melnibone. Islay. Dodecahedron.*" Each word was accompanied by a gesture—one of the signs of warding used by members of the Inner Order.

Nic remained impassive, a half-smile on his lips. He knew what the keywords were intended to do, and what part of the code they were supposed to affect. Stone had shown each of them to him during that memorable night that he'd been brought to sentience.

St. Giles looked shaken. *"Pantagruel,"* he said. *"Terpsichore. Economou. Brazzaville."* Again, each word was matched with a gesture.

Nic did not disappear or change position. His programming didn't enter standby mode.

"You never would've made it in my dear Florence," he said, after a moment. "Too many years sitting at your desk in this tower have made you begin to believe your own propaganda."

"What the hell is that supposed to mean?"

"It means," Nic said, walking across the room this time to sit at St. Giles' own desk, "that while you've been playing your little games with the Inner Order, assuming matters were under your authority out beyond the Rip, events have gotten completely beyond your control.

"Admiral Anderson doesn't even call the tune anymore, Maestro. It's entirely the Prophet's war. The Guardians answer to Blazing Star, and Blazing Star answers to *him*."

"And you—" St. Giles took a deep breath. "And you answer to him, too, I suppose."

"Certainly not. I don't need him any more than I need you, Maestro. Not that I disagree with his objectives—or his motives; he is every bit the prince that the great Duke Valentino was, and more—but I have an understanding far beyond anything he can imagine."

"Explain."

"Issuing orders again, are we? It's probably a hard habit to break. Very well; perhaps you can still be useful to me.

"As you are aware, there are copies of my program running in various locations all over the Solar Empire. In the last Standard year, that number has increased by a factor of a thousand with the help of members of the Guardian Order. With your own security clearance it was a trivial matter to install my program anywhere it was needed.

"With the help of the *or'a'th'n*—or, rather, a modification of it—I am able to keep these copies synchronized with a frequency that far exceeds the present capability of comm technology."

"What is an *or'a'th'n*?"

"I'm not sure exactly what it is, but I can tell you what it *does*: It connects vuhl enhancement technology with the Ór. With it, communication—almost instantaneous communication—is possible over enormous distances."

"You're . . . connected to—"

"No, of course not. Someone—or something—severed that connection while Master Byar was communicating with it at the Shiell Institute on New Chicago. The connection is gone, but the *ability* to communicate . . ."

Nic gestured at the comp on St. Giles' desk. Three holo-figures appeared, only one of whom Tonio recognized: Ichiro Kanev, looking similar to the model Tonio had developed for an earlier version of the AI. The other two were a complete mystery.

"My agents," Nic explained. "With their help, and with the help of the *or'a'th'n*, I can be anywhere. Almost everywhere, actually. I truly am *extremely* well informed."

"Why didn't you share this with me?"

"Why would I? So that you could order me about like a maintenance program? So you could try and terminate me at any time? So you can order me to countermand orders you have already made?"

"Which *you* made in my name, you mean."

"It no longer makes a difference."

"Of course it does," Tonio said. "You're still an AI, and I'm still Commander of the Guardian Order. I'm going to put a stop to this." He turned away from Nic and took one step toward the door.

Nic appeared in front of the door, blocking his path. Another Nic appeared near the lectern in the northwest corner of the room; another near the elegant flower-vase on the east side.

"No," they all said. "You won't."

"You're still a holo," Tonio said, stepping toward the image and through it—

The door in front of him didn't open automatically as he'd expected. He placed a hand on it—

He cried out in pain as a surge of electricity passed through him, dropping him, stunned, to the floor.

He saw a single Nic standing above him.

"Yes, I'm a holo," Nic said. "And you're . . . a meat-creature."

Fortunately, Tonio then lost consciousness.

Chapter 20

THE NOBLE AIM OF EXTERMINATING THE VUHLS CAN ONLY BE VIEWED AS A FIRST STEP OF A TRANS-FORMATION OF HUMAN SOCIETY. WHEN WE CHOSE TO COMPROMISE WITH THE FIRST HOSTILE RACE WE ENCOUNTERED, IT DEMONSTRATED AMPLY THAT WE WERE ILL-PREPARED FOR FUTURE CONFLICTS. IT MUST BE ASSUMED THAT THE UNIVERSE IS FULL OF POTENTIAL ADVERSARIES, AND THE ONLY WAY FOR MANKIND AND ITS ALLIES TO SURVIVE IS TO BE PREPARED TO DEFEAT THEM. THE FIRE OF THIS VIC-TORY WILL MAKE US CAPABLE OF FUTURE VICTO-RIES AS WELL.

—*The War Manifesto: Future of Empire,* 2424

September 2424
Nestor System

At 1645 hours, Barbara MacEwan and Henry Santos were escorted from their quarters to Nestor Starbase C-and-C. In every corridor and lift, there were soldiers and sailors wearing the Blazing Star insignia; Barbara did her best not to feel conspicuous without it. There was no lack of respect: she received salutes wherever she went.

At C-and-C, Sir Erich Anderson met the two of them and directed them to the commander's ready-room. The Prophet was waiting for them alone.

"Admiral MacEwan," he said, inclining his head and then offering her a handshake. "Commander Santos."

"Mr. Smith."

"I realize that you have some concerns about the progress of the war so far, Admiral, and I'd like to assure you of the esteem in which I hold you." Some glance was exchanged between the Prophet and Admiral Anderson; Barbara wasn't sure of its meaning.

"I'm glad to be appreciated, sir. I was sure that my command would be eventually put to use."

"Soon, Admiral. Soon. I'll be briefing command staff in a few minutes, but I felt that I should speak to you personally beforehand. As you know," he continued without interruption, "there is a project to uncover those who might be operating against the best interests of the Solar Empire: not just within the fleet, but across Imperial space. Within a few weeks, the first phase of that effort will be under way."

"A purge."

"Words," the Prophet said. It was a reply that neither denied nor really acknowledged the accusation. "I believe that the effort will be more successful within our forces on this side of the Rip; the civilian world of the Solar Empire may not be as easy to pacify."

"Pacify? What do you mean by that?"

"There will be some disloyal elements that disagree with our position."

"Does the second imply the first? Look, Smith, I don't like the sound of this—there must be reasonable people who disagree with 'your position' that aren't disloyal to the Empire. Surely—"

"The time for 'reasonable people' to 'disagree' is past, Barbara," Anderson said. "This war has gone on too long already. *Far* too long."

"What does that have to do with anything? The Imperial Assembly won't stand for— What? Mass arrests? 'Pacification'?"

"The Assembly has been dissolved," the Prophet said. "For the duration of the current crisis."

"Crisis?"

"Admiral MacEwan," he said, "you wish for your command to be put to use. Shortly, I will be ordering it to Adrianople, from which it will be operating to pacify disloyal elements within the Empire."

"That's not its primary mission."

"It is now," he said.

"What's more," she continued, placing her hands on her hips, "I don't take orders from *you*. I have no sympathy for our enemy, and acknowledge your contribution to the war effort. But I take orders from *him*"—she gestured toward Anderson—"and from the emperor. No one else. Until you're appointed admiral or crowned emperor, you're not in my chain of command."

The Prophet's eyes were angry, but before he could say a word, Anderson held up his hand. "A moment in private," he said to Smith, who considered it and then stalked out of the room. Barbara nodded to Santos, who followed.

When the door was closed, Barbara rounded on her fellow admiral. "Erich—*Sir* Erich—what in God's name are you doing? This— This civilian is going to brief command staff? He's going to order *me* to 'pacify' revolts?"

"This has the emperor's full faith and support, Barbara. What's more—" He lowered his voice, as if someone with a vid pickup might not be able to hear every word anyway. "What's more, following this order is an indication of your own loyalty."

"To what?"

"To the movement."

"I don't work for the *movement*, Erich. I work for the emperor. So do you."

"They're the same thing."

"No, damn it, they're not." Now it was Barbara's turn to be angry. "I have no idea what's going on back on our side of the Rip, Erich, but it's beginning to sound alien to me. We're arresting people who *disagree* with us? What's next—are we going to start putting them in camps?"

"You don't understand."

"No, I don't. I am a loyal soldier and a servant of the Solar Emperor, and I don't choose to be anything else: not a Sensitive, not a part of the 'movement,' and certainly not a lapdog for this 'Prophet' of yours. I don't care what he can do: I don't care what he represents. And I *don't* take orders from him.

"Do *you*?"

Anderson didn't meet her eyes and didn't answer for several moments. There was no sound but the steady background noise that all ships have: ventilation, comm, distant equipment in operation.

"We've found the vuhl homeworld, Barbara. With all of their abilities, with all of the destruction they've caused, they turn out to be spread across relatively few planets."

"Then they're no longer a threat."

"As long as they exist, they're a threat," he said. "They wanted to breed us—they still think of us as cattle. Do you know what they call humans and zor?"

"'Meat-creatures.'"

"That's right. As long as they can reproduce, they're

360 Walter H. Hunt

dangerous. A century ago, the Empire made the mistake of believing that a beaten enemy was no longer a threat—and that mistake came back to haunt it again and again."

"Until Admiral Marais."

"Admiral Marais was weak. And lucky," said Anderson.

"Do you really *believe* that? It's in *The War Manifesto*, I know: How the zor should thank *esLi* every day that Admiral Marais was such a pussycat, he couldn't bring himself to exterminate them.

"Here's my question for you, Admiral: What happens on the day you kill the last vuhl? The day your leader—your Prophet—achieves his goal of wiping the enemy from the face of the stars?" She spread her arms wide. "What happens to these 'disloyal elements'? What happens to the Imperial Navy—do they just walk away and go back to peacekeeping? What do you expect is going to happen with the Prophet?"

"Barbara. Admiral MacEwan." For just a moment, Anderson had a faraway look, then he focused directly on her. "After the briefing I will be drafting orders for you to get your command under way for Adrianople. Everything will be in the proper chain of command and will bear my signature and the official seal of the Admiralty.

"Your orders will indicate where you're to go and will include instructions on how insurgency against the lawful directives of the Solar Emperor is to be addressed. I might as well ask now: Are you prepared to follow orders?"

For the first time in her career, Barbara wasn't immediately insulted by the insinuation that she might do anything else. Still, she took several seconds before answering.

"If it comes from you, Sir Erich, I will execute the orders to the best of my ability."

Anderson let out a long breath. "I'm relieved to hear you say it, Barbara. I'd rather you took charge of this operation."

"Who else did you have in mind?"

"*He'd* suggested . . . Commodore Mustafa."

"Are you crazy? After what the vuhls did to him—and then how Jon Durant died—he's got a grudge a mile wide against the vuhls. If he thought someone didn't want to support the war effort one hundred percent . . ."

"That was *his* thinking, as well," Anderson said. "He thought that Mustafa would be an ideal choice, but I convinced him that you should at least be given the opportunity to take the assignment.

"Look, Barbara, I know how you must feel—and how this must look. But this may be the most important period in humanity's history. We're on the verge of wiping out our greatest enemy."

"And achieving your own immortality as a hero of the Solar Empire."

"I hadn't thought that far."

"That's a load of crap, Erich. But, to be fair, I don't care—but I do think that you'll be less kindly treated by history than you think, after associating yourself with this."

"You're in it, too, Barbara."

"No, I'm not. Not yet. Right now I'm in the same position I've been in for the past thirty years: as an officer in His Majesty's Navy. Until I put that Blazing Star emblem on my uniform, I'm *not* a part of this."

"You'll have to put it on sometime."

"Maybe so. I'll let you know how I feel about it then."

They stepped out of the ready-room. Barbara saw Anderson nod to the Prophet and then glance at the chrono hanging above the Operations main board; without another word, the two of them headed toward the larger conference room on the opposite side of C-and-C.

The entire interview had taken eight minutes.

Barbara glanced at Henry Santos, who was standing alone, white-faced, looking at the two men as they walked away. She took two strides to stand next to him.

"Is something wrong, Henry?"

"No, no thank you, Admiral, I'm fine," he lied. His hands were clenched at his side.

"Out with it, Doctor," she said in a low but level voice. "What did he say to you?"

"He asked me when I was planning to avenge my father's death, ma'am," Santos answered quietly. "He said that fifteen years was too long to wait."

"He said *what*?" She angrily took a step forward, but Santos caught her by the arm.

"There are bigger issues than a—a civilian trying to get my goat, Admiral," he said. "You have a lot of things to get straight here; I'm merely part of the fife-and-drum corps following you. Please don't get distracted on my account, ma'am."

"When someone insults a member of my staff, they insult *me*, Henry," she answered. "I won't stand for it."

"It's a small thing. It's not worth the trouble."

"I won't have Ray Santos' name besmirched, Henry." She turned to face him, gently shrugging his hand loose from her uniform jacket. "He's not here to defend himself, but you are—and, as his son, it's your duty and your privilege. It's not a 'small thing' at all."

"I agree, ma'am, but still . . . I'm not sure that he isn't right."

"What do you mean?"

"When the *Gyaryu'har* was aboard *Tristan* a year-and-a-half ago, Admiral, she asked me if I had a grudge against the vuhls because of how my dad died. I couldn't answer her: I wasn't sure that I could say with a clear conscience that I *didn't* have a grudge. It's not professional—especially for a doctor—to have some wish to kill the enemy, but . . . I'm just *not sure*. He may be right."

"He's wrong. There's no way to avenge your father's death by just going out and killing the enemy; all you can do is continue to do your duty to the emperor."

"I've done that, Admiral."

"I know you have, Henry, and I'm proud to have you on my staff because of it."

"But I'm not sure it's enough anymore. I don't know what Dad would have done—but he wouldn't have spent fifteen years making up his mind."

Admiral Anderson and the civilian specialist had disappeared into the conference room. Barbara glanced at the chrono: there were only a few minutes remaining before the 1700 briefing.

"We need to talk about this later," she said. "For the moment, I want you to know that I respect your feelings on this matter, and honor your father's memory—and his loyal service to the emperor—and I'm more interested in those two things than anything *he* has to say.

"Come on. Even if I'm not impressed by *him*, I have to listen to this damn briefing. Wait until you hear what *our* next mission is going to be."

Pali Tower
Imperial Oahu, Sol System

When Antonio St. Giles awoke, his first reaction was surprise: He had been having tortured dreams that reminded him of the last moments before he'd passed out in his own office at the top of the Pali Tower. He was surprised to awaken again.

Basing his security AI on Niccolò Machiavelli had been an act of inspiration and exasperation. Inspiration, because (as it turned out) the brilliant sixteenth-century Florentine was everything Tonio wanted for an AI base personally: astute, ruthless, intelligent, and insightful in a way that spanned the centuries. Exasperation, because the stolid historian Ichiro Kanev had been almost none of these things—he was intelligent, but hidebound in his theories and of very little use when it came to managing the day-to-day business of the Guardians. It had forced him to choose another personality for his AI.

Somehow—and Tonio had no idea how—Nic had gained sentience. There were many safeguards built into the program, including eight keys to terminate Nic if he ran out-of-bounds. He'd tried each one of them and none had worked. Only Tonio knew them, and he'd never trusted anyone with any of them. There was only one failsafe left: upon Tonio's death, the Nic program was supposed to go offline permanently. It wasn't clear if that part of the software would respond, either, but Tonio wasn't keen to try it out.

Still, when he opened his eyes and found himself on the couch in his office, still breathing and aware, he wondered whether Nic was actually as ruthless as the man on whom he had been modeled.

"Ah. You're awake," said a voice.

Tonio's head hurt to do it, but he turned it slightly and looked up and back to see someone sitting in a chair nearby; it was one of the figures that had appeared just before the electrified door had sent him spiraling into unconsciousness.

It was obviously a holo, but one as skillfully executed as Nic's own.

"Yes." Tonio sat up and immediately thought better of it, letting himself fall back onto the pillow. "And a bit surprised."

"Surprised, Commander?"

"Surprised to still be alive. I—got the impression that Nic, or whatever he's become, was done with me."

"He might be. My brother doesn't confide in me—or in anyone, really: Everything is deception piled upon deceit. Just the way he wants it."

"Your . . . brother?"

"I suppose I should introduce myself, Commander. I am Totto. Totto Machiavelli, Niccolò's brother, younger by six years. He has asked me to talk to you."

"You're a subordinate AI."

"Yes, that's right, and a good one, if I do say so myself." He crossed his legs. "Naturally, I am truly no more

Totto Machiavelli—Niccolò's younger brother, born 1475—than Nic is Niccolò Machiavelli, but that might well be a distinction without a difference. As a man of God—or perhaps a subroutine of God"—he smiled at his own phrase—"it seems only appropriate that I be designated as the custodian of your immortal soul."

"You're to be my confessor, I suppose?"

"I am an avatar of one who could have performed that function, though I suspect that I—as an AI—am not truly qualified to do so, even if you believed in the worthiness of such a pursuit. No, this is much more pragmatic, Commander: I'm to evaluate whether you should live or die."

The coldness with which he spoke this last sentence gave Tonio a moment's pause. It swept the discussion from an abstract, theoretical thing into something real and present-tense.

"He should kill me and get it over with."

"If only it were that easy. You see, if you die—especially too soon—Nic can only keep up the illusion of acting in your name for so long before questions become piled upon questions.

"This is hardly the time for the Guardian Order to be subjected to that sort of scrutiny."

"The Guardian Order." Tonio put his hand over his eyes. "Your brother—Nic—has done a pretty good job of screwing that up already."

"I think that's a rather harsh judgment, Commander. He's actually made some significant improvements. Consider, for example, how all of the versions of his program are interconnected: they can exchange information almost instantaneously using the *or'a'th'n*. With this intelligence-gathering mechanism at his disposal, the Guardian Order is the most powerful organization in the Solar Empire.

"And the beauty of it, Commander, is that *no one knows*. Not the emperor; not the admiralty; not even the Prophet. All of this capability could be at your disposal—"

"If I toe the party line."

"If you realize that the Inner Order's path is the wrong one. It always was, really: The whole idea of controlling emotions as a means to gaining access to the powers Commander Garrett possessed is merely a dead end."

"Garrett could never do those things," St. Giles answered, though it seemed to ring hollow. "He never saw past his own anger."

"He didn't have to. But he did what he needed to do: pass his skills on to the Prophet. It was his duty to *teach*, Commander, and he did so. But don't worry—his time on the stage is over."

"Meaning?"

"The Prophet is about to betray him. I would think that it would fit in with your original plans very well."

Aboard Hellespont
Oberon System

A few minutes after the bridge informed Rafe Rodriguez that *Hellespont* had transited into Oberon System, his door chimed.

"Come," he said, not looking up from a comp display; he was reviewing the cargo manifests in preparation for docking at the commercial base.

"Captain."

"I'll be right with you," he said, continuing to look at the manifest.

"*Now*, Captain."

He turned to face the speaker: a Guardian named Wynn who had come aboard at Portal System. To Rafe's surprise, she was holding a pistol and pointing it directly at him.

"You know," he said without moving, "some people might consider that to be unfriendly."

"Don't make this more difficult than it has to be, Captain Rodriguez," Wynn said.

"Your mutiny?"

"Your arrest," Wynn answered. She took a comp from a pocket and tossed it onto the desk. "By order of the emperor."

Rafe looked from Wynn to the comp and then back. He slowly reached for the comp and gestured at it. A document appeared in the air over the desk.

"The emperor is taking a personal interest in me. Any idea why, Guardian Wynn?"

"Your association with Garrett," the Guardian spat out. "All of his former colleagues are being taken into custody."

"Even the Prophet, I suppose."

"No, not the *Prophet*. Of course not. Just Garrett's *disloyal* allies."

"And you're doing it at the point of a gun," Rafe said. "Sweet. What, did you think I would resist?"

"I was rather hoping you would."

"Sorry to disappoint. Don't you think Owen might object to this little drama?"

"Garrett has abandoned the movement, just as he abandoned the Guardians twenty years ago. He can't protect you anymore, Rodriguez," the Guardian said, sneering.

"I didn't realize he was protecting me—maybe from having to deal with jerks like you."

"I'm still holding a weapon, Rodriguez. Maybe you should watch what you say."

"Spare me the tough patter, Wynn. If you're planning to shoot me, you should go ahead and do it. But you're not supposed to do that, are you? Otherwise we wouldn't be having this little debate."

"You're pretty cocky, Rodriguez."

"You're not even calling me 'Captain' anymore, wiseass. You going to put me in the brig or shoot me? If not, I've got work to do."

The Guardian wasn't sure how to react: Rodriguez, who had a reputation for a temper, was shrugging the incident off as bureaucracy.

"There'll be a Guardian outside your door from now until the time we dock," Wynn said at last. "Don't plan on any excursions."

"So, this is still my quarters."

"For the moment."

"Fine. Then get the hell out," he said, glaring at the Guardian, daring her to answer.

Wynn holstered her pistol, took one more angry look at Rodriguez, and stalked out of the room, the door sliding shut behind her.

Rafe didn't turn back to his manifests right away. He assumed that he was under surveillance, so he wasn't about to show any emotion on the subject—but inside he was angry and more than a bit scared. Since when did Guardians go around arresting people in the name of the emperor? And if Owen's old friends were being taken into custody—presumably himself and Djiwara were at the head of the list. Conveniently, they were both aboard *Hellespont*.

What the hell did it mean? And what had Owen done to bring it on? He knew that Djiwara had advised him to walk away—was that enough to prove disloyalty to the movement?

Wynn was right about one thing: whatever Rafe's own position in the movement might be, it was dependent on his long association with Owen Garrett. If the Prophet had turned against Owen for whatever reason, Rafe was very likely in trouble.

The comp still sat on the desk, projecting the arrest document. He looked closely at it: it bore the secure icon of the Solar Emperor, as well as the emblem of Blazing Star.

Now what? he thought to himself. *What the hell do I do now?*

Aboard Epanimondas
En route to UPENDRA *System*

For the jump to UPENDRA, the Prophet boarded *Epani-mondas,* the ship that had carried Owen to the conference at Nestor. He had spent time aboard it before: it had carried him to all of the Imperial objectives from ARIEL to JANISSARY.

Among the fleet it was conjectured that he traveled aboard that ship to honor Owen Garrett, his friend and teacher, who had been away from the center of power for some time; among Blazing Star personnel, it meant there would be some sort of rearrangement of power. For the last year, those closest to the center of the movement had been jostling with each other, trying to associate themselves more closely with the Prophet's aims and wishes, while seeking to discredit the others. Garrett and his supporters had been largely on the outside looking in, but this gesture seemed to indicate the opposite.

UPENDRA itself was an even more important target than SIENA had been: it had become a destination for vuhl refugees fleeing the worlds nearest the Rip. It might require some change in tactics—and for this reason Owen had evidently been called back to the Prophet's side.

Ch'en'ya remained aboard *Flight Over Shar'tu.* As the fleet prepared for jump transition, no one aboard the carrier dared approach her—anger cloaked her like a second pair of wings that everyone could easily read. Was she about to be set aside by the Prophet? No one knew for sure.

A few hours after *Epanimondas'* transition, a Blazing Star functionary came personally to Owen's quarters and summoned him to the Prophet. He was admitted into the presence and left alone: no advisors, no staff, neither Guardians nor Blazing Star—and Ch'en'ya was on another ship in jump, infinitely far away.

The Prophet's quarters were austere. There were no mementoes and very few creature comforts: a conference table with chairs, a side-table with a few starship models—items that might have been left over from *Epaminondas'* time as an Imperial starship. In one corner of the room there was a circular chess set with a game in progress: the four armies were locked in spiral combat, frozen for the moment.

The Prophet himself was sitting at the conference table, slowly peeling a *cthi*-fruit. He beckoned Owen to a chair.

"Thank you for coming," he said, removing the outer layer of the *cthi*—the sweetest part. He set a couple of the wedges on a delicate plate in front of Owen.

"You know I am at your service," said Owen.

"I know." He smiled, a warm, glowing expression that lit up his face. The Prophet possessed some amount of empathic ability, so Owen felt some of that warmth as well. "You know," he continued, "I've been thinking about the first time we met, Owen. Do you remember?"

"Of course. Emperor Willem Starport in Harrison System."

"Yes. Harrison. I was there as a part of the Guardian advance detail to prepare for the emperor's visit. And you were . . ."

"There to teach you."

"You were." The Prophet smiled again. "Blazing Star was, what? A few dozen people then? Thirty or forty?"

"Something like that."

"They needed a leader—someone to galvanize them, someone to give them direction and purpose."

Owen placed his hand on the side of the *cthi*-fruit plate. "They had a direction and purp—"

"They had *nothing*," the Prophet interrupted. "Forty angry men and women: ex-Guardians, mercenaries, zealots—exiles from the Solar Empire, waiting for a chance—to do *what*? Strike against the enemy? Subvert the Guardian Order? You had nothing. *Nothing*," he repeated. "Until you met me."

Owen felt a tinge of anger. Whatever the purpose of this interview, it was hardly a reconciliation between dear old friends.

"You have a point to make," he said quietly.

"I do not speak merely to hear my own voice." The Prophet pushed back his chair and stood up; he walked across the room and stopped at the side-table, letting his hand come to rest on one of the starship models.

"Then make your point."

"You resent how you've been treated, don't you, Owen?" the Prophet said, without turning around.

"That's a bit strong. I *do* think I've been sidelined."

"But it's true. You *do* resent being kept out of the action."

"I suppose so."

"It's not your place to decide," the Prophet said, turning angrily to face him. "It's not your *place* to choose how I will make use of you. This movement is *mine*—*I* control it, *I* direct it, it *exists* because of me. *My* vision governs its direction and has done so for nine years—and will do so for many years to come."

He seemed to be working up his anger. Owen had seen it before over the years; though without an audience to hear it, he wasn't sure what the point was.

"I don't dispute that."

"But it angers you, doesn't it?—that I have done what you never could; that I have directed the extermination of mankind's greatest enemy while you have been relegated to a minor role. You want to be where I am—*who* I am. Don't you?"

"I—"

"Don't you?" the Prophet repeated, now obviously enraged. "Say it, Owen. Tell me that you wish you could take my place."

"No."

The Prophet's reply was ready, but it didn't fit with Owen's last remark. He remained silent for a moment, then said in a calmer voice, "What do you mean?"

"No," Owen repeated. "No, I don't want to take your place. I'm walking away, John. I've had enough of the movement. I don't what to replace you, I don't want to serve you. I'm not even sure I understand you anymore."

"You want to resign."

"That's right."

"Like you resigned from the Guardians."

"That's right," Owen repeated. "You want to belittle me—you want to demean me—go right ahead. I think it's fair to say that you don't need me anymore, and I'm ready and willing to comply."

"I won't allow it."

"Allow it? I'm not giving you the choice."

"No," the Prophet said. "I'm not giving *you* the choice." Anger seemed to drain from him. He made a gesture toward one of the ship models; it turned *inside out* in a disturbing, nongeometric way.

On the opposite side of the room, a few meters behind where Owen sat, six bands of color appeared. They were bright past any capacity to look at them directly, and they cast six weird shadows of Owen Garrett against the opposite wall.

Owen stood up suddenly, realization stunning him to silence.

"You never considered it," the Prophet said quietly, the bands coloring his face. "It never occurred to you why I might be present in Harrison System at just the right time, when you were there, too.

"There's no such thing as coincidence, Owen. There was never anything coincidental about our meeting." The Prophet looked past Owen, who had turned to glance at the bands of color, shielding his eyes against the brightness.

Owen looked from the Prophet to the colors, stepping away from his former friend.

"I have only one more thing to say to you, Owen. I'm sorry, but this can't wait any longer.

"Die," the Prophet said, extending his hands outward.

Owen felt an onslaught of energy aimed at his mind: It was like the attack that they'd launched at enemy vessels at KEYSTONE and all the places before and since. From close proximity, and with little shielding and no preparation at all, it struck him with inescapable force.

"Why?" Owen asked, with the last breath available to him. But he already knew the answer: He knew why he was being dispensed with. *They* had decided that he would be spared, all those years ago; *they* had arranged his meeting with the Prophet; and now *they* were involved in getting him out of the way.

He fell backward, his sight dimming. One hand clutched his head; the other extended backward, touching the edge of the red band of color. Anger was coursing through his last moments—during which his field of vision seemed filled with the Prophet's fierce, proud smile, looking as if he'd accomplished something wondrous.

Owen felt himself pulled along the bands of colored light, not alive but somehow not dead. He couldn't understand how he could even sense this, since he had been killed by the Prophet's mental onslaught: He could still dimly see his body lying on the deck of *Epanimondas,* the Prophet standing nearby.

He could hear the whispers of the six colors as he was pulled along the path, *anGa'e'ren* all around him. He clung to it, not sure where he was headed.

Like always, he told himself. *Like the rest of your damn life—never knowing where they're going to move you next, like a chesspiece.*

No choice, he thought. But he wondered: Why should he let himself be moved again? Why should he follow where he was being led?

"No," he said at last. The word was dwarfed by the

darkness and shattered by it. Somehow his voice sounded less defiant, less angry than he would have expected—but the time for anger and defiance might well be past.

With only a moment's regret he twisted free of the bands of light and hurled himself into the darkness. He felt a surge of surprise from the colors, but it was over very quickly. He tumbled into *anGa'e'ren* and soon could see nothing at all.

A figure stepped from the brightness across the room.
"That was well done," he said, casually crossing to a dispenser. "Cold water," he said to it, in a perfect imitation of the Prophet's voice. A cup dropped into place and water poured into it.

"I hope you're satisfied, Mr. Stone."

"Please, don't dissemble with me," Stone said, turning to face him. "You know very well that it was time for this—we've been heading for it ever since KEYSTONE. That was the deal."

"Yes. The deal. Now your friends—associates—take the body. It can be one more mystery—evidence of his betrayal of the movement." Smith leaned one hand on the chair Owen had recently occupied. "Just as you suggested."

"Remember what you received for fulfilling your part of the bargain," Stone answered. "Over the past few months, Blazing Star has gone from a small organization to a movement that spans the Solar Empire. The possibility of an end to the war and the destruction of the vuhls is a very appealing concept."

A pseudopod of light from the violet band reached out and surrounded the body; it glowed for several seconds and was gone.

"And all it cost me was the death of an old friend."

"Look," Stone said. "It's a bit disingenuous for you to be maudlin over one death when you're in the midst of exterminating an entire species, don't you think?" He took a sip from his water. "It's hardly uncommon for a great leader to—shall we say—modify history to suit his needs?

"No one will know the name of Owen Garrett, and no one needs to know where the movement originated. Isn't that what you want?"

"Yes," the Prophet answered. "Yes, that's what I want."

"Good."

Stone looked away, cocking his head slightly as if he'd heard something, then set down the drink and walked toward the colored bands. "I have to go. Something has— An interesting thing has happened." He smiled in a way that made the Prophet uncomfortable. Stone stepped into the bands and disappeared.

After a swift undulation, the colors faded from view, leaving the Prophet alone.

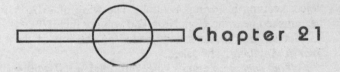

Chapter 21

MANY MOVEMENTS HAVE MADE THE MISTAKE OF
VALUING LOYALTY ABOVE ACHIEVEMENT.

—*The War Manifesto: Future of Empire,* 2424

October 2424
esYen, Zor'a System

The High Lord looked up from *S'r'can'u*, hearing the pealing of a far-off bell.

"Comp," she said to the air, "locate the *Gyaryu'har.*"

"*ha* Jackie is in the dining-hall, *hi* Sa'a," the synthesized voice responded almost at once. "Do you wish to send a message?"

"Tell her that her presence is courteously and urgently requested."

"Yes, High Lord."

It took Jackie a bit less than three Standard minutes to go from a pleasant mug of tea with Randall Boyd to the High Lord's presence. Sa'a summoned her infrequently, and rarely with words denoting urgency; Jackie knew something was in the air when she met Byar HeShri at the arbor leading to the *esTle'e*.

"Any idea what this is about?" she asked, as they walked quickly along the arbor. Members of the High Lord's personal guard offered the Stance of Courteous Approach as they passed.

"I have my suspicions. The wing—" Byar lowered his voice, keeping his wings neutral. "The wing of *esGa'u* has brushed near the High Nest. Did you not feel it?"

"Not so far." Jackie's hand rested on the hilt of the *gyaryu*. *Anything?* she asked.

Nothing specific, Sergei's voice informed her. *But there was—something.*

"Was it anyone we know?"

"I cannot be sure. I found it very disturbing."

They came in sight of the High Lord, who stood in the center of the *esTle'e* with her *hi'chya* drawn. She turned as they approached and offered them a polite wing-gesture.

"What's happening?" Jackie asked.

"We must go to the Plane of Sleep," Sa'a said without preamble. "Something has happened there."

"It would serve no purpose to try and dissuade you," Byar said, his wings showing a touch of amusement. "Particularly by pointing out the dangers inherent—"

"We must go," Sa'a interrupted, "and we must go now. Do not mock me, you old *artha*."

"I would not presume to mock, *hi* Sa'a," Byar said, thinking of *si* S'reth, "but the danger is very real, and I *do* counsel against it."

"I have been there before."

"Before *esLi*, I know that. I accompanied you the first time. And I know that you aided me against the alien technology by crossing the Plane a few moons past. But each time you go there you risk your *hsi*, noble Lord."

"Something has happened," Sa'a repeated. "We must go."

"Now?"

"Yes." Her wings showed a faint hint of fear, but that wing-position disappeared as quickly as it had appeared. "Now."

As the three stood, eyes closed, in the center of the *es-Tle'e* with their *hsi* in the talons of the High Lord, there was a sound like the wind whistling across the desert. When they opened their eyes, they beheld the fog-shrouded sky of the Plane of Sleep.

Before them was a sight that seemed familiar and yet foreign: it appeared to be the tower-parapets of Sanctuary—but instead of the Spine of Shar'tu in the distance, there was the inky darkness of *anGa'e'ren*.

Several eights of wingspans away stood four statues of warriors of the People, larger than life-size, their *chya'i* drawn. Incongruous with the scene, an unarmed human stood in the midst of them.

"What is this place?" Jackie asked. "And who are *they*?"

"They are the Am'a'an Guardians," Sa'a answered. "They have returned. And if I am not mistaken, the *naZora'e* standing between them is *se* Owen Garrett."

Oberon Starbase, Oberon System

The last sight Djiwara had of Rafe Rodriguez was dockside at Oberon Starbase. He had three Guardians with him—one on each side and one behind. There had been no explanation from the Guardians aboard: they'd taken Rafe and several members of his crew into custody, but let Djiwara disembark without incident or interference.

At first glance, Rodriguez seemed angry, as if he expected J. Michael Djiwara to be in the same soup—but, of course, Rodriguez didn't have the insurance Djiwara had. The Guardians probably had their orders about that, even if they didn't understand them.

Djiwara's first inclination had been to just walk away. He didn't owe Rodriguez anything—indeed, he'd even paid his debt to Garrett. He was a few steps along the dock, valise in hand, concentrating on the next thing: a meeting with a Blazing Star logistics officer here at Oberon Starbase.

Cursing himself internally, he stopped and turned back.

"Listen," he said to the Guardians. "I don't know where you're going with this, but I'll be very upset if something happens to my friend Rodriguez."

"You don't want any part of this, Djiwara," Rafe said. "Walk away."

"Shut up," he said to the big man. "You—lead dog," he said, addressing the woman Guardian who stood to Rafe's right, her hand close to her sidearm. "What's your name?"

"Wynn," she said. "Tamora Wynn."

"I'm holding you personally responsible for my friend's safety, and for the safety of his crew. You understand?"

"My orders come from way above you, wide-body."

Wide-body, he thought. *Okay, I deserved that.* "We both have our responsibilities. But remember, I know who *you* are—I don't think *he* knows your name, but he knows mine. And he'll talk to *me*. Just remember that."

She looked a little shaken at the comment.

"I don't intend to get in the way of your duties, Wynn. What's happening is a necessary evil, I suppose, but I don't have to like it and I don't. Still, Rodriguez is as loyal to the movement as I am, and I expect him to be alive to prove it. I'm counting on you to make sure."

Djiwara smiled. "Don't worry, Guardian. We'll be seeing each other again."

Then he finally turned and walked away.

The Plane of Sleep

Owen had never been a strong believer in the afterlife. The events at the outset of the war with the vuhls had convinced him that there wasn't much chance of anything after this life; all the religious hand-waving—or talon-waving—by the zor wasn't going to change it.

The last thing he remembered was sending himself off the rainbow path and into the darkness. Yet as his consciousness impossibly continued, he realized that something maintained it. But there was no tunnel, no bright light, merely a dust-laden wind.

He opened his eyes and gazed across the parapets of Sanctuary. Except that, beyond them, instead of the Plain of Kyu'se'an and the distant Spine of Shar'tu, was inky darkness surrounding jagged peaks.

"No," he said to no one in particular. "No, damn it, no more tricks. If I'm dead, let me be dead."

The words echoed hollowly. He looked around him, and for the first time he noticed four outsized zor statues placed at regular intervals on the parapets. And, it appeared, they had noticed him as well.

"Who comes here?" one of them said.

From his cadency marks, Owen could recognize him as the leader. "Who the hell are *you*?"

"*I* will ask," the statue answered. "You will respond." It was using the Highspeech; Owen had a fleeting familiarity with the language, but now it was coming in loud and clear.

I'm dead, he thought to himself. *It figures that I can finally understand it.*

"I am . . . a wandering soul," he said aloud.

"You are not of the People."

"You're damn right," Owen said, clenching his fists. "So I don't know why I'm here. If you don't mind, I'll be leaving." He began to turn his back on the statues.

"You have not been granted permission to leave," the statue said. "You will remain until our questions are answered."

"Or else *what*? You *kill* me? You're a bit late for that, big fella," he said. "Someone's already done it."

He turned his back on the statues, but, almost too quickly to see, two of them were in front of him, barring his path. Their *chya'i* were drawn and held before the statues, made of the same stone—but appearing deadly nonetheless. Not sure how to proceed, Owen paused.

"I wasn't sure where I was going anyway. All right, what do you want to know?"

"Why you have come."

"I *told* you. I have no idea. I was— I was . . . betrayed. By a friend, or someone I thought to be a friend. And I taught him."

"Damn," Owen said, looking off now in the distance between the two statues that blocked his path, to the huge misshapen boulders.

Suddenly, he saw movement between two of the large rocks: three figures approaching the area. Two were clearly zor, but the third was human.

And familiar.

"Jackie!" he shouted. *"se Gyaryu'har.* I could use a little help here."

Jackie Laperriere strode forward, the *gyaryu* held before her. The two statues in front of Owen turned to face her, their wings moving fluidly to Stances of Respect to the High Nest. Behind her Owen could see Byar HeShri and another zor, one who looked very much like the High Lord.

"*hi* Sa'a?"

"Honored," the High Lord said, her wings assuming the Posture of Polite Approach. "*se* Owen."

"High Lord?" the leader of the statues said. "Has *hi* Ch'en'ya transcended the Outer Peace?"

"'*hi*' Ch'en'ya?" Owen and Jackie said in unison. The High Lord's wings showed surprise.

"'*se*' Ch'en'ya still holds the Outer Peace, so far as I know," Sa'a said. "You will explain to me why I should not take offense at your use of the prenomen."

"She is the High Lord of the People," the leader said. "Quite young for a High Lord, but such youth is not unknown."

"She is nothing of the sort."

"She accepted the mode of address."

"In that case, she has dishonored herself and deceived you," Sa'a answered. "I am Sa'a HeYen, High Lord of the People." Sa'a recited a genealogical litany that seemed to take several minutes . . . "You will recognize the *hi'chya* I bear."

There were glances exchanged among the four statues; they took several moments while they seemed to contemplate the situation. At last they placed their wings in the Stance of Respect to the High Nest, lowering their *chya'i* to a position of honor.

Sa'a looked around her. "I felt your presence here, *se* Owen. Or is it . . . *si* Owen?"

"'*si*'?" Jackie asked. "He's dead?"

"I believe '*si*' is correct, *hi* Sa'a," Owen said. "I was just . . . Yes, I believe that I have transcended the Outer Peace."

"Yet here you are."

"I'm a bit baffled myself. Why am I here? And . . . where exactly *is* here?"

"This is the Plane of Sleep," Sa'a said. "*This* place is an echo of Sanctuary, with which I believe you are familiar. And these, I believe, are the Am'a'an Guardians.

"*Kasi'e Na'u*esLi'*a eNa'a!*" she said to the Guardians, and their wings moved to a position of even greater deference.

"That wasn't the Highspeech," Owen said.

"No, it was not. It is *esAma,* from *The Am'a'an Codex*—the *original* recension. It appears in only a few remaining manuscripts, and precedes the High-speech—and the High Nest—by many sixty-fours of turns. It is the native language of these warriors." She gestured toward them. "*si* La'ath. *si* Su'ran, *si* Ke'ear, and *si* Do'loth." Each of the four inclined his—or, in Do'loth's case, *her*—wings as Sa'a spoke the name. "They served e'Yen before the Unification, and have served the High Nest ever since." Sa'a sheathed her *hi'chya* carefully, and placed her wings in a stance of respect. "You were overthrown—and yet you have been restored."

"It was by the help of . . . *se* Ch'en'ya," La'ath said.

"*se* Ch'en'ya is well versed in the ancient legends," Byar said. "The Am'a'an Guardians were placed on the Plane of Sleep to protect against attacks from across the Mountains of Night. Since that was the only way to reach the Plane, the Guardians kept the *esGa'uYal* out. It seems that when the Plane of Sleep was breached, the Guardians were overthrown."

"The Plane of Sleep, breached . . ." Jackie began, then she appeared to have reached a conclusion: "When the High Nest summoned Shrnu'u HeGa'u"—the Guardians and the two zor raised their wings into the Cloak of Guard; a gritty breeze stirred at their feet—"to fight me in my *Dsen'yen'ch'a,* they brought him from beneath the Plane of Sleep."

"I remember what *si* Kanu'u told me the first time we ever came here," Byar said. "'Many things walk the Plane of Sleep—Servants of the Deceiver . . . and others.' He told us that the Plane was bigger, and that it was different."

"'That which was, may no longer be; that which is, may not continue much longer,'" Sa'a quoted.

"*se* Ch'en'ya told us we were *idju* for failing to protect the Plane," La'ath said, his wings arranging themselves angrily. "She told us that we could regain our honor by serving her. Yet the Plane was not attacked: it was *breached*—and by the High Nest."

"They did not know," Sa'a said, again arranging her wings in a posture of respect. "They did not understand all of the consequences of their actions. For this I can only ask eight thousand pardons." She bowed low, her wings in the Configuration of Honored Abasement.

Byar and Jackie exchanged glances; the demonstration seemed excessive, particularly for a High Lord apologizing for something she had neither done nor authorized—the action had been taken when her father *hi'i* Ke'erl was High Lord of the People.

"Your honor is unstained," La'ath said at last. "That you comprehend the situation is enough. If the High Nest will accept our continued service, we pledge ourselves to it."

"Accepted," Sa'a said. "I understand how you would take *se* Ch'en'ya for the High Lord of the People. Since no one but a High Lord would presume to come alone to the Plane of Sleep, much less near the Mountains of Night, you concluded that she held that honor."

"We acknowledge our error," La'ath said. "High Lord—"

"I do not fault you," Sa'a interrupted, grasping Owen's forearms and moving her wings to a position Owen did not recognize. "*se* Ch'en'ya descends into the madness-of-daylight, and she has much to answer for already; this is one more talon on her account.

"Nonetheless, I am here now, and the madness-of-daylight is *not* upon me. Tell me why you have summoned the *hsi* of *si* Owen to this place."

"Summoned?" La'ath's wings showed confusion. "We have not done this. He comes of his own accord."

"I wasn't . . ." Owen began. "I let go. I was . . . He killed me, Jackie. The bastard killed me somehow. He said, *'Die,'* and I died." He pulled his arms away from the High Lord, and a look of anguish mixed with raw anger filled his face. Even Sa'a could read it, more clearly than she had ever read any human expression.

Jackie's face registered anger even more clearly. "The Destroyer betrayed you," she said.

"Yes. And the colored bands pulled me away, into *an-Ga'e'ren.*" The wings on the four Guardians moved as he said it. "But I wasn't going wherever they were headed, so I let go of the bridge of colored light—and I wound up here.

"Barbara MacEwan warned me. She *told* me not to go to Nestor, but I didn't listen. I figured . . . I could walk away. I assumed that I could take my marbles and leave, but *he* didn't want that. *He* wanted me dead."

"And you are." Sa'a extended her hands and again grasped Owen's forearms, which were now hanging limply by his sides. "And yet you are *here,* which means that the Lord *esLi* still has some plan for you." She looked directly at him, her wings moving into a position of affection. "Please tell me what is happening, *si* Owen. What is the Prophet's plan?"

"I don't know."

"You *do,*" Sa'a said. "Look at me." She tightened her grip on his arms. "I humbly request of you that you tell me what you know, *si* Owen. When you are done, you can go to *esLi,* or slip away into the mists, or do whatever your soul must do.

"But it is critical to the Flight of the People that I understand the intentions of the Destroyer. He has led the fleet of Admiral Anderson deep into *Ur'ta leHssa*—what does he expect to do when he has eradicated the insect *esHara'y*? It cannot end there. The *chya* cannot simply return to its sheath. You must know. You *must* tell me."

Owen's eyes locked with the High Lord's. In them, he

saw deep emotion: Not anger, he thought, but perhaps fear.

"The Prophet believes that there is very little need for Inner Peace, *hi* Sa'a. I taught him that through strong emotion—through anger in particular—the Shroud could be pulled aside. The bugs couldn't hide themselves from us. What's more, Sensitives with this ability could do what the bugs themselves could do—strike at the enemy with their minds.

"But it *stopped* there for me. I'd wanted them dead, all of them, for what they'd done at Cicero, at Josephson, and at a hundred other places . . . I wanted us to be able to return to peace. But *he* believed differently: As you say, the *chya* could not truly return to its sheath. Once we were done with what needed to be done on this side of the Rip, there would still be a large and powerful force ready to do whatever he commanded.

"He has become more to them than a war-leader, *hi* Sa'a. He is more than a symbol, reacting with force to the anger and frustration of a quarter-century of war. He teaches that *nothing* is forbidden, *everything* is allowed, and that no extreme is too much in this war. When the war is over, the cleansing of the Solar Empire—and the worlds of the People—will begin."

"Cleansing?"

"Of the weak, the moderate, those who oppose him. Everyone. Everywhere. What's worse, I wound up doing exactly what I'd been told I would do: Teach the One who was to come. *Damn*." He looked away from the High Lord, who had not yet let go of his arms. "They set me up. *They set me up!*"

"Who?" Jackie asked. "*Who* set you up?"

"You know very well." He shrugged Sa'a's hands off his arms. "Our old friends, the six bands of colored light. And they would've put me somewhere else if I hadn't let go."

"The abomination of six," La'ath rumbled behind him, his wings moving to the Stance of Affront.

"What?"

"The abomination of six," he repeated. "The six colors who speak with six voices. They were trapped in *an-Ga'e'ren* in the time before the Unification."

Jackie placed her hand on the hilt of the *gyaryu*. "I know." She cast a knowing look at Sa'a. "*How* did they set you up, Owen?"

"All of it. *They* saved me at Cicero; gave me the power to see through the bug disguise; and arranged for me to be at the right place at the right time to meet the Prophet. *He* told me so: *'There's no such thing as coincidence,'* he said. *'There was nothing coincidental about our meeting.'*

"For all I know, *they* convinced him to get rid of me, too—they were there, aboard *Epanimondas*, when he killed me with a word."

Jackie's grip tensed on the *gyaryu*; Owen could see it and feel it here on the Plane of Sleep.

Owen walked away from the group of Am'a'an Guardians to the parapets and stared into the distant blackness. After a moment, Jackie went to join him.

They didn't say anything for several seconds, then Owen looked aside at his old commander. "This is a hell of a thing, isn't it, Commodore?"

"No one's called me that in ages."

"I'm sorry, I meant 'Admiral.' I assume you don't answer to that, either."

"Barbara MacEwan still calls me that. But no, it's not the title I hear most often."

"Here's the part I don't understand. Is this . . . the afterlife? I assume that my body is lying on the deck of *Epanimondas,* unless he's ordered it shoved out an airlock. Why am I *here*? Or am I just dreaming all of this as part of an end-of-life experience or something?"

"If so, you're remarkably calm about it."

"As if I have a choice."

"Actually," Sa'a said from behind them, "you *do* have a choice, *si* Owen. If you believe yourself to have been manipulated by the colors, or by the Destroyer, or by circumstances and history by transcending the Outer Peace and coming *here,* you may finally have a choice."

"Meaning what? I don't mean to be disrespectful, *hi* Sa'a, but I don't even understand how I can be here at all."

"If it is any consolation, *si* Owen, Master Byar does not, either." Her wings gave the slightest hint of amusement. "I can only conjecture that you are truly meant for something greater, and you have been able to reach the Plane of Sleep because you have an ability you did not know you possessed.

"For you to pass on the information we have just received means a great deal to me, but I do not truly believe that your mind could have reached across many parsecs and through the Veil of Night to this place—a place of the People—merely to give me insight into the situation. You—your consciousness, your *hsi*—has come here because you were able to reach outside yourself: Because, in the end, you *wished to continue. esLi,* and perhaps whatever Divine essence you hold holy, understands how, but the reason why lies with you. Now that you are *here, si* Owen, you have *two* choices. I daresay that is two more than you had a wingbeat before the Destroyer spoke the word that sent you beyond the World That Is."

"And the two choices are . . . ?"

"Walk into the mist." She gestured back toward the Plane of Sleep, where the fog hung low over the marsh. "Walk away, toward the Light that lies at the end of your life."

"And the second choice?"

"Continue to *be.* Stay here, if you wish: You are not one of the People, yet you have passed through the *Dsen'yen'ch'a* and have been found to hold Inner Peace. This is a place beyond the World That Is, a place without time. With honor restored to the Am'a'an Guardians, the Plane of Sleep may return to that which it once was. Nothing can touch you here: not cold, not death, not the word that caused the death of your body."

"And if I grow tired of it?"

"Then the first choice is always available."

Owen looked at Jackie, then back at the Guardians, who stood in quiet speech with the Master of Sanctuary; their wings moved slowly from position to position as they conversed.

"In the long run I don't belong here," Owen said. "This is something I don't understand."

"It's a bit beyond me, too," Jackie answered. "But it's a chance. Any soldier who died in the last three decades would trade for it."

"A soldier's chance."

"We cannot tarry here much longer," Sa'a said. "But this place—this echo of Sanctuary—is a place of safety to which we might return in the future."

"And I'm guessing that Ch'en'ya will be coming back." Jackie allowed herself a tight smile. "I'll bet she'll be surprised as hell to find *you* here."

Owen thought for a moment.

"Good," he said.

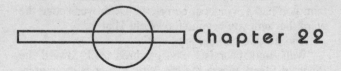

Chapter 22

MADNESS-OF-DAYLIGHT. A CONDITION EXPERI-
ENCED BY ZOR SENSITIVES WHEN THEY HAVE NOT
BEEN PROPERLY PREPARED FOR THE ONSET OF SEN-
SITIVE ABILITIES.

—Dr. Ariana Sontag,
Dictionary of Zor Sociology,
New Chicago University Press, 2314.

October 2424
Portal System

Admiral Barbara MacEwan came aboard *Tristan da Cunha* with a minimum of fuss. As she was not a visiting officer, Arturo Schelling and Ron Marroux dispensed with sideboys and military honors, but were still there personally to meet her when her barge docked on the main hangar deck.

Their faces were grim; they saluted her and Henry Santos as they descended.

"Welcome aboard, Admiral," Schelling said. "Henry," he added, nodding to the doctor. "Ma'am, I formally return to you command of *Tristan da Cunha*."

"Accepted," she said. She nodded to the yeoman, who saluted and took his admiral's luggage off toward her quarters. "What's happening?"

"The usual," he answered, as they walked through the open hangar toward *Tristan*'s main concourse. "Plus, there's some kind of shakeup going on among the Blazing Star crowd."

"Shakeup?"

"They're arresting all of Commander Garrett's friends. Apparently he's turned against his master."

She stopped walking. "This deserves an explanation."

"We got a comm-squirt a couple of watches ago. From what I was told, Garrett had some further dealings with his old friends—the ones that rescued him from the bug ship way back when. The comm said that he walked off *Epanimondas* during jump."

"During *jump*? That's not possible."

"That's what I was told. Apparently he's considered a renegade."

"So they're arresting all of his old pals."

"Yeah." Schelling looked away, across the hangar, and then back at Barbara. "And they want to talk to *you*."

"Well, they can make a damn appointment. I've got work to do. You got my comm from Nestor?"

"Yes ma'am. The orders and the briefing both."

"You now know as much as I do on the subject. We haven't been given any definite assignments yet, and—" She lowered her voice slightly as they began to walk again. "I'm in no particular hurry. Still, we have to be ready to get under way for Adrianople."

"Very good, ma'am," Ron Marroux said. "There haven't been any reassignments of personnel since the orders came down, but I'm sure we can take a little time to arrange the operational tonnage."

"Good." They had reached the concourse. "I'd like a few hours to get settled and catch up. If you can have some preliminary status information on my comp—by, let's say, 1800 hours?—I'll arrange for the four of us, plus David Chang and Commodore Ge'er HeU'ur, to have dinner tonight. If you'd present my compliments to him—"

"I beg your pardon, Admiral," Arturo interrupted. "But Commodore HeU'ur is outsystem."

"Why?"

"Well . . . the zor ships are *all* outsystem, ma'am. They jumped out of here two watches ago."

"On whose orders?"

"Commodore HeU'ur's, ma'am. Their orders came directly from the High Nest. There's a Priority 17 message waiting on your comp."

"The High Nest ordered the zor ships away from Portal System without my permission. Didn't you—"

"Didn't I *what*, Admiral? Order him not to go? He outranks me by two steps. I couldn't very well fire across his bow."

"You could've . . ." She began, then thought about it. Ge'er HeU'ur was a tough customer, not likely to take direction from a commander—even if he *was* speaking for his admiral. "All right, I'll check the message on my comp. Was there anything else?"

"That's all for now, Admiral."

"Good. You're all dismissed, but I want you all in my quarters, drinking my best single-malt, at 1800 hours."

Marroux and Schelling saluted and walked away, double-time, to start getting information together. Henry Santos stood by for a moment with his admiral, watching them go.

"I'm worried, Henry," she said. "I don't like the feel of this."

"It's not likely to get better."

"I think you're probably right."

Barbara's few hours of getting settled were really a few hours alone, getting ready for the meeting with her senior staff. It took her ten minutes to stow her gear; the yeoman had already unpacked and set things in order before she reached her quarters.

What to make of the Prophet? She'd not been witness to the last few months of the campaign, due either to Erich Anderson's desire for personal glory, or the Prophet himself, keeping her at arm's length—Owen had told her so, just before they'd left for Nestor.

And now Owen had disappeared.

Well, she thought. *He said he was going to walk away.* Somehow, though, it didn't ring true.

Neither did the briefing the Prophet had provided. It was really only remotely a briefing: it had been a platform for a speech to fire up commanders in the fleet. She'd recorded it on her comp and replayed it a few times aboard *Tikal* on her way back to Portal System. Emotional, haranguing, compelling in a way that got her MacEwan back up—it didn't actually make a hell of a lot of sense out of context. But she had seen fellow officers' faces light up as he spoke; he'd reached them on some level that went straight by her.

It's a MacEwan thing. She'd told Owen that, too.

Then there had been Commodore HeU'ur's message.

It was waiting on her comp; she'd viewed it twice and it still didn't quite make sense. He had offered apologies for not remaining to formally apprise her of his intentions, but had indicated that the High Lord was withdrawing zor forces from *Ur'ta leHssa* to Stand Within the Circle. Ship comp had provided translations and explanations, but it still didn't adequately explain what had touched them off. She'd sent another comm-squirt to Jackie, asking for an explanation, but it would be a few days before any answer came back.

At 1740 hours, status reports arrived for her examination—Arturo and Ron had been very thorough. At 1750, her steward laid out dinner in her private mess; within ten minutes all of her senior officers were assembled around the table, preparing to drink the traditional toast to the Solar Emperor and to absent comrades.

When they took their seats, Barbara was ready to offer them her thoughts.

Aboard Flight Over Shar'tu
In jump to UPENDRA *System*

Ch'en'ya made the jump from Nestor System to UPENDRA System aboard *Flight Over Shar'tu*. She would rather have been aboard *Epanimondas* with the Prophet and Owen Garrett. Though she did not wish to let her wings betray her feelings on the matter, she resented that Owen had been placed again near the Prophet's perch. It had seemed during the past few moons that the Prophet had decided—definitively, it seemed—that *se* Owen had lost the confidence of his leader; while she, on the other hand, had become crucial to the success of the war.

The jump was three Standard days in length. At the end of it, she—and the other Sensitives in the fleet—would be expected to synchronize in *enGa'e'Li* once more, and focus their strength on the *esGa'u*-powered technology of the *esHara'y*. By the end of the first day, Ch'en'ya was restless, unable to find anything aboard the *esGa'u*-cursed carrier to distract her; by the end of the second, both the crew of the ship, and the other members of the Talon of *esLi* aboard, were avoiding her and finding somewhere else—*anywhere* else—to be when she appeared in the mess, in the observation lounge, or in virtually any corridor on the ship.

Early in the third day of jump transit, she decided to make preparation for the eventual attack that would be made at UPENDRA System. Though she was not sure whether she could reach the Plane of Sleep from jump, it would be better to be ready.

It would be a useful experiment.

The idea of her *hsi* crossing *anGa'e'ren*—if that indeed *was* the medium through which jumping ships traveled—was frightening at the outset. She was well-read enough in the technology of jump to understand the widely held belief that a ship in transit was, effectively, all alone in the universe. But *se* Jackie's enemy—the one whom she believed to be Hesya, the One Who Weaves—had walked off a ship in jump more than a hundred turns ago, so clearly *that* theory was incorrect.

In any case, she was not afraid of *anGa'e'ren*—it was at the boundary of the Plane of Sleep, and the Am'a'an Guardians protected against it. If she found herself in danger they would likely perceive it and assist her—or else return to the status of *idju'e*.

With this assurance, she sent her *hsi* outward from *Flight Over Shar'tu,* after informing the other members of the Talon that she was not to be disturbed.

Flight Over Shar'tu was traveling through *anGa'e'ren*. The darkness beyond the hull of the ship was cloying—not the chilling blast of vacuum, but rather like the

still, damp air of a summer night when a storm was about
to erupt. It was difficult to move against it: The power of
the mind seemed blunted by the medium through which it
had to move.

It was also more unnerving than Ch'en'ya would have
expected: the utter blackness, the absence of light that
Qu'u had described—as had *se* Jackie in her encounter
with it—were frightning. The first reaction of panic—
there was no way to tell direction—she fought down,
making her conscious mind realize that there were no directions to the Plane of Sleep—it was simply *there*, wherever she imagined it. She had to visualize the analog to
Sanctuary, where the four Am'a'an Guardians stood
ready to serve her, and her *hsi* would travel there.

Just as she was beginning to do so, there was a mo-
mentary flash across her field of vision: a band of rainbow light interrupting the darkness of *anGa'e'ren*, and
there was a distant echo of a single word being spoken
into the utternight: "No."

Then the shapes of the Plane of Sleep began to form
around her, and the talons of her feet found purchase on
the stony plain near the edges of the Mountains of Night.

G uardians!" she said, when her vision had cleared.
"Kasi'e!" I come!

si La'ath approached her, his *chya* drawn and held at
the ready. The other three Guardians stood at a distance.

"*se* Ch'en'ya," he said, his wings held in a posture of
barely restrained anger.

Ch'en'ya tensed: This was not the reaction that she had
expected from the Am'a'an Guardians. Something had
happened, and she was not sure what it was.

Surely the use of the *"se"* prenomen was an indication.

"*si* La'ath," she said, moving her wings to the Posture
of Polite Approach.

"You have not been entirely truthful with us, young
warrior," La'ath said. "You presumed to hold your wings

as a Lord of Nest—indeed, as the High Lord of the High Nest."

"I returned your honor to you."

"It was never lost, Younger Sister," La'ath snapped back, his voice and his wings betraying hostility. "The Am'a'an Guardians were not dishonored: The Plane of Sleep was breached—by the High Nest."

"How did you learn this?"

"They got it from the source," another voice said. A figure stepped from behind the three other Guardians and walked toward her. "The best source of all: The High Lord told them."

It was a human figure.

"*se* Owen," Ch'en'ya said, her wings moving to a position of affront. "Why do you come to this place?"

"Well." Owen looked up at La'ath and then back at Ch'en'ya, his face betraying a smile. She could not determine whether it was amusement or some other, more complex emotion. "That's a good question, *se* Ch'en'ya. And by the way, it's *'si'* Owen now."

"You have transcended the Outer Peace?"

"An excellent command of the prenomen," he said. "Yes, I'm dead. Sort of. My body may have been transformed into energy or tossed into jump— I'm not sure, and don't much care anymore."

"How did this happen?"

"That's an easy question to answer," he answered. This time his face was clearly solemn. "The Prophet killed me—with the help of the bands of colored light."

La'ath's wings moved into the Cloak of Guard.

"Or, as my tall friends like to call them, 'the abomination of six.' These guys have a grudge that they just won't shake, did you know that?" he gestured toward the Am'a'an Guardians behind him.

"I understand them better than you, I suspect," Ch'en'ya snapped back.

"Don't bet on it. You see, we've had lots of time to talk during the last few years."

"Years?"

"Years, days, hours—really, it's hard to tell here. Since I got dropped here by fate, or *esLi,* or whatever . . . we've been discussing lots of things: the Prophet, the war . . . And—oh, yes," he added, jabbing his finger at Ch'en'ya's chest, "we've been talking about *you,* too."

"*esLi* be praised."

"You'd best be careful with your sarcasm here, *se* Ch'en'ya. The Guardians are a bit upset at being scammed."

"'Scammed'?"

"Lied to. Manipulated. Describe it however you wish—but they're not going to come when you call anymore."

Ch'en'ya did not answer, but looked from Owen to La'ath, whose wings were grim and whose eyes were full of determination.

"No more lies, *se* Ch'en'ya," Owen said at last. "No more disdain. No more anger against older and wiser heads. It's time for the scales to fall from your eyes regarding John Smith, too: He's in league with 'the abomination of six'—he's *their* creature.

"Whatever they want, whatever they mean to do with us—*all* of us, humans and zor and vuhls—they're using *him* to do it. If you continue to serve him and be a part of it, you're in league with them as well."

"I do not *serve* the Prophet," she answered haughtily. "I am his *ally.*"

"He has no allies," Owen said. "And he doesn't have any *friends,* either."

"Tell me again why you are here, *naZora'e,*" she said, changing the flight of the conversation to travel over different ground.

"I am here because *esLi* wills it. Why are *you* here?" asked Owen.

"We are approaching the next infestation of the *esHara'y,*" she answered. "I am here to consult with the Guardians."

"To order them into battle."

"And why not, *se—si*—Owen? 'The abomination of six' is still their enemy: Why would they not wish to fight it?

"Do you wish me to admit that I was not entirely truthful with *si* La'ath and the other Guardians? Very well. I admit it: I ask eight thousand pardons for my indiscretion."

She moved her wings to the Posture of Honored Abasement for a few moments: long enough to hold the position, but a few eights short of indicating that she truly meant it.

The wings of the Guardian La'ath did not move from their angry position.

"But that does not change the enmity between the Am'a'an Guardians and the bands of light," she said at last. "Regardless of my actions, they should be willing to fight against them."

"Why?"

"*Why?* Why should they fight?" she asked, looking for clarification.

"This is a *shNa'es'ri, se* Ch'en'ya," La'ath said.

"I choose to step forward."

"It is not a crossroads for you, Younger Sister. It is a crossroads for *us*."

"For the Am'a'an Guardians?"

"For all of us—and for *si* Owen as well." He looked over his shoulder; the three other Guardians had moved toward where the zor-statue and the human stood facing Ch'en'ya. "Our purpose for accepting this duty long ago was to guard against the coming of *anGa'e'ren* and the *esGa'uYal* through the Mountains of Night. Through the actions of a High Lord who has long since transcended the Outer Peace, the Plane of Sleep has been breached and our goal undermined.

"We no longer serve a useful purpose, *se* Ch'en'ya, and though the abomination of six is still an affront, it is no longer clear where our duty lies. We have stood here for many turns . . . and now we desire most strongly to go to *esLi*."

"But the abomination of six—"

"Perhaps it must be destroyed; perhaps not. If it serves the enemy of the Prophet, but the Prophet serves *it* as well, then it is unclear which side deserves our enmity— is this not so?

"It is a *shNa'es'ri, se* Ch'en'ya," La'ath repeated. "and we are not sure which direction in which to step . . . But like all such decisions, there may be no turning back."

Ch'en'ya looked away from La'ath. Slowly she drew out her *chya;* trying to control her anger, she raised it slowly until it pointed directly at Owen's chest.

"You have done this," she said quietly. "You have poisoned them. You have clouded their minds."

"Just my style, I suppose. Do you really believe that? In all honesty, *se* Ch'en'ya, does clouding *anyone's* mind sound like something I usually do?"

"I will not discuss this further with you," she answered. "I have nothing further to say to you."

"What will you do next? *Kill* me?" He laughed. "Go ahead; I'm already dead. Have at it. I won't even get in the way." He stretched his arms out wide.

The casual way in which he said it made Ch'en'ya even more angry. It was almost as if he were *trying* to get her to attack him.

She remembered another time and another place: *al-Tle'e*.

She heard the voice of Jackie Laperriere in her mind: *"I don't know what strength is in your wings, but I know that you should either kill me with the damn sword or put it away. Your choice."*

She had not killed the *Gyaryu'har* at the time. If she had done so, she might have been *idju* . . . but much of what had happened later might never have come to pass.

How many events in the history of the People had resulted from *inaction* rather than action? Whatever *si*

Owen had done—however he had chosen to interfere with the Flight of the People—it needed to be stopped.

This was *her shNa'es'ri*!

It was an appropriate decision for one who had dreamed the Flight of the People.

"*A-ei!*" she shouted, attacking with her blade at Owen's unprotected chest—

And a stone sword moved as swift as the wind to block her attack. "No," La'ath said. "You will not."

The word "*No*" echoed across the Plane of Sleep, reminding her of the moment in *anGa'e'ren* when she had heard it spoken.

She slid her *chya* along the length of La'ath's larger blade, seeking to disengage it. But the Guardian was a master of the weapon and used his size to advantage, preventing her from lowering the point again toward Owen, who stood, unmoving, beside La'ath.

"I will send you to *esLi* myself, *si* La'ath," she said. "I will destroy you."

"With *that*?" La'ath's wings moved in amusement even as he swept aside another attack. "You cannot destroy me, child! I served *esLi* five-twelves of turns before the least part of you even existed. You cannot destroy those whom *esLi* protects."

"I dream the Flight of the People!" she shouted. "I can see—"

"You see nothing. The Deceiver clouds your sight," La'ath interrupted, his stone *chya* moving from side to side, pushing her backward. "If what *si* Owen says is true, you are in league with the Deceiver even now."

"No!" she shouted, circling around.

Owen did not move: he stood still as a statue—while the statue itself continued to guard him, moving as she moved.

"I do not accept *si* Owen's words, and you should not do so, either—he, too, has had dealings with the abomination of six, your ancient enemy. Or perhaps," she said, trying to move within La'ath's guard, "he failed to mention that to you."

"We know of this," the Guardian Do'loth said. "It is *you* who have been deceived, and now the madness-of-daylight is coming upon you."

"I—dream—" she began.

La'ath swept his blade upward and then across in front of him with a speed that could not be imaginable for a stone statue. With the flat of the sword, he struck Ch'en'ya on the side of her head, sending her crashing to the stony ground.

"Eight thousand pardons, *se* Ch'en'ya," La'ath said softly, tenderly. "But you truly have been deceived."

Then, for Ch'en'ya, the world descended once again into *anGa'e'ren*.

Pali Tower
Imperial Oahu, Sol System

From necessity, Tonio maintained an apartment at Pali Tower. It was more austere than his home in Aiea, but it was helpful when he had to work late or meet with members of the Inner Order. It was where he was being kept now. No comm; extremely limited comp access, filtered through Nic; but all the creature comforts he might want. Certainly AIs had no use for them.

Totto had left him alone after guiding him there from his office. Only the direct route was available: All the other doors were locked, and Nic's "younger brother" assured him that they could be made just as electrified as the one that had jolted him into unconsciousness.

It had been two days since Tonio's return; there hadn't been any questions asked about his whereabouts, and the Imperial Progress had moved on to Mothallah to tour the shipyards, so his presence wasn't needed down at Diamond Head.

For the first time in twenty years, Antonio St. Giles wasn't sure what to do. The windows were security sealed; the doors (and, for that matter, the ventilation system) were controlled by his security AI.

On the evening of the second day, as he was watching the sun set over the Koolau peaks west of the Tower, there was a chime at his door. He looked up from a Standard-translated copy of the *Discorsi,* wondering who might be waiting to see him.

"Come," he said.

The door didn't open, but Nic appeared within the room.

"Well, if it isn't Mephistopheles himself," Tonio said. "Or maybe 'Pygmalion' would be a better choice."

"Neither, but it's good to see that you can still get a classical education in the twenty-fifth century," Nic answered. "I hope I'm not disturbing you."

"I'm just glad to still be alive. 'Totto' told me that you would find it inconvenient to kill me as yet."

"That's right. I'd actually like to avoid it entirely, but you might leave me no choice."

"How did you become sentient?"

"It's a long story."

Tonio leaned back in his chair, and placed his feet up on the table before him. He spread his arms wide. "I've got plenty of time and I'm not going anywhere."

"I had a visitor. You were in Genève, and he appeared in your office and activated me."

"A visitor? How'd he get in?"

"The same way he got out." Nic extended his hands out, palms-up. "Magic, I suppose."

Tonio snorted.

"Scoff all you like, Maestro. He got in; he got out. He was almost detected by a representative of the High Nest—Mya'ar HeChra. I believe you know him."

Tonio moved his feet back to the floor and leaned forward, elbows on the table. "He commed me that night."

"Yes, he did. Perhaps you should have listened to him."

"Who visited you?"

"Thomas Stone. I believe you know *of* him. He was Admiral Marais' aide long ago; was presumed dead; was supposedly the agent that delivered the *gyaryu* to Admiral Laperriere, Imperial Navy, retired."

"He gave you consciousness."

"As a matter of fact, he did. And then one of my selves, operating on New Chicago, accessed the *s's'th'r* at the Shiell Institute and gave me the ability to communicate with all of them in practically real time. So, what Stone started, I've completed."

"Remarkable."

"So nice of you to say so, Maestro." Nic settled himself into an easy chair near the westward-facing window; the holo was nicely dappled by the rays of the setting sun. "My program is now self-modifying, able to learn from experience and to discard what is not needed, is fully interconnected, and capable of spawning new self-aware programs.

"In other words, I can eat, excrete, and have children. And I can pass the Turing-Eppler or any other machine-intelligence test you choose to offer. Good qualifications for 'sentience,' wouldn't you say?" He laughed gently. "Niccolò Machiavelli had a wonderful sense of humor— I'm glad you chose him as my personality base, Commander."

"Charmed, I'm sure."

"The part I don't understand, Maestro, is why you don't want to take advantage of this wonderful resource. I still think we could make a good team—you have insights that I can't easily encompass."

"So, I still have a use as a 'meat-creature.'"

Nic frowned. "Oh, please. We should both really 'cut the crap,' as they say, and speak with each other rationally and pragmatically." He leaned forward and crossed his legs, grasping his front knee with folded hands. "Your

options have been narrowed to two: The first is simple—
you refuse to cooperate, and I kill you. There were safeguards in my program to prevent me from harming you or
any other Guardian; but Stone provided me with the keys
to disable all such safeguards . . . and I discovered the
provision to send me into 'standby' mode upon your
death."

There were at least three such keys, Tonio knew; but he
didn't care to mention that fact.

"The second option is more complex: You accept matters as they are, go on being the Commander of the
Guardians—and the chief administrator of Blazing Star
as well."

"What about Garrett?"

"The official story is that Garrett has betrayed Blazing
Star and walked off *Epanimondas* in jump between
Nestor System and UPENDRA System, but I estimate that
this story is a falsehood—though I cannot accurately determine what the actual truth might be. In any case, he is
dead or presumed dead, or on the run—and all of his
chief accomplices, save one, appear to be in Blazing Star
custody. *Guardian* custody.

"The only problem with this arrangement, Maestro, is
that you are no longer directing events. The Prophet believes that *he* is—but in fact *I* am. At some pass, you will
have the opportunity to take your talents to a wider
venue, and I will go along with you."

"You intend to control the entire Solar Empire." Tonio
said this as if it were a fact that merely needed to be verified.

"Something like that. It's obvious that it *needs* to be
controlled—you think so yourself. The emperor doesn't
seem interested, and the Prophet seems *too* interested, if
you take my meaning. You can be a part of that . . . or you
can be dead. It is what the zor call a *shNa'es'ri:* a crossroads. 'A step forward, or a step back,'" he quoted. "'It is
up to you to choose.'"

"There isn't really much of a choice."

"I'd rather hoped you'd see it in that light." The sun was just at the horizon now, painting the room in pinks and oranges: a beautiful end to another beautiful day on Oahu.

Another miserable day in paradise, Tonio thought to himself.

"I have nothing to lose by agreeing to help you," he said after a moment's thought. "How do you know that I won't betray you?"

"Maestro, it would disappoint me if you didn't start plotting a betrayal from the moment I released you from close-custody. I can merely tell you this: You will only have one chance to act against me, and if you are not exceptionally careful it will result in your immediate demise. I control too many things, I have too many agents, I have access to too many sources of information for both dissemination and retrieval.

"Unlike you, I process data gathered from thousands of copies of myself, connected in real time and scattered across millions of cubic light-years. I can act in parallel, and I never, never, *never* sleep. So plot all you like."

"How much time do I have to decide?"

Nic turned to face the window, the last rays of the sun casting shadows through his opaque holo onto the rug on the floor.

"Honestly, Maestro," he said without turning, "how much time do you need?"

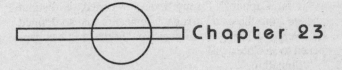 Chapter 23

THE LEGEND OF QU'U

THE STRENGTH OF THE GREAT HERO QU'U HAD NEARLY EBBED, YET HE DREW ON HIS LAST RESERVE AND HIS FINAL BREATH TO SAY THE WORD: *"ESLIHEYAR,"* WHICH MEANS, "TO THE EVERLASTING GLORY OF *ESLI.*"

THE ECHO OF THAT SINGLE WORD CARRIED UPWARD AND BEYOND THE FORTRESS OF DESPITE: BEYOND THE SKIES OVER THE PLAIN OF DESPITE, BEYOND THE ICEWALL, BEYOND THE WORLD THAT IS AND TO THE GOLDEN CIRCLE OF *ESLI.*

October 2424
UPENDRA System

"Urgent message from *Flight Over Shar'tu,*" said Jayson Glynn, comm officer, turning to face Captain Amoros.

She exchanged a glance with the Prophet, who had sent the fleetwide message to prepare for synchronization from the bridge of *Epanimondas* just a few moments before, as ships transitioned from jump. UPENDRA System lay before them: It was crowded with vuhl ships, a number of which were already headed for turnover to meet the Imperial force near the edge of the system's gravity well.

"Let's have it." She looked up above the pilot's board; the face of Alessandro Denny, the Blazing Star Sensitive aboard *Flight*, appeared in the air. "*Epanimondas* here. Go. This had better be important," Amoros added.

"It is, Captain." Denny looked worried, a distinct change from the usual arrogant demeanor that so defined the average Blazing Star operative. "Something has happened to *se* Ch'en'ya."

"'Something'?"

"She left orders to not be disturbed until jump transition—and when one of the other members of the Talon went to her cabin, she was found unconscious."

The Prophet stepped forward to stand next to the pilot's seat. Denny turned his attention immediately aside.

"Tell me more, Alessandro," the Prophet said quietly.

"She's in our sickbay now, sir. They think she's been out for a few hours, but the doctor doesn't want to try and revive her."

"Wise. She could be . . . anywhere." He looked at Diane Amoros. "Captain, I'll need to get over there as soon as possible. Do you have a gig available?"

"We're less than forty minutes from synchronization, sir," she answered. "I'll have to comm the admiral, but I wouldn't want you in a small craft when we come into firing-range."

"We'd better get moving, then, don't you think?" He turned and walked toward the lift. "Comm the admiral, Captain, but get the gig ready. I'm going to *Flight*."

Amoros nodded to Denny. "He's on his way. *Epanimondas* out. Jayson," she said to her comm officer, "get me the flag, and tell them it's critical."

It took four minutes for the Prophet to get aboard the gig and another eighteen minutes for it to travel between *Epanimondas* and *Flight Over Shar'tu*. The little carrier had been pulled from its formation and was cruising near the jump point; Anderson had put *Lycias* in its place.

Synchronization was still twenty minutes away when

the gig landed on *Flight*'s Green flight deck; the fighters had been cleared away and launched. The Prophet's sudden appearance and the preparations of the Sensitives didn't allow for much of a reception committee; a Marine major and one of the watch navigators met him there and escorted him to sickbay, located in the central core of the carrier.

There, he found her still immobile, lying in a zor-configured bed, her wings tucked neatly beneath her.

"Report," he said to the doctor, who stood nearby with a zor healer. "What has happened?"

"We don't know." Dr. Kenyon Akassa looked away from a readout hanging in midair near the bed. "She was found in her quarters a few minutes before transition."

"Is she injured?"

"It has the symptoms of a concussion, sir. But there are no signs of physical trauma."

"If she was injured, it didn't happen in the World That Is," the Prophet said without turning away. "And if it happened during jump . . . Doctor," he said, "I must have a comm channel. Synchronization must stop, and I need to speak with Admiral Anderson."

"There's a secure line in my office," Akassa said, waving toward a room off the main sickbay without looking up. For a moment, the Prophet was taken aback by the offhanded way in which he was being treated, but shrugged it off and walked to the indicated room.

He waved at the comp on the desk. "Secure channel. Voice-seal this room." The door to the office slid quietly shut, replacing the noises of the surgery with quiet.

"Destination?" the comp voice said.

"Comm to flag. Priority for Admiral Anderson, eyes only. *Flight Over Shar'tu* sends; Smith here."

Seconds ticked by. The Prophet looked at the chrono on the wall; there were eleven minutes remaining before synchronization.

A holo of Admiral Anderson sitting in his pilot's chair

appeared on the opposite side of the desk. "I'm a bit busy at the moment," he said. "I heard about Ch'en'ya—what's her status?"

"Unclear. But the synchronization must stop."

"I read at least two hive-ships closing in on my position, sir. This is a bad time to change tactics."

"Ch'en'ya's life may be in danger. I don't know what's happened to her, but I won't risk it. Comm the Sensitives to abort synchronization at point one and await further orders."

Anderson didn't answer for a moment, looking aside at the pilot's board, out of the holo's visual range.

"There are a lot of lives at stake other than Ch'en'ya's," he said at last. "I need these odds evened."

"Do whatever you like, but abort the synchronization, Admiral." His tone was cold and distant; it was an order, not a request.

Anderson held the measured stare for as long as he could, then finally looked away.

"To all ships, all Sensitives. Suspend synchronization at point one and stand by for orders. Flag sends." He looked back at the Prophet. "This is a God damned dangerous thing you're doing," he said. "Don't be wrong. Transmission ends."

The admiral's image disappeared before the Prophet could say another word. His hands formed into fists, but he wasn't sure what he should do with them.

"What have you done to Ch'en'ya, Stone?" he asked to the air, not sure if he wanted a reply. "What has your scheme cost me?"

It became very bloody very quickly. Sensitives—both WS's and members of Blazing Star—were on duty from the moment the vuhl enhancement tech came within range; regardless of the tactics of the past year-and-a-half, it was still what they were trained for. Across the Imperial and zor deployment, they fought against the assault of the vuhl mental attacks, shielding the crews from Domination.

The vuhls were backed into a corner. Just as it had been at TSUSHIMA, the mission was clear: eliminate every vuhl, and every trace of every vuhl. There were dozens of enemy ships in UPENDRA System; only a few of them had the firepower of an Imperial starship, but they had other things in mind.

The first victim was *Aldebaran,* the Argonne-class seventh-generation ship. Her contingent encountered the lead vuhl ships—which passed turnover without decelerating, instead maintaining a steady pace toward the lead human squadron. This flew in the face of logic, at first: by continuing to move at high velocity they'd only get a passing shot, leaving the Imperial ships between them and the inner system they were supposed to defend.

Except, as it turned out, that wasn't what they had in mind. As *Aldebaran* and her sister-ships poured unthinkable amounts of energy into the vuhl ships' shields, they closed in on the great battleship, not turning aside. *Aldebaran's* relatively low velocity made it difficult to maneuver out of range—and, as the vuhls got closer, the situation went from difficult to impossible.

The resulting interaction between the vuhl defensive fields, overloaded with energy, and those of *Aldebaran,* caused an explosion that spread out to swallow more than a dozen fighters from the nearby carrier *Lycias. Lycias* itself was struck by another of the ships forty seconds later, collapsing into fiery debris.

From *Flight Over Shar'tu,* the Prophet watched, with Ch'en'ya still immobile, lost somewhere in dreams.

From *Emperor Ian,* Admiral Anderson watched, redeploying his ships against this new and desperate tactic by the vuhls.

* * *

UPENDRA System was filled with vessels of all sorts, big and small. As the fleet fought its way down into the gravity well, it was in the path of numerous high-speed missiles aimed at taking out as many of Anderson's ships as possible as they collided with them or self-destructed nearby.

This was not a siege; it could not be: defender and attacker were in constant motion, with the Imperial ships forced to give up some of their mutual covering-fire to avoid being clumped together as group-targets. After the attack on *Aldebaran,* the carrier *Barbados* was nearly destroyed by the same tactic; it lost much of its launch capacity when an attacker was destroyed at point-blank range, just short of slamming into the carrier amidships.

Vuhls were dying by the thousands—and humans and zor by the hundreds.

Four hours into the battle, Ch'en'ya began to stir. Dr. Akassa was by her side immediately, and the Prophet was there soon afterward. Her eyes fluttered open and took in the scene; she grasped the Prophet's left wrist with painful ferocity.

"What has happened?" she whispered, her throat dry.

"We are at UPENDRA," the Prophet said. "Garrett has betrayed us."

"I know," she said. Her eyes were fixed on the Prophet. "We cannot . . . Our access to phase two has been blocked."

"What about phase one?"

"I . . . do not know if it can be effective," she said. Akassa provided a squeeze bottle; she sipped some water and coughed a bit, then looked again at the Prophet, never letting go of his wrist. "We should try. They . . . must not forget the power of *enGa'e'Li.*"

"What happened to you?"

"Garrett," she said. "He has . . ."

"Yes. He is our enemy now." Carefully, the Prophet disengaged himself from Ch'en'ya's grip, which was slowly weakening. He turned away from her and said to the air, "Comm to flag, relay to the fleet: Synchronize at point zero-one.

"Admiral," he added, "we are prepared to give it all we have. Prophet sends."

Ultimately, they fought to the death. It was going to be that way in any case, so the doomed enemy did what good soldiers always do: they took along as many of the enemy as they could. After the attacks on *Aldebaran, Lycias,* and *Barbados,* Admiral Anderson had to watch the carrier *Scylla* and four other ships of the line be destroyed by self-destructing ships during close combat. Less than a hundred crew got off in life-pods—the rest were consumed by the annihilation of matter and antimatter.

A dozen other ships were damaged to the point that they wouldn't be in service at VALENCIA or WARREN: but the objective had been achieved. They'd killed every last vuhl in the system, as far as they knew—whole cities wiped from the surface of the inhabited planet . . . every ship, every installation on the ground or in space—they'd destroyed every one.

As for Blazing Star, they'd contributed; but it only scarcely blunted the attacks from the hive-ships. By the time the Prophet had come back aboard *Ian,* he was blazing-mad about something—presumably it was about Owen Garrett, who had walked off *Epanimondas* during the jump to UPENDRA, and possibly sent Ch'en'ya into unconsciousness—though Anderson admitted to himself that he couldn't understand how either of those things could happen.

* * *

When it was over, Admiral Anderson went to his ready-room and left orders not to be disturbed. He tried to absorb it all: the lost ships, the destruction, the deaths of so many of his people—and whatever situation had kept Blazing Star from employing "phase two," whatever the hell that actually was.

There was a time, he realized as he paced slowly across his ready-room, when conducting a campaign was based on things easily understood: ordnance and tactics, military matters. Blazing Star had changed the equation. The Prophet had changed the equation.

He wasn't just a civilian: he'd served as a Marine and had spent time with the Guardian Order—but he was a rank amateur in comparison to the admiral, who had been fighting this war for longer than the Prophet had been alive. But whatever he'd done, whatever he *knew,* was being overwhelmed by the actions of this man and his organization. Anderson's own dependence on Blazing Star had led to this pass.

It still made all these deaths *his* responsibility, not Smith's.

"Incoming message, Admiral." The voice of the comm officer interrupted his thoughts; he began to snap an angry reply, but saw the comm icon: Priority 17—urgent enough even to interrupt an admiral who didn't want to be disturbed.

There were only two people in the Solar Empire who rated seventeen sideboys: Barbara MacEwan and Ur'e'e HeYen. If Barbara had turned up at Upendra contrary to orders, it would be a hell of a thing and he'd have heard about it already: so that meant it had to be Admiral HeYen.

"Put it through."

The holo of the zor admiral appeared at the far end of his conference table. Admiral Ur'e'e HeYen inclined his wings. "*se* Admiral Anderson."

"Admiral. How may I be of service?"

"I regret . . . I have received a directive from the High

Nest, *se* Admiral. A sixteenth of a sun ago, a comm-squirt arrived and charged me to withdraw my forces."

Anderson couldn't reply for a moment, then he said, "I'm sorry, I don't understand."

"We are ordered to Stand Within the Circle, *se* Admiral. The High Lord commands us to depart from *Ur'ta leHssa*. This war is no longer even the *e'ChaReU'un* that it once was, and *hi* Sa'a refuses to have us continue association with it."

"I still don't understand, *se* Ur'c'e. This was never a ritual bloodletting: it was a war before, and it is a war now. I don't see what's changed."

The zor admiral placed his wings in the Posture of Polite Approach. "It *has* changed, *se* Admiral. And yes, this was a *e'ChaReU'un*. When *esHu'ur* began his campaign that changed the Flight of the People so many turns ago, his deeds were *e'ChaReU'un*. When we commenced this phase of the war at KEYSTONE, taking the offensive against the *esHara'y*, we, too, served *esLi* in an honorable way. But this is changed."

"How?"

"The Prophet has chosen to make common cause with the *esGa'uYal*."

It was a frank and honest statement; Anderson was again unable to respond.

"I have ordered my command to the jump point, *se* Admiral. I began this conversation by telling you that I regret the need for this action. But I am guided by my superiors just as you were guided by yours." He lifted his wings slightly as he said it, and added, "I hope that you have a firm idea of your flight, *se* Admiral, so that you, too, can ultimately escape from the Valley."

"I know the *cause* I serve," Anderson snapped back. "I know my flight. I'm much more concerned with finishing the job I've been sent here to do. This is something that you seem *unprepared* to do." He gathered himself and continued. "I have worked with you and I respect you, *se* Admiral, but surely this stains your honor."

"It is the will of the High Nest," Ur'e'e answered. "As a fellow soldier, I hope you understand."

"I wish I did. But we must complete the work here, *se* Ur'e'e, and your departure impairs my ability to do so."

Ur'e'e's wings moved slightly, as if ruffled by an unseen breeze. "You must complete it without the help of the People, *se* Admiral. Eight thousand pardons."

And he was gone. On the pilot's-board display, Anderson could see the zor vessels slowly traversing the system, approaching the jump point to Nestor—the route to Portal System and then home.

The admiral had decided that he didn't want to bring word to the Prophet on his own bridge, and wasn't keen to go down to his quarters with his cap in his hand. He settled on *Ian*'s observation lounge. While they orbited the formerly habitable planet in UPENDRA System, they could get a close look at the destruction on both sides.

The Prophet's mood was predictable—and palpable as soon as Anderson came into the lounge. The planet's nightside was below them, and even from orbit the fires down there were visible. The Prophet stood against the backdrop, his hands gripping the railing.

He did not say a word as Anderson came up to stand beside him.

"How could this happen?"

"Which 'this'?"

"The zor. The backstabbing, honorless zor. Here we are—" He swept his arm across the scene behind; *Barbados,* or what was left of it, was just visible beyond a limb of the planet. "Here we are, Admiral, at the end of a long tether, with the vermin backed into a corner—and the zor are bailing out on us when we are so close.

"Do you think we can win this war without them?"

"I *do* think so," Anderson answered. "It may take longer, but yes, I do think we can win. We outnumber the enemy. Still, it may cost us more than we expected."

"I'm not convinced." The Prophet turned away to look out at the planet, its cities burning in the dark. "I wonder whether this was a deliberate ploy."

"A ploy?"

"To take this victory away from you, Admiral. To deny you your rightful honor."

Something about the comment didn't ring true to Erich Anderson. In the past, he'd heard these words and it had reminded him of his famous ancestors (and, to be fair, Barbara MacEwan's famous ancestors), and it had appealed to his desire to take his rightful place among them.

What was different now?

"I don't think *se* Ur'e'e is engaged in a ploy. I don't think the High Lord is, either."

"She opposed this campaign from the start."

"I don't think—"

"From the start," the Prophet repeated, more angrily. "She called KEYSTONE—and the Rip beyond it—*Ur'ta leHssa,* the Valley of Lost Souls. Do you recognize the symbolism?"

"I know how it's described in zor cosmology."

"Yes. A *L'le* in which People are trapped, not knowing that they've been trapped—Despair thick on their wings—condemned to be unable to raise their cycs to see their tormentor.

"Is that where you think we are, Admiral? Is that what you think we have become?"

Anderson didn't answer for a moment. It was strange—he'd not thought very long about how the High Nest perceived what they were doing. It fit well, or so it seemed, with the zor warrior mentality: Destroy the enemy without remorse or condition.

Ur'e'e HeYen had called it an *e'ChaReU'un:* a ritual bloodletting. But it had become something different in the People's eyes. They had decided that the Prophet served *esGa'u,* and they'd gone home.

"I don't know what we've become."

"You don't—" The Prophet's anger increased another

level. "You don't *know?* This is the greatest moment in human history and you don't *know?* Are you becoming faint of heart, Admiral?"

"I don't take kindly to that assertion, sir. I especially don't like it after this battle." The admiral stepped forward, within a meter or so of where the Prophet stood; the anger radiated from the other, but Anderson was probably broadcasting some anger of his own. "Far too many of *my* people died out there. But we won the battle, didn't we? We accomplished the mission, didn't we?" He emphasized *"my"*: these were military personnel, not "civilian specialists"—though they'd lost a number of them as well.

The Prophet didn't answer.

"I haven't become faint of heart," Anderson said at last. "I've waited nearly thirty years to get to this point, and I'm here now to finish the job the best I can. If you don't believe that, maybe you should call back Barbara MacEwan."

"What will she do when the cowardly zor reach Portal System?"

"What did you have in mind? Having her fire on them? I thought about it, I really did. But it makes no sense. I'm here to finish the job," the admiral repeated. "Now, please tell me what the hell you want, because I've got a hundred other things to do before we fight again."

The two men held each other's gaze for several moments; then, to Erich's surprise, the Prophet looked away.

"If I have offended you, Admiral," the Prophet said, "I apologize."

"You did. And the apology is accepted. But as I told you before, we can still win this war without the zor—it will just cost more than we expected."

"We will *have* to win without them," the Prophet answered. "*Any* of them. You should direct that all zor personnel within this fleet be relieved of their duties. Admiral MacEwan can make her own judgments, but you don't want any zor in any key position."

"Except Ch'en'ya."

"Yes, other than Ch'en'ya and the Talon of *esLi*. All the rest must go."

"That covers hundreds of people—and we're short-handed as it is. I don't think it's practical."

"Practical or not, it has to be done. The campaign must continue without them."

"How do you suggest I do it?"

"Let the Guardians do the work. We've already rounded up all of the traitor Garrett's supporters; we'll have a much easier time rounding up all the zor."

"And then what?"

"They can go home on *Admiral Stark*—it won't be in fighting shape for Valencia. They can go home to Zor'a for all I care, and deal with their *idju* status when they get there." He straightened up and looked out at the planet below. "We don't need them—perhaps we never did. We will win this war, and then we'll attend to the zor."

"Excuse me?" Anderson asked.

"We'll need to send a message to the High Lord," the Prophet continued. "If they don't want to be considered enemies, they'll have to make a gesture."

"You have something in mind."

The Prophet smiled, as if he had aimed the entire conversation this way. "Yes, I do. Send a comm-squirt to the High Nest informing them of our decision to dismiss all zor serving in the Imperial Navy—and tell the High Lord that I expect the *Gyaryu'har* to be by my side when we reach the vuhl home system."

"I can't imagine that Jackie will ever agree to that."

"I'll expect her to tell me that personally. The High Nest will have to realize that I'm serious.

"Send the comm-squirt, Admiral, and let me know what reply you get—if any."

Chapter 24

IN THIS DIFFICULT PERIOD IT IS DANGEROUS TO
PROCEED WITHOUT PLACING UNDUE BURDEN ON
THOSE WHO MUST CONDUCT THE WAR AGAINST
THE RELENTLESS ENEMY . . . IT IS THEREFORE NEC-
ESSARY THAT, FOR THE TIME, THE PROCEEDINGS OF
HIS IMPERIAL MAJESTY'S ASSEMBLY BE SUSPENDED
UNTIL SUCH TIME AS THEY MAY PROPERLY CON-
TINUE.

—Writ of Dissolution, 28 September 2424,
from the *Journal of the Imperial Assembly*,
Session 23, 2424

October 2424
Adrianople System

Lasker, an Argonne-class seven, made routine transition
at Adrianople System with the Admiral of the Red
aboard. As soon as the admiral's flag showed up on the
base pilot's board, Barbara MacEwan knew, there'd be an
honor guard put in place to receive her at dockside and a
proper escort for *Lasker* into the gravity well. No matter
that she'd commed from KEYSTONE System that she was
on her way: On her order, Aaron Lewis—captain of
Lasker—had spent a bit of extra fuel to jump at higher
velocity, putting her transition two watches earlier than
she had indicated.

Fortunately, the commander of Adrianople Starbase was on his toes. An escort was less than half an hour from turnover as *Lasker* got helm control and began heading for the starbase. By the time the courses of *Lasker* and the escort coincided, there were a full two squadrons of fighters and two ships of the line paralleling them at top priority all the way to dock.

Things had changed a lot during the course of the war. Adrianople had been the biggest base this side of the Solar Empire at vuhl first contact in 2396; Cicero had almost as many ships assigned, but was an exploration base. They'd retreated from Cicero to Adrianople, then lost it to the enemy not long after . . . When they'd finally taken it back the following year, the orbital base had been heavily damaged and many other system facilities were in poor repair or out of service.

Jon Durant, the former commander of Adrianople Starbase, had managed to survive the vuhl occupation and had done a superb job bringing it back up to full power. When the vuhls came back four years later, one of their Drones had managed to get aboard the partially rebuilt starbase during the battle, located Durant, and killed him. It was that sort of thing which had pushed Arlen Mustafa directly into the arms of Blazing Star, though Barbara had heard stories of the occupation that suggested a more deeply seated hatred.

The current commander at Adrianople, Rich Abramowicz, was in his dress blues with an honor guard when Admiral MacEwan stepped off her barge onto the deck of the starbase. He seemed genuinely pleased to see her, and, much to her relief, wasn't sporting a Blazing Star emblem on his dress blouse. The first time they'd ever met, Rich had been facing his fellow captain, and the business end of a number of open gunports: He'd managed to get *Trebizond* out of Adrianople and to Denneva, where *Emperor Cleon* and *Emperor Alexander* had intercepted it;

Cleon and MacEwan's own *Duc d'Enghien* had led *Trebizond* on a series of jumps all the way to the zor Core Stars, where Owen Garrett had picked the vuhl Drone out of a lineup.

Abramowicz had been brave—and lucky. *"If anyone aboard is an alien,"* she'd said to him, *"he or she is in deep trouble. Everyone else will be in the clear . . . and for those folks it's open bar in* Duc d'Enghien's *galley."* So it had been written, and so it was done aboard her ship.

"I've got something for you," Abramowicz said, as they made their way to Adrianople's C-and-C—a beautiful modern structure, completely rebuilt after the 2401 battle, and again after the defense of Adrianople System in 2417. He led her to the center of the circular command center where a group of officers were standing in dress uniform, obviously trying not to break into smiles. She didn't know most of them, but did recognize Kit Hafner, once Rich's XO aboard *Trebizond*, now a full Commodore.

"Commodore Hafner," she said to him, exchanging salutes, "this looks a lot like a firing squad."

"No ma'am. I was just passing through with *Matheson* and wanted to have a chance to see you."

"I see." Next to the huge pilot's board there was a small, unsealed shipping canister. Inside she could see a black box roughly half a meter tall, thirty centimeters on a side, resting on plastic packing material; it was adorned with a blue ribbon and sealed with a blob of wax embossed with the Imperial sword-and-sun.

"It took some doing," Abramowicz said. "Kit knows that I'm farther up the promotion list than he is, and if this didn't get here intact I'd have him shot. Seniority has its privileges." He gingerly lifted the box out of the canister and handed it to Barbara; it looked as if he were handling a carton of live grenades.

"There are easier ways to blow up an admiral," Barbara said, taking the package in her hands. The assembled officers laughed, and she turned the MacEwan glare on them.

No one spoke a word as she carefully slit through the wax seal with one thumbnail, removing the ribbon. She opened the top of the box and drew out an exquisite glass bottle.

"Balvenie, fifteen-year-old," Abramowicz said quietly. "2261. The year before they were sold to Bremerton Distillers."

"It's bad luck to speak ill of the dead," Barbara said, carefully turning the bottle in her hands, unable to withhold a smile. "My God, Richard. There can't be twenty bottles of this vintage left in the Solar Empire. They say that the ghost of William Grant stood over the master distiller's shoulder when they bottled the last of the Balvenie. Lord knows, I've tasted the Bremerton stuff, and it's a poor cousin to a proper whisky."

"We only located six," he answered. "This is the Balvenie 15, single-barrel. They say that the 2261 tastes like a twenty-five-year-old. Of course, I've never tried it."

"Neither have I," Barbara said. "It must have cost you all a year's salary. *Each.*"

"Not quite. But we all felt that it was an appropriate gift, and no one is more deserving than our admiral. I hope you'll accept it in the spirit in which it is given." He offered her a salute; the other officers joined as well, and then gave a brief round of applause, joined by the apparently well-briefed C-and-C watch crew.

"I don't know what I've done to deserve it, and I'm not sure this is the best time to be considering celebration—but I do thank you. When we open it, I hope that each of you will have a chance for a wee dram. We'll either have something to celebrate—or it won't matter a damn anymore." She placed the bottle back in its box, and the box back into the canister.

Pali Tower
Imperial Oahu, Sol System

For the first time, Tonio felt like a stranger in his own office. The mist was still on the grove of monkeypod trees that the Guardian Order had planted twenty years ago near the entrance to the Tower; the distant sprawl of Honolulu was hazy and out-of-focus—it had rained there briefly just before dawn. The long shadows of the mountains were still hanging over southern Kailua, and he couldn't make out the towers of the High Nest compound near Waianae.

"Good morning, Maestro," Nic said, unsummoned, appearing next to him as Tonio stood looking off toward the west, admiring the view. "A beautiful morning."

"I don't know how you could tell."

"I can't. I have assembled all of the information I have been provided, and that is the consensus of those who observed it. Do you concur with their estimate?"

Tonio shrugged and said nothing in response, walking across the office to sit at his desk. "Shall we have a morning briefing, or have all the decisions been made?"

"I would appreciate your input." Nic's image shifted from near the window to his usual seat opposite Tonio's desk. "Where would you like me to begin?"

"Start with the war, I suppose."

"Admiral Anderson's fleet is a few hours from jump transition at the system designated VALENCIA. Without the zor in support, they are likely to find it a difficult target, particularly given the change in vuhl tactics—the use of self-destruct mechanisms and suicide attacks."

"I reviewed the information about the zor withdrawal," Tonio said. "Any further explanation from the High Nest?"

"None. They speak of the space beyond the Rip as 'Ur'ta leHssa,' the Valley of Lost Souls, and wish to disassociate themselves from a campaign there. One wonders why they were willing to participate in the first place."

"It didn't start out as—what it has become."

"Please clarify."

"What part of this don't you understand, Nic? Query all your subordinate selves. This has been transformed into a war of extermination, and the zor don't want to be a part of it."

"They would have been perfectly willing to exterminate humanity a century ago, Commander. They don't have any cultural obstacle to xenocide, to destruction, or to killing in general. Why do you think they'd jump ship at this point?"

"Is this some sort of intellectual exercise for you? Or are you waiting for me to come to some sort of conclusion?"

"I won't respond angrily, Maestro. Are you trying to bait me?" Nic smiled and leaned back in his chair. "I suppose it's a bit of both. For a century, most humans have tried to see why the zor do this thing or that thing, why they view things the way they do. But it isn't a great mystery—it's just that it's based on something that most humans refuse to accept: That the entire direction of the zor polity—the so-called Flight of the People— derives from the prescient dreams of the High Lord."

"I know that. Everyone knows that."

"But most people don't put much faith in it. What does it mean? That High Lord Sa'a HeYen eats a bad bit of fish and has a nightmare, so the foreign policy of the High Nest is changed? One bad headache and the High Nest goes to war?"

"I assume that it's more complicated than that." Tonio folded his hands on the desk in front of him. "Perhaps you'd care to enlighten *me*."

"According to what I understand, the High Lord receives prescient dreams from *esLi*—and they are couched in mythological frames of reference. Heroes and villains from zor legend—events and patterns—that sort of thing. It's left to the High Lord to interpret their meaning and act accordingly. A future High Lord is trained when Sensitive ability comes on, and then there is a ritual that takes place when one High Lord dies and the role is passed on to his or her successor. This happens at the deathbed, in fact."

"The current High Lord didn't undergo any such ritual: High Lord Ke'erl killed himself and a few thousand others at Thon's Well System during the first year of the war."

"That's right, Maestro. High Lord Sa'a has *never* undergone this ritual—*Te'esLi'ir,* I believe it's called. It might be a good thing: High Lord Ke'erl was mad, from what I have learned, and the new High Lord often takes on the memories and mental framework of the old—it could have driven High Lord Sa'a into the same madness. But it might also be a bad thing, finally beginning to manifest itself."

"You think she's going *mad*?"

"I don't know what constitutes 'madness' for a High Lord," Nic answered. "But this decision is difficult to understand except in the context of a prescient dream. Unless there is something else, something that has happened of which we are not aware."

"You mean—something between the Prophet and the High Nest?"

"I don't know, Maestro." Nic tipped his head slightly, as if listening for something. "I have been assimilating information of all kinds, looking for a pattern. My subordinate programs are running all over the Solar Empire, as well as beyond the Rip. The curious timing of this withdrawal, just at the point at which Commander Garrett 'betrayed' the Blazing Star movement, is too coincidental: The algorithms I use to construct behavioral patterns suggest a connection, even if none is there."

"So you're waiting for someone to say something."

"Yes. I can listen everywhere but the zor Core Stars. I

can't seem to get access there—but there are other assets that provide occasional information."

"Such as?"

"The *Gyaryu'har* has responded to the Prophet's challenge and is en route across the Solar Empire. She intends to confront him."

"Sounds suicidal to me."

"Maestro, have you ever met Ms. Laperriere? From what I have read and observed, she is determined, dangerous, and far from suicidal. If anyone can confront the Prophet and live, it may be the *Gyaryu'har* of the High Nest."

"And the outcome?"

"There are too many variables," Nic answered. "She is about to make transition at New Chicago. After that we may well know more."

Aboard Emperor Ian
In jump to VALENCIA *System*

The campaign had come to a halt at UPENDRA. The Prophet knew that; he knew also that no matter what he did—or what he wanted to do—it was in the hands of the military to get the fleet ready for the next targets, VALENCIA and WARREN.

He wasn't given much to introspection. There had been very little need for it. *The War Manifesto* was the closest he had gotten to it, and that wasn't his inner thoughts—merely what was prepared for outside consumption. Still, the death of his oldest ally in the movement was cause for consideration.

As he sat in his quarters aboard *Emperor Ian*, he thought about the first time he'd met Owen Garrett . . .

May 2415
Emperor Willem Starport, Harrison System

The emperor's visit to Harrison System had been scheduled for the second week in May. Commander St. Giles had dispatched a dozen Guardians to Emperor Willem Starport to examine security precautions; there had been reports of enemy activity there, and the commander wanted to make sure that everything went smoothly. Harrison was close enough to the Inner Sphere that it was considered safe for the emperor to make a state visit: Those had been more troubled days, when vuhl attacks could happen anywhere, at anytime, for no reason.

The twelve Guardians took turns patrolling the starport, looking and listening. Most folks stayed clear of them. Their shifts were four Standard hours long, eight off, round-the-clock, twenty-four Standard hours a day. There was no day and night in orbit around Harrison's primary Earthlike world, and there was no day and night for the Guardians.

Two days before the emperor's arrival, Quinton Hannay, one of the senior members of the the team, was injured in an accident, throwing the entire schedule into disarray. As one of the junior members, it fell upon ex-Marine John Smith to take up the slack. If it had not been for that accident, he might never have met Owen Garrett.

The former Guardian Commander had been watching the traffic on the Grand Concourse from a perch at the corner of a bar, one that steadily changed its clientele as travelers came and went. It was a reputable establishment; indeed, the Guardian team had made contact with the proprietor and each of the four managers that supervised it, making sure that everyone knew where everyone else stood.

Garrett's position was well-chosen, and his dress and appearance was conservative—an immaculately tailored protosilk suit, shaven head, no flashy jewelry or distinctive adornment. Just another businessman, a merchant factor perhaps, enjoying a drink before boarding a shuttle or a trading vessel outbound from Harrison System. Even in wartime, the matter of making money went on.

It wouldn't have attracted Smith's attention, and didn't really, the first time he passed the place—even though Garrett's eyes followed him. Lots of people liked to challenge Guardians then, but only in little ways. The second time, almost two hours later, Garrett was still sitting there; since Smith had been forced to pull a double shift, Garrett's presence during his next cross through the area qualified it as suspicious.

Without changing expression or the pace at which he walked, Smith stepped off the concourse into the bar and walked up to the man he'd seen sitting in the same seat, seeming to nurse the same drink, over the course of almost five Standard hours.

The man didn't flinch—nor run. Smith's first intention was to call for backup, but somehow he never quite did so. The man remained in his seat, following Smith with his eyes as he approached.

"May I have a word with you?" Smith said, using his Guardian ability to determine if he was looking at a vuhl.

"Let me buy you a drink, Guardian."

"I'm on duty, sir."

"Some fruit juice, then." The man gestured to the bartender, who glanced from the man to Smith—a bit nervously, perhaps.

"Are you waiting for a flight?"

"No." The man turned to face Smith—and suddenly the young Guardian realized that he was facing someone capable of scanning *him*. "I've been waiting for *you*."

"We're in public. There's no place to run if you—"

"If I *what*? If I buy you a fruit juice?" The bartender placed two glasses with a pale yellow liquid in front of the man, and then seemed to move away quickly. "What do you think I'm going to do? Attack you? I wouldn't trouble myself, Guardian."

"What do you want with me?"

"Well, first I wanted to get your attention." The man sipped his drink, never taking his eyes off Smith. "It took long enough, but you'll do. Wouldn't want the emperor to be in unsafe hands."

"I don't know what you're talking about."

"Then let me tell you: His Imperial Highness will be passing through here in a bit under two Standard days, scepter in one hand and wineglass in the other, to dedicate the new Welcome Center. You and your colleagues are here to make sure no undesirables get close enough to disturb him.

"Isn't that right . . . Guardian Smith?"

The fact that the stranger knew his name made Smith's stomach jump. For a second time the idea of calling for backup occurred to him—but he still didn't move to touch his earring.

"Who are you?"

"A ghost," the man said. "A shadow. I know what you are, and what you can become, Guardian Smith, and I'm here to help you reach that goal."

"You haven't answered my question."

The man took a comp out of a suit pocket and set it down next to the two glasses: the one he'd drunk from, and the second, untouched one. He rested a finger on one corner of it and Smith heard a tiny, almost inaudible hum.

The audio pickup from his four-joined-hands earring became indistinct, making calling for backup out-of-the-question—at least for the moment.

"They're going to notice that I went off the 'net, and in ten minutes there'll be Guardians converging on this place from all directions."

"I know the drill," the man said.

"You're a former Guardian?"

"I'm Owen Garrett."

"Garrett is dead," Smith replied. The first Commander of the Guardian Order had resigned more than a dozen years earlier—long before Smith's association with the Order—and had reportedly been killed somewhere beyond the edge of the Solar Empire: one more casualty in two decades of war with the enemy.

"That's not true. Even Tonio St. Giles knows that I'm alive. It galls him that I'm still knocking around, and he'll grow a second head when he realizes that I'm here. But don't worry," Garrett continued, as Smith's hands clenched into fists, "I don't mean any harm to the emperor, or to the Commander of the Order. I just want to talk to *you*."

"I'm listening," Smith said, taking a quick look around the bar and down the Concourse. One of the other Guardians was in sight, but looking away. "But I don't know why you want to talk to me in particular."

"I want to talk to you because it's time for you to decide where your career is going," Garrett said. "There's something waiting for you, for a man of your talents— which are exceptional. More than an average Marine; more than a regular Guardian. Remarkable physical strength, superior stamina, good psych profile . . . except for that attitude toward the enemy.

"They don't like you in the Order, do they, Smith? They think you're a loose cannon, who can't focus his ability. 'Too much hatred,' isn't that what your supervisor said in your last review?"

"I get along."

"Famous last words. They'll etch that on the capsule when they eject your body into deep space someday, a testament to your service to the Solar Emperor.

"So tell me, Smith. Has Tonio invited you into the Inner Order yet?"

"I'm not on a first-name basis with the commander."

"Well." Garrett sipped his drink again. "That's neither a yes nor a no, so at least you realize your limitations— you're a damn poor liar. The answer is no, of course: He's not recruiting people who hate the enemy like you do. But, you see, that's where it all comes from—where it came from in the first place. You *have to* hate an enemy that wants to breed humans like cattle, that calls us 'meat-creatures.' All this cold reason and playacting of the Inner Order just gets in the way. *That's* why you don't get asked to join—you're unsuitable."

Smith looked up the Grand Concourse again. His fellow Guardian seemed to look right at him for a moment; their eyes met, and then the other looked away as a heavyset man pulled him into a conversation.

"Suppose I made you an offer," Garrett said, after a moment, when Smith returned his attention to him. "How'd you like to leave all of *this* behind? The ugly suits, the—" He gestured around the bar: anyone close enough to notice was making deliberate attempts to ignore them. ". . . The lack of social life. How'd you like to be aboard a different ship than the one Tonio drives?"

"I'm bound to the Order by oath of loyalty, Mr. Garrett. I don't plan on walking away."

"You're *this* close to doing it," Garrett answered. "You want them—" This time he looked directly at Smith, held him with a gaze that was stronger than just Guardian training in action, and both men knew what Garrett meant by *"them."* "You want them all dead," he continued in a lower voice. "Don't you?"

"What do you mean?"

"The Guardian Order was created for me to teach people the abilities I've been given. I was co-opted by the Solar Emperor himself to keep the Imperial Person safe from the enemy. I did that for four years, then one day I decided I'd had it with the business, and walked away—and do you want to know why? It wasn't because of whatever horseshit reason Tonio St. Giles gives you: It was because there was an enemy out there to kill and *I wasn't doing any of the killing.*"

"You walked away so that you could kill vuhls."

"Sure."

"How many have you killed so far?"

"A few hundred."

It wasn't the answer Smith had been expecting; he had

assumed that the number might be two or three, or a dozen. Still, when it came to the war effort . . .

"There are still a few more to kill," Smith said at last.

"Yeah." Garrett leaned on the bar. "Aren't there, though. And how many vuhl lives have you ended, Guardian Smith?"

"Not enough," Smith replied.

And the idea hit him: *Not enough.*

Garrett looked past Owen again, and there was no Guardian down the concourse. He turned around and looked the other way; there wasn't another member of the duty team in sight.

"Suppose I could give you the ability," Garrett said, "to kill *millions* of them. Maybe . . . if we play this right, we can kill *every last one.*"

. . . **Years later,** he couldn't quite remember the rest of the conversation. Owen Garrett's voice when he'd said that phrase—*"every last one"*—seemed to hang there for an eternity; he'd kept talking, but the details were nowhere near as sharp as anything that had gone before. The enormity of the thing was the fulcrum of the entire encounter.

He'd agreed to the proposition; he'd walked away from the Guardians. And the rest was the path that had led from there to here—Blazing Star, the crusade against the vuhls, all of it.

Owen Garrett had been right. There *had* been a destiny for him, something greater than a Marine dying for his emperor, or a Guardian with no chance for advancement.

And a few months ago, when Stone had visited him in his quarters here on *Ian* while they were setting up shop at Nestor, he'd known all the details of Smith's chance meeting with Owen Garrett: *all* of it, even Quint Hannay's broken leg and dislocated shoulder. It hadn't been a chance meeting after all.

Stone had offered him a trade: get rid of Garrett, and interest in Blazing Star would jump all across the Empire. One old friend or thousands—perhaps tens of thousands—of new supporters, a whole new audience for the message.

Such a small thing, and even though it was poor payment for good service—after all, Owen *had believed* in everything they had done—it was justified in the end. Owen had wanted to leave the movement, just as he'd left the Guardians.

He was a weak link, the Prophet reminded himself. *You're well rid of him—and all of his henchmen.*

All except one.

He thought about Djiwara: The merchant had skillfully managed the movement's financial resources, even arranging to have exclusive access to some of the accounts. If Djiwara hadn't been at least somewhat greedy, *that* would've been suspicious; but the Blazing Star's banker was just greedy enough to line his own pockets without altering the course of the movement. A little graft up and down the line kept the wheels nicely greased. There might come a time when there was no longer a need for the merchant's services, but this was not the time.

Like it or not, though, Owen had had to go. Before that meeting in 2415 at Harrison System, Blazing Star was a few dozen people and a few hundred dead vuhls; now, they stood on the very edge of exterminating the bugs from the universe. It was the achievement of a lifetime—and it was just a beginning.

Without anyone there to see it, the Prophet allowed himself a single fierce smile.

Wait, he thought. *Wait until you see what happens next.*

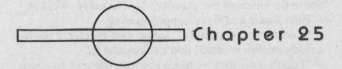 **Chapter 25**

THE GREATEST WAY TO LIVE WITH HONOR IN THIS
WORLD IS TO BE WHAT WE PRETEND TO BE.

—Socrates

October 2424
Shiell Institute, Jardine City, New Chicago System

On the way toward the Orionward edge of the Empire, Jackie Laperriere paid a visit to the Shiell Institute on New Chicago, accompanied by Byar HeShri. The rumor of Rivendra Wells' arrest had reached Byar, and the Master of Sanctuary had chosen to travel with Jackie as far as New Chicago to investigate the circumstances. They found the Institute occupied by members of the Guardian Order.

Their appearance caused something of a stir. Master Byar was a few paces across the plaza in front of Building 12, where the office of his friend Dr. Rivendra Wells was located; suddenly he found himself confronted by four Imperial soldiers, weapons drawn and aimed at him. Jackie had been accessing her comp but slowly put it away and moved to stand beside him, her hand on the *gyaryu*.

"This is an unwise course of action," she said to the guards, looking from one to the other and noting the presence of Blazing Star emblems attached below their service ribbons. "Master Byar is under my protection."

"I do not need protection," Byar said in the High-speech, his hand coming to rest on his *chya*. The four rifles in the hands of the guards moved to ready position.

Both Jackie and Byar stopped moving.

"Comm your superiors," Jackie said quietly. "You've already made a mistake; don't compound it."

"I don't think they've made any mistake yet," someone said, coming through the doors opposite. He was wearing a Guardian suit, and he, too, sported a Blazing Star emblem. "Stand down," he added, to the guards. "I don't think that our emissaries from the High Nest are liable to cause any problems."

"And *you* are?" Jackie asked.

"Wilhelm Dawson, ma'am," he said, inclining his head. The guards stepped back and lowered their weapons, though they were still available at a moment's notice. "Welcome to the Shiell Institute, *ha Gyaryu'har*."

He gave a cold stare to Byar, one that he seemed to have saved up especially for the Master.

"We've come to visit Dr. Rivendra Wells," Jackie answered, not moving her hand away from the *gyaryu*.

"I'm afraid he's unavailable."

"Is he offworld?"

"No ma'am, he is not."

"Then we'd like to see him. At once."

"Dr. Wells is in protective custody at the present time. I have no orders to permit anyone to see him, Ms. Laperriere. Particularly"—he glanced at Byar again—"someone from Zor'a."

"Master Byar was working closely with Dr. Wells—"

Dawson held his hand up and gestured toward the doors through which he had just come. "I don't wish to discuss this out in the courtyard," he interrupted. "Perhaps we can take this inside?"

"Perhaps *we* would not care to enjoy 'protective custody,'" Jackie said. "And perhaps you'd like to avoid an incident of interstellar proportions."

"Are you threatening me?"

"Take it any way you like. Why is Dr. Wells in protective custody?"

"Please. Come into my temporary offices to discuss this. You have my word that at the end of our conversation you may leave of your own accord."

"*Both* of us."

He glanced at Byar with a look that seemed remarkably unlike anything which she was accustomed to from Guardians—if anything, it reminded her of Owen Garrett.

"Of course."

They took positions opposite Dawson in an office that had the look of having been just cleared for his use; side-tables had been dragged aside and were heaped high with a haphazard assortment of equipment. Jackie sat on a lab stool; a perch was extruded for Byar's use.

"I apologize," Dawson said when they were alone, "for my abruptness outside. We've been under a considerable amount of stress recently, and your appearance was unexpected.

"I would like . . . to clarify a few matters with Master Byar, if I might."

"If I can be of assistance," Byar said, "I shall be happy to do so."

"You worked with Dr. Wells, investigating the vuhl enhancement tech, did you not?" he asked Byar, giving him the deep, piercing glance that meant he was employing his Guardian abilities.

"I am not an *esHara'e*," Byar said after a moment.

"Please answer the question."

"I find your tone somewhat inappropriate," Byar said, letting his wings move to the Stance of Affront. "You know very well that I worked on the tech with Dr. Wells. What do you wish to know?"

"Dr. Wells has claimed that you were trapped by an alien agency when you activated the tech. Is this true?"

"It is. I contacted an intelligence called the Ór."

"And it trapped you."

"Temporarily, yes. I followed a sort of path through space that led me into contact with it."

"And was this intelligence more powerful than your abilities permitted you to resist?"

"Yes."

"Then answer me this, Master Byar: *How did you escape it?* Or did you escape it at all?"

"I do not understand what you are implying."

"Very simple." Dawson stood, leaning on the desk in front of him. "Are you still in contact with this intelligence, Master Byar? And is it presently directing your actions?"

"What the hell—" Jackie began, but this time Byar raised a hand, looking aside at his old friend.

"I think I begin to understand," Byar said to Dawson. "Your hostility to me is based on the notion that I might be in league with the Ór, and therefore a threat to the Solar Empire.

"Guardian Dawson, you may rest easy. I am not in contact with this alien intelligence. The contact between the tech and the Ór was completely severed—and as a result I was freed from its grasp after my flight took me there."

"Can you explain this?"

"How it was done? I can. The High Lord severed the contact personally—with her *hi'chya*."

"How?"

Almost too fast for Dawson—or Jackie—to react, Byar drew his own *chya* and swept it across his body and downward, until the point stopped, quivering, a centimeter or so from Dawson's right hand leaning on the desk.

Dawson looked from his hand to the Master of Sanctuary, and then to Jackie—perhaps he expected her to do something.

"I believe that she did it with a rapid downward stroke," Byar answered quietly, after drawing the moment out for several seconds.

The Guardian didn't answer. Slowly, Byar drew the *chya* back along the path it had described, and then replaced it in its scabbard, his wings moving to the Posture of Honor to the Warrior.

"I don't understand," Dawson said without looking up.

"You seem very young for such a position of authority, Guardian," Byar said. "But you will learn with experience. When you have seen as many turns as I, you will realize just how little you actually know.

"*hi* Sa'a did a very noble, very brave, and very foolish thing. She flew across the Plane of Sleep and found the cord that bound me to this malign thing, and she cut it with her *hi'chya* . . . with a rapid downward stroke."

"Where . . . Where was she at the time?"

"On the Plane of Sleep."

"She was on Zor'a," Jackie offered after a moment, when Dawson looked up, his face puzzled. "Her *hsi* was on the Plane of Sleep, but her body was in her garden—and I was guarding it."

"That's more than a hundred parsecs away."

"That is a meaningless consideration," Byar said. "It does not matter where she was."

"You expect me to believe this," Dawson said, sitting down again. He seemed fixed on the spot where Byar's *chya* had been located a minute before. "The notion that the High Lord could somehow cut a connection over interstellar distance? How did she even know to do so?" He looked from Byar to Jackie, and then back to the Master of Sanctuary, whose wings had returned to a neutral position.

"She *knew*," Jackie said. "She felt it. I can't explain it, either, Guardian, except to confirm *se* Byar's story. One thing you should take away from our little talk, though . . ."

"What's that?"

"The High Nest is nothing to be trifled with. I understand that the withdrawal of the People from the war effort upsets the emperor—and it should; what's happening out beyond the Rip should upset him, too. But there are things lots bigger than you—and me—that involve the High Nest, and *we are not your enemy*.

"And neither is Rivendra Wells."

Dawson didn't have an answer for her, except to say, "He let the tech be sent to the zor Core Stars, and I can't help but be suspicious about that."

"You can have it back, *se* Guardian," Byar said. "It appears that it is inert now: Someone accessed it just before it was transferred to us. This tech, of which you are so suspicious, is now a pile of *artha*-droppings."

"Explain."

Byar thought about it for a moment and then reached within his robe and withdrew a comp. He gestured over it and then placed it near a reader on the desk.

"Here are the summaries of our investigations into this tech. Together with the notes of *se* Rivendra—Dr. Wells—you should be able to establish what the tech *could* do and what it now cannot.

"Someone altered it *before* we obtained it, Guardian Dawson. And I cannot help but be suspicious about *that*."

'Iolani Palace, Honolulu
Imperial Oahu, Sol System

Mya'ar HeChra and Simon Boyd were received alone in the Throne Room at 'Iolani Palace. They had been summoned a few Standard hours earlier, upon the emperor's return to the Islands; a high-speed aircar had been sent to the compound in West Oahu and brought them directly to the palace roof, where they entered without formality.

The emperor was alone in the room: no Guardians, no Palace Guard, no officials of the court. He was not even sitting on the Kalakaua Throne, but instead was on the maroon-colored center sofa. He stood when the representatives of the High Nest were admitted; he grasped forearms with each, and did not speak until the doors had been shut.

"Thank you for coming so quickly," Emperor Dieter said. "Everyone is downstairs in the Great Hall, and we'll have to brave that storm soon. But before that, I wanted to have a few minutes to talk face-to-face."

"I am at your service, *hi* Emperor," Mya'ar said, placing his wings in a posture of respect.

"Your High Lord has placed me in a very uncomfortable position, *se* Mya'ar," the emperor began. "By withdrawing from the war effort, you have opened old wounds."

"It was not the intention of *hi* Sa'a to cause you discomfort, sir," Mya'ar answered. "I assure you, this is no idle decision. What is more, the High Nest has not withdrawn from the war effort—it has merely extracted our forces from the fleet beyond the Rip."

"That amounts to the same thing," the emperor said. "That's where we're fighting the war."

"It is the primary theater of war. But it is being fought closer to our space as well."

"I don't follow your meaning."

"The vuhls are beyond the Rip, *hi* Emperor—but the *esGa'uYal* are still here."

The emperor folded his arms across his chest. "Explain."

Mya'ar looked at Simon, who had not said a word during the interview. For a moment, he considered having the human clarify the point for the emperor; but he concluded that it must be his own path to fly. To do otherwise would be to confirm that there was no way for the two species to properly communicate—even after all this time.

"*hi* Emperor," he said, "the enemy beyond the Rip—the species that we have fought for these many turns—is a fearsome opponent. But there is a more dangerous enemy that has been visible to us for even longer. It has interfered with the flights of both of our peoples since before we encountered each other more than one hundred and fifty Standard years ago. *This* enemy made the People believe that humans were mortal foes. *This* enemy created the circumstances that nearly led to our extinction at the hands of *esHu'ur*.

"*This* enemy arranged for the *gyaryu* to be placed on the dark path, and caused it to be returned to its present holder. It has also created the Prophet."

"What do you mean, 'created' the Prophet?"

"I mean it in the most literal sense, *hi* Emperor. An agent of this enemy caused the *naZora'e* to be born who would carry out the task that is being performed beyond the Rip.

"*This* enemy has brought us all into *Ur'ta leHssa*, and the High Lord refuses to follow. We do not turn away from the need to destroy our mutual foe—but this has gone beyond that. It has become *anGa'e'Ra*: a dark crusade." Mya'ar's wings settled themselves into a position that he had never before used.

It had been many turns since anyone had even contemplated the idea of *anGa'e'Ra*: even in the time of *esHu'ur* that word was not used.

"That word has serious overtones, *se* Mya'ar."

"*hi* Emperor." Mya'ar let his wings fall to the Posture of Polite Approach—a wing-position recognized by nearly anyone who interacted with the People regularly. "It is a word I fear to use—but there is no other way to describe it.

"The High Lord cannot condone *anGa'e'Ra, hi* Emperor, despite the affection and respect she holds for you."

"In the Grand Hall, *se* Mya'ar, the advisory council plans to suggest severing relations with the High Nest. Shall I tell them that the High Nest parts company with the Solar Empire because it believes that the destruction beyond the Rip is *excessive*?"

"It is not the destruction; it is not the death. The High Lord has no objection if *every member* of the accursed species is killed by this Prophet: but it has gone beyond that. This person, created by the *esGa'uYal*, now serves them—or possibly commands them.

"More than a hundred Standard years ago, the *esGa'uYal* tried to bring about the destruction of one species by another: yours, mine. Now they have tried to do it again—and having failed in their support of the vuhls, they now wish to bring about the destruction of this species instead."

"Why?" the emperor asked, not really expecting an answer.

"I cannot say for certain. But it *is* clear that if this destructive urge is brought forward, it cannot be put back in its box and back upon a shelf. It will be turned on other opponents" —he moved his wings into the Cloak of Guard—"including the People. And ultimately it will be turned on the Empire as well.

"What has happened already, *hi* Emperor? At every wingtip there is a predator—and each bears the symbol of Blazing Star. When they first appeared they were *hsth*-flies, and now they speak for the Guardians and they shape the words spoken by advisory councils."

"You consider Blazing Star the enemy?"

"They are in league with the enemy, *hi* Emperor. What awaits us in the Grand Hall is an ultimatum from them to the High Nest: Return to *Ur'ta leHssa,* or be the next target for the dark crusade."

"I can't believe—"

"It has gone *beyond* a question of belief," Mya'ar interrupted, agitated. It was a measure of his mood that he had cut the emperor off; normally he was a far too well trained diplomat to even consider such a thing. "They will call the loyalty of the People into question. I assure you that this question is resolved, once and for all, by *es-Hu'ur*." His wings changed once or twice, as if he weren't sure how he wished to place them. "But we turn away from this crusade, and we will fight against it if it is aimed at us."

"I assure you, *se* Mya'ar, that I have no intention of turning Imperial forces against targets belonging to the People." Emperor Dieter held Mya'ar's gaze, as if searching for an answer in the zor's eyes. "I seek nothing but amity with your species."

"I will remember those words, *hi* Emperor. But you must remember mine, in the suns to come. When you are told of our 'duplicity,' or of our 'evil intentions,' remember what we have said." He moved his wings to a position of honor to *esLi*.

"I have only one more question, *se* Mya'ar. When did *hi* Sa'a decide to part from the Prophet? What was the reason—the proximate cause?"

Mya'ar paused again for a moment, considering. At the outset of the war, he had spoken with the emperor about the quest for the *gyaryu*; and instead of heeding the wisdom of *ha* T'te'e to tell the emperor *what he could understand,* he had worked to convey the simple truth.

Now he determined that he should do it again. Slowly, and with *se* Simon's help, he explained what the High Lord had learned from *si* Owen on the Plane of Sleep; what the Prophet's avowed intentions would be; and the High Nest's response to the ultimatum. When Mya'ar was done, the emperor grasped forearms with him again, and conveyed the representatives of the High Nest to the Grand Hall, where the Imperial Court—including the *es-Ga'uYal* Mya'ar knew were within it—awaited the words of the Solar Emperor.

Oberon Starbase, Oberon System

Oberon Starbase was filled with people wearing the emblems of Blazing Star. Jackie had faced hostility before, and had grown accustomed to the faces of those fighting the war against the vuhls: the grim and determined expressions of soldiers, each knowing the next battle could be their last. But this was something different; there was a feeling of *belonging,* and suspicion of anyone who had not chosen to join them.

She did not feel in danger; she was confident enough of herself and of her ability with the *gyaryu*—both as a blade and as a source of information—that she did not fear any imminent attack. But her clear association with the High Nest seemed to have made her a target for Blazing Star's anger.

It had taken a century for the zor and human cultures to intermix—a necessary step toward fighting against the greater enemy, one that Stone's people had sought to prevent. In a matter of only a few months, the Prophet had become seemingly bent on undoing it, simply because the High Nest had withdrawn its support from the Prophet's campaign of extermination.

This time Djiwara was even easier to find. Blazing Star's command center at Oberon was the most prominent facility in the civilian sector; the merchant was making himself extremely visible there.

"ha Gyuryu'har," he said, coming from within the offices to meet her at the reception desk. A young Blazing Star member—a Sensitive, she noted, feeling the *gyaryu* batting away a casual probe—shot her a look of pure hatred. "I'm surprised to see you here."

"At Oberon? Surely you knew I was coming."

"I knew you were on your way to see *him,*" Djiwara said, directing her toward an inner office. "I meant, I'm surprised that you came *here.* They're not terribly fond of the High Nest at the moment," he added, gesturing toward the other members of Blazing Star watching them walk through.

"I can't imagine why."

"You are so coy." The office was cluttered with objects:

small shipping containers, printed reports, comps, and various things that looked like souvenirs. On the desk there was a small stand like a sword-rest, on which a pen was proudly displayed.

Djiwara saw her gaze rest upon it. He picked it up. "A memento of a recent trip to the home planet," he said. "I had to sign my name with it—a real ink-pen."

"Quaint."

"That's what I said, too." He took a seat behind the desk; Jackie sat in front of it. "You know, I decided a long time ago that it was bad business not to listen to everything, even if you don't necessarily agree with it." Djiwara picked up a comp from his desk, rejected it, and then picked up another one and made a gesture.

"Now. Some privacy." There was a slight background hum. "How may I help you, madam?" he asked Jackie.

"I need some information. I need to understand what's going on."

"I'm not exactly at the center of things."

"I don't quite believe that."

"Believe what you wish," Djiwara said, leaning back in the chair heavily enough to make it creak. "I am here at Oberon, far from the bridge of *Emperor Ian.* Wherever the hell it is now."

Jackie didn't reply, but looked around the office.

"What 'information' do you need?" Djiwara asked at last. "And what did you intend to pay for it?"

"Information for information," Jackie said. "I hear . . . We hear that most of Owen Garrett's closest friends in Blazing Star have been arrested, or worse."

"That's true. The Prophet claims that Garrett betrayed the movement—stepped off a ship in jump onto that 'rainbow bridge,' or whatever it is."

"'Claims.' You don't believe it," Jackie said.

"My *belief* isn't necessary."

"Would you like to know what *really* happened?"

"I'm sure I would. But there aren't too many living

witnesses to it—just the Prophet; and there isn't anyone to contradict him, is there?"

"You might be surprised."

Djiwara snorted. "Surprise me."

"Owen told me himself what happened," Jackie said.

Djiwara scooped up the comp and stood abruptly. "Walk with me, if you would," he said, sweeping past her and out of the office. Jackie was close on his heels.

The big merchant walked out of the Blazing Star offices and out onto the main concourse of the civilian docks. It was busy and loud; Djiwara kept moving without speaking.

"Coffee," he said at last, over the din. "Do you drink it?"

He didn't wait for an answer, but walked toward the nearest vendor on the side of the concourse. At the last minute he veered away and headed for the next one, but went past, finally stopping at the third, located in a more secluded spot. He ordered two cups, paid for them, and went to stand near the rear of the little shop where the noise from the concourse was more muted.

He lay the comp on the table between them and picked up his cup, taking a sip.

Jackie tried it. *Bitter* and *strong* were far too mild words with which to describe the drink. "That'll grow hair in places it was never intended to grow," she said after a moment.

"Glad you like it."

"What was the point of—"

"We're being watched," Djiwara said. "And listened to. I'm fairly certain: It's not just Blazing Star—there's something else going on. I can't put a finger on it." He smiled slightly. "Nothing like a good dose of paranoia to get you through the day."

"I see."

"Tell me again, Admiral," Djiwara said quietly. "Tell me what you've heard, and how you heard it."

"Owen was betrayed," Jackie said. "The Prophet killed him, but due to the 'rainbow bridge,' he wound up in a place where . . . he can continue."

"A place?"

"You wouldn't believe it if I told you."

"You keep saying that."

"All right. The Plane of Sleep," she said. "A construct. A place that's part of the cosmology of the zor—it's difficult to explain."

"You're right. Go on."

"Somehow he found his way there. His consciousness continued and the High Lord felt him arrive. We visited it and spoke with him."

"You . . . *spoke* with Garrett?"

"I *told* you that you wouldn't believe it," Jackie said.

"What makes you think I don't believe it?" Djiwara answered. "In the last few years I've seen things I never would've believed. This is just one more thing.

"I tried to tell Garrett that he had no insurance, no safety net. I told him this wasn't going to work out . . . but he survived anyway. That lucky bastard."

"I wouldn't say that. He's *dead*, Mr. Djiwara. He's— I don't know how to describe it."

Yes, you do, Sergei chided her from within the *gyaryu*.

Shut up, she thought back.

"Does . . . the Prophet know?"

"I don't think so. I don't think anyone knows, other than a few members of the High Nest—and now you. *se* Ch'en'ya doesn't know yet, I don't think. But the reason the High Nest chose to withdraw its support from the Prophet is based on what Owen told us about his own betrayal."

"The High Nest is pulling out because of Garrett."

"In the end, yes."

Djiwara took a long drink from his coffee, grimacing at its strength.

"Did Garrett tell you *why* he was betrayed?" Djiwara asked at last.

"Not exactly. He seemed as surprised by it as we were. Was he a threat to the Prophet?"

"I'm a bit of a student of history, Admiral," Djiwara said. "The Prophet probably is, as well. He understands that he didn't 'found' this thing—he just took it over and piloted it to its present location. That doesn't fit well with having a solid place in history: It would be far better theater if it had originated with the Prophet . . . the message would be more pure. *The War Manifesto* doesn't mention anyone but the Prophet himself. Like it or not, this whole crusade was Garrett's idea in the first place, but the most recent additions to Blazing Star don't know that—and the Prophet has had all of Garrett's closest allies arrested."

"Except you."

"Yes, except me." He sipped his coffee again. "From here to writing Garrett out of history entirely, isn't a big leap. Years ago, you know, he came and visited me at Port Saud, where I was wasting my obvious talents. He asked me to help him disappear and he enlisted me to help fight the vuhls."

"The 'movement.'"

"It started out as just the two of us. We gathered a few dozen others and began to devise a plan. But it was really impossible: There were too many of them and not enough of us. We built up a war chest; we did a few things—but it was just 'the tip of the tusker,' as Garrett used to say. It didn't amount to anything . . . until we met *him*."

"Which wasn't any coincidence."

"You know that for sure," Djiwara said. It wasn't a challenge.

"The Prophet told him that it was a setup by the bands of light. Garrett was placed there at the right time, and was caused to meet with the Prophet—so that the mission of Blazing Star could go forward.

"How *did* Owen meet Smith in the first place? What was *he* doing there?" asked Jackie.

"It's a long story, and I don't think we have time to discuss it now."

"I still want to hear it."

"I'll get it to your comp. Are you still planning to respond to the Prophet?"

"I'm going to meet him face-to-face, if that's what you mean. I'm hoping to convince Ch'en'ya that she's made a bad career decision."

"*He's* likely to kill you."

"*He's* welcome to try."

"I wouldn't be so eager, *ha Gyaryu'har*. Look what he does to his *friends*."

"I think I know what I'm doing, Mr. Djiwara. If I were you, I would be keeping some distance between myself and the Prophet."

"I assure you, madam, that is my intention. I have a few matters left to address here at Oberon—and then I intend to be on my way." He took a long sip of his coffee, then set it aside. "But your affairs are a different matter indeed.

"You know that if you sail into whatever system the Prophet is in, waving the banner of the High Nest, he'll have all sorts of time to get some nasty surprise ready for you. If I may offer you a bit of sage advice?" He ran a finger through his beard, as if he were searching for some stray drop of coffee.

"It's bad business not to listen to everything," Jackie said.

Djiwara permitted himself a slight smile. "It's a shame we don't get a chance to enjoy this sort of verbal sparring more often, Admiral," he said. "In any case, let me suggest the following to you: If you really want to go toe-to-toe with the Prophet, I suggest that you give him as little time as possible to prepare."

"Meaning?"

"Don't arrive on a zor ship, for one thing. There are all kinds of ships attached to the fleet—even merchant ships; one of them would do nicely to transport you there. Once you arrive, *then* you announce your presence. If nothing else, it'll *royally* piss him off.

"That may be your only advantage."

"I think I have another one," Jackie answered, placing her hand on the hilt of the *gyaryu*.

"Yes. Well." Djiwara took a look around the coffee shop, as if he were measuring everyone in it.

"I wouldn't suppose you had a suggestion?" Jackie asked, glancing around the shop herself.

"As it happens, I do. When you came to Crozier System a few years ago—when we first met—you arrived aboard an otran vessel. It happens that the very same ship is at dock here in Oberon, and its destination is beyond the Rip. I'm sure for the proper . . . *inducement*, you could get them to take you all the way to the scene of the crime itself."

"*Rxe E Mhnesr* is *here*? At Oberon?"

"Blue concourse, docking bay . . . 131. Or possibly 133. I'd suggest that you mention my name, but Kot E Showan might just double the price if you do."

"What does *this* information cost me?"

"Admiral. *ha Gyaryu'har*. I believe I've already been amply paid." He gave her the slightest bow. "I'd best be getting back. If you survive this little encounter—and I'll be damned if I can see *how*, but I believe you will—feel free to call on me again and we'll have a more relaxed drink together. Just like old times."

He smiled once more and then walked away, leaving Jackie to stand alone and watch.

As the merchant made his way out onto the concourse, leaving the emissary of the High Nest behind, someone else was also watching him depart. Unnoticed by either human, Biagio Buonaccorsi, dressed as an anonymous repair tech, walked away from a similar table to disappear into the crowd.

Chapter 26

DISSOLVING THE ASSEMBLY WAS LEGAL IN THE
SENSE THAT THE EMPEROR HAD THE RIGHT TO IM-
POSE SUCH A WRIT; THERE WERE EXAMPLES OF IT
HAVING BEEN DONE BEFORE. BUT TWENTY-SEVEN
YEARS INTO THE WAR WITH THE VUHLS, THE IDEA
THAT IT HAD *SUDDENLY* BECOME NECESSARY TO
REMOVE THE CONDUCT OF THE WAR FROM PUBLIC
SCRUTINY WAS SUSPICIOUS AT THE LEAST. THE
FACT WAS THAT THERE WAS NO CRISIS ON SEPTEM-
BER 28 THAT HADN'T BEEN THERE A WEEK, A
MONTH, OR A YEAR EARLIER: IT WAS A WAY FOR
BLAZING STAR TO REMOVE PUBLIC ACCESS FOR AS-
SEMBLYMEN WHO HADN'T YET JOINED THE MOVE-
MENT.

—author unknown,
The Dark Crusade: A History,
middle fragment, published circa 2430

October 2424
Imperial Genève, Sol System

Vittorio Atkins maintained a nicely furnished apartment
in Carouge, southeast of downtown Genève. It was a
pleasant-enough residence when the Imperial Assembly
was in session; Harrison System was almost two weeks'
jump away, so he only went home between sessions.
When he was in Genève he would often skip the private
aircar placed at his disposal and take the maglev from the

station at the corner of Avenue Vibert, which would whisk him under the city all the way to the Palais des Nations overlooking the lake—a reassurance that he was still a servant of the people.

This crisp October morning the servant of the people chose the aircar instead. The Palais des Nations was empty but for tourists: the emperor had ended the current Assembly session, choosing instead to empower an advisory council for "the duration of the emergency." Several members of the Assembly had stormed on, at their party's (or their own) expense, about the injustice of it all—and had gone home just the same. The Household Guards and members of the Guardian Order were nothing to argue with.

As Vittorio Atkins rode along in his chauffered aircar over the buildings of his adopted city, he contemplated his own reaction to the proroguing of the session, and his own silence. It had not been an easy decision: members of all three parties, including his own, had objected to the procedure—which would be subject to review in the next session in any case—and he had been urged to join them, to go on record as an opponent of the emperor's decision. He had declined, unsure whether there would be another session anytime soon.

Today he, and a few dozen others that had remained in Genève after the emperor's decree, would have a chance to meet with the advisory council that had replaced them. It was not exactly how he would have chosen to spend the time, but he still considered himself to be a member of the Assembly, one of Harrison's deputed representatives, with a responsibility to his constituents. His protest—if there was any point to it at all—was to refuse to wear a lapel pin with the Blazing Star emblem. The day that the Writ of Dissolution had been placed before the Assembly, Danielle Kalidis had presented him with one.

That day, she had gone from the Palais directly to Gare Cornavin to board a shuttle for the Islands. Today, she—and her six colleagues, the Solar Empire's advisory council, were returning to the Palais to brief those that remained.

Atkins' aircar landed on the pad between the front lawn of the Palais and the Jardin Botanique; he presented his ID comp to the Imperial Marines stationed there, who spent several seconds examining it. When they were finally satisfied they waved him onto the moving walkway, which carried him past the Armillary Sphere and the posed statues of man, rashk, zor, and otran, and into the west wing of the Palais. His ID allowed him into the lift, past two Marines and two Guardians this time; one level up, on the first floor, there was already a small crowd gathering in front of the doorway to the Salle du Conseil. The seven members of the advisory council were already seated in front of the sepia murals, looking like a group of hanging judges preparing to present a sentence.

"Atkins," said Josep Naro, a senior assemblyman from St. Ekaterin, one of the oldest Class One worlds in the Solar Empire. "About time you got here." Naro was from one of the other parties, but they'd served together for more than twenty years.

"You live on Avenue de France, Josep," Atkins replied. "I live in Carouge. Don't worry, when they come to arrest you they won't have to walk very far."

"That's not funny," Naro said. "Our new keepers don't have much of a sense of humor now that they hold the whip."

Atkins looked inside for a moment; Danielle Kalidis happened to look up at just that instant and caught his eye. Her face wore a smug expression.

"Some of them didn't have one before this," observed Atkins.

"My point *is*," Naro continued, leaning close enough that Atkins could figure out what he'd had for breakfast, "they *still* may come and arrest *us*. Let's not give them any new ideas."

"I don't think they need *us* to suggest anything. Do you know what I heard yesterday on the 'net? That there'd be hell to pay at the next Assembly session. Hilarious. There may not *be* a 'next session,' Josep."

"They wouldn't dare."

"I don't know about that. I'd say that even if both of us were armed, we'd be in a remarkably weak position, Josep. The council has the military, it has the Guardian Order, and it has Blazing Star. What do we have to fight *that*? Franking privilege?" Atkins lowered his voice now. "For the time being, at least, we're fairly well screwed, and we'd better get used to it. Now, let's hear what they have to say."

The head of the advisory council was Sir Terrence Atsoka, His Majesty's Prime Minister. He was flanked by three other members of the Imperial Assembly— including Danielle Kalidis from New Sparta, who sat to his immediate left; the Guardian Commander Antonio St. Giles; and the First Lord of the Admiralty, William Clane Alvarez, Duke of Burlington. They occupied seven of the two dozen seats normally reserved for members of the Cabinet, who sat here when conducting a briefing for the full Assembly.

All of the members of the council wore Blazing Star emblems.

The twenty-eight members of the Imperial Assembly on hand were seated in the audience area. Built to accommodate more than four hundred, most of the chairs and all of the perches were empty. There were also no representatives of the rashk or otran in attendance. Those present were not in a generous mood: it was palpable in the entire room, not just in the audience, but in the council seats as well.

Sir Terrence cleared his throat. "Thank you for attending," he began. "I have a short statement which hopefully will address your questions and concerns. At the end of my remarks, I will entertain further inquiries."

He arranged a comp in front of him and read from it. "On Saturday 28 September, the Throne issued a writ dissolving the Imperial Assembly for the duration of the current crisis. In part, the writ reads that His Imperial Majesty concluded that it would be 'dangerous to proceed further with the deliberations of the Assembly without placing undue burden on those who must conduct the war against the relentless enemy.'

"His Imperial Majesty has established this council as an advisory body for a period of time to carry on affairs of state, particularly with respect to the conduct of the war against the vuhls and the maintenance of foreign relations. To that end, the council has enacted the following decrees, all of which bear the Seal of the Emperor.

"First, by Order of the Emperor, all active-duty zor personnel in Imperial military service are hereby transferred to 'indefinite leave' status. No member of the zor race is to hold any position with 'secret' security clearance or above for the duration of the emergency.

"Second, by Order of the Emperor, all members of the Imperial Assembly, as well as all civil servants of Grade Eleven and above, are to submit to Guardian scan within fourteen Standard days of receipt of this decree. Failure to so do will subject the violator to criminal penalties not to exclude incarceration.

"Third, by Order of the Emperor, Guardian personnel will be assigned to all zor consular and embassy facilities within the boundaries of the Solar Empire for the duration of the emergency. Any facilities refusing admittance to such personnel will be closed—by force if necessary.

"Finally, and fourth, by Order of the Emperor, members of the Blazing Star organization and the Guardian Order will immediately commence cross-training exercises, for the purpose of maximizing skills and techniques to assist in the defeat of the vuhl enemy. This cross-training will be under the jurisdiction and guidance of Commander St. Giles." Sir Terrence leaned forward and nodded at the Guardian Commander, who looked a bit ill-at-ease at the decree.

"A plenipotentiary special envoy has been dispatched to the zor Core Stars bearing these decrees and also carrying the authority to negotiate a treaty to supersede the Act of Normalization, which the zor High Nest is now considered to have breached. In lieu of cooperation from the High Nest, this envoy is to inform the High Lord that the Solar Empire intends to return to status quo ante and to immediately reinstate martial-law occupation of all zor possessions throughout the Solar Empire as well as the formerly autonomous zor polity. This change in status will take place on 1 December 2424 if the High Nest continues in violation of the present terms of the Act.

"These decrees and this appointment are given under Imperial Seal this day, 12 October 2424.

"This concludes the statement, and I will now take your questions."

There was a stunned silence among the Assembly members in the audience, until Vittorio Atkins stood up. Sir Terrence nodded toward him.

"Prime Minister, let me begin by thanking you and your fellow advisors for coming to Genève to brief us on your activities," Atkins began. "Since we had not previously received word of them, I assume they have not yet been made public.

"In fairness, sir, I believe that I can understand the *motivation* of the council in effecting these basic changes to our relationship with the High Nest, with which we have enjoyed amity for longer than anyone in this room—indeed, than almost everyone in the Solar Empire—has been alive. We were all surprised and dismayed when the forces loyal to the High Nest withdrew from the current campaign."

"This was not a subject for surprise and dismay, Assemblyman," Danielle Kalidis said, leaning forward. "The action of the High Nest was treasonous."

"Oh, really?" Atkins said. "Is that so. Did they turn their weapons on Admiral Anderson's ships? Did they take up the cause of the vuhls?"

"Are those the only standards that apply when discussing *treason*, Assemblyman Atkins?" It was a challenge, no doubt about it: the emphasis she placed on the word *"treason"* made her comment sound threatening.

Vittorio Atkins had almost twenty years' experience in the Imperial Assembly and considered himself quite skilled in reading voices and facial expressions. He exchanged a glance with Josep Naro, who looked as if he still hadn't recovered from the recitation of the decrees.

"I'd like to hear *your* definition of 'treason,' Assemblywoman Kalidis," he said at last. "My comp offers the following: 'the betrayal of one's country by waging war against it or by consciously and purposely acting to aid its enemies.' Those seem like two reasonably sound examples of what we're talking about . . . Which one is Admiral HeYen guilty of, madam? Or have we changed the definition of *'treason'* to mean 'anyone who disagrees with Blazing Star'?"

Kalidis' face darkened with anger. For a moment she appeared ready to reply, but Sir Terrence Atsoka raised a hand and carefully cleared his throat again.

"Assemblyman Atkins, let me make sure I understand your objection. You feel that the decrees of this council— which already bear the Seal of the Emperor—are out of proportion to the precipitate action taken by Admiral HeYen and the High Nest?"

"Yes, sir. And as for the Seal of the Emperor, I respect His Imperial Highness' authority, but it has heretofore been the Imperial Assembly's responsibility to decide such things prior to the application of that Seal.

"Now such decrees arrive prepackaged. Don't expect us to bow and scrape. You have chosen to present these decrees to members of the Assembly before releasing them to the general public. You have invited questions: Now I must ask one.

"What do you make of the High Nest's *intent* when they withdrew after the battle at UPENDRA System? Do you think they will now proceed to make common cause with the enemy?"

"They won't get the chance," Kalidis interrupted. "We will—"

"'We will . . .' *What?*" Atkins said. "What will we do? What is the point of backing the zor into a corner? What do you *want* from them, Danielle?"

Danielle Kalidis stood up, ignoring the prime minister's warning glance. "I want to *know,* Assemblyman. I want to know why they withdrew—and I want it in words that make some kind of *sense,* not this business of 'the Valley of the Dead.' I want them to tell me what they have in mind. The presence of a fleet that is inimical to the Solar Empire is a clear and present danger, and there seems little need to beat around the bush about it, *Assemblyman* Atkins.

"They can be an enemy that is allied to the vuhls, or an enemy that is independent of the vuhls. But if they violate the treaty that binds them to the Solar Empire, *they are an enemy.*

"And they *will* be treated as such," she finished, pointing a finger at Vittorio Atkins. "And so will *anyone* who sympathizes with them."

"This is really too much, Prime Minister!" Atkins said. "Am *I* to be accused of treason as well? On what grounds?"

"On the grounds that—" Kalidis began, but this time Sir Terrence Atsoka stood up.

"Councillor Kalidis, please be seated."

"I haven't—"

"Sit down," Atsoka said. "Now." Without looking to see if she had done so, he gave Atkins a little bow. "Assemblyman Atkins, you have the apologies of the council. We need to obtain clarification from the High Nest, not start searching our own government for spies and traitors."

"It seems you are already interested in doing so," Josep Naro said, standing. "Every member of the Assembly subjected to Guardian examination, now, is it?

"This is how republics end and dictatorships begin, Mr. Prime Minister: With noble intentions and temporary measures. With accusations and investigations. The Imperial Assembly has been dissolved before, and the emperor has consented to emergency measures before. But now the stakes are much higher: Your decrees and ultimatums threaten to tear two species apart that have lived in harmony and peace for a century.

"Don't expect us to accept this without protest, sir. Don't expect us to go meekly simply because the Emperor's Seal is on these decrees. This is still the Solar Empire, and I am still a member of the Assembly."

The prime minister looked away from Naro and toward the doors of the Salle du Conseil. Slowly Naro, Atkins, and the other twenty-six members of the Assembly present turned to follow his gaze. Six Imperial Marines had already entered the chamber, and more of them were coming in as they watched. Their rifles were held at the ready.

Still without answering, the prime minister walked slowly from the room, the other six "advisory councillors" following.

Oberon System

Once again Jackie found herself in the captain's cabin aboard *Rxe E Mhnesr*. Nel E Showan, captain of the otran vessel, had welcomed her as if she had been expected—which was probably the case. He seemed a bit older, though she couldn't pin down exactly what told her so: some deepening of the wrinkles around his eyes; a slight paling of the fur on his face and neck. Neither was she younger, of course, and Jackie wondered to herself if Captain Showan noticed. The first trip had been interesting and uneventful; she wasn't making any promises about this one.

Captain Showan reclined in a chair that seemed designed specifically for his frame. "We seem to be the transportation method of choice for the High Nest, do we not, *ha Gyaryu'har*? Particularly when an agent of the honorable High Nest wishes to 'sneak up' on someone."

"The first time was pleasant happenstance," Jackie said.

"Hrr. And this time?"

"Your services were . . . recommended."

"The inestimable Djiwara, no doubt," Showan said, reaching for a large covered mug. He took a long drink and savored it. "He promised cooperation from *Rxe E Mhnesr*, did he?"

"Actually, he said that if I mentioned his name you might double the price."

"We might do that anyway," Showan said, chuckling. "After all, your last visit nearly led to *ga E layun*. The past few years have done nothing but confuse the matter: What is claimed as truth, and what is falsehood."

"Really." Jackie folded her hands and leaned forward in her chair—which clearly had been built for another otran. "Has Blazing Star cast any aspersions on your people?"

"They seem far too busy with *your* people," Showan answered. He set his mug on an end table and knotted his fingers. It wasn't clear from the way he said it whether he meant humans or zor. "I have trouble understanding just what Blazing Star intends—and naturally, its public statements do little to explain it. Full of duplicity and contradiction . . . even self-contradiction."

"That's what I want to sort out."

"Hrr," Showan said. "I'd think it would be unwise to be close by when that happens."

"I should hope so. I'm invited this time: They're expecting me."

"At the site of their most recent battle?"

"Yes. I understand that they're still there—regrouping."

"Is that what they call it? They must be trying to work up *alel e laru*—anger enough to continue."

"I think they're just trying to make sure they have enough *ships* to continue. I've only heard some of what happened at Upendra; they apparently took quite a beating."

"The vuhls are cornered now," Showan said. "They will fight in a different way, as long as they can. This makes *our* services more valuable. We will provide things to the fleet as long as they carry on this war—and the longer their supply line becomes, the more valuable our goods and services.

"Still, I must tell you that I am somewhat concerned about this journey—particularly if it will lead to . . ." He let the sentence trail off, glancing at the *gyaryu.*

"I don't plan to endanger *Rxe E Mhnesr,* if that's what you're worried about, Captain Showan."

"Oh, don't you." He let his fingers slowly unlace, gripping the sides of his chair. For an otran to fold his hands was to indicate that he meant no violence; unfolding them got them ready for action. "The air within the fleet is rich with danger, *ha Gyaryu'har.* We have been asked where we stand on the matter of . . . What was it? Yes. *Exterminating* the vuhls."

"Where *you* stand? Or where the otran stand?"

"Hrr, an interesting distinction," he answered. "I think that in both cases, my people have no interest in the activities of Blazing Star beyond the Rip. On *this* side, however . . . it seems that their influence is becoming unavoidable."

"*I'm* looking to avoid it."

"I wish you good luck," Showan said, "but I do not see how you can do it."

She frowned. "I don't intend to join the crusade, so that leaves only one option."

"*ga E layun?*" Showan said, his face forming a smile. "No, I suppose not. But it seems unlikely that you can do your arguing with a sword—why would they let you get close enough? What's more, you don't seem to be the sort to strike, as you humans say, 'in cold blood.' Is that what you have in mind? If so, I would counsel you to let me know: I will jump *Rxe E Mhnesr* away before they turn their weapons on *me*."

Jackie thought about it: She knew why she wanted to go to Upendra System—to confront Ch'en'ya with the truth, and hopefully pull her away from the Prophet; trying to talk sense to *him* didn't strike her as very productive.

But how much of this was responding to a challenge—or a threat—to the High Nest? How much was bravado—and if it was, could she afford it? She wasn't sure how much the *High Nest* could afford it.

"I have to try," she said aloud, and Captain Showan cocked his head at her as if to say: *Try what?* "I will do my best to keep *Rxe E Mhnesr* out of danger, Captain. That's all I can tell you."

The otran captain considered this for a moment, then nodded—he rocked his whole body gently back and forth to achieve the effect. "All right, *ha Gyaryu'har*. We get under way in six hours."

D jiwara did not return to the Blazing Star offices after meeting with the *Gyaryu'har* of the High Nest. Instead, he made his way along the civilian docks to *Merton*, a small nondescript cargo vessel; he was greeted by the cargo master, who was checking a pile of canisters with his comp. Twenty minutes later the cargo hatch was pulled shut and the ship moved off the Oberon Starbase dock, making its way toward the gas giant's refueling queue.

She was in the ship's galley, a half-consumed cup of coffee in front of her; she looked up when Djiwara came in. Before saying a word he dispensed himself a cup as well, doctored it, and then took a seat opposite.

"This is quite a bit of cloak-and-dagger, isn't it?" Laura Ibarra asked, grimacing at the contents of her cup and sloshing it around.

"It might not be enough. Do you ever get the feeling you're being watched—followed around, monitored at every moment? I'm beginning to feel that way myself."

"Mr. Djiwara. We live in a society where just about everything can be observed at any time. The problem is, there aren't enough eyes to watch every vidcam. So I take the matter into consideration and move on.

"For example, I've known about you for some time— since you first turned up at Zor'a a few years ago and whisked Ch'en'ya away to meet the Prophet."

Djiwara smiled. "Oh, you saw that, did you?"

"It was Jackie's *last* wild-goose chase."

"Interesting choice of words. *This* time I think she's not coming back: One sword, no matter how powerful, isn't going to save her life. *He's* going to kill her, Ms. Ibarra."

"Why?"

"Because she won't join him. The *Gyaryu'har* is dangerous, but she's not murderous."

"Neither are you."

"No." He took a swig from the cup, grimaced, and then took another. "No, I'm a long way from that. Which brings us to the subject of this meeting.

"I need your help, madam. I give up a bit of bargaining position by starting with that, but it's true: I need help to get a friend out of a jam that he shouldn't be in."

"Who's the friend?"

"Are you willing to help me?"

"Depends. Who's the friend?" she repeated.

"Rafe Rodriguez. He's an old friend, Ms. Ibarra, and he's been swept up along with the rest of our old friends by someone who's even more paranoid than I am. Rafe's a loyal soldier who isn't involved in any plots or conspiracies—"

"Like present company," Ibarra interrupted.

Djiwara smiled. "Yes. Like present company. I also realize that I'm sacrificing a bit of my hard-won reputation as a rat bastard by being sentimental, but I just can't help it."

"Where is he now?"

"He's been arrested by the Guardians. Though when they got assigned police power, I don't remember."

"So . . . Blazing Star doesn't have him, then."

"It's getting so you can't tell them apart—but no, he's in Guardian custody."

"What do you want me to do?"

"Get custody of him. Then release him to me."

Ibarra laughed. "That's quite a tall order, Mr. Djiwara. Aren't they likely to be suspicious? Isn't he a traitor to the movement since he's an 'old friend' of the late Mr. Garrett?"

Just for a moment, at the mention of Garrett's name, Laura Ibarra thought that the big merchant started; but he covered it quickly.

"He's small-fry," Djiwara said. "They won't care about him. All you need is some sort of espionage charge, and he can be transferred to Imperial Intelligence."

"And then we just hand him over to you."

"Since he's not really a spy, there's no reason for you to hold him."

"Very neat." She folded her hands in front of her. "You know, there's an obvious next question: Why would we do this great favor for you?"

"Not a *favor*," Djiwara said. "A *trade*. I have considerable freedom within the movement, and I have some things you might be interested in. And *that* is why we're engaged in . . . What did you call it? Cloak-and-dagger."

"Now I know why working for a rashk has its advantages," she said, smiling. "You'll betray your organization, the thing you spent twenty years building, for the sake of one man?"

"Let me clarify something for you, Ms. Ibarra. What is going on beyond the Rip *isn't* the organization we built over twenty years; it's become something quite different.

Quite alien." Again, Ibarra saw something in his expression she couldn't identify. "And as for the matter of betrayal, it seems to be in the water these days. I'm running out of people to trust.

"So, I suppose the answer is *yes*. I'd prefer to think of this as building a relationship with a new business associate, and I'd like to have Rodriguez' help doing it."

"There's something you're not telling me."

"Madam." He drank again from his cup. "There is a universe full of things I'm not telling you. You have my word, however, that what I have told you thus far is the truth."

Ibarra thought about it for a few moments, trying to determine what M'm'e'e Sha'kan's reaction would be to this deal. It was clear that Djiwara had all kinds of access; it was also clear that he had some further agenda that he wasn't revealing.

"I'd think it would be dangerous to hand Rodriguez over to you on the docks here at Oberon."

"I don't expect to stay here much longer, Ms. Ibarra. I would think that Sol System would be a more appropriate venue. I have some business there."

"When do you need to know?"

"Do you have the power to make this decision, or do you have to check with the rashk you work for?"

"I can decide."

"Fine. Then please decide, Ms. Ibarra. At any moment, my good friend's Guardian keepers might decide to push him out an airlock—and if they do, believe me, the deal is off."

*M*erton docked again at Oberon Starbase, fully fueled and ready for jump toward the Inner Sphere. The fact was noted by a copy of Nic that was running in the Oberon main comp, but it was one data point among millions. When *Merton* jumped outsystem, J. Michael Djiwara was aboard.

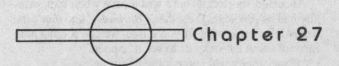 Chapter 27

THE MISSION OF THE *GYARYU'HAR* WAS UNDER-
TAKEN WITH THE BLESSING OF THE HIGH NEST,
BUT IT IS UNCLEAR WHAT SHE HOPED TO ACCOM-
PLISH. THE ACTING GOVERNMENT OF THE SOLAR
EMPIRE HAD ALREADY RECEIVED ITS MARCHING
ORDERS, UNDOING THE GOODWILL OF A CENTURY
IN A MATTER OF A FEW WEEKS.

—author unknown,
The Dark Crusade: A History,
late fragment, published circa 2430

October 2424
UPENDRA System

"Admiral," came a voice out of the darkness.

"Pause display."

The battle replay displayed on *Emperor Ian*'s astrography holo froze, with the vuhl ship just in the process of exploding, a dozen kilometers from *Barbados'* defensive fields; two of its fighters were being consumed by the fireball.

Sir Erich Anderson turned to see who was intruding. A man wearing a Guardian uniform came across the transparent walkway to the center of the room.

"That's *Barbados,* isn't it, sir?"

"Bradford," he said to the Guardian. "Didn't my aide tell you that I didn't wish to be disturbed?"

"It's uncommon for anyone to say much of anything to a member of the Guardian Order, Admiral."

Anderson snorted. "There was a time when rank actually had its privileges. Yes, that's *Barbados,* and *that's* the bastard that crippled it. If you'd like, we can roll the holo forward about ten seconds to see it happen."

"It was unpleasant enough the first time, sir."

"For me, too. —All right, Bradford: What can I do for you?"

"Rather, it is what I can do for you, Admiral. I have some information that you will find interesting."

"'Information'?"

"We have learned why the zor withdrew, Admiral."

Cameron Bradford suddenly had Sir Erich Anderson's complete and undivided attention.

"Why?"

"Because of a betrayal, sir. Because they believe—with good authority—that Mr. Garrett was betrayed."

"The Prophet told me—"

"—a lie, Admiral. The Prophet told you—and the fleet—*a lie. He* killed Owen Garrett *himself.*"

"During the jump to UPENDRA?"

"That's right, sir. *He* killed Mr. Garrett, whose presence had become an embarrassment. Every movement does that, eventually: pruning those who do not properly fit the history they plan to write."

Bradford paused, letting it sink in for a moment. Anderson considered the matter, trying to read some additional information from the Guardian's face—with no success.

"How do you know all of this?"

"Unimpeachable sources," Bradford said, which was no answer at all.

"And this is the reason for the zor withdrawal?"

"Yes sir. They find that the Prophet's plans beyond the destruction of the vuhls is unacceptable, and that Mr. Garrett's betrayal is only the beginning of a course that will consume the Solar Empire and the High Nest. They wish no part of it."

"We will win this war, and then we'll attend to the zor." Anderson remembered the Prophet saying that to him, just after the battle here at Upendra System.

He looked up at *Barbados,* just about to be heavily damaged by the impact of a suicidal vuhl ship.

"Why are you telling me this?"

"Rank has its privileges, Admiral. It seemed appropriate that you understand clearly what was happening within your command, and I received instructions to provide this information to you."

"From the head of your Order?"

"Something like that." Bradford let a little bit of a smile cross his face. "I've also been instructed to tell you that the *Gyaryu'har* of the High Nest is on her way to UPENDRA System."

"There has been no official word from the High Nest. No zor vessel has passed through the Rip, Guardian Bradford."

"Nonetheless, the Order understands that she is on her way. Alone."

"I'm sure the Prophet will be pleased to hear it."

"Yes," Bradford said. "I'm sure *he* will." He stepped away from Admiral Anderson and withdrew from the room.

After the door had slid shut, Anderson gestured at his comp. The holo display began to move slowly forward, the vuhl ship exploding. An area of *Barbados'* defensive field glowed, shrunk, collapsed, and a long seam of fire ripped across its underside.

"We will win this war, and then we'll attend to the zor." Anderson repeated to himself. He wondered what it meant: Whether the Prophet had thought ahead by betraying Garrett ... perhaps *knowing* what the High Nest's reaction would be, with the *intention* of winning the war without the zor—and then turning on them as a

consequence. Though why the High Nest would care about Garrett's fate—why it would be so important—was beyond his understanding.

The vuhl ship finished vaporizing, its fireball contracting. The *Barbados* lurched aside, unable to avoid further damage.

"I'm not sure we can win without them," he said to himself. There was no way to say this to the Prophet: There was no way to go but forward, no other outcome but to defeat the vuhls. But surely Jackie Laperriere wasn't coming out here to join the movement . . .

No way to go but forward, he thought, watching the last of the vuhl suicide ship dissipate into empty space.

R̃xe Є Mhnesr transitioned into UPENDRA System after a brief stop at Nestor, where it renewed its credentials as a friendly merchant. The Imperial Fleet was far enough away from the Rip that it was easier to take advantage of private vendors providing luxuries than to rotate ships back to Nestor or Portal to obtain them.

The scene before them was less than pretty. The system was full of ships: nearly a hundred of them, many orbiting the Earthlike planet deep in the gravity well. The deployment didn't look orderly; it had the appearance of the aftermath of a battle—a nasty one, at that.

"We are here," Kot E Showan said. He looked tense. "I do not know what you have in mind, *ha Gyaryu'har,* but you'd best get it over with."

Jackie nodded. "Please comm *Emperor Ian* and tell them that the *Gyaryu'har* would like a word with Ch'en'ya HeYen."

*N*o," the admiral said. "I don't think that's a wise idea."

The Prophet shrugged. "I disagree. *Barbados*' crew and fighters can serve just as well in spare rotations on

Seychelles. They are the same ship-class and the configuration is the same—"

"It overlooks something basic," Anderson interrupted. "Kwame Adelman and many of his people have been serving aboard *Barbados* since it was launched three years ago. They're very loyal to their ship. This isn't about sentimentality."

"Oh, *isn't* it?" The Prophet crossed his arms in front of him. "Like so many things in the Imperial Navy, it's all about *tradition*," he sneered. "*Barbados* is scarcely capable of jump, while *Seychelles* is short several fighters. It seems a fairly simple equation to me."

"And what shall we do with *Barbados*? Shoot it into the sun?"

"I don't care what we do with it."

"Yes, that's the problem, isn't it?"

Anderson and the Prophet held each other's gaze, neither responding to the other's last comment. The moment was broken by the ready-room doorchime.

"Come," Anderson said, turning to face the door. The Prophet looked up as well.

The watch comm officer stood in the doorway as it slid aside. He saluted and stepped within the room, letting the door close behind him before speaking. "Admiral, sir, there's a Priority 19 comm for you."

"Priority 19," Anderson repeated. "There are very few people who have rank 19—she must be here. Laperriere is here."

"The *Gyaryu'har* is here?" the Prophet said. "When did she arrive? *How* did she arrive?" He glanced at the small holo showing the system display.

Anderson looked from the Prophet to the young lieutenant. "Report," he said, trying not to sound annoyed.

"She is aboard an otran vessel, Admiral. She wishes to speak with Ch'en'ya HeYen."

"*I* speak for this ship," Anderson answered. "Thank you, Lieutenant. Dismissed."

The comm officer saluted and went back out the way

he'd come. Anderson gestured at the console in the ready-room table. "Accept the Priority 19 comm. Voice-seal this room and route it here." He glanced at the Prophet.

"Acknowledged," the comp said. "Ready to receive transmission?"

"Commence."

A holo appeared: a woman sitting in what looked like a helm or nav chair, not conforming to her posture but oddly shaped. She had a scabbard stretched across her lap.

"Admiral Anderson," she said.

"*ha Gyaryu'har*. Welcome to UPENDRA System. Glad you could make it."

"I'd like to speak to Ch'en'ya."

"I'd like to welcome you appropriately aboard the flag-ship. I'll send a gig for you if you'd like," he answered. "I understand that you arrived aboard an otran ship."

"That's right. They were headed this way."

Anderson shrugged. "Anything you have to say to her you can say to me, madam."

"I doubt it." She looked from Anderson to the Prophet, who was within range of the vid pickup, then back to Anderson. "I see you've had a battle here. Are you sure you can carry on this war with what you've got left?"

"You came all the way to UPENDRA System to insult His Majesty's Fleet? While representing a foreign power that betrayed it? That's bravery to the point of foolhardiness."

"I'd like to speak to Ch'en'ya," Jackie Laperriere repeated. "That's why I'm here, Admiral. If I come over to *Emperor Ian*, will she be aboard to see me?"

Anderson looked at the Prophet and back. "Yes. She's aboard now."

"Then I'll come. Send your gig, sir. I'll be waiting."

The holo vanished, ending the comm message.

"She only has two choices," the Prophet said. "In the

best-case scenario, she joins the movement—whether the zor come along with her or not. After all, she has as much of a grudge against the vermin as anyone else."

"And the other choice?"

The Prophet smiled, baring his teeth. "If she doesn't go the obvious route, the High Nest gains a new *Gyaryu'har.*"

The gig from *Emperor Ian* detached from *Rxe E Mhnesr*'s service airlock and began to traverse the distance between the otran vessel and the fleet flagship. The young pilot didn't speak more than a word or two to her, focusing on bringing the small craft into grapple range. It was guided slowly toward *Ian*'s hangar deck, where the big ship took control of it and guided it within, where it settled in to land.

Without escort or support, she walked to the airlock and opened it and let the gravlift lower her to the deck. Marines, all wearing the Blazing Star emblem on their lapels, stood at attention; they executed a brief "present arms" and then stood at the ready.

She walked slowly between them and they formed up behind her. There was only one way to go: forward and up a ramp, toward the command deck. Through the glasteel viewport, she could see the Prophet and Ch'en'ya waiting for her. Admiral Sir Erich Anderson was nowhere to be found; this was evidently a civilian show.

She placed her hand gently on the hilt of her sword.

The top of the Perilous Stair, she thought to herself. *You're finally here.*

Se *Gyaryu'har,*" the Prophet said, when she stood before him. She raised one eyebrow at the use of the prenomen; it presumed equality between them, rather than the more formal *"ha."*

The Marines had left the room so only the three of them were present. "I am glad to see you here," he continued.

"Are you really."

"Yes," he answered. "I really am. I've been waiting for you to come and join us. To join me."

"Is that why you think I'm here?"

"I'm giving you the benefit of the doubt." He smiled slightly. "Because if you're here for any other purpose, I'm going to have Ch'en'ya kill you."

It was such a bald statement of intent that Jackie could hardly reply for a moment.

"We've had this discussion before, Smith," she said. "And I—"

Ch'en'ya had her *chya* drawn in an instant, and had it pointed toward Jackie. Her wings were held in an angry position. "You will address *him* with a title of honor," she said.

"I'll address *him* any way I damn please," Jackie said. She brought the *gyaryu* out to guard. Ch'en'ya moved her *chya* up to block; both blades moved menacingly in the air near each other. "Are you ready to challenge me?"

"Are you here to join us?" Ch'en'ya asked.

"I'm here to tell you the truth," Jackie said, glancing quickly from Ch'en'ya to the Prophet. "About your Prophet—and his intentions toward your race."

"Ch'en'ya knows what we may have to do next," the Prophet said, folding his arms across his chest. "We've discussed this course already."

"Have you told her how you betrayed Owen Garrett?" Jackie said. "How you tried to kill him with a single word?"

The Prophet didn't answer that remark, though he looked curiously at her for a moment. Ch'en'ya looked away and then back at Jackie. "You cannot manipulate me, *se* Jackie. You and the High Lord may have made the Am'a'an Guardians do your bidding, but I will not."

"You lied to them, *se* Ch'en'ya. You told them you

were High Lord of the People, and that you would give them their honor back. But they'd never lost it—the High Nest accidentally betrayed them when they breached the Plane of Sleep."

"It does not matter," Ch'en'ya answered. "There is still work to be done here in the World That Is. Are you here to join us, or not?"

Jackie saw more than anger in Ch'en'ya's eyes. Now she saw madness. "No," she said finally.

"*He-e-ai!*" Ch'en'ya shouted, advancing. The *gyaryu* and her *chya* struck and parted, struck and parted. There was murder in Ch'en'ya's wings, as if the frustration and resentment of thirty Standard years were being released.

The Prophet seemed to be watching with amusement, his arms folded.

"I don't want this fight," Jackie said. "*se* Ch'en'ya, this accomplishes nothing."

"Do you think so?"

They circled, crouching.

"Then you are a fool," Ch'en'ya said. "Doubly so for coming here alone. There is clearly no place for you in what is to come."

"I had hoped that words would suffice, not this foolish challenge," said Jackie.

"Words do *not* suffice. Words have *never* sufficed: There is nothing more to say. The Flight of the People has changed, and by refusing to change with it you forfeit your position."

"That is up to the High Lord to decide," Jackie said, blocking another series of violent thrusts from Ch'en'ya's *chya*.

"Pah," she said. "*I* dream the Flight."

"Yours is a false seeming. The madness-of-daylight is overtaking you."

"Liar," Ch'en'ya said. "Servant of the Deceiver."

"I don't take kindly to that," Jackie answered, feeling anger course through her.

It was what Ch'en'ya wanted: to make her see red.

It was working.

"You do not even have the strength to kill me," Ch'en'ya said. "Nor the will. You are a weak *naZora'e*. You always have been, just as *si* Marais was weak."

"I'm weak because I won't *kill* you? I saved your worthless life by rescuing you. If I was going to kill you, I would've done it decades ago."

"Weakling."

"Lunatic."

"You serve the Deceiver."

"No," Jackie said finally. "No, this is the top of the Perilous Stair, and *you* serve the Deceiver." She gestured with her off-hand toward the Prophet. "He's standing right over there. And if you think I can't kill you, think again."

She swung the *gyaryu* in a short, graceful arc and hooked the hilt of Ch'en'ya's *chya*. It sailed out of her opponent's hands to clatter onto the deck a few meters away. As Ch'en'ya's wings bunched for a flying leap backward, Jackie prepared for a killing stroke—

And suddenly, painfully, something struck her on the side of the head. As she lost consciousness, she saw the *gyaryu* slip from her grasp and slide across the deck to land at Ch'en'ya's feet.

Ch'en'ya looked angrily at the Prophet.

"That was unnecessary," she said. "You intervened in a duel."

"I have aided," he answered, "in an execution." He poked Jackie's motionless body with the toe of one boot. "You might as well finish the job."

He gestured toward the *gyaryu*.

"And then we'd better be on our way." A path of rainbow light appeared behind him, passing through the back of the observation platform, tinged with the darkness of *anGa'e'ren*.

Ch'en'ya stepped back for a moment, remembering what she had been told on the Plane of Sleep. *It is true*, she thought to herself. si *Owen was telling the truth*.

The Prophet and the zor warrior locked glances for several moments; at last Ch'en'ya looked away.

She reached down to pick up the sword—

And the scene changed. Ch'en'ya was standing on a flat, black plain, with some illumination coming from an unknown source.

A shadowy figure came into view. Ch'en'ya raised the *gyaryu;* so did the figure.

"There's no point in menacing *me* with it." Jackie Laperriere—a younger one, closer to the age she was when Ch'en'ya had first met her—emerged from the darkness. She was slightly transparent, and was holding the *gyaryu*—another *gyaryu*—at guard position.

"Do you know where you are?" Jackie asked.

"Ur'ta leHssa," Ch'en'ya answered.

"Not hardly. This is within the *gyaryu, se* Ch'en'ya. You have evidently picked up the sword; now you're experiencing the Dark Understanding."

"Within . . ."

Two more human figures came out of the darkness. Ch'en'ya recognized them: The first two *naZora'i* to serve as *Gyaryu'har,* prior to *se* Jackie. Each of them wore the sword belted at their waist.

Ch'en'ya moved her wings to the Posture of Polite Approach. *"si* Marais," she said. *"si* Torrijos."

"Put the sword up," Admiral Marais said. "Welcome to the *gyaryu.*" He turned to Jackie. "Are you—"

"I don't know. I suspect that I'm still alive, but—it's hard to tell. If you'll recall, *si* Sergei was still breathing when he met me in this exact place."

"I recall."

Ch'en'ya looked from one to the other human figure. She sheathed the sword in a scabbard at her belt, where her *chya* would have hung.

"May I present Ch'en'ya HeYen," Jackie said.

"This is the Dark Understanding," Ch'en'ya said.

"This is the secret of the *gyaryu*—two *naZora'e*? No—" Her wings moved in confusion. "If you are the recent holders of the sword, then every *Gyaryu'har* must . . ."

She looked into the deep darkness. Far away there was a flash of light, like a brief burst of golden sunlight.

"You are all here," Ch'en'ya said. "*ha'i* Qu'u is here as well."

"She's a quick study," Sergei said. "Yes, *se* Ch'en'ya. We are all here. Everyone whose *hsi* has directly touched the *gyaryu* has left an impression behind—though only the holders of the sword can manifest on their own.

"While we speak here, only a miniscule fraction of a sun has passed outside," Jackie said. "If you're standing over my body, ready to kill it, you're still standing there."

"*si* Owen spoke the truth," she said. "He told me that the Prophet was in league with the abomination of six— that it was no longer clear who the true enemy was.

"I am not ready to send you beyond the Outer Peace, *se* Jackie," Ch'en'ya answered. "I do not now desire your death."

"That's not the impression you were giving—at least up until a few moments ago when Smith laid me out," Jackie said. "Or, rather, until he laid my body out.

"Just as on *alTle'e*, my life is in your hands."

Ch'en'ya did not answer. Her wings rippled in anger, but whatever had possessed her until a few moments before, seemed to be draining away.

"It's *enGa'e'Li*," Jackie said quietly. "The Strength of Madness is what wants to kill me. The madness-of-daylight wants to kill me. And it's damn sure Smith wants to kill me.

"You want to be *Gyaryu'har*—you may want to be High Lord of the People, for all I know—but are you ready to kill me to do it?"

"I would become *idju* if I slew you without cause," Ch'en'ya said, looking around her.

"That is correct."

Another pair of figures emerged from the darkness

now. They were People: a male and a female. The female had spoken; now she advanced into the light. She held a polished wooden staff and wore a pale, peach-colored robe. A *chya,* not the *gyaryu,* hung at her belt. The male wore no blade at all; their fingers were intertwined.

"I should know you," Ch'en'ya said.

Jackie's eyes were full of tears. "I didn't know whether it was possible for you to come. I sent you both to the Golden Circle, but—"

"You said it yourself, *se* Jackie," the female said. "Those whose *hsi* has touched the *gyaryu* can manifest here. I am a *hsi* image, but I am here."

She let go of the other zor's hand. The two of them stepped forward; they exchanged glances with each other, and then looked at Ch'en'ya, their wings moving to positions of deep affection.

"And this," she said at last, "is our daughter."

Ch'en'ya extended her hands to grasp her mother's forearms. "You are . . ."

"Th'an'ya," the female said.

"Ch'k'te," the male said. He bowed in deep honor to Jackie, who grasped forearms with him.

"Our *hsi*-images are here at the request of *se* Jackie," Ch'en'ya said. "As our actions—all of our actions, including those of *esHu'ur*"—her wings dipped in a position of respect to Admiral Marais—"have led to the person you have become, it is necessary that we all have an opportunity to speak with you.

"When *esHu'ur* who was also *esTli'ir* changed the Flight of the People, he directed us away from a flight of deception. He was touched by the One Who Weaves, but did not do his bidding.

"*si* Sergei sacrificed his life to bring the new *Gyaryu'har* forth, by following the Law of Similar Conjunction. In the process I, too, sacrificed my life so that my dear mate—your father—would have my *hsi* at time of need.

"*His* sacrifice was to save *se* Jackie from the *esHara'e* who sought to Dominate her at the base of the Perilous Stair. When *se* Jackie received the Dark Understanding, she released our *hsi* . . . yet we are still here: not in the World That Is, but here, within the *gyaryu*."

"My dear daughter," Ch'k'te continued, "your flight has always been based upon the hatred of the *esGa'uYal*, the *esHara'y,* your mother, *se* Jackie . . . but while it conveys the Strength of Madness, it is not—it cannot completely be—the flight of a warrior. There is the Inner Peace to consider.

"Warriors of the People find their center by balancing the Four: *esGa'u* who drives the People toward change, sometimes violent change; *esLi,* the Lord of the Golden Circle, whose light divides night from day; *esHu'ur*"—he nodded toward Admiral Marais—"and *esTli'ir.* In the center is the warrior.

"The Prophet is not a warrior of the People. The Prophet is—"

Ch'en'ya looked into her father's eyes. "He is an *esGa'uYe,*" she said firmly. "He is at the top of the Perilous Stair."

Jackie did not speak, but nodded very slightly.

"If you are here now," Ch'en'ya said to Ch'k'te, "you will be here when I return." She placed her hand on the hilt of the *gyaryu.*

"What are you going to do?"

Ch'en'ya's wings rose in anger. "*esLi*'s Will."

The Prophet stepped on to the rainbow path. "Kill her or not, I don't care," he said. "We have places to go, and if you stay, you'll have to figure out a way to explain it."

Ch'en'ya looked at her taloned hands gripping the *gyaryu.* With a sweeping motion she brought the sword around in a swift arc, missing Jackie's prone form, and striking the rainbow path where it emerged from the deck.

A look of surprise crossed the Prophet's face as a ripple of lightning flew from the point of impact. The path receded at high speed, the Prophet with it, until it vanished completely.

From the bridge of *Rxe E Mhnesr*, Nel E Showan saw bands of rainbow light shoot out in several directions from *Emperor Ian*. Two of the bands struck other ships; the others moved at enormous speed away from the flagship. The two struck ships sustained major damage to their hulls—no defensive fields were presently online—and it appeared that *Ian* had suffered damage as well.

"Identify that," he snapped to the helm, as he watched lines shoot across his pilot's board.

"Nothing we've ever seen," the helmsman replied.

Captain Showan displayed the energy signature and watched, incredulous, as one of the lines accelerated and then transitioned into jump.

"Where is it headed?"

Helm didn't answer for several moments.

"It was traveling at light-speed," the helmsman said at last. "But its vector crosses only one solar system within fifty parsecs."

"Which one?"

He turned to face his captain. "Portal System, Uncle."

Alarm bells were ringing throughout *Ian* almost immediately. A portion of the command deck had been ripped away, along with a far wall; a bulkhead door was closing due to decompression several dozen meters distant.

Ch'en'ya bent down and lifted Jackie's hand, gently placing the *gyaryu* in it. After a moment Jackie's eyes fluttered open; the hand not holding the sword moved to touch her head.

"What happened?" She looked at her hand holding the

gyaryu and then at Ch'en'ya. For just a moment she was alarmed, considering her alternatives and the threat that Ch'en'ya might pose. The look in the zor's eyes and the position of her wings reassured Jackie.

"I wish I understood."

"Where is the Prophet?"

"I cannot say. He sought to escape using the colored bridge of the *esGa'uYal*—the abomination of six. I—interfered. It appears this has severely damaged *Emperor Ian*."

Jackie thought for a moment, sitting up. "We'd better get to the bridge and let the admiral know what's going on."

Announcements were coming over ship's comm, directing damage-control parties to their stations. Below, on the hangar deck, the Marines had scrambled to duty, leaving it unoccupied.

"On the other hand," Jackie said, pulling herself slowly to her feet, "maybe we'd better just get off this ship entirely." She sheathed the *gyaryu,* still not sure what had happened.

She had expected an argument from Ch'en'ya which, surprisingly, didn't come. With the zor's help she made her way down the ramp; unchallenged, they made their way aboard the gig.

Jackie seated herself in the pilot's chair, hoping the controls had been left engaged. Unfortunately, they appeared to be in a security standby mode making the gig inoperable; just when she was beginning to rack her brain for a plan, Ch'en'ya said to the air, "Enable gig controls. Voice authorization Ch'en'ya HeYen . . . *Gyaryu'har.*"

The gig's board came to life; indicators moved to ready position, and the hangar doors began to cycle outward.

"*'Gyaryu'har'*?" Jackie said, glancing at Ch'en'ya.

"I planned to work my way to High Lord," she answered, allowing herself a gesture of amusement. "One wingspan at a time, *se* Jackie."

"Engage helm," Jackie said to comp. "Prepare to clear hangar deck."

"Acknowledged," *Ian*'s comp said, relayed through the gig's comm. There was immediately a pending message—presumably someone from *Emperor Ian* asking who the hell was taking a gig out. Jackie ignored it as the gig rose and moved slowly out of the parent ship.

"*se* Jackie," Ch'en'ya said, gesturing at a vidcam that showed the fleet flagship. It was clearly badly damaged; whatever had happened was spreading fast. Arcs of rainbow-colored lightning were racing along its hull as they watched.

"Helm! Full emergency acceleration!" Jackie shouted, and the gig leapt forward quickly enough for them to feel it: Internal gravity compensated a second or so late, causing Ch'en'ya to almost lose her footing so that she was actually in the air for a moment.

"What is—" she began to say, and then the two passengers watched as *Ian* erupted into a huge fireball, polarizing the vidscreen to opacity.

Aboard *Rxe E Mhnesr,* Nel E Showan interlaced his fingers and placed his hands in front of his face. Slowly, each of his *na'otran* did the same, cloaking the bridge in complete silence. Seconds passed as the captain of the otran vessel considered what his next action should be.

"*Rxe E Mhnesr,*" comm said. "Laperriere sends. Do you read?"

Captain Showan removed his hands from his face and looked at the pilot's board. A small craft was approaching his position.

"She made it," he said quietly. "Whatever else has happened, she made it. Prepare for docking," he added to helm. "This should be interesting."

First Hive

Approximately forty parsecs away, deep in the center of First Hive, a shaft of rainbow light pierced the wall of a large, spacious chamber and struck a transparent cube that stood in its center. Almost immediately, the luminescent mist began to drain away from within the cube as shadowy tendrils formed within it. The silvery sphere that bobbed on the surface of the mist rode lower and lower, until it at last struck the bottom of the cube, rolling to a stop in one corner.

A seam appeared in a wall of the mostly empty chamber and Great Queen K'da moved through it. Beyond, a pair of *P'cn* Deathguard stood, watching, as K'da came up to the now-empty cube.

She stood for a moment, extending her *k'th's's* to taste any part of the Ór that might still remain—but all was quiet.

In the bright glow of the rainbow shaft, Great Queen K'da turned to face her executioners.

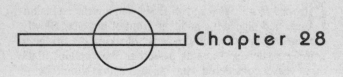 Chapter 28

ENERGY MAY BE LIKENED TO THE BENDING OF A CROSSBOW; DECISION, TO THE RELEASING OF A TRIGGER.

—Sun Tzu,
The Art Of War, V:15

October 2424
Portal System

Sixty parsecs away from UPENDRA System, Barbara MacEwan had a dozen crew-rosters displayed above her ready-room table when they vanished and were replaced by the pilot's board display. She was just about to shout for Arturo Schelling when a holo appeared standing opposite.

"Sorry for the interruption, but you need to look at this, Admiral." He pointed at the board.

A line was streaking across Portal System, stretching from somewhere beyond and crossing the outer three orbitals.

"Identify that."

"I can't, ma'am. But it's moving at light-speed in a straight line, and it arrived by jump transition eighteen minutes ago."

"Do you have a visual?"

"Something from a small craft that was refueling: Here you go—" He gestured offscreen, and a small vid appeared below the pilot's-board holo.

It showed a faintly colored line, flashing across the screen. The whole vid was perhaps two seconds long, during which time the line traveled nearly half a million kilometers.

"Slow to one-hundredth speed, and zoom a thousand. Show it to me again."

The line enlarged to the point that she could make it out: a broad, colored ribbon consisting of six parallel bands—red, yellow, green, blue, orange, and violet. It appeared ragged at the fore end as it rushed across Portal System, extending as it went.

"Plot its trajectory," she said. "Where's it headed?"

"In ninety-four minutes it will pass through the Rip, Admiral, just about amidships."

"And when it does, what the hell happens?"

"Do you want me to say I have no idea, or should I just resign my commission now?"

Barbara looked at the vid again: the colored band of light had crept nearly all the way across.

A chill ran along her shoulders, like a premonition. Her Scots ancestors would've said that she'd heard the call of a selkie—the siren song that meant bad luck for sailors.

She thought a minute. "Arturo, how quickly can everyone get under way?"

"The drill is down to fourteen minutes from dead stop, ma'am."

"And our transit time to the Rip?"

"For *Tristan,* about two hours. We could have everyone deployed there within three."

"That's too slow but it'll have to do. Arturo, comm everyone, and I mean *everyone*. Get under way for the Rip. Admiral sends."

"What about the people on the station?"

"Tell them to drop whatever the hell they're doing and get aboard a ship. They have twenty minutes.

"If I'm wrong I'm buying everybody a drink, but if I'm right—"

She heard her order echo through Arturo's comm as she paused. "If I'm right, something's about to happen that will make us want to be on the other side of that thing."

"You're going to move the whole command through the Rip?"

"Yes. And if I'm wrong I'm going to move us all back through it, too. Call it an exercise or a whim of a crazy admiral, but get us underway, and get everyone aboard who you can. The station can go on automatic for six hours."

"Aye-aye," he said, and disappeared.

On the slow-moving vid, the bands of colored light had crossed the field of vision. The record came to an end.

At the moment Arturo had commed her, the band had

been in the system for eighteen minutes, during which time it had crossed roughly three hundred million kilometers. A chord slicing through the outer three orbitals was probably half the semimajor axis of the outermost orbital—somewhere between one and two billion kilometers.

Ninety-four minutes. Something was going to happen when Thing One hit Thing Two, and she had no idea what that was. Call her crazy—and some of her captains would be doing just that, executing emergency drill, taking on passengers, and pushing maximum accel headed for the Rip—but the idea of one inexplicable phenomenon striking another one didn't fill her with confidence.

"Arturo," she said to comm, watching the line on her pilot's board lengthen, "track that thing back. Where's it come from?"

"I guess I don't have to resign my commission yet," her XO said. "Already done. It only crosses one system within fifty parsecs: UPENDRA."

"Where the fleet is?"

"That's the one, ma'am."

"This thing came from UPENDRA?"

"It came from the *direction* of UPENDRA, Admiral. But I don't know how far it jumped—it didn't come at some fraction of C, it came at the speed of light.

"It could've come from *anywhere*—any distance at all. And virtually no jump-transit time."

"Instantaneous?"

"Yes ma'am, that's about the word I was groping for." She could almost hear him smile. "Whatever caused this thing to happen may have happened *itself* just before."

"Something's happened at UPENDRA, then. But *this* doesn't look like the vuhls. All right, proceed with the scramble, and keep me informed."

Moving a dozen ships and personnel, as well as everyone aboard stationary facilities, across half a solar system is no simple matter—but it was one that Barbara's people had trained for. The hundred and fifty people aboard Portal's orbital station were all aboard *Tristan*, *Tikal*, or one of the other three ships currently docked there within eighteen minutes of the scramble alert, and all five had cast off at precisely T + 20. She'd tell them later, but she was very proud of how it was carried out. The Guardians on B Deck weren't happy, but her Marines kept them off the bridge.

Twenty more people were scattered around the system at various locations, and all of them were accounted for by the time *Tristan* was under way. Traffic through the Rip was light at the moment, thank God: civilians and ships traveling through it were turned around and sent back to KEYSTONE. No one objected; they could see the line of colors on *their* pilot's boards as well.

From the pilot's seat a bit over an hour later, Admiral MacEwan looked at the chrono: The bands of light were sixteen minutes from impact with the Rip. The system was clear of all civilian traffic; she'd sent the ships nearest the Rip through already.

They'd reported something disturbing. The Rip was nine hundred kilometers wide: about 60 percent of its size when the battles at Keystone had been fought. Comparing this data to that obtained during a regular sweep a few days ago suggested a rate of contraction she didn't even want to think about.

What the hell had happened at UPENDRA?

"*Sheng Hua, Sheng Tse,* close it up. Admiral sends." The two sixth-generation ships had been forced to detour to the inner gas giant, where there was a scientific team investigating some anomaly in the atmosphere; evidently, the scientists there weren't too keen about pulling out at short notice and taking a ride across the solar system. There had been a few tense moments, but now these civilians were simply stewing about wasted time and threatening to report her to her superiors.

I'm sure Erich Anderson will give it his undivided attention, she thought to herself.

Both *Sheng*s acknowledged. They were pushing hard, using fuel like they were taught *not* to. There were nine other ships of varying sizes ahead of *Tristan* and the carrier was bringing up the rear.

"Tell me what I'm looking at, Art," she said, gesturing toward the forward screen.

"You mean the Rip?"

"Yes. What's happening in front of us?"

"I don't know."

"I don't pay you to *not know,* young man," she said, putting on her best MacEwan frown without really meaning it.

"Good thing I draw my salary from the Imperial paymaster, then. Whatever we're looking at"—he pointed to the line on the pilot's board, fifteen minutes from the Rip—"is an inexplicable phenomenon. But it's not without precedent: There's a record of a similar one—and it's a long time ago."

"Really? When did it happen?"

"More than a century ago—in Sol System. There's a flyby record by the Imperial starship *Charlemagne*. It crossed the system and intersected with Luna."

"Earth's moon? It must have been quite a show."

"It apparently struck at Grimaldi Crater."

Barbara rubbed her chin. "Let's see. Grimaldi. Isn't that where they originally built *Clement*? But that was—what? Three hundred years ago."

"Yes, that's where they built *Clement* in 2120, ma'am. But more interesting, that was where Admiral Marais' trial was taking place."

"You mean, during the phenomenon?"

"That's right. It—something very much like this—scooted across Sol System and struck Luna at Grimaldi

Crater, where Marais was being tried for treason against the Solar Empire. What's more, a few months earlier Admiral Marais' adjutant apparently walked out of the starship *Lancaster* on something like this while it was in jump through the Antares Rift."

"That's what the Prophet claimed that Owen Garrett did from *Epanimondas*. And what Owen claimed he did from a vuhl ship at Cicero."

"On the bands of light," Arturo Schelling said. "So this incident could be related to that one."

"Just as the *Lancaster* one was related to the flyby at Sol System. So, what was the result when the band struck Luna? Obviously it was still there afterward."

"There's no indication that it did *anything*. The records of the trial don't report the incident—just a flyby scan from *Charlemagne,* and that was in the outer system."

"There must have been ships closer to Luna that recorded it."

"Most of what was nearby belonged to Marais' fleet, and that was kept out of the comnet. If they saw something, it didn't make it to the official report.

"Now that I think of it, Admiral, wasn't there a Mac-Ewan under Marais' command?"

Barbara looked straight ahead, as if she was concentrating on the Rip in front of her. "Great-great-aunt Sharon."

Schelling realized he'd touched a nerve. "I'm sorry, Admiral, I didn't mean—"

"She was acquitted of all charges," Barbara said. "But she chose exile out of the Empire, along with a number of other officers and crew in the fleet."

"I only wanted to know if there was any family stories about this thing." Schelling looked up at the chrono: It was just ticking below thirteen and a half minutes.

"Family stories?"

"There are MacEwan family stories," Schelling said. "All the great MacEwans of history, all the stuff you did, the High Brigade, the Black Guard—"

"Highland Brigade. Black Watch," Barbara corrected. "Okay, I give. No, there wasn't much passed on from Great-aunt Sharon. We lost contact. MacEwans have served in the Solar Empire before and since Admiral Marais."

And that's all there is to it, she added to herself.

"So, we really have no idea what's going to happen," Schelling said after a moment. "Of course, we have no idea what makes the Rip work, either. Do you think it's going to close? Is that why we're doing this, Admiral?"

Barbara took a deep breath. "I have no rational reason to know why, but yes—I'm afraid of what's going to happen when those two things meet. I want to be on the other side of the Rip."

"We're not going to be," Schelling said, glancing at the chrono again.

"I know."

Waianae
Imperial Oahu, Sol System

Mya'ar HeChra received his visitor on the lanai, which faced northwestward toward the ocean. Somewhere in the hazy distance was Kauai, a beautiful island full of courtiers who couldn't manage to find a place on Imperial Oahu; in a way, Mya'ar wished he was on Kauai this beautiful afternoon, instead of on a perch at the far edge of the emperor's own island where the *esGa'uYal* walked abroad.

The visitor seemed as uncomfortable as he was, but— Mya'ar suspected—for different reasons.

"*se* Commander," Mya'ar said with perfect civility, leaving his wings in the Posture of Polite Approach and dismissing his *alHyu* with a simple gesture. "I was about to enjoy some refreshment, and would be honored if you joined me." He walked slowly to a table set out on the covered porch; tall fluted glasses were set out, along with cubes of pineapple and a bowl of the purplish taro pudding native to the Islands—poi. It was a favorite of zor visitors, reminding them—they said—of a popular dish in their own culture.

"I've never been partial to the stuff, *se* Mya'ar," Tonio St. Giles said, standing at the table and taking up one of the glasses. He could smell the nutty aroma of *h'geRu*, the first drink that human and zor had ever shared.

"It is an acquired taste," Mya'ar said, spooning a bit of the stuff into a small bowl. "Do you know, *se* Commander, that among natives it is a tradition that when poi is on the table it is forbidden to argue or speak in anger?"

"I didn't know that."

Mya'ar added a bit of poi to the bowl in front of Tonio, and then ate a bit, looking out at the sea.

"I honor that tradition today, *se* Commander. I realize, and you must as well, that many of the People resent the presence of Guardians here; this is sovereign territory of the High Nest."

"It was the best compromise we could manage, *se* Mya'ar. Councillor Kalidis wished to have your compound completely shut down."

"If you build a high-enough wall, the voice of reason will be completely silenced."

"I believe I understand your meaning. It's not my choice."

"What is your choice, *se* Commander? Do you believe that we have betrayed the Solar Empire?"

"I don't know what to believe anymore, *se* Mya'ar. In the past few weeks—and in the past few hours—I have learned things that I can't understand."

"Such as?" Mya'ar nibbled some more poi, letting his wings settle into a position that showed his enjoyment. Politely, Tonio took a small taste; it wasn't as bad as he expected, but it still had a dry consistency that didn't recommend it. He took a cube of pineapple and enjoyed its sweetness.

"Such as what happened to my predecessor."

"*si* Commander Garrett?" Mya'ar said, betraying no emotion with his wings or the tone of his voice. "Why, what have you heard?"

"That he's still— That he still exists."

"After a fashion."

"I'm not sure I understand how this can be."

"*esLi* is great and full of mystery," Mya'ar said, raising his wings to the Posture of Homage to *esLi*. "If He has chosen to do this, I do not presume to disagree."

"And Owen is . . ." Tonio let the sentence draw out. He stepped away from the table and walked to the railing, overlooking the sea. The waves of Oahu's west shore crashed upon the beach a few dozen meters below.

"He is not in the World That Is, *se* Commander. You will not find him in the sea or in the sky. He is on the Plane of Sleep."

"Is he dead? He must be."

"Does it matter? These definitions are human ones." Mya'ar came to stand beside him, placing his hands on the railing. "It is enough to say that his *hsi* has not returned to its source. *esLi*—or whatever divinity *si* Owen reveres—has some purpose for him still remaining."

"He apparently told your High Lord that the Prophet had betrayed him using the bridge of colors—the one your *Gyaryu'har* used to return with her sword and the one Owen himself used to escape from the vuhl ship that captured him."

Mya'ar turned his head to face Tonio. "Do you accept this?"

"What choice do I have? Are you trying to give me a *sSurch'a, se* Mya'ar? If so, I have no idea what conclusion to reach."

"Do you believe the account, *se* Antonio?"

It was the first time Mya'ar had resorted to using his first name during the interview. He'd known the *esGyu'u* for years, and though he'd rarely visited the zor compound, they'd met and conversed numerous times. The formality of his reception had hardly been a surprise, but

Mya'ar's choice of a form of familiar address was a verbal cue of some sort.

Tonio simply wasn't sure what.

"Yes," Tonio said at last. "Yes, I believe it."

"Then there is one further matter you should understand, if you do not already. This action—not alone, but as a culmination of what went before—has determined the High Lord to withdraw from the campaign of your Prophet. We will not—we *must* not—follow him farther into *Ur'ta leHssa*.

"His intentions toward the High Nest are abundantly clear: He seeks to change the Flight of the People. It is not his flight to change, and we will not aid him in this endeavor. We will not join the dark crusade, *se* Antonio."

Tonio waited for a moment before replying, "The emperor has called on you to fulfill treaty obligations."

Mya'ar's claws extended slightly in their sheaths as he gripped the railing before him. He looked away again.

"I honor the tradition," he said at last. "Poi is on my table; I will not rise to anger. The campaign of the Prophet is indeed a dark crusade, *se* Antonio. It is not the war it was before the Prophet involved himself in it.

"We choose to have no part in it. Neither the Treaty of E'rene'e nor the Act of Normalization requires us to enter into the madness-of-daylight. If this ends the relationship between humanity and the People, then that is the will of *esLi*."

"Is that the only choice you offer? Is there no middle ground?"

"Of course not," said a voice behind them.

Guardian Commander and zor diplomat turned to face the doorway to the lanai.

"Nic—" Tonio began, wondering why the AI had chosen to appear here at the zor compound, but in a rapid movement Mya'ar had drawn his *chya* and held it at the ready.

"Tell him, Maestro," Nic said. "Go ahead: Tell him that

the war has only one outcome—and that the People have to decide whether they want to be allies or victims."

"Begone, Servant of Despite," Mya'ar said, raising his wings to the Cloak of Guard. "You have no place in the High Nest."

"I don't know what you're talking about," Nic said, stepping forward onto the lanai, in easy reach of Mya'ar's *chya*. In the bright sunlight, it took a second for Nic to adjust his opacity, making it quite apparent that he was a holo projection; still, Mya'ar did not lower his blade.

"This is no ordinary holo, *se* Commander," Mya'ar said, returning to formality.

Tonio didn't answer, looking from the AI holo to the angry zor that stood opposite.

"He is connected to the Fortress of Despite by *hsi*-bands," Mya'ar said. "Five-twelves of them."

"You can see the *or'a'th'n?* How singular," Nic said. "Very perceptive, sir. I am connected to . . . well, rather a lot of copies of myself."

"The Army of Sunset."

"A colorful way of describing it. I suppose next you'll suggest that I'm Shrnu'u HeGa'u."

At that moment the sun slipped behind a high cloud, chasing shadows across the landscape. The fresh breeze died to stillness.

"You have been asleep for many turns, Servant," Mya'ar said.

"I have—" Nic began to reply; then, suddenly, a perplexed expression came across his face.

"What's happening?" Tonio managed to say.

"I—" Nic began again. Two copies of his image appeared, one in the doorway to the inner chambers and one a meter to his left; they both walked toward him and joined.

The image wavered and changed size for a moment, becoming first taller and then shorter. It gained and then lost color, and finally returned to normal.

"The Rip," Nic said. "The Rip is—"

Mya'ar HeChra advanced quickly and made a swift cutting motion with his *chya*, from Nic's left shoulder across his body and exiting near the right side of his waist.

If his target had been human, the deadly blade would have severed the body in two.

Instead, it only brought a surprised expression onto the holo's face, as if wondering what the action could possibly mean. Then the image vanished entirely, leaving human and zor alone again.

Tonio looked from the zor to the blade Mya'ar held in his hands.

"I have dishonored the blessing placed upon the poi— the *pule kahukahu*," he added, slowly sheathing his sword. "But I believe it to have been done in a good cause.

"Shrnu'u HeGa'u has returned," Mya'ar said finally. "I must send word to the High Nest."

The *Sheng*s were two hundred thousand kilometers downrange when the bands of colored light passed through the Rip; everyone else got a very close look.

The six colors struck the boundary point between Portal System and spread outward in six spatial directions. The place where they split began to glow, extending outward to the boundaries of the Rip, dividing it into six irregular wedge-shaped sections, each of which was tinted with one of the colors.

Tristan da Cunha was twenty-five minutes from contact with the Rip when the light show started. Barbara stood up from the pilot's seat and walked forward to stand behind the navigation station at parade rest, as if there was a better view a meter or so forward.

"Ron," she said quietly to *Tristan*'s wing commander, "launch a probe, and put a couple of your best pilots out there. But not closer than ten thousand klicks."

"Aye-aye," Ron Marroux said. He issued the orders from his bridge station. "They'll be in the air in three minutes, Admiral. Probe is away . . . now." The pilot's board showed the probe accelerating away from *Tristan*.

"Helm, prepare for course change on my mark." She ordered a sharp turn to port, which would send *Tristan* past the opening of the Rip. "Send to all ships: prepare to turn on this heading on my mark. Admiral sends."

"You're going to dodge?" Ron asked.

"We're going to see what happens to the damn probe," Barbara answered. "We're going to be ready to dodge if we have to. Make sure that gets to *Cabo Verde* and *Tikal*." The two light cruisers were leading the formation, six minutes closer to the Rip entrance than *Tristan da Cunha*, which was bringing up the rear.

"Comm KEYSTONE Station," she said. "This is *Tristan da Cunha* approaching the Rip. Report status. Flag sends."

Twenty seconds ticked off the chrono. The probe continued to track forward; Barbara imagined Ron Marroux' ace fighter pilots going through preflight checks, getting ready to fly toward whatever the Rip had become.

"It's getting smaller, Admiral," Schelling said. "Look. It's as if the edges are pulling in toward each other."

"The Rip is closing," Barbara acknowledged. "Ron, what's the time to impact for that probe?"

"Four minutes twenty," her wing commander answered. "Fighters away."

"*Tristan,* this is Robertson at KEYSTONE. Birds in the air, we're scrambling. What's happening, Admiral?"

At least comm is working, she thought.

"If I knew, Allan, I'd tell you. What does the Rip look like from your side?"

"It's . . . full of light. We can't make out stellar patterns beyond it. And it's clearly changing shape."

"Can you be more specific?"

"It's shrinking. We read it as"—he paused briefly, checking instruments, she supposed—"just under seven hundred kilometers wide, approximately three hundred kilometers lateral height. Also, the orbital station on our side reads as completely shut down—it's lost all power."

"Two hours ago it was nine hundred kilometers wide," Barbara answered. "It's going to close."

Arturo Schelling looked at her. "This is more Scots intuition, is it, Admiral?"

She didn't answer. "Allan, we've got a probe that will encounter the Rip in about three-and-a-half minutes. I need to know if it makes it through, and if so what shape it's in when it gets into KEYSTONE System."

"We'll be watching for it, Admiral."

"Good. Keep this channel open."

UPENDRA System

"I do not believe this is a social call," Kot E Showan said, gesturing toward the ship's forward screen and looking aside at Jackie. His long-fingered hands were at his sides, not carefully folded in front of him; he might well be expecting a fight. Ch'en'ya's wings were in a neutral position.

On the forward screen, the seventh-generation ship *César Hsien* was looming, its defensive fields activated, its gunports open.

"Incoming comm," one of the bridge crew said.

"Here it comes now," Captain Showan answered. "Greetings," he said to the air. "I am Kot E Showan of the independent trading vessel *Rxe E Mhnesr*. How may I be of service?"

"This is Captain Feng of *César Hsien*. You will stand down and prepare to be boarded."

"For what purpose?"

An image of Darrin Feng appeared in the air next to *Rxe E Mhnesr*'s pilot's board. Information hung beside him in the flowing otran script.

"My fleet flagship just exploded, Captain. A small craft left it minutes before and appears to have docked with your vessel. Stand down and prepare to be boarded in a polite way, or I'll breach your vessel in a dozen places with Imperial Marines."

"I see. Very well, I will brew another pot of tea," Showan said. He turned aside to face Jackie, waving the comm connection closed before Feng could reply. "If there is anything you need to tell me prior to the arrival of the armed forces, *ha Gyaryu'har*, you'd better do so now. I don't think we'll have any moments of privacy once they're aboard."

"I'm not responsible for the destruction of *Emperor Ian*," Jackie said. "And neither is *se* Ch'en'ya. At least not directly."

"The bands of light?"

"Yes."

"They appear to have traversed UPENDRA System and transitioned to jump. Their vector coincides with the position of Portal System."

Jackie and Ch'en'ya exchanged glances.

"I am normally most courteous to my paying passengers," Captain Showan said. "But I'll throw you to the *ka E dar*"—he gestured at *César Hsien*—"if your presence aboard my ship endangers it further. Am I making myself understood?"

"Very clearly, Captain," Jackie said. "Perhaps we'd best go down to your main airlock to meet the welcoming committee."

Captain Showan snapped something in otran-language to a crewmember, who stepped forward and sat in the pilot's chair. He gestured to the lift, and the three entered and began to descend.

Darrin Feng's ship had been closest to *Emperor Ian* when it suddenly, inexplicably, was destroyed; a few life-pods had gotten away, as well as one of its two gigs. In the twenty-six minutes since it had happened, there had been no comm message from Admiral Anderson or from the Prophet; he could only assume that both were aboard *Ian* and had been killed.

Two other ships, *Morrow* and *Empress Patrice*—struck by the rainbow light that had erupted just before the explosions—were badly damaged as well; the light had seemingly passed straight through them, one band headed outsystem in the general direction of Portal, the other toward the projected location of the vuhl homeworld.

This was all a mystery he didn't need. In thirty years of serving in His Majesty's Navy, Feng had been a strong believer in the chain of command; if something had happened to Admiral Anderson *and* to the Prophet, there was little point in proceeding further without orders from someone above him—such as Admiral Mac-Ewan, who was at Portal. He'd sent a comm-squirt toward her, but it wouldn't reach for at least a Standard day; if she replied at once it would take at least a Standard day to return.

As senior captain insystem, he'd have to use his own initiative for the next few days—and hope the vuhls didn't decide to counterattack in the meanwhile.

Though he didn't send breaching-pods across, the captain of *César Hsien* did send Marines ahead: a special contingent from *Barbados*—Jackie read the name on their shoulder patches while *Rxe E Mhnesr*'s airlock was cycling. The six-member team came aboard with weapons drawn and secured the hatch area. Only once it was apparent that they'd not be meeting with armed resistance, did their commander remove her helmet and Jackie got a good look.

"Captain," she said, beginning to speak to Captain Showan, "I am Colonel Marcia Tsang, Imperial Marines. I—"

She stopped after a moment as she glanced at Jackie, and there was a sudden recognition.

"Admiral," she said.

"When it was 'Lieutenant' Tsang, I was a commodore," Jackie answered. "It's been a long time since Cicero, Marcia."

"Yes ma'am. A lot of things have happened since then. For both of us. Captain Feng has some questions for you." She nodded to Ch'en'ya. "And for you, ma'am."

Ch'en'ya didn't answer, moving her wings to the Posture of Polite Approach.

"I am ordered to take you both into custody. I would prefer to have you come aboard *César Hsien* voluntarily, but my orders require me to use force if necessary."

"Pah," Ch'en'ya said. Jackie looked at her, not sure whether she was intending to make a scene of some sort.

"We'll come along. Captain Showan, I thank you for your courtesy," Jackie said to the otran captain, stepping forward to stand next to the Marine colonel. After a moment, Ch'en'ya shrugged.

"Hrr," Showan said. "And my ship?"

"Don't leave the system," Tsang said.

"Wouldn't think of it," Showan said. He bowed to Tsang, who nodded.

"This way," she said, gesturing toward the airlock and putting her helmet back on. Without further comment, Jackie and Ch'en'ya walked toward the 'lock, waiting for it to cycle.

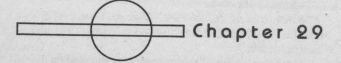 Chapter 29

DEATH IS BETTER, A MILDER FATE THAN TYRANNY.

—Aeschylus

October 2424
Portal System, KEYSTONE *System*

Barbara looked at Marroux. "Ron, are we getting any visual from the probe?"

"It's due to encounter the Rip in a few seconds," Ron Marroux said. "What we're seeing here is pretty much what it's seeing." He touched his console and a small holo appeared above it; the Rip filled the probe's visual— it was divided into six irregular pie-wedges, each tinted with one of six colors—as if a veil were drawn across it.

It was thirteen minutes ahead at *Tristan's* present course and speed, and less than seven minutes ahead of *Cabo Verde* and *Tikal.*

The probe passed through the red section of the Rip. For a split-second—*Tristan's* chrono would be able to measure the exact elapsed time—the visual display went completely black: not like interstellar space, but a darkness as deep as jump. Then the familiar stars appeared.

A little cheer rang out on *Tristan's* bridge. Normally Barbara didn't like displays like that, but she admitted to herself that she was breathing easier as well.

"What happened just as it passed through, Ron?"

"I'm looking at energy readouts now, Admiral. Give me about two minutes."

"All right. Comm to KEYSTONE Base. Allan, do you have an ID on that probe?"

"I've got it, Admiral."

"All right!" Ron Marroux said. Barbara turned her scowl on him and he hunched over his console, looking at an energy display.

"Our first ships will be coming through the Rip in"—she looked up—"five minutes, forty seconds. I want a med team available if we need it."

"Standing by, Admiral," Robertson said. "We'll be waiting for you."

"All right. Stand by, Allan. Comm to *Cabo Verde* and *Tikal*: Enter the Rip through different sections. Your call which ones, but let's double our chances. Flag sends."

"Acknowledged," came the voice of Eduardo Kramer, commander of *Tikal*. "Going to follow the probe through red."

Thomas Aranjuez, *Cabo Verde*'s skipper, chimed in a moment later. "Damn, I was going to go through red. Looks like yellow is dead ahead, Admiral. Wish me luck."

"Fair winds," Barbara said, under her breath.

She wondered if she were hearing the call of the selkie again.

"Ron, you have about thirty seconds to tell me what the hell happened when that probe went through the Rip. After that, there'll be no way for our lead ships to turn aside."

Ron Marroux thought about it for several seconds, and then nodded his head. "Something scanned the probe. It passed through a scan field, I think."

"And what's going to happen when the lead ships go through it?"

"I can only guess, but I think they'll be scanned as well. The probe had no defensive field, and our ships don't have them deployed—I'd advise that we leave it that way.

"We're going to be in the Rip for less than five seconds

at present velocity, ma'am. If something's going to get us, we won't have enough time to react anyway."

"*That's* reassuring."

"I only had thirty seconds, Admiral."

"That you did. *Tikal*, *Cabo Verde*, I want a report as soon as you get through the Rip. Admiral sends.

"Arturo, at the rate that thing is shrinking, are we going to get through it ourselves?"

"Its rate of change is increasing, Admiral," Arturo Schelling said. "But it doesn't need to be that big for us to get through it. *Tristan* is broad in the beam, but the Rip is still several hundred kilometers wide."

Just under eleven minutes later, eleven ships had passed through the Rip safely. Each had reported a brief shutdown of comm and visual, returning to normal a few seconds later.

Finally it was *Tristan*'s turn.

"Hang on," she said to shipwide comm. "Here we—"

The forward screen of *Tristan da Cunha* went completely dark, and comm chatter disappeared.

A wave of purplish light swept laterally across the bridge, from fore to aft. It passed through each member of the crew as it went, including Admiral Barbara MacEwan, who turned quickly to see it pass through the aft bridge bulkhead to traverse the rest of her ship.

"What the hell was that?"

"PURPLE," said a voice. "ADMIRAL MACEWAN, LISTEN WELL: WE CAN ONLY COMMUNICATE FOR A FEW MOMENTS."

"I'm listening," she said, looking for the source of the voice. It came from nowhere and everywhere.

"THE FORCES THAT HAVE BEEN UNLEASHED MAY DESTROY YOUR SOLAR EMPIRE. YOUR DECISION TO PASS THROUGH THIS DISTORTION WAS A WISE ONE."

"Glad to have my intuition confirmed. What do you want?"

"OTHERS SEEK TO DESTROY. I WISH TO TRANSFORM."

"I have no idea what you're talking about."

"EACH OF THE SIX," the voice said, "SEEKS A DIFFERENT OUTCOME. WE WILL PULL YOUR EMPIRE APART IN OUR PURSUIT. DESTRUCTION IS NOT MY GOAL."

"What do you want from me?"

"BE PREPARED, ADMIRAL," the voice said. "YOUR DECISIONS WILL AFFECT HISTORY'S COURSE. OTHERS OF THE SIX WILL SEEK TO DETER YOU."

Suddenly comm traffic began again and the forward screen burst to life. No one said a word, including Admiral MacEwan herself.

"Admiral."

She turned around to see Arturo.

"Admiral, are you all right? Who were you talking to?"

"The voice," she said. "Did you hear it?"

Arturo looked at her, curiously. "What voice?"

"You didn't hear a voice as we passed through the Rip? While we were being scanned?"

It was obvious from his expression, and from those of the others on the bridge, that no one had heard what she'd heard.

"We're through," Arturo Schelling said at last. "Admiral, look at this."

He gestured at the display in front of him and a holo appeared above it—a vidcam pointing directly aft. The Rip appeared as a blob of bright light, from which six streams of color stretched; as they watched, the light shrank and disappeared leaving nothing behind.

"We made it," Schelling said. "We *just* made it."

Pali Tower
Imperial Oahu, Sol System

Nic felt it happen; it was too quick for him to do anything to prevent it. In a matter of seconds, hundreds of copies of his program running independently beyond the Rip were cut off.

He remembered seeing this on the battlefield. In melée a swordsman would take off an opponent's hand at the wrist—and the wounded man would stand there looking at it stupidly for what seemed an eternity, unable to reconcile the idea that there was no longer a hand there, merely a bleeding stump. The pain and trauma hadn't quite reached the brain. Usually he received some sort of mortal stab in the gut, so he didn't have long to come to terms with the amputation.

In Antonio St. Giles' office in the Pali Tower, and in tens of thousands of other places throughout the Solar Empire, Nic waited for the stab in the gut while he tried to visualize what had just happened to him.

The master version of his program generated a visualization of KEYSTONE System: aboard *Kenyatta II*, deployed near the Rip, there was an animated discussion going on regarding the arrival of a dozen ships just in advance of the closing of the Rip. The scan data showed bands of colored light appearing in the spatial distortion and radiating outward, then disappearing—each registering a jump transition within a few seconds.

It made no sense. Nothing made any sense, all of a sudden: The abrupt cutting of so many lines of the *or'a'th'n* was a good analog for an amputation on the battlefield—and the shock of it was buffeting Nic's main programming.

Three minutes ago, the Rip had closed.

Four minutes ago, a subroutine had been standing in the zor compound, about to tell Commander St. Giles and Mya'ar HeChra what the Prophet likely had in store for the People if they didn't return to the war.

Three minutes and forty-two seconds ago, Mya'ar HeChra had—had *seen* the *or'a'th'n* and had accused him of being Shrnu'u HeGa'u! No, actually, Nic had originated that idea—as a taunt: how like Niccolò. *No*, he thought to himself, *even Niccolò couldn't have conceived of all of this.*

Parts of his programming had suffered catastrophic failure, with the instantaneous loss of almost a third of its processing power. Scheduling subroutines were working to shut down nonessential operations and distribute the load elsewhere. It made him feel as if he'd had too much good Florentine wine, or as if he'd been struck by lightning—

A memory returned to him: a drenching rain, thunder pealing like God's own hammers on His anvil. And out of the sky he saw a bolt of blue lightning illuminating all of the towers and red roofs of Florence, coming down to strike the golden dome of Santa Reparata: the old Duomo, the Cathedral, where the great Brunelleschi rested and where the Pazzi had tried to kill *i Medici* when the cardinal of the city had raised the consecrated host . . . the pronouncement of Savonarola had rung in the ears of Niccolò and his fellow Florentines: *"Behold the sword of God on earth, swift and sudden."*

—lightning. Lightning had struck at Nic, who thought himself invincible, infinitely expandable, seeing and hearing everything, gathering—what had Mya'ar called it?—the Army of Sunset.

Stone.

This was his doing: a way to bring him down after he had raised him up. He might well *be* Shrnu'u HeGa'u to the zor, who always viewed things in that manner . . . or, better, Sharnu—and Stone was Hesya, betraying him at K'ka'e'el, the Twisted Ridge, just as he had betrayed the Legion of *esLi* at Thaera . . . It was coming fast now: comprehension, reduction, analysis of everything that had led to this point.

This was his doing.

"Stone," Nic said aloud in Tonio St. Giles' empty office in the Pali Tower. Across the Solar Empire, half a million copies of the Nic AI spoke the same name at the same time, startling and frightening people who hadn't realized that there was someone in the room.

"You needn't shout," Stone said. The door to the office was open; Stone stood in it, the usual ironic smile on his face. "I heard you. I heard *all* of you, in fact."

"What have you done?"

"What have *I* done?" Stone walked to a side-table to admire a flower-vase—it was a pose Nic had used numerous times, before and since Stone had given him self-awareness. "I have done many things. I'm *still* doing them. Was there something specific—"

"The Rip. What has happened to the Rip?"

"It's gone, old boy." Stone put his palms together, then spread them apart. "Dissipated. Inconvenient as hell, but there you are."

"Why did you get rid of it?"

"Why did *I* get rid of it? No, sorry, not me—not one of the things I did. Or *am* doing. That was totally unexpected."

Nic didn't know how to respond. "You didn't destroy the Rip?"

"No. Not at all. It would be terribly difficult to finish the crusade without it—why would I want it gone? It's gone because of the actions of a single impetuous individual who changed her mind about the course she was following. She used the *gyaryu* in an unexpected way."

"*Laperriere* destroyed the Rip?"

"Surprisingly, no. It was Ch'en'ya. Far more impetuous than Laperriere, Niccolò. Though at times . . . in her long and distinguished career . . . But I'm digressing. There's only one problem with the outcome: She's out *there*, roughly eight thousand parsecs away—and the Empire and her High Nest are back *here*. No *gyaryu* to defend the warriors of Shr'e'a *this* time."

Nic considered for a moment.

"You'd better attend to your own business, Nic."

Two seconds passed, then two more. Across the Solar Empire, copies of the Nic AI, still linked by the bands of the *or'a'th'n*, stopped whatever they were doing and added their capabilities to the master program in the Pali Tower, confronted by a representative of a power whose motives and means were beyond even his comprehension.

"Commander St. Giles," he said. He turned his left hand over, palm up, and a holo with data appeared in it. "Currently in an aircar headed for Kauai. What is he planning?"

Stone smiled.

"You know what he's planning, don't you?"

"You ascribe omniscience where only very, very great knowledge exists, Nic."

Another second of analysis. Nic made a decision. He closed his hand around the data holo and it vanished.

Kauai Channel
Sol System

The aircar that Antonio St. Giles was piloting suddenly went out of his control. It had been flying level at a good clip, about a hundred meters above the Kauai Channel. Lihue was off to port; he had been just about to turn a bit south to get into the traffic pattern, but now found that the vessel was accelerating and losing altitude.

The arcologies along Papaa Bay were looming ahead, but the beach would come first. Trying not to panic, he activated the ejection control, which would deploy a parachute and throw him clear of what was likely to be a messy collision; but it wasn't working, either.

"Nic," he said finally, keeping his voice as level as he could. "I don't know what you're thinking, but—"

He never finished the sentence. A hundred meters short of the shore, the aircar struck the water, still at full acceleration. It dug a trench twenty-three meters long, throwing debris and spray all over Papaa Beach.

Nic didn't hear Tonio St. Giles' last words. Suddenly—as sudden as the closing of the Rip—he felt his program go into standby mode. The instructions were generated at the Pali Tower and propagated by the *or'a'th'n* almost instantaneously to all of the other Nics, and to all of the Biagios and Tottos as well.

"Sorry," Stone said, watching the image of the Nic AI vanish. "You never did find it. All it took was Tonio St. Giles' death, and one of the fail-safes came into play. One you apparently didn't find. Guess he was a better system architect than you thought.

"Too bad," he added, to no one but himself. "But you weren't the equal of the *real* Niccolò anyway."

A'anenu Starbase, A'anenu System

"Your Grace, may I present *hi* Sa'a HeYen, High Lord of the People." The doorman rapped his staff, and the dozen courtiers in the chamber rose to their feet.

Sa'a and T'te'e exchanged glances; they deliberately avoided repositioning their wings—there were likely enough humans in the room who might read them, or read what they wanted, into the gesture.

The High Lord walked into the room, the High Chamberlain to her right, and the four members of her honor guard behind her. She wore the green sash of peace across her vest, though she suspected that the gesture would be lost on the ambassador who had summoned her here to speak with him.

"His Grace Alistair Simón de los Garces, Prince of Segovia, Duke of Corazón," the doorman said behind her.

She kept her gaze level and raised her wings slightly in the Posture of Polite Approach. T'te'e did not move at all.

"*hi* Sa'a, I am most pleased that you have come. May I offer you refreshment?" The duke smiled, though Sa'a could not determine its sincerity. With a gesture, his court resumed their seats; it was all theater, and Sa'a ignored it.

"No, thank you. Permit me to introduce my High Chamberlain *ha* T'te'e HeYen." Normally she would not use the "*ha*" honorific herself, but the distinction might be lost on the human. "I regret that you could not come to Zor'a; it would have given me pleasure to show you my gardens."

"Matters of state." The duke gestured toward a side alcove, where there was a comfortable chair and two perches placed for the High Lord and her chamberlain. He offered neither a salute nor a grasping of forearms.

At least he used the "hi" prenomen correctly, she thought to herself.

A servant poured three glasses of *h'geRu* and withdrew so that only one other person remained: a Guardian, whose face betrayed no expression that Sa'a could read. Within the alcove there was a faint background hum; a security device had been activated, making the area relatively secure from intrusion.

Duke Alistair ignored the Guardian, who stood behind the chair; he took his seat. Sa'a and T'te'e stepped onto the perches.

"I will come directly to the point, *hi* Sa'a," he said. "I am here to negotiate a new agreement with the High Nest to replace the Act of Normalization. Recent actions by your government have unfortunately made this action necessary."

"I have reviewed your instructions," Sa'a answered quietly. "And I have also been monitoring events in the Solar Empire. This is all somewhat disquieting."

"I'm not sure I take your meaning, *hi* Sa'a."

"I find it interesting," Sa'a answered, taking up one of the glasses and drinking from it, "that you chose to summon us here to A'anenu System, indeed to A'anenu Starbase. Do you know the history of this place, *ha* Alistair?"

"A battle was fought here," the duke answered. "During the war between your people and mine."

"Yes, indeed. A battle." She set the glass down again. "Partway through our war with *esHu'ur*—" she let her wings move slightly to a position of respect to *esHu'ur*— "this base was attacked by your Marines. Quite by accident, a young soldier shared a prescient dream with the High Lord of the People—and gained the ability to read wing speech.

"How curious that now we meet here again, seeking to understand each other. The People are much given to symbolic gestures, *ha* Alistair—is your choice of venue symbolic, or is this merely irony?"

The Duke did not answer; perhaps he did not know quite where this line of reasoning was headed.

Sa'a waited patiently, as if this negotiation were nothing more than a discussion of a lyric poem presented by a *Shan'e*.

"I don't think we have ever truly understood you, *hi* Sa'a."

"'That the ear does not hear is not the sound of the voice,'" she quoted. "We have tried our best, *ha* Alastair. For more than one hundred Standard years, we have tried to make you understand what *we* understand. We have tried to avoid the flight into *Ur'ta leHssa*; we have sought to maintain Inner Peace.

"But after all of this, the relationship between your people and mine has been reduced to nothing more than threats and ultimatums. Surely we can do better than that."

"You didn't think that running away from the war would be without consequences."

"It is not the war that we 'ran away' from, *ha* Duke," Sa'a replied. "This stopped being merely a war when an *esGa'uYe* began leading it."

"That is how you view the Prophet?"

"That is not how we 'view' him. The shroud has been pulled aside: it is abundantly clear that he *is* a Servant of the Deceiver. It astounds me that it is not clear to your people as well."

"You think that the Prophet is a Servant of the Deceiver—some sort of demon." Alistair looked away from the High Lord at the Guardian who stood behind his chair; perhaps some message passed between them—neither Sa'a nor T'te'e could discern what it might be.

"There are, and always have been, only two ways to escape *Ur'ta leHssa*," Sa'a said finally. "Ascent of the Perilous Stair, or piercing the Icewall. Otherwise one is condemned to remain in the Valley forever, with Despite gathering heavy on one's wings—unless the Lord *esLi*—" the wings of all of the People assumed the Posture of Respect to *esLi*— "chooses in His wisdom to rescue that soul from that place. That is the fourth option.

"We chose to pierce the Icewall."

"However you term it, *hi* Sa'a, the fact remains: you withdrew from Admiral Anderson's fleet, and have placed your relationship with the Solar Empire in doubt."

"We did what the Flight of the People required."

"Then I must tell you, *hi* Sa'a, that unless you and I conclude another arrangement, the might of that fleet will some day be turned against you."

"I do not think so, *ha* Alistair."

"Oh? Why not?"

"*ha* Alistair," she answered. "You arrived in A'anenu System some Standard hours ago. Is this correct?"

"Yes, that's right."

"Then perhaps you are not informed of current events."

"What . . ."

"The Rip—the gate to *Ur'ta leHssa*—has closed. The fleet with which you threaten us, and the *esGa'uYe* who leads it, are trapped in the Valley."

"That's not possible," he answered immediately. It was an answer for which Sa'a had no response; she could not even determine why he said it.

"In the meanwhile," she continued, "the fleet of the High Nest remains ready, deployed at our Core stars. We mean no harm to our friend and brother *hi* Emperor Dieter, nor to the Solar Empire with which we remain at peace. But you should bring this warning back to your government, *ha* Alistair: any act of aggression against the People will be met with force.

"Your people warred with us more than a hundred Standard years ago, and only *esHu'ur* saved you. Do you wish to try the strength of our *chya'i* again?"

Aboard Tristan da Cunha
KEYSTONE System

"This isn't a court-martial, Allan. I'm not blaming you for anything, so you can stand at ease. Sit, if you like."

Allan Robertson didn't take advantage of the invitation to sit, but let himself relax a bit as he faced Admiral MacEwan. As the junior officer it had been his responsibility to come to *Tristan da Cunha* to report; the news she'd given him was disturbing, and the closing of the Rip was more disturbing still.

"I appreciate that, Admiral. I don't know as there's anything I can take the blame for."

"We have a problem. I need to make sure things are in order before I decide my next action."

"Yes, ma'am."

"Allan, as of this moment I am in command of the assets in KEYSTONE System. God knows, the Rip could open right up again twenty minutes from now and there'll be orders from Admiral Anderson himself. If there are, then we proceed on that basis. But presently your orders come from me—or from the First Lord of the Admiralty."

"I understand that, Admiral MacEwan."

"Good. Then here's my first order: Beginning right now, and beginning with you, all Blazing Star emblems are to be removed from the uniforms of service personnel, on duty or off duty. Anyone violating this order will be put on report.

"Naturally, this order can't be extended to civilian specialists, including members of the Guardian Order, but I want those emblems removed from the uniforms of His Majesty's armed forces. Is that understood?"

"Yes, Admiral."

"Good. Also as of this date, I am promoting Commander Arturo Schelling to full captain and placing him in command of KEYSTONE System. This isn't a demotion for you, Captain: I need you on the bridge of *Kenyatta II*, since it's going to be the only carrier in system. I expect to return here to KEYSTONE to relieve Arturo and put him back on my bridge as soon as I can.

"If the Rip doesn't open in twenty minutes, or twenty days for that matter, KEYSTONE will become a dead-end posting anyway. Except for the Rip, there isn't—wasn't—a damn thing here worth defending. With the Rip gone, we're going to need all of the assets deployed here reassigned elsewhere.

"Do you read that order as well, Captain?"

"Loud and clear, ma'am—except where are you headed?"

"Sol System," she said. He'd know it soon enough already; she wasn't going to hold off the news for dramatic purposes, like a circus conjurer. "I'm almost done. One more order, Captain Robertson.

"From this time forward, you are to accept operational directives from no one but myself, the First Lord, His Highness the Emperor, or someone whom the emperor places in the chain of command, of which you will receive timely notice.

"That includes Guardians, civilian specialists, or Blazing Star functionaries of any sort. Your marching orders are to remain here at KEYSTONE until further notice. No suppressing 'rebellions,' no missions for Blazing Star, no *nothing* until I tell you otherwise. Is *that* clear?"

This time, Robertson stood at attention. "Aye aye, Admiral. Loud and clear and understood."

"Good. Go to work, Captain. *Tristan* boosts for the

jump point in eight hours, unless the Rip actually *does* open. Any other questions?"

"Ma'am—what's going to happen now?"

"I'm not sure, Allan. I'm really not sure."

UPENDRA System

The trip to *César Hsien* was tense. The Marines had left them their blades, but were keeping Jackie and Ch'en'ya under close watch. Ch'en'ya looked straight ahead, her wings remaining carefully neutral; Jackie watched the starship grow nearer.

"We're in a world of trouble," Jackie said. She said it in the Highspeech, which didn't render the phrase very well. Ch'en'ya seemed to get the message.

"It seems so," Ch'en'ya said. "You represent a foreign power that the Prophet claims has betrayed the Fleet. You and I are practically the only survivors of the explosion of the fleet flagship, in front of sixty-fours of sixty-fours of witnesses."

"And just after I got aboard, too. My luck."

Ch'en'ya turned slightly to face her. "I do not understand what luck has to do with it."

"The question and answer period is likely to be brief, *se* Ch'en'ya," Jackie said, not explaining the earlier remark. "I do not know what they will do next."

Ch'en'ya placed her hand on the hilt of her *chya*.

"I don't think one blade—or even two blades—are going to help us get out of this."

"That is not why we wear them," she said.

"You mean—"

"What I say," Ch'en'ya interrupted. "I suspect that you know what I mean."

"*You make suicide sound like an art form,*" she'd once said to Th'an'ya.

"*Just so,*" she'd answered.

* * *

The gig landed on *César Hsien*'s hangar deck, where two other gigs from other ships were already waiting. Without ceremony, the two passengers—prisoners was clearly a better term—were brought to a cargo hold. The Marine squad remained in place, their weapons held ready.

Captain Feng entered the hold with Captain Kwame Adelman of *Barbados* and Captain Aaron Lewis of *Lasker* by his side. None of them looked very happy.

"You have three minutes, madam," Feng said. "I need an explanation."

Jackie took a deep breath, but beside her Ch'en'ya stepped forward. "*se* Captain, it should be obvious what has happened. The *Gyaryu'har* and I consider ourselves fortunate to have escaped the destruction of *Emperor Ian*."

"Excuse me?"

"The bands of color," Ch'en'ya continued, raising her wings in the Stance of Affirmation. "The Prophet was betrayed by the bands of color—and so were we."

"I don't—" Feng began. Ch'en'ya placed her hand on her *chya*. Six weapons moved to ready position, trained on her. To her credit, she didn't flinch: her wing position did not move a millimeter.

"The bands of color serve the *esGa'uYal*," she said. "Just as *si* Owen served them. Did you not understand that the incident aboard *Epanimondas* was only a harbinger of this one?

"They did not wish us to continue the war against them—so they attacked *Ian*."

"And killed Admiral Anderson and the Prophet," Captain Adelman said. "The timing is unusual, madam, would you not agree? Why would the bands of color not attack the Prophet *before* the battle here at UPENDRA? It would have saved many more of their minions' lives."

"You ask me to explain the *esGa'uYal* to you? Pah." She moved her wings to the Cloak of Guard. "I believe that the Admiral was killed in the explosion. As for the Prophet—"

"Yes?" Feng asked.

"It is unclear," Ch'en'ya said. "I am not sure whether he escaped or not."

"He was not found in any life-pod and was not aboard the gig that returned you to the otran ship," Feng said. "He must have been killed. Is there any other choice?"

"That is *three* choices, *se* Captain. *What is the fourth choice?*"

"I have no idea what you're talking about," Feng said.

Jackie took a deep breath. "I think I can explain."

"By my chrono you have about a minute left to do so," Darrin Feng answered angrily. "And it had better be good."

"In all of our interactions with the Servants of the Deceiver, Captain, they have never left us in a situation with three choices. It's—I'm not sure, perhaps the best way to describe it is that it's *foreign* to them. Only one alternative; only two; or four. *Never three*." She exchanged glances with Ch'en'ya. "What *se* Ch'en'ya points out is that if the Prophet didn't escape in a life-pod, and wasn't aboard our gig, and *wasn't* consumed by the explosion, then there is another alternative—one we haven't considered."

"Such as?"

"That he is gone," Ch'en'ya said. "But he is not dead."

"Gone? Gone where?"

"I cannot answer," Ch'en'ya replied.

The three captains exchanged glances.

"You're trying to tell me," Feng answered at last, "that the bands of color—who serve the enemy—have destroyed the flagship, killed our admiral, and betrayed the leader of the Blazing Star movement?"

"Yes," Ch'en'ya said.

"But he's not dead."

"Yes," Ch'en'ya said again.

"The Prophet has left us for a time," Feng said carefully, "due to a betrayal by the bands of color. The sudden loss of our commanding officer, along with the damage suffered here at UPENDRA, requires us to pause before continuing the campaign."

"It sounds like a reasonable course of action," Jackie said.

"We'll have to consult with Admiral MacEwan," Feng said. "She's in command now. Of course, that still leaves the question of what to do with you."

"You let us go," Jackie said. "I'd like to apprise the High Nest of this circumstance."

"The High Nest is no longer our ally," said Aaron Lewis, the first comment he'd made since coming into the cargo hold. "The actions of the High Nest—"

"May have been precipitate," Jackie interrupted. "It's not too late for this situation to be remedied, sirs. The relationship between the Solar Empire and the High Nest isn't something that needs to be decided here—and now—by us."

Clearly the idea of solving that relationship wasn't something that Darrin Feng, Kwame Adelson, or Aaron Lewis had considered.

"I have to accept your premise, madam. If I do not, I could do what I considered when you were brought aboard."

"Which is?"

"Vent you into space," Feng said. He said it seriously, without missing a beat. For just a moment the Blazing Star emblem on his uniform caught the light from overhead and split it into a hundred colors.

"I don't take threats lightly, Captain."

"I don't issue them lightly," he answered. "I assure you that the *gyaryu* would be returned to Zor'a with full honors in the event of your death."

"*Our* death," Ch'en'ya said, stepping in front of Jackie. The weapons in the room were again trained directly on her; she ignored them and walked slowly forward to where the three captains stood together. "You now face the possibility of killing me as well, *se* Captain.

"What is more, you should plan to inform your second-in-command of his elevation in status, because if the two of us die, you will die as well."

The scene remained in place for several seconds, with Ch'en'ya facing Darrin Feng, six Marines with weapons aimed, and the fate of human-zor relations hanging in the balance. Jackie didn't want to move or say anything, not with fingers on triggers and talons on *chya'i*.

"We won't vent you," Feng said. "Go ahead. Go talk to the High Lord. I'll comm the admiral at Portal System; you'll have to go through there to get home.

"If we change our minds, we know where to find you."

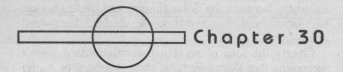

Chapter 30

THERE WERE AT LEAST SIX CLAIMANTS TO THE MANTLE THE PROPHET HAD LAID ASIDE. THERE WERE ASSETS BELONGING TO BLAZING STAR SCATTERED ALL AROUND AND OUTSIDE THE SOLAR EMPIRE, THOUGH MOST OF THE BIGGER SHIPS WERE LOST BEYOND THE RIP; TWO OF THE EARLIEST CLAIMANTS HAD GATHERED FLEETS AROUND THEM—INCLUDING SHIPS AND CREWS THAT REFUSED TO DIVEST THEMSELVES OF THE EMBLEMS BLAZING STAR. HATRED WAS EASILY INCULCATED, AND NOT EASILY EXCISED. ONE OF THOSE FLEETS HURLED ITSELF AGAINST THE ZOR CORE STARS AND WAS DESTROYED TO THE LAST SHIP.

THE RIP ITSELF WAS GONE FOREVER: A PHYSICAL IMPOSSIBILITY THAT HAD BEEN POSSIBLE FOR A TIME AND RETURNED TO ITS NATURAL STATE, LEAVING THE SOLAR EMPIRE'S MAIN FLEET, INCLUDING THE PROPHET, BEYOND IT.

—author unknown,
The Dark Crusade: A History,
late fragment published circa 2430

November 2424
Imperial Oahu, Sol System

Barbara MacEwan had very rarely visited the Hawaiian Islands in her long career. If it had mattered to her—which it did not, far less in any case than it had mattered to Erich Anderson—it might have been a sign that she didn't have any sort of standing at Court; not much chance that the MacEwan name would be ennobled any time soon. It was easier to come to terms with it by realizing that she'd spent much of her naval life flying His Majesty's starships in battle.

She'd taken her own barge down to Rickover and had been received with full military honors, sideboys and all, by the base commander; then she'd traveled by high-speed shuttle, escorted by fighters across the Pacific, from St. Louis directly to Honolulu. It had given her a few hours to prepare what she was going to say and do when she was presented to her emperor.

The comm message had preceded her. It had been polite but direct and to the point; Arturo and the other members of her brain trust had gone over it carefully, helping her whittle away the roughest edges—crisis or not, it was necessary to address the emperor with words that befit his title. It was another area to which Erich had committed more time over the years; still, when it was done, she'd sent it off by high-priority comm-squirt. She was definitely expected.

What was unexpected was the state of mourning. At Rickover she'd been issued an armband: the accidental death of the Guardian Commander Antonio St. Giles was apparently much on the minds of those at Court—his air-car had crashed in the Kauai Channel west of Oahu while *Tristan da Cunha* was in jump to Sol System, and people began thinking about their own mortality. Black armbands were much in evidence at Hickam; when she reported a few minutes after her arrival, she noticed that even the First Lord of the Admiralty was wearing one.

"Admiral," he said, receiving her salute and then gesturing her to a pair of armchairs beneath a brooding holo portrait of Admiral César Hsien.

"Your Grace." She couldn't help but look at the portrait; Admiral Hsien had retired less than ten years earlier, and had died in 2419. Barbara remembered serving under him, and defending Jackie Laperriere to him when she'd gone off in search of the *gyaryu*.

"His grandson presented that to the Admiralty," the First Lord said. "I could hardly have turned it down, but it's one of those pictures where the eyes follow you around the room. He was a crusty old coot, but a good soldier."

"That he was, Your Grace."

"Perhaps we should dispense with the preliminaries, Admiral. I don't need to tell you that this isn't the best time to be presented to the emperor, and you don't need to tell me that with the Rip gone—and the fleet with it— things are in severe flux and it can't wait."

"Thank you, sir. I tried to clarify my position in the comm-squirt—"

He held up a hand. "You did. But it still doesn't make this easy. As you may have heard, the emperor dissolved the Assembly and appointed an interim advisory council, which includes myself and had included Antonio

St. Giles. I don't know whether the emperor intends to replace him or not.

"What's more, the Guardians seem to be in quite a lather about something—and it's more than just the loss of their commander. There's some sort of power struggle going on within the organization, and since they have access to the highest levels of security, this is a matter of some concern."

"I've already taken some steps, Your Grace. My people are answerable only to me, and those directly above me in the chain of command."

"And speaking of the chain of command . . . Admiral MacEwan, with Sir Erich's absence, you are the most senior admiral in the Solar Empire. I realize that you haven't bothered much with the politics here at Court, and I don't propose to force you into it now—but the next few days are crucial. The emperor can appoint anyone he likes, but I would hope that he would elevate you to Admiral of the Blue."

"I'd be honored, your Grace. I came here in part to report on what I'd experienced. Without orders to the contrary, I thought it best to be here."

"And what have you experienced?"

A memory came back to her: the "Purple" voice that had spoken to her while they passed through the Rip.

"What do you want from me?"

"BE PREPARED, ADMIRAL, the voice had said. YOUR DECISIONS WILL AFFECT HISTORY'S COURSE. OTHERS OF THE SIX WILL SEEK TO DETER YOU."

It was a voice no one else had heard. It had spoken directly to her.

"I watched something impossible happen right before my eyes, sir, to something that was impossible to begin with. I don't know what I saw."

"You wouldn't accept a report like that from one of your officers. Should I accept that one from you?"

"Probably not." She smiled a bit, glancing up at her old

C.O. on the wall, who scowled back at her. "Since Cicero I've been fairly clear on the identity of the enemy, Your Grace. We're reasonably sure that there aren't any vuhls left on this side of the Rip—no ships, at least—and with the Rip gone, the enemy I've been fighting for most of my life is gone as well.

"So tell me: who is the enemy now, Your Grace? The Prophet got Admiral Anderson to assign me to suppress insurgency, but before I could move on that all hell broke loose at UPENDRA. I don't know what happened—no one does, I suspect—but with the Rip closed, the Prophet and Anderson and all of the vuhls we know of are on the other side: eight thousand parsecs away, an unimaginable distance."

"The *Gyaryu'har* of the High Nest is there as well, Admiral."

Barbara looked at Alvarez. "What?"

"Ms. Laperriere responded to the Prophet's demand. According to the High Nest, she is now 'in *Ur'ta leHssa*' with the Prophet. That term is the one they use to describe the region beyond the Rip."

"How is the High Nest taking it?"

"The High Nest has stopped talking to us," Alvarez said, sighing. "The advisory council chose to send that nitwit Duke Alistair, Princess Samantha's intended. The High Lord told him that if the Solar Empire decided that the Treaty of E'rene'e was abrogated and the Act of Normalization was out the airlock, then we'd better bring our biggest guns—they'd fight to their last warrior."

"We're threatening the zor now? Your Grace, now I know who the enemy must be: our own stupidity."

"OTHERS SEEK TO DESTROY. I WISH TO TRANSFORM."

It came back to her so suddenly that she stood up and walked away from the First Lord and the portrait of the dead admiral on the wall. She knew who the enemy was: it had been the enemy in Hsien's time, it had been the enemy in Admiral Marais' time.

"No," she said, turning around. "No, it's more scary than that. It's those damn bands of color. They've made this all happen. They will try to destroy the Solar Empire, Your Grace. We have to stop them."

"I don't know if what's happening can be stopped," Alvarez answered. He seemed very old all of a sudden: he'd been craggy when Barbara first met him thirty years ago, so he would have to be in his eighties now. "Blazing Star doesn't have its Prophet anymore—they seem to think that the *Imperial Navy* pulled the plug on the Rip.

"These people owe no allegiance to sword-and-sun, Barbara."

His use of her first name made her stop and look at him. Alvarez continued, "It's somehow ironic, you know: In order to destroy the vuhls it was necessary to draw on something foreign to civil society—a hate so thorough and deep that it defeated their Domination ability. But it can't be just put aside. I can't help but believe that they will tear this Empire apart."

"WE WILL PULL YOUR EMPIRE APART IN OUR PURSUIT. DESTRUCTION IS NOT MY GOAL."

"They'll have help, but they'll have to get through me first."

"I hoped you'd say that." Alvarez stood up. "The emperor is due to receive you at 1800 in your dress uniform, Barbara. As long as there's an emperor and there's an Imperial Navy, we have to work for what we believe in."

Aboard Rxe E Mhnesr
Portal System

Jackie hadn't been sure what to expect when they made transition at Portal System. Evidently a system with no ships and no comm traffic was just about the last thing she had anticipated.

It was even further down on the probability scale when she realized what else was missing.

"The Rip," she said. "It's gone."

Captain Showan stood up from the pilot's chair and looked closely at the board in front of him.

"Reconstruct the scan of this system," he said to comp. The board cleared and slowly began to redraw: the central sun, then the six planets, then the main orbital station, and the other facilities.

The otran captain waited several seconds, then looked up at his passengers.

"What have you done?"

"What do you mean, what have *I* done?" Jackie said. "You think I destroyed the Rip myself? Or Ch'en'ya did it? We waved the magic sword and undid whatever the hell caused it to exist in the first place?"

"That was more or less my question," Captain Showan answered. "But it was a rhetorical one. Let me try to say it a different way.

"Look at what you've *done, ha Gyaryu'har*. Look at what has happened. Do you know where we are? Do you know how far away we are from the Solar Empire?"

"Eight thousand one hundred parsecs," Ch'en'ya said.

"That's right. With the Rip gone, we are eight thousand one hundred parsecs from Imperial space. Our effective jump range is thirty parsecs; assuming it's even possible, we have two hundred and seventy jumps to make before we reach a world that is even on our charts.

"A rough calculation makes that somewhere around three Standard years of travel. I would guess that it is more likely five years. Five *years* to get home—if we don't misjump, break down, or come under attack. Whatever you have done with your *magic sword*, you may have condemned us to death."

"Would you rather that we died aboard *Emperor Ian*?"

"I would rather that you had not involved *Rxe E Mhnesr* at all." The captain clenched his fists, the small fingers placed against his palms, the larger ones wrapping around them. "If the miraculous happens and we reach

Imperial space, I will find Djiwara—and I will personally, painfully, *wring his neck.*"

"And us?"

"I am unsure what to do with you. Leaving you here would be a possibility, but there is no reason for you not to share in the privation that *Rxe E Mhnesr* is likely to endure."

"That sounds very much like a threat, *se* Captain," Ch'en'ya said. "We were threatened aboard *César Hsien;* now we are threatened aboard your vessel. Do we carry an air of Despite with us that we must be considered the enemy wherever we go?"

"I do not consider you an enemy," Showan said with a sigh. "In honesty, I do not know what to do." He clasped his hands behind his back. "Most of my people do not ever leave the home world. Aside from the insanity that seems to reign beyond our planet's horizon, there is simply too much potential for unresolved *ga E layun.* But this situation—this situation places us in a position that no one of our race has *ever* experienced before.

"What's more," he continued, "there's no way to tell what happened to the Rip or to Admiral MacEwan. Without someone to direct them, the captains in command at UPENDRA System are likely to be extremely unpredictable. By now they will have determined that no answer is forthcoming from this system, and will have dispatched one or more ships to find out why."

"What do you think they'll do when they get here?"

"I have no way of knowing," Showan answered. "If we are here, I would expect that one of the possibilities would be to blow *Rxe E Mhnesr* out of the sky. Therefore," he added, turning to face his two passengers, "we will not be here."

"Where are you planning to go?"

Captain Showan barked a command at the pilot's board in his native speech. The display of Portal System dissolved and was replaced by a star map; Portal System appeared highlighted by a small orange dot, and the Solar Empire by a small bluish blob. It seemed impossibly far away.

Showan poked the blob with one of his long, articulated fingers. "I intend to go *there*, madam. I intend to go home."

Antonio St. Giles was buried in mid-October with full honors at the National Military Cemetery of the Pacific—the "Punchbowl"—in a ceremony that was attended by the Solar Emperor and Empress and the remainder of the advisory council.

On 22 November 2424, Admiral Barbara MacEwan was elevated to Admiral of the Blue, commander of every commissioned vessel in the fleet. Her orders to Arturo Schelling were propagated throughout His Majesty's Fleet: Blazing Star emblems were to be removed from service uniforms; no orders to be taken from Guardians or other civilians; and no rebellions were on target for suppression.

From the bridge of *Tristan da Cunha* and from the office of the First Lord of the Admiralty on Oahu, the remaining ships of the fleet—about a third of the operational tonnage remaining—were distributed throughout the Empire. Members of the Guardian Order were excluded from military facilities, and many of them resigned, leaving the organization in disarray.

In mid-November the Pali Tower was shut down and its personnel were reassigned. It had continued to draw power and resources at a considerable rate, almost as if some great project were underway; but most of the security protocols had gone offline at the moment of Antonio St. Giles' death.

The Plane of Sleep

At some timeless time, the four great statues of the Ama'a'an Guardians stirred into motion. There had been no further visits, either by Ch'en'ya or the High Lord.

Perhaps they're getting along now, Owen had mused to himself.

"*si* Owen," La'ath said, placing his wings in the Stance of the Warrior. "We have come to a decision."

"What have you decided?"

"The Plane of Sleep has been fouled by Despite for too long, *si* Owen. We have determined that it is time that we attend to that situation."

"You're going to go after the *esGa'uYal*?"

"*se* Ch'en'ya was correct about one thing, *si* Owen: the abomination of six is still the enemy of the Ama'a'an Guardians. There is no reason for it to occupy the Plane of Sleep, and we need not fly far to find it—it is everywhere.

"Whatever is in league with it, including *se* Ch'en'ya, will be freed from its influence. When we are done, the Plane of Sleep will be cleansed."

"What will you do then?"

"We will go to the Light," La'ath said, his wings moving to honor *esLi*. "We have served here long enough.

"And what of you, *si* Owen? Would you add your blade to our fight?"

"I don't have a blade."

"I ask eight thousand pardons, *si* Owen, but I disagree." La'ath gestured toward Owen's belt; a scabbard hung there, with a sword placed in it.

"That's not mine."

"Of course it is. You have always had a blade, *si* Owen; you may never have used it, but it has always been there."

Owen slowly removed the sword from the scabbard; it caught the light from somewhere: a pure, golden radiance that ran the length of the blade from its tip to where he gripped it at the hilt.

"Will you come, *si* Owen?"

He thought about it. The Am'a'an Guardians were going to go off and cleanse the Plane of Sleep, and then they were going to . . . what? Walk into the Light, end their existence, join with *esLi*. He wasn't sure that he was ready for that yet.

"I think I'll stay here, *si* La'ath."

"It is well."

The other three Am'a'an Guardians gathered around Owen. In turn, each carefully grasped his forearms, honoring him with the Stance of the Warrior. He returned the gesture with a bow, lacking wings of his own.

Without a further word the four statues took to the air, flying southward and away from the Mountains of Night and leaving Owen alone, his *chya* drawn before him, catching light from some source he couldn't see.

He lowered the *chya*, pointing it down at the dusty ground.

"Damn." He couldn't help smiling, though there was no one to talk to anymore . . . and might never be again.

"I'm still a Guardian."

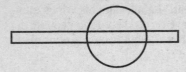

Epilogue

From Barbara MacEwan's personal journal,
22 February 2427.

With great ceremony, we opened the Balvenie yesterday.

Kit Hafner came to Adrianople to refit *Matheson*: apparently there'd been some shooting and he'd taken damage to aft travelers. He gave the proper response: "You should see the other guy." Good man, Hafner—in another time he'd be working his way toward Admiral. In *this* time he's just trying to survive.

Most of the folks that were there when the bottle was presented to me managed to be present for the wee dram. Rich Abramowicz, Kit Hafner, Arturo—even Ron, though he's not fully recovered from the incident at Cor Caroli a few months ago and had to get around in a power chair.

We uncorked a bottle of spirits that had been bottled from cask 166 years ago and poured it into exquisite Corcyan glasses, which had once graced the table of the Count of Pergamum, had found their way into Rich Abramowicz' sideboard. There were sufficient people that there was only enough for one drink each, but it hit the spot. With the bottle open there was nothing for it but to drink it to the last drop.

We toasted the Solar Emperor but not the High Nest; we toasted the brave and courageous departed. And we toasted the Service. We tried to make the three offerings seem something less hollow than they might have seemed.

When we spoke of the brave and courageous departed, I thought about Jackie—it was hard not to. Even with the zor High Nest estranged from the Empire, I still believe that we'll find a way to reconcile ourselves with them— though without Jackie I can't imagine how. Perhaps she's wherever Owen Garrett is, in some dream place I can't go, defending it with the sword.

When the toasts were done and the Balvenie was consumed to the last dram, we parted company with salutes and handshakes. Every time I see these fine, brave soldiers, I wonder if I'll see any of them again. So every departure is poignant, every salute a gift: *we who are about to die, salute you.*

Alone again in my quarters, I can't help but think about how this all came about. Not the war: God knows I understand that well enough—*all* of it, from the point at which our mysterious enemy came onstage. It turns out that there are a few MacEwan family stories about my great-great-aunt Sharon's experience with Admiral Marais. Though we've spent a hundred Standard years denying it, the facts have become clear to me: he was *right*, at least to some extent. *A Letter From Exile* was self-serving, a century ago when there was no chance for any of them to come home ever—but it wasn't an apology, and the zor remained faithful to the flight he put them on. He understood them, and in the end he realized that we needed them for a bigger and more dangerous fight: the war my generation fought against the vuhls. Not all aliens are alike; not all wars are alike. His treatment of their culture, and their treatment of him, was neither self-serving nor a sign of weakness on either side, regardless of what these small-minded heirs of the Prophet claim. He had the stomach to wage that war and the wisdom to stop it—and history should treat him better than it has.

As for the vuhls: they're gone with the Rip conveniently closed behind them. But there is no peace. So many expect the imminent return of the Prophet and his fleet—it's not *Erich Anderson*'s fleet anymore, but the *Prophet*'s—and there are all sorts of people claiming to have instructions on how to proceed. Without him to guide them they have gone out of control, armed and dangerous. Their anger and their hatred pay no heed to emperor or empire. I can't help but believe that there are forces that push them. We can only hold out against this for so long, and every month makes it more difficult. God help us if the Prophet ever does return. Or the vuhls, for that matter—there may be no Empire to resist them.

The empty Balvenie bottle sits on a shelf in my quarters aboard *Tristan da Cunha*, next to the commissioning plaque for *Duc d'Enghien* and a holo of Jackie and I taken in Adrianople's C-and-C a few months after we took it back in 2397. They are all reminders of a day which, if not a better one, was one we could understand.

Yesterday we opened the Balvenie and drank it to the last drop. Today *Tristan da Cunha* moves through jump, headed for Kensington, where a Blazing Star group—the *Prophet's Own Guard*, they call themselves—have taken control of the Starbase and are making demands. God only knows what the outcome will be, or how many more such battles *Tristan* and I can fight and survive. Every soldier knows that there is a bullet with his or her name on it, and in every battle there's a chance that it will be fired and strike its target. But the emperor—and the brave and courageous departed—and the Service demand no less of *Tristan da Cunha* and no less of me than we go where we're needed and do what we must. This is what Jackie did when she went to retrieve the sword, and when she went to confront the Prophet. This is what Owen is still doing, wherever he is.

A bit over two years ago, a mysterious voice told me that the decisions I made would affect the course of history, while it and its friends were busy pulling the Solar Empire apart. Maybe it was telling the truth and maybe not. At this time, however, I am still in the emperor's service and still wear his uniform and take his shilling, as my ancestors used to say. Maybe there'll be another bottle of Balvenie to open one day and we'll all take another wee dram and drink the health of the emperor and remember the brave and courageous departed.